See So That
We May See

See So That We May See

Performances and Interpretations of Traditional Tales from Tanzania

PETER SEITEL

From performances tape-recorded by Sheila Dauer and Peter Seitel

Indiana University Press
BLOOMINGTON AND LONDON

This book was brought to publication with the assistance
of a grant from the Andrew W. Mellon Foundation.

Manufactured in the United States of America

Library of Congress Cataloging in Publication Data
Seitel, Peter.
　　See so that we may see.

　　Includes index.
　　1.　Tales, Hava.　2.　Oral tradition—
Tanzania.　I.　Dauer, Sheila.　II.　Title.
GR356.72.H38S44　398.2'09678　79–3036
ISBN 0–253–15917–2 cl.　1 2 3 4 5　84 83 82 81 80
ISBN 0–253–20242–6 pa.

CONTENTS

Preface

Following a discussion with Okot p'Bitek, noted East African poet, critic, and sociologist, I chose to develop this book as literary interpretation and to drop certain features of social science discourse I had previously included. Description of Haya society and culture is therefore presented as part of the interpretation of meaning in the tales rather than as an end in itself. The reader will note that there are few words that could be called jargon and few devices (such as formulas, flow charts, or statistical summaries) that could be labelled academic or analytic.

The goal has been to synthesize the approaches of aesthetics and ethnography, of entertainment and interpretation. It would be a breach of faith to present entertainments from Haya oral tradition in a nonentertaining, incomprehensible or disrespectful way, or in any way that does not address their rich theatrical nature. I have tried to use modes of discourse that combine these orientations and discard those that do not.

In order to allow the Haya tales to occupy an aesthetic space in the book in their own right (with the interpretations serving as maps of this space), I have chosen to use a system for the presentation of oral texts developed by Dennis Tedlock. This format is the clearest way we have in print to convey some of the theater and poetry of storytelling performances. For these tales do not come to us in typescripts or in dictated versions recorded in longhand. The stories in *See So That We May See* were all performed in people's homes before appreciative audiences of fellow Hayas.

When a Haya audience says to a Haya narrator, "See so that we may see," they are agreeing to participate in the telling of a tale. They agree to entertain a world where a different causality is in effect, where animals and even trees may speak as humans; moreover, they agree to follow the development of the story, so that, for example, character A, who has undergone experiences m,n,o, and p, is a different character (in the minds of the audience members) by the time he enters situation q. Through this participation the audience "sees" what the narrator "sees" as he or she tells the tale. The audience's participative effort is a crucial component of the story's vitality. A living performance is conceived by the mingling of the teller's and audience's creative energies and is nurtured by their collaborative participation.

In a similar way, reading tales in the Tedlock format requires a participative effort from the reader. It says to him or her: "If you are willing to make the effort to participate in the performance of this tale by following a few simple conventions, you will hear with your 'mind's ear' and 'see' more vividly what the narrator 'sees.'"

I thank the following Americans for their advice and encouragement: J. David Sapir, Herb Shore, Ralph Rinzler, Roberta Heller Faul, Maxine Miska, Marta Schley, and Steve Zeitlin. In addition to the narrators included herein, I thank the following Tanzanians for their advice, patient instruction, and warm hospitality: Dr. Israel Katoke, Dr. Godwin Kaduma, Richard Mutembei, the late Felix Kataraia, and the late Godfrey Ngaiza. I thank Bonnie Whitehead for typing the final draft. And I thank two people without whose aid I could not even have begun this project: Winifred Kisiraga and Sheila Dauer.

See So That
We May See

1

The World of the Tales

THE LANDSCAPE

If it is possible to discover a center of gravity in the social landscape—a place where many of a person's feelings originate and grow, the hub around which a family's daily activities turn, the same locus that is the setting for important activities throughout a person's life, from birth through youth and maturity, old age and, finally, death—if it is possible to say where this center is, then for Haya society it is the cooking hearth.

The hearth consists of three large stones that enclose a cooking fire in the innermost room of a traditional Haya round-style, windowless, grass-thatch house. The stones are called *mahiiga*, a word that also names the social unit of the extended family itself. It is an ancient word; its origins can be traced to the language that the Bantu people spoke before they migrated into eastern and southern Africa apparently over two thousand years ago.

The hearth is dimly lit and private. Every meal is cooked here and eaten in a space close by. Family members sleep in portioned-off spaces arranged in an arc around these three stones. The fire's warmth drives out the chill of a rainy season in the 3,500- to 5,500-foot altitudes of Hayaland. Children are conceived and born in close proximity to it, and it is at the hearth that a parent or grandparent will try them with riddles and entertain them with stories, some of which are included in this collection.

Hayaland, with a population of about 550,000, is located in the West Lake region in northwestern Tanzania. The original inhabitants of this area were hunting and gathering peoples who probably spoke a language related to those spoken today by the Khoisan (Bushman) peoples in southern Africa. Historians speculate that sometime before the first millennium, Bantu-speaking people migrated to the area, bringing with them the skills of ironworking and agriculture.[1] The original inhabitants were driven out or emigrated. Beginning about 1500, a series of invasions from the north set up a conquest state in Hayaland. The ruling group consisted of the invading peoples, who were pastoralists. The ruled group was the indigenous peoples, who were agriculturalists and fishermen. Over time, the invaders took up agriculture as well as the language and aspects of the culture of the indigenous group. This system evolved into a society similar to a caste system in which there are two unequal sets of clans: ruling clans, which provide chiefs, and nonruling clans, which do not. The first Europeans reached Lake Victoria, the eastern border of Hayaland, in 1861. In 1890, the Anglo-German Treaty established the area as part of the German East Africa colony. The World War I peace treaty of 1919 awarded Britain possession of this part of German East Africa, and it remained a British colony until Tanzania (at the time named Tanganyika) achieved independence on December 9, 1961.

Hayas are primarily farmers. They cultivate plantains as their staple food crop, but also raise cattle and other livestock, as well as millet, beans, potatoes, corn, tomatoes, and cassava to supplement their diet, and onions and hot peppers to flavor it. Hayaland's principal cash crops are tea, which is grown principally on large tea estates by hired workers, and coffee, which is grown by individual farmers. Coffee is marketed through a farmers' cooperative that exports the beans or roasts them and manufactures instant coffee at its factory near the town of Bukoba, a port on Lake Victoria. Besides tending banana and coffee plants, rural Haya men often engage in other commercial activities such as fishing, fish marketing, storekeeping, cattle trading, watch repair, bicycle repair, or beer brewing.

For many Hayas, the cooking hearth is no longer located at the innermost point in a house. Following the rectangular house style that became popular in the early twentieth century, it tends to be located elsewhere, often in a separate cooking shed at the rear. But many traditional, round-style houses are still to be seen in Hayaland, and they are the only kind of house represented in the tales.

An acquaintance with Hayaland, its people, and their literature is well begun at the hearth, for it is the center of the social world described in the tales. It is a setting for significant action in eight of them: *I Shall Be Drinking from Them; Teaser; The Bride's Relish; I Ate Minnows, Little Minnows; Kyusi, Kyusi, Good Dog!; Crested Crane and Dove; Blocking the Wind; and Satisfaction.*

Located outside of and surrounding the area that includes the hearth is an outer, ring-shaped room. The rear portion of this room is traditionally used to house livestock—cattle, goats, and sheep. It is the location of events in three tales: *Open and Let Them Come In, Squeezer,* and *It Was Haste That Killed Her.* The front area of the outside room is used to receive guests, as in *Mutele, You've Left Me, You've Gone.*

Outer and inner rooms are separated by a permanent, columned, circular wall with a front doorway that is closed off by a movable wicker screen. The boundary between inner and outer rooms, with its screen, plays an important part in *Blocking the Wind* and *Greens of the Cow Pasture.* Outside this room is the circular wall of the house itself, with a tunnel-shaped vestibule and door in the front. The front door boundary figures in the action of *Open and Let Them Come In* and *What Was It That Killed Koro?*

Except for the hearth, the floor of a house is covered with soft, dried lengths of grass. This covering is changed periodically for the sake of cleanliness. Women and girls cut and gather the grass in untilled fields, as in the tales *Child of the Valley* and *The Serpent of Kamushalanga.* A good-sized traditional house can be twenty to thirty feet high.

Outside the house and in front is a packed-earth front yard where children play, coffee beans are spread to dry, and guests are initially received. Movement from the hearth to the front yard characterizes the tales *I Shall Be Drinking from Them* and *Kyusi, Kyusi, Good Dog!* At the rear of a house is a walled bathing enclosure (see *The Bride's Relish* and *Greens of the Cow Pasture*) and, in recent times, a structure that houses a latrine. Traditionally, every time one defecates, one digs a small hole in the ground in the banana grove, filling it in with earth afterwards. Proper disposal of human wastes prevents occurrences such as the one in *Mutele, You've Left Me, You've Gone.*

Surrounding each Haya house and its outside activity spaces is a plantain grove. On this plot of land, which averages about an acre, a family's staple food supply is grown. The use of manure—

primarily that of cattle—and mulches of grass and of already harvested banana plants allows this intensive form of agriculture. As-
sorted vegetables grow in the spaces between banana plants, and
coffee plants grow in their shade.

A village is composed of individual houses, each with a surrounding grove of bananas. It may vary in size from several to several hundred households. Outside the village are open fields in
which women grow supplemental crops: potatoes, groundnuts, and
beans. Millet, which is central to the action of *Teaser* and *Blocking
the Wind*, appears to have been the staple crop in the past. Many
people still grind millet to make porridge, primarily in the southern, less fertile regions of Hayaland.

Outside the fields are the pastures for cattle and other live-
stock. Tending the livestock is work for men and young boys (as in
Open and Let Them Come In). Pastures are a setting for *Child of the
Valley* and *Greens of the Cow Pasture*.

Beyond the fields or interspersed among them are rivers,
springs, and swamps composed of marshy ground and floating papyrus stands. This is the setting for the main action of *Nchume*.
Swampy areas are also a habitat for elephant grass and the home of
wild pigs, which are hunted by parties of men and dogs, as in the
final episode of *Magezi*.

Outside the village at a greater distance is the wilderness.
These grassy steppes are the home of wild animals. Although there
are not so many in modern times, one can still spot hippos in the
rivers, hunt wild pigs that destroy crops, and hear occasional reports of rogue elephants and leopards on the prowl. Passage
through the wilderness and its attendant dangers is a theme that
appears in several tales: *Give-Him-Sweetness-If-He-Cries*, *The Water of
Ikongora*, and *Have You Not Seen Luhundu?* The wilderness as a place
devoid of civilization is the setting of *Three Brothers* and *Who Was the
One Who Ate It?*

Lake Victoria is a fishing ground for Haya fishermen, but it
appears in their literature as an alternate world, a dwelling place of
spirits, whether one journeys out onto the lake, as in *Woman-of-
People-Forbidden-Horn* or beneath its surface, as in *I Ate Minnows,
Little Minnows*. This other-worldly quality does not appear to apply
to Lake Ikimba, a much smaller body of water to the west of Lake
Victoria. Lake Ikimba, however, as the tale of that name suggests,
does have its mysteries. It is traversed by floating islands (papyrus
stands) and is home for a fish with "breasts" that can breathe air (a

lungfish with what we interpret as vestigial "legs"). Moreover, the lake does not like strangers, and it can, they say, turn blood-red to demand a human sacrifice. It was possibly an execution place in times gone by, as in the conclusion of *Child of the Valley*. The other world can also be reached by going up above, as in *Squeezer*, or by going underground, as in several Haya epic songs.

This is Hayaland seen from the inside out: cooking hearth at the center; surrounded by outer rooms for guests and livestock; surrounded by the outside activity areas of the house; surrounded by the banana grove; then the village, the fields, the pastures; a quasi wilderness of swamps, rivers, and copses of trees; and finally the wilderness itself. Or moving on an alternate plane, one may visit the world of the spirits in or on Lake Victoria, up above in the sky, or below in the ground.

These separate domains can be thought of as "fields" in the sense of gravitational or electromagnetic fields. That is, in each domain an individual is subject to varying kinds and degrees of influences.

At the cooking hearth, a female, domestic force is at its highest level. In *I Shall Be Drinking from Them*, a woman stands at the hearth against her husband and the social pressures of a male dominant society to create a reproductive miracle. The same theme is stated more equivocally in *The Strong One* and burlesqued in *Blocking the Wind*.

As one moves outward from the hearth, the level of domestic force decreases, and when one reaches the agricultural fields where women plant their crops, a new force begins to exert influence: the wilderness. This is an antidomestic, anticivilized force that reaches its high point when one reaches the wilderness itself.

In *The Glistening One* the landscape is fully laid out: the wilderness, where Leopard's rule is law; the house, where women hold sway; and the fields, the place in-between where neither is dominant and strategic encounters occur. Even as siblings move outward from the civilizing restraints of the home, antisocial behavior can emerge. Witness the tragic tales *Three Brothers* and *Child of the Valley*.

For a child, the center of the world is the cooking hearth. It is the only "inside." But as one grows older, two other centers become important: a political one and one associated with marriage. The traditional political "inside" was the court of a chief. It was here that a chief—one of seven in all of Hayaland—lived with his advisers, his wives, and his servants. The palace was said to be a sophisticated place, as contrasted with the rural areas surrounding it. The people of the palace (*abakale*) differentiated themselves from the *abakigemu*, "people of the banana groves." The former were supposedly more knowledgeable and better spoken. They dwelled in a world of beautiful appearance and dress—a world, depending on one's viewpoint, seen as wisely governed by a knowing monarch or as a place where people were subject to the despotic whims of whatever chief happened to be in control. Chiefs lost their formal political power when Tanzania gained independence from Great Britain.[2]

The chief's court appears in a central position in *Look Back and See What Lugeye Does!* and is one of two centers in *Lusimbagila Bestows on All* (the other is the hearth). *Teaser* and *Little Leper of Munjolobo* have the same dual-centered landscape consisting of hearth and palace. In these two tales a young girl permanently moves out from one and into the other as a chief's bride. A similar landscape becomes the setting for comedy when a woman moves, not as a bride, but as the chief's adopted mother in *Greens of the Cow Pasture*.

At marriage a woman moves from a world centered on her own family's hearth to a new world centered at the hearth of her husband's family. This move is traditionally the most significant one a woman makes. Despite planning by the two families involved, and despite the extensive discussions that precede a marriage, a woman does not really know for certain what she will find when she enters there. Each household has its own field of forces; one must act within them and negotiate them on one's own. A woman may find her new family eats unconventionally (*I Ate Minnows, Little Minnows*) or is disbelieving of her word (*It Was Haste That Killed Her*).

A man also enters the inside in connection with marriage. He goes to the family of a prospective bride and takes from there a woman. He must be careful and self-controlled in this, lest evidence of undesirable tendencies follow him and spoil his reputation and his endeavors. This is what occurs in *Mutele, You've Left Me, You've Gone* and probably also happens in *Salute Leopard, Who's Living in the Past*.

This, then, is the social landscape of Hayaland as it appears in the tales: a primary center is inside at one's own natal hearth (outside are the banana grove, village, fields, pastures, and wilderness); secondary centers are the chief's court and the house of one's spouse's family. It is an historical outcome of Haya society's economic and intellectual interaction with the environment in eastern Africa. Expressed metaphorically in the tales, it appears in an abstract, ideal form that everyone recognizes as the creation of artistic imagination. The landscape is a particular view of the world that indicates places which are important to the life of an individual and to the continued existence of society, an aspect of an ideology by which Hayas comprehend and interpret their lives. Into its spaces and dimensions people are born, live, and die.

LIFECYCLE

The traditional place for a Haya baby to come into the world (Hayas would phrase this "to be taken out from inside") is near the hearth, though many women now give birth in hospitals. The act of giving birth is regarded as an important test of a woman's self-control: she should not allow herself to cry out in pain. She should keep it inside, as a warrior does. She traditionally gives birth in an upright, squatting position (celebrated in women's songs) as attendant women receive the child and perform the required ablutions and rituals. Unlike many other African societies, Hayas regard the birth of twins as an event of extraordinarily good fortune.

The first years of a child's life are spent in his mother's care playing in the front yard, being carried to the fields on his mother's back as she goes to work, staying with her as she prepares meals. Storytelling is one way to make the time pass while the family waits for the evening's food to finish cooking.

Young girls learn basic economic skills from their mothers. As children and adolescents, they are sent to fetch water and to gather grass for the house floor. They learn cooking and agricultural skills. As they reach marriageable age, girls begin to do fancywork, such as basket weaving, sewing, crocheting, beadwork. At the same time, they learn to give cosmetic attention to their appearance. All of these activities can be called by the same name, *oku-shemeza*, "to make (something) pleasing," and are preparations for courting and marriage.

Young boys learn basic economic skills from their fathers. As children, they play with toy cattle made from twigs and bananas. When they are old enough—about ten or eleven years old—they are entrusted with taking the goats to pasture. This is the occasion for a group of boys to meet and to engage in verbal dueling, which often contains underlying sexual meaning. The verbal banter is regarded as training in the use of artistic and intentionally ambiguous speech.

A marriage between young people is arranged by the two families involved, although the match may be initiated by the couple themselves. Each side has a spokesman who is well versed in artistic and strategic speech. Over the course of weeks or months, terms of the marriage are decided: how much money is to be paid to the bride's family ("brideprice"), the outfitting of the final ceremony, and various other matters relating to the couple.

After the orderly progression of ceremonies, a bride comes to live with her new husband and his family. She is immediately "hidden inside" in the groom's house, behind the wicker screen in the doorway to the inner room.

Traditionally, she may remain there for up to six (some say nine) months, doing no agricultural labor and having no outside social life. The length of her stay "inside" depends on the relative wealth of her husband's family, that is, on their ability to feed an adult who does not produce food. It is hoped that during this initial period of marriage, the bride will become pregnant. She will thereby fulfill her reciprocal obligation to "feed" the groom's family with offspring. They feed her, she "feeds" them—in addition to the emotional satisfaction that children bring, they are future workers.

Although Hayas apparently practice no formal collective initiations for youths of either sex, the regimen that a Haya bride undergoes in connection with the period she is "hidden inside" can be seen as initiation into adult society. For several days, and especially on the night before she will make the final journey to the groom's house, she is given formal instructions by her father's sister and other female kin about what she should and should not do in her new household. While she was living in her own father's house, she may have been the much sought-after, beautiful, talented, agriculturally and domestically diligent, bridewealth-producing, grown-up child of her parents. On entering the groom's house, however, she loses all of this. She becomes economically dependent on her new family of in-laws and does no agricultural or domestic labor. Moreover, she has cost the in-laws the amount of bridewealth paid to her family. She has been stripped of her prenuptial status as a sought-after marital prize and is now the lowly newcomer who must learn to live and work in the groom's family and prove her worth. This may be a difficult process, depending on the relative temperaments of bride and in-laws, principally that of her mother-in-law. At the end of her seclusion, the bride emerges as a full-fledged adult to assume womanly duties in the fields and at the hearth and to begin to bear children.

At the same time the bride is being "hidden inside," the groom often journeys outside to a distant locale. There he works to accrue wealth of some sort in order to gain some measure of economic independence from his father. Traditionally, this wealth was in the form of cattle, goats, and sheep, but currently it might be money earned in wage labor. His absence can compound the bride's problems with her in-laws since he is unavailable to mediate between them or to take her side.

The new bride may thus find herself in a difficult situation with her in-laws. No wonder she is a central character in many women's tales. In addition to the six tales in the section entitled "The New Bride," she appears in *Blocking the Wind*, *Kibwana* (as a European), and *Have You Not Seen Luhundu?*

Haya marriages are often polygynous, an arrangement that appears to generate a degree of domestic friction. The competitive jealousy between wives of the same husband is proverbial. It is at the center of dramatic conflict in *Crested Crane and Dove*.

A woman's prestige increases with childbearing, realized profit from her agricultural and domestic labor, and advancing age. When a bride first arrives, she speaks to others haltingly, like one who is ashamed. During the ensuing years, her confidence may grow, until, after menopause, she assumes the status of a woman who "fears no one" and "speaks like a man." One of the best narrators in this collection, Laulelia Mukajuna, happens to be such a woman.

SOCIETY

One element in the social environment of Hayaland is so taken for granted that it is virtually invisible in the tales, although it is present in some way in each. A clan, specifically in Hayaland a patrilineal clan, is a unit of people who form a recognized group by virtue of their genealogical descent from a single ancestor, the descent being computed only through the male line. In other words, a person inherits his or her clan affiliation from his or her father, and all people with the same clan affiliation have it by virtue of father-son links back to a common ancestor. In actual practice, the genealogical tracing is rarely done. It is usually enough to know the name of one's father's clan, which is the same as one's own.

There are two commonly recognized symbols associated with each clan. First is a *muziro*, "prohibited thing," or taboo. This may be a kind or part of an animal or plant or some other object from the natural world. In the distant past this object is said to have killed a member of that clan and thereby to have established the prohibition. Different clans that have the same prohibited thing are said to be related to one another. The social significance of this relationship lies in marriage: with certain exceptions, one may not marry someone who has the same prohibited thing. That is, one may not marry someone from one's own clan or a clan that is related to it. The prohibited thing appears in the title of *Woman-of-People-Forbidden-Horn*. The symbolic horn would usually identify a specific clan that has this as a prohibition. The central character named Woman-of-people-forbidden-horn would be a member of this clan, but, in fact, no such Haya clan exists.

The second symbol associated with a particular clan is a *mulumuna* (literally "sibling of the same sex as the person speaking") or "clan sibling." This is an animal that is related to a clan by virtue of a behavioral trait shared by the animal and by members of the clan who performed assigned duties at the court of the chief. The Bajubu, for example, provided the chief with water to wash his face, and their "clan sibling" is the hippo. The symbolism of the "clan sibling" is evoked in a genre of poetry called *eby'ebugo*, self-praise poems recited by a groom and by warriors in times gone by. It appears in the song in the tale *The Glistening One*, as told by Winifred Kisiraga. The particular use of the symbolism is explicated in the introduction to that tale.

The clans of Hayaland are divided into smaller branches called *mahiiga*, "hearth stones," or sub-clans. A sub-clan is composed of members of a clan who are descended from one living or recently deceased patriarch. The "depth" of a sub-clan in genealogical time varies from three to five generations. The sub-clan is associated with a particular village where the patriarch was given a parcel of land by the chief.

Traditionally, only men could hold land, and they held it at the pleasure of clan leaders and chiefs. In this traditional, feudallike system called *nyarubanja*,[3] a chief distributed land to men who, in turn, parcelled it out to their sons and others, who would cultivate it and pay tribute for its use. (This situation is foregrounded in *What Was It That Killed Koro?*) As one can imagine, with seven chiefdoms, which might change chiefs faster than generations succeeded one another, and with grantees of land free to redistribute land-for-tribute relationships as they saw fit, within certain limitations, the *nyarubanja* system became quite complex. The independent Tanzanian government abolished it in favor of a system more consistent with the institutions of a modern state. The transition is still being sorted out in the courts.

The principal institutions of power in traditional Haya society were dominated by males: the clan structure, the system of landholding, and the political bureaucracy. But there is a force or a tendency in Haya society that stands in opposition to these male structures, namely, the feminine principle which is centered at the hearth—the only power that can produce new members of families, clans, and society.

The male principles of duty and obedience and the female principles of love and nurture oppose one another in some instances and are complementary in others. Since most of the tales in this collection are told by women, the female principle is profoundly in evidence. For example, nurture not only sustains life in the tales, but also acts against the forces of a hostile wilderness, as in *Give-Him-Sweetness-If-He-Cries* and *The Glistening One*. A mother's devotion to her offspring can cause her to stand against her own husband and social opinion, as in *I Shall Be Drinking from Them*. This principle is turned on its head in the ribald tale *Kibwana*, told by Laulelia Mukajuna, where a mother makes a delicious stew of her only child.

The last example shows that the female principle is not all sweetness and warmth. It is also cunning, determination, perseverance, and sometimes strong desire. The tales portray all of these characteristics. They also give voice to a woman's ambivalent feelings about clans: she is protected by her own, she may be oppressed by the women who have married into her husband's clan, and she glorifies the patrilineal clan of her mother, to emphasize the importance of the female blood tie. The latter relationship is evident in the traditional formula that marks the conclusion of tales: "I finish you a story. I finish you another. At your mother's brother's they're eating beer bananas and bean leaves. At my mother's brother's the bananas are growing fatter and fatter." This is a boast, self-praise for having told the story well, as a warrior would chant his own praises after a victorious battle. The food imagery says: I have higher prestige than you. At your mother's family's farm the staple food reserves (unpicked plantains) have been exhausted: witness the fact that they're already eating the bananas which were to be used for making beer and the leaves of the bean plant (the beans themselves have already been eaten). At my mother's family's farm, however, the plantains are so plentiful that there are many still growing fatter and fatter on the unharvested plants. The formula asserts the importance of the female blood link in claiming social prestige. The analogy with a successful warrior is apt, for in chanted self-praise (*eby'ebugo*), one's mother's clan re- ceives equal emphasis; behaviorial traits—like good soldiering and good speaking—are said to be inherited through the female line.

FOOD

The storytelling formula also indicates that for Hayas, as for all cultures, food has symbolic significance. The symbolism of food plays a role in almost all the tales collected here. It is at the center of the action in tales like *Greens of the Cow Pasture*. It may even appear in a transformed state, like the putative cannibalism in *What Was It That Killed Koro?* or the excrement in *Mutele, You've Left Me, You've Gone*.

Haya cultural ideas about food can be divided into three areas: first, the ownership of land that produces food; second, the labor of cultivating and preparing it; third, the act of consuming it. Each area is governed by certain ideological principles, and each area holds implications for social prestige.

Land ownership is traditionally a male domain. As briefly described above, under the feudallike *nyarubanja* system, land was distributed by the chief to prominent and worthy men, thence to their clansmen and clients, and so on down the line. Symbolic and social implications of this system are expressed in the Haya aphorism *Akulisa niwe akutwala*, "the one who feeds you is the one who rules you." The verb "feed" in this context refers to providing land for growing food. The proverb means that the person who provides one with the land that sustains him is the same person to whom one owes allegiance and, moreover, the person who has the socially sanctioned right to control many aspects of one's behavior.

In this system, the chief is the ultimate landowner and also the ultimate ruler. He "feeds" his people and rules them. The same principle applies to each point of land distribution down the line: at each level, the distributor "feeds" the distributee and, therefore, rules him. The lowest level of distribution is from father to son. A father apportions a plot of land from his own holdings when his son marries. At that point, and before it as well, the father provides land that feeds the son; this is said to be a basis on which a Haya father "rules." A son owes his allegiance to his father, and through him to his clan, and through the clan to the chief.

The connection between feeding and ruling can be used rhetorically, as in the following context. If two people are arguing over one's right to dictate the behavior of the other, the one who refuses to comply can ask, "*Wandisa?*" "Have you fed me (today)?" That is, if you fed me you could rule me, but since you do not, you cannot!

The position of women in this ideology is to be ruled, since they cannot (traditionally) own land. While an unmarried girl lives with her parents, she is ruled by her father and through him by the clan because she is "fed" by them. When she marries and goes to live with her husband, she is then ruled by him and his clan because they now provide the land which she cultivates.

As one might expect, tales do not portray exemplary instances of people being ruled as they should be. Instead we find interesting violations of the norm that lead dramatically to new situations where the norm is reasserted.

A good example of this is *Blocking the Wind*, in which a wife improperly rules her own husband until the husband's sister sets things straight. There is also *She's Killed One. We've All of Us Come*, in which a wife who refuses to be ruled is chastened and almost killed by the trouble she stirs up.

Cultivation of all food crops except plantains is traditionally women's work. Men tend the perennial banana plants; some herd cattle, hunt, or fish. Harvesting all food crops, preparing meals, and serving them are also part of a woman's economic role.

Cooking and sharing out food has both economic and symbolic significance. Economically, these acts literally sustain the lives of family members. Symbolically, cooking and sharing food define and reaffirm the existence of the economic unit—the *eka*, "household," composed of the people who share the same hearth and home.

Cooking one's own food and having no one to share it with is a sign of social isolation, of not being included in a domestic group. The motif of cooking for one's self is used to heighten the aloneness of characters in *Kibwana* and in *The Serpent of Kamushalanga*. It seems to increase the attractiveness of the handsome prince in *Kibwana*; his vulnerable isolation puts him in need of feminine shelter (p. 180).

The third area of food symbolism, eating, is by far the most elaborated. Many varieties of food have symbolic significance, and their consumption as well as the amounts in which they are eaten, and even their relative proportion in the individual's diet, all have cultural meaning. Kinds, amounts, and combinations of foods that a person eats make symbolic statements about what kind of person he or she is. This is as true in Haya society as it is in our own, where styles of food consumption have implications of class, ethnic, and age-group affiliations.

In Haya symbolism of eating, the more discriminating a person is in the kind of food he eats, the higher social prestige he or she has. This can be nicely illustrated by the opening line of the Haya epic song *Kajango*, which goes *Nyamwemanyo tolya bya bana, tohunyahunya*, "The one who knows himself does not eat the food of children, he does not eat a bit of this and that." This succinctly states the association between dietary discrimination (that is, not eating the food of children and not eating a lot of different foods) and prestige (that is, the highly valued quality of self-knowledge).

But the meaning of this line extends deeper, for when a knowledgeable Haya hears these words, he knows it is a symbolic reference to the clan of the Bankango. The forbidden thing (*muziro*) of the Bankango is the intestines of all animals, and the Bankango's clan sibling (*mulumuna*) is the hawk (see p. 16). They have produced dynasties of chiefs, but it is said they were not always rulers. Centuries ago, when the ancestors of certain other ruling clans invaded Hayaland, they elevated the Bankango to the status of rulers. And the reason that they were chosen from among other clans, it is said, is that they "ate well." They ate as befits the rulers of men. They share this characteristic with their clan sibling, the hawk, who does not eat a bit of this and that as other birds do; he eats only meat. That is why in this particular context, discriminating eating is a reference to this ruling clan.

The chief himself is the most discriminating eater of all. He eats nothing—in public, anyway. In many societies in Africa and elsewhere, the ruler must not be seen eating by the people he rules. This is part of a geographically widespread complex of ideas known among students of society as "the divine kingship."

The clans whose male genealogical lines produce chiefs are more discriminating eaters than are the clans who do not produce rulers. Adult members of the ruling clans (*balangila*) do not eat fish of any kind. Members of the nonruling clans (*bailu*) do. Marriages between these two groups were traditionally prohibited, except those of the hypergamous type—men from the ruling group marry women from the nonruling group, but not vice versa. When a hypergamous marriage occurs, the woman's sub-clan takes on a semi-royal status (*enfula*) and from then on abstains from eating fish.

Adults are more discriminating eaters than children. Among ruling clans, children are allowed to eat fish until the time they become adults. Children of all clans eat food left over from the night before (as in *I Shall Be Drinking from Them*). Adults, especially men, would not eat this. Children are also fond of "sweet things"—sugar bananas, wild fruit, candy—but a self-respecting adult would not eat them (ideally, of course). The child whose name is given to the tale *Give-Him-Sweetness-If-He-Cries* is an example of this association between children and sweet foods. In this particular tale, "sweet things" are fed not to children but to leopards, who, as we shall see later, are the incarnations of noncivilized eating.

Women are more discriminating than girls. Adult, married women may not eat goat meat, *ensenene* (a kind of grasshopper that comes once a year to Hayaland), or the flesh of the lungfish. The first two prohibitions appear in the tales *Kyusi, Kyusi, Good Dog!* and *Crested Crane and Dove*, respectively. The lungfish may be eaten only when a woman has just given birth; it is said to increase the amount of milk in her breasts.

Men are more discriminating than women—or at least they are supposed to be—despite the fact that women are traditionally prohibited goat, *ensenene*, and lungfish. A woman might eat a bit of leftover food or some raw vegetable while she is working in the fields, two categories of food a man should not admit to eating.

As this last pair of discriminations and nondiscriminations indicates, the symbolism of eating is more of a rhetorical than of a categorical nature. One should follow the rules, and one must not admit to not following them, if he wants to be thought of as a discriminating person with high social standing. When a man claims he eats *only* plantains, meat, and milk, he is speaking about his high prestige, not about his personal tastes in food. The statement means he has enough of the prime land needed to grow bananas and enough cattle to eat only these foods. We can assume the speaker is royalty and eats no fish. When others have to supplement their diet with beans, vegetables, or cassava, he does not. The traditional closing formula for storytelling (see p. 11) is another statement of this sort.

The symbolism of eating is rhetorical and traditional. It specifies the kinds of food a person should (claim to) eat or not eat so as to place oneself traditionally on his or her best social footing. The actual diet of most Hayas is varied, and the word "vitamins," pronounced as the British do, is part of the vocabulary of many Hayas.

If the chief and the hawk are at the top of the ladder of eating vis-à-vis prestige, at the bottom is the dog, least discriminating of all consumers. An untrained dog will eat almost anything, Hayas observe, even excrement. Dog's eating habits are proverbial. Say someone eats like a dog, and you are asking for a fight. It is no wonder that a gluttonous bride tries to pin the blame on a dog for her own improper eating in *Kyusi, Kyusi, Good Dog!* It would be eminently believable of him. And a deliciously unthinkable act, an abomination that, were it known, could shatter a person's prestige, is to eat the meat of a dog. That would be bad eating squared, so to speak, but this is what happens in the droll tale *Who Was the One Who Ate It?*

Leopard is also an infamous eater, and his fault lies in his uncontrollable appetite for meat. He will do anything for it, and this invariably (in the tales) gets him into trouble. Leopard's appetite for food is one of the defining features of his character—he is a *mululu*, "glutton." His gluttony is embellished in the tales by attributing to him a desire for many different kinds of food in addition to meat: raw field crops in *The Glistening One* and "sweet things" in *Give-Him-Sweetness-If-He-Cries*.

Gluttony appears frequently in the tales. Gluttons do not share food or respect other food-related obligations. Sometimes they cook for themselves in secret and eat alone. Their punishment for this is to be expelled from their social group, to be separated from the family relationships that their gluttony has violated. The reversed mirror image of the glutton is the character who arouses pity by having to cook for him or herself. In the instances described above (p. 13), the characters are unjustly expelled from their respective social groups and therefore cook and eat alone. The glutton, on the other hand, cooks and eats alone and is therefore justly expelled.

Food and its associated activities are the principal subject of several tales and are used symbolically in others. For a better appreciation of the centrality of food, we may look to two additional features of Haya social life: the natural rotation of the seasons in Hayaland and the cultural expectation of reciprocity in social relationships.

The annual growing cycle begins in about mid-September with the onset of the light rainy season. At the beginning of the season, rain falls every other day or so for a short period. It grows gradually greater in frequency and duration, and then it ceases rather abruptly in December or early January. About a month or so into the light rains, *ensenene* drop down from the northeast. *Ensenene* are a particular kind of grasshopper that appears only once a year from no-one-knows-where and are avidly prepared, cooked, and eaten. Further details about *ensenene* can be found in the introduction to *Crested Crane and Dove*, where this food is at the center of the action.

After the light rains comes a short but intense dry season that lasts about four to six weeks. This is the hottest time of the year. The equatorial sun's intensity seems magnified by the absence of wind in this season, clear skies, and the thinner air of the highland altitudes.

About the end of February, the heavy rains arrive. They come slowly, but build until it rains every day for varying periods, sometimes for several days without stopping. During these three seasons—light rains, short dry season, and heavy rains—there is an adequate supply of food. Crops have been growing and maturing; some have been harvested.

Around the beginning of June, the rain tapers off, skies become clear, and a long, windy, dry season begins. This lasts for three to four months and can be a relatively lean time that taxes the food reserves of Haya farmers. Four tales are set in this season: *Blocking the Wind*; *The Woman "Full Moons"*; *Kulili Your Brother of Only One Mother*; and *Satisfaction*. The relative scarcity of food can awaken dormant stresses among kinsmen and evoke behaviors that in fatter times are kept in check. If the previous heavy rains have been insufficient, or if the light rains are delayed overlong, there may ensue a time of hunger, called *enjala*, literally "hunger." If this grows longer and more intense, it can become a famine, called *eifa*, "death."

Drawing boundaries of food distribution during these times may not be an actual problem, but it is treated problematically in

the four tales cited above. These tales speak of gluttony, its consequences, and the nature of kin ties. This kind of gluttony is tanta-
mount to placing one's desire for food above all else, including familial relationships. It signifies that one has lost control of his
appetites and is ruled by them. Nowhere is the glutton who refuses
to share food within or outside his own household treated sympa-
thetically. His punishment is separation from the social group.

These tales also explore a problem inherent in marriage: husband and wife cannot live like brother and sister—they cannot have
the same diffuse and enduring solidarity that comes from a blood
relationship. "Blood is thicker than water," to cite a Haya proverb.
In the abstract setting of a lean, dry season, this complex of ideas
about sharing and kinship can be explored.

As a dry season wears on, staple food reserves, unharvested
plantains, become fewer and fewer. One who lacks the prime
acreage to produce sufficient plantains that will sustain him
through the seasons must turn to crops planted as a hedge against
famine, like cassava. Increasing the variety of one's diet, if it is
known, decreases one's prestige. This is one reason a family eats in
private. Guests are not received during meals, unless invited. What
a family eats is not a public matter, and the person who can truth-
fully boast that he eats only milk, meat, and bananas has a royal
plot of land.

The ideal of formal reciprocity in social relationships is expressed among Hayas in many different ways. All seem to be based
on the simple axiom that one returns good for good and bad for bad.
The plots of several tales are structured by the symmetry of reciprocal actions (*Lusimbagila Bestows on All*, *Open and Let Them Come In*,
Blocking the Wind, *Kibwana*, and *What Was It That Killed Koro?*).

In real life formal reciprocity means debts and generosity are
repaid, favors and services returned, promises honored, mutual respect exchanged in customary practices.

Formal reciprocity structures expectations about social interactions outside the family, but not within. If someone outside the
family fails to fulfill a formal reciprocal obligation, and a fairly
clear-cut case can be made about it, sanctions can be taken. Within
the family, however, there are no expectations of formal reciprocity.
Love, respect, and unmeasured, untallied generosity ideally structure relationships. Can one ever repay a parent? "Can you surpass
your father (in giving)?" a Haya asks.

When a family sits down to eat together, for example, after

they have ceremonially washed their hands, a mound of steaming plantains has been placed in the center, and a stew has been shared out in individual portions, one person may take a piece of meat from his own portion and add it to the portion of someone else. This is a gracious act, done out of affection, not because one fears he cannot finish. The recipient must not reciprocate by giving the donor a piece of his own food. To do so means he disdains a gift from that person. Within the family, actions are not governed by reciprocity; they are expected to be characterized by undifferentiated love.

This is why gluttony is such a problem. There are no specific rules that govern the sharing out of food within a family—either reciprocal or hierarchical. It is all a matter of spirit (Hayas would say "heart"). There are no legal sanctions that can be taken against a glutton.

In three stories, *The Woman "Full Moons"*; *Kulili Your Brother of Only One Mother*; and *Satisfaction*, gluttonous husbands murder people because of a desire not to share food. Yet the punishment for this act is not, as one might expect, the reciprocal act of the murderer's execution. It is rather the dissolution of the marriage. Family is the framework within which the tales develop, and their logic is that gluttony brings separation. Within this framework, the murders are merely "objective correlatives" of antisocial gluttony.

SOME CONCEPTUAL CATEGORIES

Concepts such as the expectation of reciprocity, the fact that it applies only outside the family, and the areas of the Haya social landscape with their attendant forces, all form part of a set of Haya terms for attributing motives to human behavior. There is an additional interpretive concept that is so primary, so far-reaching, and so productive of meaning that its significance can be seen in every one of the tales collected here. It is simply that all things have an inside and an outside.

Inside/outside is a way of viewing the world that points out culturally important boundaries: inside and outside a person, a family, a house, a clan, a village, the earth itself. It can be seen in Haya words used to describe various social entities. A significant personal insult is *oku-terwa omwizo*, literally "to be hit inside." A child of a woman of one's own clan, who is not a member of one's own clan because of patrilineal descent, is called *omwihwa*, "one who is taken out (from inside the clan)." Private matters are *eby'omunda*, "matters of inside (the house)." It appears in Haya proverbs: "That which you take from inside (a womb) causes pain," that is, children are a lot of trouble (see the lesson the narrator draws from *I Shall Be Drinking from Them*, pp. 65–67). Also about children, "It sickens but does not cause vomiting," that is, no matter how much trouble children are, you can never totally divest yourself of them.

The inside/outside principle appears also in the basic plot structures of all of the tales included here. Simply stated, dramatic conflict develops when something is placed inside at the beginning of a tale and by the end is gotten out, or is placed outside at the beginning and eventually is brought in. There are many possible variations, depending on the nature of the thing in question, whether it is brought in or out or goes of its own accord, and the kind of boundary crossed. A single story may include several things to be brought in or out and several boundaries to be crossed. Sometimes these are dealt with one after the other, but often insides and outsides are combined in more complex ways.

Plot development in the tales seems to be divided into five basic acts. First, an initial situation that sets the scene, introduces the characters and the relationships between them, and portrays action that results in the second act, displacement. Displacement is so called because in this act, we find something is located inside which should, or wants to be, or is in danger of getting outside; or something is outside which might, for some reason or other, get inside. The third act is attempted or gradual mediation, in which someone tries to take out what is inside, or what is outside tries to come in, or what is inside tries to come out. This action is repeated by the same character at different times and places, or by different characters at the same place. The fourth act is successful mediation, in which something that has been outside successfully gets in, or inside successfully gets out. The final (optional) act is result, in which someone is rewarded or punished, depending on the terms of the plot.

The sequence was discovered by comparing plot development in about 120 Haya stories—those in my own collection plus the published collections of Rehse and Cesard. The five acts do not fit all tales perfectly, but almost all do involve the inside/outside principle. All tales in this collection are formed according to the five-act sequence described above.

This recurrent pattern of plot development points to the importance of inside/outside. Note that all songs in the tales (not all tales have songs) occur in the acts attempted/gradual mediation and successful mediation; that is, just at the time when something is trying to cross or actually is crossing a boundary between inside and outside. This marks the crucial point of the tales; the discourse changes from prose to poetry.

Dramatic action occurs on significant boundaries, most of which we have already encountered. The house is invaded by Leopard (*Open and Let Them Come In*) and a man-made monster (*Mutele, You've Left Me, You've Gone*). A bride is forced out of her husband's house by her in-laws (*Woman-of-People-Forbidden-Horn*), a wife by her gluttony (*Crested Crane and Dove*), an adulterer by the aggrieved husband (*What Was It That Killed Koro?*). A secret gets out of the house helped by a dog (*Kyusi, Kyusi, Good Dog!*), and gets in helped by a bird (*Kulili Your Brother of Only One Mother*). Cat enters following man, but when it gets inside, it goes to live with woman (*The Strong One*).

Both a bride and the dawn are brought into the palace (*Teaser, Little Leper of Munjolobo, Look Back and See What Lugeye Does!*). A chief himself is taken out (*Lusimbagila Bestows on All*), and a chief's "mother" cannot keep herself in (*Greens of the Cow Pasture*).

Leopard is lured from fields into a village by women (*The Glistening One*). Two children come out from an animal's house into a human village of their own accord (*It Was Haste That Killed Her*). And a secret from the wilderness is brought in and almost let out in a village (*Who Was the One Who Ate It?*).

The wilderness is crossed by a wife for her husband (*Have You Not Seen Luhundu?*), by a mother for her child (*Give-Him-Sweetness-If-He-Cries*), and by a child for his father (*The Water of Ikongora*).

The tales *Squeezer* and *The Serpent of Kamushalanga* introduce a new boundary: a character's body. In these tales, an animal becomes a handsome groom. Outside, in appearance, he was an animal; inside he is a person. The action of the tales concerns the emergence of an inner reality.

Although they do not undergo such dramatic transformations, protagonists in the other tales as well are characterized by an outward/inward, apparent/real contrast. The tale of *Crested Crane and Dove* describes a distinction between inward qualities and outward appearance. Crested crane is beautiful on the outside, but a stupid glutton on the inside. The dove is homely on the outside, but a self-controlled, knowing Haya wife on the inside.

Characters who bring brides and the dawn to the chief's palace are outwardly insignificant creatures—a small bird, a little leper, and a dog—but inwardly have the cunning and perseverance to succeed. The same can be said of the youngest child in *The Water of Ikongora.*

The cat mistakes outward physical appearances for inward realities in *The Strong One* when he surmises from man's weak exterior—he has no claws, horns, or tusks—that he poses no threat to the lion, for whom the cat has been standing guard. The opposite situation characterizes Kibwana, a chief's son who is so beautiful on the outside that a chiefdom almost falls, a queen would desert her husband for him, and the daughter of the Kaiser himself wants only to be seen with him as her consort. On the inside, however, at various times in the story, he is as unfit to rule as he is to be a complete husband.

The inside/outside person boundary is important for understanding character motivations. According to Haya theories about what motivates people to act, inside every person are appetites or desires (*amailu*). Under normal conditions, an appetite is kept inside; it is controlled. But in some situations, control weakens, the appetite comes out into the open, and the person acts in an unusual or antisocial way. The tales explore various appetites and the conditions which allow them to emerge.

The collection of tales can be seen as a catalogue of Haya desires, although probably not a complete one. In addition to food, there are appetites for sex (*Squeezer, Kibwana,* and *Blocking the Wind*), knowledge (the temptation to see a "sweet thing" in *Look Back and See What Lugeye Does!*), seeing a loved one who is greatly missed (*Have You Not Seen Luhundu?* and *Nchume*), progeny (*I Shall Be Drinking from Them, Kibwana*), revenge (*Lusimbagila; She's Killed One. We've All of Us Come*). There is an appetite "to be seen with" somebody of high prestige that motivates the chief's retinue and the Kaiser's daughter in *Kibwana* and the cat in *The Strong One.* The uncontrollable urge to be seen among one's riches drives out the unlucky queen mother in *Greens of the Cow Pasture.* The desire "to make something pleasing," which includes fancywork, cooking, and sex, lures willful maidens to marriage with chiefs (*Teaser, Little Leper of Munjolobo*) the way that Leopard is lured through his appetite for food (*The Glistening One*).

Control stands in opposition to appetite. Self-control regulates the flow from inward feelings to outward behavior. Inside, one may feel desire, fear, vengefulness, or curiosity, but he or she must not let this interfere with the pursuit of the proper course of action. Hayas call this virtue *oku-nyikila*, "to persevere," or *oku-gumisa omwoyo*, "to harden or tighten (one's) heart." Self-control and perseverance in the face of overwhelming external opposition are widespread principles in the tales. Characters who have control succeed and characters who lack it fail. Even Leopard succeeds in eating a young girl, paradoxically, only when he manages to control his perpetual craving for food (*Open and Let Them Come In*).

Control of another person, the power to influence his or her behavior, is also the subject of a significant number of tales. One form that this power takes is the explicit, socially sanctioned dominance of one category of person over another. The chief rules his followers. Parents rule the behavior of their children. In-laws rule a new bride.

Where the dominance relationship is more equivocal or where an expected pattern of dominance may be reversed, one character may gain control by using the other's appetite. Women use Leopard's gluttony to control and finally to defeat him in *The Glistening One*. An apparently insignificant leper and a bird win out over the objections of an unmarried girl by making use of her desire "to make (something) pleasing" in *Teaser* and *Little Leper of Munjolobo*. And a new bride controls her husband because she is the source of gratification for his appetites in *Blocking the Wind*.

Two mental processes represented in the tales bear special attention because they mark significant turning points in the action. These are coming to a decision, and being perplexed or confounded. Often, just before he or she embarks on a new course of action, a character in a tale says "No!" To a Haya audience this means he or she has come to a decision regarding which course to follow. "No!" signifies that several alternatives have been considered, but all have been rejected except the one that is then carried out.

When a character is said to be "confounded"—and this occurs in about half the tales—the Haya word used is always the same, *oku-shobelwa*. The word describes an intellectual predicament, usually, but not always, on the part of a single character. Typically, the character has been acting and thinking within a certain framework or logical domain; that is, with certain assumptions about the nature of things, with certain prescriptions for action, with certain values. The character is then confronted with a situation or with information that cannot be assimilated into the framework. This unexplainable oddity "confounds" him, and the action must then shift to a new framework, a new logical domain.

The cat, for example, has been instructed by his blood brother, the lion, to watch over him as he sleeps. But the lion has stipulated that the cat need only be concerned with "strong ones," as the lion himself is a "strong one" and does not worry about any others. One by one, the cat warns the lion about all the animals, but the lion rejects each warning because the animal in question is not a "strong one." The cat is confounded. How can he warn the lion if there are no "strong ones"? The cat's framework is inadequate to deal with this contradiction. The framework must then shift. It does. A man arrives (*The Strong One*).

"Confoundment" is a mental state, but its occurrence in a tale is as significant for the logic of plot development as for the psychology of character portrayal. Confoundment signifies that all possibilities have been exhausted for action and interpretation of action within a given frame. The frame then shifts, in the above example, from the domain of animals alone to the wider world of animals plus humans.

A shift in the opposite direction occurs in *Look Back and See What Lugeye Does!* The chief sends out a messenger to bring back the dawn. He goes, but is outsmarted and returns empty-handed. "My lord," he says, "it has beaten me." A second is sent, but meets the same fate. "My lord . . ," he says, "it has confounded me." At that point the dog comes forward to volunteer. Confoundment marks the place where the human frame is replaced by humans plus animals.

In several instances a character's confoundment does not lead to a new framework of action. The old framework is inadequate, but there is nothing that can replace it. The character has been confounded and remains that way. The possibilities have been exhausted. He or she is powerless to act.

This completes the outlines of our sketch of Hayaland, a vision that is framed, as it were, by Hayas themselves, in the perspective of their own oral tradition. The rural world that has begun to take form is built upon the three-stone foundation of the cooking hearth. Located at the economic and symbolic center, the innermost space in the social landscape, the cooking hearth and its surrounding areas in the inner room are the place of food preparation and consumption, sex and childbearing, and the exchange of knowledge in riddles, tales, and secrets of the family group. The cultural complexities of food and sex account for the central concerns in a majority of tales; the social implications of knowledge account for a significant minority. Themes that involve the symbolic triad of food, sex, and knowledge, and a fourth member, political power, are played out in the spaces and dimensions of the Haya landscape.

Tales in the collection have been grouped according to the kind of imagined event that forms the central dramatic action. A rough approximation of an individual lifecycle seems most apt for some tales, Chapters 3 through 7; other groupings fit the remainder, Chapters 8 and 9. The juxtaposition of similar tales interilluminates central dramatic themes, increasing the range of one's insight into imaginary events. The reader should note that the final tales in Chapters 3, 6, and 8 would be puzzling, if not incomprehensible, without the context of meaning created by the other tales in their respective chapters.

2

Storytelling Performance

When food for an evening's meal has been placed on the hearth and has begun to cook, members of a household sometimes fill the time until dinner with riddles and tales. Riddling and storytelling often go together, before or after one another or mixed in between. As an activity, riddling has more overt verbal give and take. But both entertainments rely on audience collaboration for their success.

In riddling, participants agree to follow a sequence of rules: one person assumes the role of questioner; others try to answer the riddle question he or she poses; if they cannot, they acknowledge defeat and request the answer; the questioner may then demand a village in payment; others propose a certain village to be given; the questioner usually accepts and gives the answer, but he or she may hold out for a bigger village. Of course, these property transfers are purely imaginary.

Riddling play is invoked by a formula that requests and grants a promise of cooperation:

Questioner: Koi!
Others: Lya!
Questioner then asks the riddle.

(The words *koi* and *lya* appear to have no lexical meaning in this context; in other contexts *lya!* means "eat!") This formula may or may not be repeated each time a riddle is asked, but it will almost certainly begin a riddling session. A would-be questioner must receive an acknowledging "lya!" to his "koi!" If he does not, he cannot proceed.

Storytelling also requires cooperative interchange among participants, but of a different kind. The terms of the storytelling agreement are spelled out in its opening formula:

Narrator: *Nkuha lugano* or *Nkwitila lugano*
Audience: *Nkuha lundi* or *Nkwitila lundi*
Narrator: *Lufa*
Audience: *Nkulu y'eirai*
Narrator: *Nkaija nabona*
Audience: *Bona tulole* (*Bona lubona,* "See [thou] Seer," has also been recorded)
Narrator: *Nabona . . .*
   Translation
Narrator: I give you a story *or* I finish you a story.
Audience: I give you another *or* I finish you another.
Narrator: It's done.
Audience: The news of long ago.
Narrator: I came and I saw.
Audience: See so that we may see.
Narrator: I see . . . (here begins the story)

This is the opening in its most extended form. It is composed of two parts. The first, "I give you a story . . . the news of long ago," is about swapping tales in a storytelling session and about the long ago nature of the narrated events. As a rule, several tales are told at a single sitting. If several good storytellers are present, they will alternate playing the role of narrator. Parents encourage children to try their narrative competence in telling a tale. The second part of the opening, "I came and I saw . . . I see . . . ," is about "seeing" events in a tale. The narrator "sees" them and helps the audience "see" them also. This collective visualization of events is part of the cooperation that supports successful storytelling performances. We shall return to it shortly.

The two parts of the opening may be used separately, together, or not at all. The absence of an opening means that the situation in which narrator and audience find themselves has already been defined as a storytelling situation by preceding performances or by a request that a certain tale be told. Precise wording also varies, but the first part, if it is spoken, is about swapping stories and "the news of long ago," and the second, if it occurs, is about "seeing." The second is used more frequently than the first.

When an audience responds to the narrator's "I came and I saw," it almost always says, "*bona tulole*," which I have translated as "See so that we may see." *Oku-bona* usually means "to see with the eyes," but in other contexts it can mean "to see something in a certain way," that is, to have a particular opinion. *Oku-lola* means "to see" also, but in the sense of the English expression "Let's see," or "We'll see." *Oku-lola* could thus be translated "to appear to some-one," and the opening phrase *Bona tulole* could be rendered, "See and let it appear to us," or "See and let us see."

The expression appears as "See so that we may see" (an equally correct rendering) to indicate the active role members of an audience play in a successful storytelling performance. They help a narrator to project his images on an imaginary screen seen in their collective mind's eye. The narrator projects these images by "seeing" them himself. He describes events as though they were occurring at that very moment; he becomes one character, then another, and "sees" the events of a tale as they do.

The performance temporarily erases differences in the time and space between events in a tale and their reenactments in the storytelling present. This marked suspension of temporal and spatial distinctions is achieved with an audience's collaboration and for its aesthetic enjoyment. As a storyteller shifts his or her approach from description to impersonation, the events of then and there become visible here and now. Grammatically, the narrator alternates between third-person narration-about and first-person impersonation-of. This is the central feature of a storytelling performance, whether the tale told is a centuries-old folktale, a political incident that has taken on legendary significance, or an interaction of earlier in the day that is worthy of retelling later in the evening. The third-person/first-person shift profoundly influences the way a storyteller recreates the events of a tale and the way an audience is entertained by that recreation.

When a performer impersonates a given character in a tale, he identifies his intellectual capacities with those of the character and behaves as he, she, or it would in that situation. This is the method that generates spontaneous dialogue within a tale, voice intonations, gestures—all the modalities of storytelling. The variety, depth, and balance of these ad lib embodiments and enactments create richness in a story's texture and meaning.

The audience's role is to see what the narrator sees. They do this by "going along with him," by interpreting and integrating the many and complex statements he makes into a coherent picture. The audience follows the unfolding of a tale by understanding the changing relationships among characters. They interpret statements made by one character in one way, statements made by another character in another way, and statements made in the authorial voice in still another. The audience keeps track of the implications that a preceding event holds for a succeeding one, and they supply cultural connotations to objects, characters, modes of address, and intonations that appear in a tale. They move with the tone and rhythm that a narrator establishes for a performance, so that a narrator's voice modulations, pauses, or hurried lack of pauses make meaningful contrasts to an established norm. If an audience "sees" what a narrator "sees," they will be moved and entertained by his or her performance.

Hayas say that the most important attribute of a well-formed story is that each significant element must be present and in its proper order. This applies not only to tales but to any kind of narration—an account of one's travels, for example, or conveying a dictated message. Adults teach children to keep remembered items in a particular order by sending them with messages from household to household. Children are also encouraged to narrate simple tales to sharpen this skill. Remembering and narrating details in their proper order requires practice and concentration (try learning and performing a complex tale, and you will recognize this). The most frequent mistake in Haya storytelling appears to be the introduction of an incident before its proper time.

Some Haya tales have a marked spatial order as well as a temporal order. A narrator often specifies that protagonists set out from a place like "here" and journey to a place like place N. If the characters engage in a repeated activity—singing a song, for example—the narrator will locate instances of that activity at particular points along the way. The spatial sequence, constructed from locations along a familiar route, helps an audience to visualize the events.

The action of a Haya tale often concludes with words like, "And when I saw these things, I came to tell you about them." This, along with the dramatic resolution that directly precedes it, is called the *empendekelo*, the "breaking off" of the tale. It can also be called *okw-itila*, "to finish (the tale) for (someone)," as in the opening *nkwitila lugano*, "I finish for you a story." The finishing of

the tale shifts the audience's frame of reference from the world of
tales, where the narrator has "seen" the imaginary events, back to
the world of everyday reality.

The conclusion of a tale may include a statement of the lesson,
as the narrator sees it, that the tale illustrates. Such a statement is
called *okw-itulula*, a word which also means to decant a liquid, usually millet beer, so as to separate out the sediment. Stating the lesson directly might be seen as separating out the cultural values expressed in a tale from the dramatic action that embodies them.

Cultural values have developed from historical conditions in
Hayaland. Often tales reflect a past reality; sometimes they incor-
porate elements from the present. But the concerns they address
are resonant with aspects of contemporary everyday life.

Tales can speak to the contemporary situation because the categories that structure imagined events also form part of the repertoire of categories Hayas use to interpret everyday affairs. The stories are simpler and more abstract than situations in the real social
world, but they are understandable in similar terms. Social dominance, social reciprocity, and sexual appetite, for example, are parts
of both imagined tales and the real social world. Concepts used to
comprehend them in one domain are useful in the other as well.

The two worlds, to a degree, are understandable in the same
terms. This commonality establishes the constitutive and rhetorical
relationship between social reality and the reality portrayed in the
tales. Tales are metaphors for aspects of social life as understood by
Hayas. They are abstract, artistic statements that objectify and
grant perspective on the culture they describe. They enable Hayas
to hold aspects of their social world at arm's length, so to speak, to
examine them, to communicate them to one another, to reconfirm
them, to think about changing them, and to entertain themselves
with those images of their own lives.

INTERPRETATION

The point at which storytelling art and meaning intersect is
the storyteller's view of the world as seen through each protagonist's mask. The two sides of storytelling, the significance of events
as they are perceived and communicated by a narrator, and the
spontaneous, aesthetic experience of the performance itself, reinforce one another through a narrator's ability to interpret and enact

imagined events from different points of view. Rich performances proceed from rich interpretations.

If we would have Haya stories live in a non-Haya setting, reveal to us their intrinsic cultural value, show us how they are comical, tragic, well wrought, and insightful, then we must confront the intelligence that informs descriptions and enactments of events in the tales. Such an intelligence is like an optical lens through which both narrator and audience see events. It brings an event into cultural focus. It indicates aspects that are significant and necessary to comprehend the event. It helps an observer to construe actors' motivations and to understand the causes of those motivations. In short, the intelligence we seek interprets human activities the way Hayas interpret them.

The interaction between the interpretive intelligence of a storyteller and the sequence of events in a tale produces cultural meaning and aesthetic performance. The synthesis of conceptual categories and linear narrative is a "language" in the sense that it creates and conveys meaning. Meanings here depend on the tale as a whole rather than on individual words, so that the "language" of storytelling is a more abstract, generalized level of communication than the language itself, of which tales are composed. For example, the tale *Have You Not Seen Luhundu?* tells the simple story of a husband who leaves his new bride to seek fortune. He becomes lost and stays much longer than expected. The wife follows, singing to people she meets to ask the husband's whereabouts. She finds him and they return. This is the sequence of events.

A Haya interpretive intelligence directs one's attention to certain features of the depicted situations. First, what is the bride's motivation? It is a desire to see a loved one whom she has not seen for a long time (like the siblings in the tale of *Nchume*). The bride pushes on through the wilderness in an act of perseverance. Inward resolve conquers external forces that would frustrate it. She successfully mediates her husband's position from being lost outside to being recovered and brought inside again. These categories—desire of a certain kind, perseverance, outside and inside spaces in the landscape—are part of an interpretive intelligence. Applied to the sequence of events, they yield a statement: the bride, motivated by a strong desire to see her lost loved one, persevered to go outside and bring him back inside. This statement made by the tale in Haya storytelling "language" expresses a more abstract level of

meaning than the literal description of events. It is based on interpretations of events in the tale according to a set of categories that
storytellers and audiences use to "see," and also to understand, similar events in the real world.

Part of our task in presenting the tales is to describe the conceptual categories in a Haya interpretive intelligence and to show
how they are realized in particular sequences. Much of the description has been done in the preceding chapter. The remainder is to
be found in forewords and notes to individual chapters, where it is
also shown how the categories combine to create and convey cultural meanings.

It might be argued that the existence of an interpretive intelligence and a narrative "language" is based on circular reasoning, for
both the primary evidence for their existence and the phenomenon
which they are said to explain are one and the same: namely, a
collection of tales. However, the existence of the categories has
been demonstrated in other areas of Haya verbal art and culture (a
kinship term here, a proverb there, see p. 19) and shown to fit
homologously with more substantial features of Haya society, such
as the traditional house type, the settlement pattern, and the social
organization of the economy. Moreover, categories in an interpretive intelligence and "language" account for a rich variety of narrative detail with relatively few concepts (e.g., appetite, control, perseverance, inside/outside), which can combine to form a wide range
of meanings. As a working hypothesis, these concepts led to the
discovery of three underlying character motivations that are un-
named in the texts of their respective tales: the cat's motivation "to
be seen with" someone of higher status in *The Strong One*, the reluctant maiden's desire "to make things pleasing" in *Teaser* and *Little
Leper of Munjolobo*, and sexual desire, the source of the husband's
craziness in *Blocking the Wind*. These discoveries have been tested
with several Haya speakers and found to be correct. Evidence internal to the tales shows an interpretive intelligence at work that is
rich in expression, elegant in structure, and methodologically useful. External evidence and corroboration answer the charge of cir-
cularity.

But in a larger sense, our interpretations may be judged by
how much they augment a reader's enjoyment and appreciation of
the tales collected here. For if the ability to tell and to enjoy narrative is universal (as it seems to be), and if the reader is not out of

sympathy with Hayas in regard to basic social values, then, should our interpretations, in fact, illuminate what Hayas find entertaining about the tales, the reader will see the tales' aesthetic force enhanced by the interpretations. In any event, that is our goal.

METHODOLOGY AND PRESENTATION

The translations and interpretations included here have developed over a ten-year period. For eighteen months, 1968–1970, during fieldwork that was focused on different but related subjects, Sheila Dauer and I compiled a collection of folktale performances.[1] These were transcribed by Ma Winifred Kisiraga and Ta Elias Kaishula, both of whom narrated tales as well. Dauer and I checked transcriptions with Ta Elias Kaishula and Ma Winifred Kisiraga and asked our Haya associates to explicate words, concepts, and sometimes actions that seemed especially interesting.

After leaving Tanzania and completing work on Haya conversational use of proverbs, I began a process that ultimately led to the interpretations included here. The rhetorical literary analysis of Kenneth Burke gave direction to the investigation. It sought in Haya folktales a "rhetoric of motives," a set of Haya terms for objectifying and construing the motivations of human action in society.[2] The process of extracting cultural meaning from the tales was based on the analytical work of V. I. Propp in his *Morphology of the Folktale*, where formalist methods enable one to discern recurrent patterns of plot development and so to isolate units for comparison among texts.[3] Having found comparable units, I was able to discern in the single unit of a particular tale a combination of elements; moreover, particular combinations could be seen as recombinations of elements in other tales. This insight was guided by structuralist analyses of Claude Lévi-Strauss.[4] As in Lévi-Strauss' analyses, the recombinations of elements suggested the workings of a philosophical system; but unlike his mythic results, which speak to humanly imposed order in the cosmos, our folktale results speak to the motivations of human actors in society.

The results of the formal (syntagmatic) and structural (paradigmatic) analyses were a set of elements, or cultural categories, and ways of combining them to make sense in an apparently Haya fashion. These categories and combinations (termed "interpretive

intelligence" and storytelling "language." respectively, above) were
developed from both texts and from other ethnographic data. The
proper combination of cultural categories produces a statement that
has meaning to a person who shares the culture. As with a language, if one knows the words and the way to combine them properly, he or she can produce statements meaningful to a speaker of
that language.

In the present context, categories and combinations produce
interpretations of tales, that is, retellings of them in terms of abstract cultural concepts. The test of validity for these statements is
to ask a person who shares the culture whether or not the statements validly interpret the events of a tale in Haya conceptual language. This was done in an extended written correspondence between Ma Winifred Kisiraga and me and with two subsequent trips
to Hayaland in 1973 and 1975.[5]

The first tale to be significantly interpreted was *Kibwana*. The
interpretation centered on the several aspects of marriage which are
set in opposition to one another in the events of the tale and also on
the food-sex metaphors present in the text. Ma Kisiraga accepted
most of the statements I had constructed with elements analyzed
from texts. Some she augmented considerably, and a few she rejected completely.

This interchange developed the central concepts of appetite,
control, and perseverance. My trip in 1973 filled out the interpretations of the other tales in this regard. At that time, Ma Kisiraga
supplied the last, most puzzling, but now quite obvious reading of
a character's motivation: the cat's desire to be seen with beings of
high prestige in *The Strong One*.

The interpretations grew in completeness based on further
analysis and the addition of the confirmed elements. In 1975, I was
able to return to test a more complete set of interpretations. Besides
further consultations with Ma Kisiraga and several other Hayas, I
was fortunate to be able to confer with Mr. Richard Mutembei,
Educational Director of the Lutheran Mission in West Lake District, who is regarded as an expert in matters of Haya traditional
culture. I played tapes for him of performances that seemed crucial
to the interpretations. I think it is accurate to say that we agreed on
the aptness of almost all the interpretations, while we differed
somewhat on the emphases given certain elements. The present
interpretations should be regarded as having been made by an out-
sider to Haya culture, guided by the methods of analysis at hand
and by the patient instruction of Haya colleagues. When I have

erred, it is because I have imperfectly understood their instructions.

I could not confirm every element of every interpretation of every tale included here. In general, elements that are framed in Haya concepts—appetites, settings, social statuses and roles—have been discussed with Hayas. Elements that speak to the workings of a symbolic system—logical inversions, other symbolic transformations, and generic patterns in story plot—have not been confirmed with Haya speakers, although they are based on a knowledge of Haya language, ethnography, and oral traditions. In general, I have marked semiotic interpretations with words like "seems" and "appears to be."

The interpretive process thus follows the trail of symbolic explication blazed by Victor Turner, who demonstrated the importance of indigenous exegesis of symbols (the necessity of asking the people who use symbols for explanations of their meanings rather than an anthropologist's relying solely on his or her own interpretive powers). We have added to this interpretive methodology the descriptive linguist's test of a valid model, which is its ability to generate statements that are acceptable to a native speaker.

Validity with respect to Haya culture is one value that is asserted for the interpretations. But as has been pointed out, they may equally be judged by the degree to which they nourish a reader's appreciation of the tales. For to project the tales in a medium accessible to non-Hayas is our primary objective.

ORAL LITERATURE
ON THE PRINTED PAGE

Our project in cross-cultural entertainment must necessarily confront one mediation process beyond that required by the barrier of language and culture. This is the mediation needed to transform a verbal performance into the written word, for the tales collected here are enacted and enjoyed by Hayas as oral literature. They embody the modalities of living performance—the unfolding of a story through time, significant pauses in the flow of narration, changes in the pace in which events are depicted, the tonalities of the human voice, singing, clapping the hands and snapping the fingers to reinforce rhythms in the tale, and mime. The art of oral literature also partakes of a cooperative, mutually supportive interchange between performer and audience, a focusing of collective creative energies that resurrects imagined events from cultural tradition. The impossibility of completely translating this multidimensional aesthetic experience to the printed page does not unseat our endeavor.

A way of mediating Haya oral performance for English readers has been developed. Like actual storytelling, it embodies a creative interchange between performer and audience. In effect, it invites the reader to employ his or her "mind's ear" as well as "mind's eye" in reading the tale, that is, to participate in the recreation of the oral modalities of traditional storytelling performances, and in so doing, to experience the imagined events as closely as possible to the way a Haya narrator, with the help of a Haya audience, projects them.

To this end, tape-recorded storytelling performances have been transcribed according to a system based on the one developed by Dennis Tedlock in an innovative book of Zuñi narratives, *Finding the Center*.[6] Aspects of performance such as pauses, voice quality and intonation, and, to a degree, gestures, are clearly indicated according to a simple set of notations described below.

The notational system is designed to increase a reader's understanding, appreciation, and enjoyment of a tale. I have tried not to overburden the transcription with complex notations and have therefore tested and omitted certain features which might distract the reader's eye from the flow of narrative images.

Pauses between narrative phrases are represented in four ways. A narrator's normal pause for breath, about one second in duration, is marked by a downward move and a return to the left-hand margin:

He says, "Now what shall I do?"
He takes one of his men
and says, "Now go . . .
to the man's house, inside there . . .
Go and find the dawn for me."

A pause that is clearly present but of a shorter duration than a normal pause—usually about a half-second long—is marked by a downward move without a return to the left-hand margin:

This one comes out
        and that one comes out
                from inside the calabash.

A pause that is longer than a normal one and lasts about two seconds is marked with a circle:

When she had gone . . .
and entered the forest . . .
she meets in there—a leopard.
o
The leopard says, "What are you searching for?"

A pause longer than two seconds is marked with a double circle:

He snaps his fingers in frustration. What you have tasted, she
    had not yet tasted. It doesn't pain her. But he, who had
    already tasted it, is pained.
oo
He's miserable.

Note the convention of indenting when a single narrative line is longer than a single line on the printed page. Double-circle pauses can sometimes signal that the narrator is searching for a word.

A rising intonation at the end of a line is indicated by three dots (. . .). After one or a series of rising intonations, a falling intonation is marked with a period. This rising, rising, falling intonation sequence is found frequently in the tales:

They set out one day to travel . . .
o
Twelve o'clock passed . . .
                one o'clock . . .
                            three o'clock . . .
                                      and
    they hadn't gotten food . . .
                or even water.

Words spoken in a LOUDER voice are printed in capital letters. The letters in words that are d-r-a-w-n o-u-t are separated by dashes. Words spoken in a DEEP VOICE are indicated with small capital letters. Lines that are spoken with a sing-song intonation—something like whining but not nasalized—are printed in italics:

THE ONES WHO HEAR SAY, "MY LORD PROVIDER,
STOP KILLING PEOPLE.
THE BIRD HAS BROUGHT HER.
They jump up and run out of the p-a-l-a-c-e.
They take out a l-e-a-t-h-e-r c-a-p-e.
                                They take out a s-e-c-o-n-d
      c-a-p-e.
Eh-Eh: They take out a s-e-d-a-n c-h-a-i-r.
THEY FIND THE GIRL CRYING FOUR PATHWAYS OF
TEARS.

   Songs that appear in the tales are indented and follow the ty-
pographical conventions of poetry.
   When other features are noted, such as gestures and audience
comments, no special notation is used. In general, I have tried to
make the conventions as easy as possible to follow and to use ty-
pographical symbols in ways that do not contradict their conventional meaning.
   Lines are numbered for reference according to the following
arbitrary convention: each spoken line that returns to the left-hand
margin counts as one line. Thus, for the purposes of reference, the
line quoted above, "They set out one day to travel . . . " counts as
a single line, as does the line that follows it,

"Twelve o'clock passed . . .
                        one o'clock . . .
                                    three o'clock . . .
                                                and
      they hadn't gotten food . . .
                        or even water.

This is counted as a single line because it begins at the left-hand
margin and does not return there. The lines in songs are not numbered. They can be referred to by specifying the lines they fall
between.
   The title given to a tale is taken from a significant, repeated, or
memorable line or is the name of a central character. Haya tales do
not have formal titles. They are referred to—as in a request for a
telling of a specific tale—by one of the methods already described
or by a short summary of the events in the tale. "Tell the story
about how dog brought the dawn," someone might ask, or equally,

"Tell *The Dawn of Lugeye*." The titles that are found in this collection could be used in Haya to request them from their tellers.

NOTES ON THE TRANSLATION

All but two tales were originally performed in Haya; the final two in Chapter 9 were performed in Swahili. Several aspects of the Haya language have no direct correspondence in English, a situation that required certain choices among English alternatives to be made and followed as consistently as possible throughout the collection. In Haya, for example, there is a third-person animate pronoun that does not specify gender, like the words "person" or "child" in English. The child in the tale *Give-Him-Sweetness-If-He-Cries* is nowhere specified as either male or female. Given the alternatives, I have chosen the masculine pronoun because "him" is as close to being an unmarked pronoun as we have in English (the Haya is truly unmarked). Keep in mind, though, that Haya does not specify the gender of the child. In other instances I have tried to indicate the unmarkedness of gender where none is specified.

Like other Bantu langauges, Haya has a system of noun classes. Each class is characterized by a particular noun prefix. So *mu-haya* is a Haya person, *mu-jungu* is a European person, *mu-ganda* is a person from Uganda. A leopard is *em-pisi*, a hyena is *em-pumi*, a chicken is *en-koko*. There are fifteen or so noun classes in Haya, depending on how one defines the term. This feature of grammar would not concern us, were it not for the fact that Hayas sometimes change the regular class of a noun to another class by changing its prefix in order to convey a connotational meaning. *Em-pisi* is leopard, but sometimes he appears in the tales as *eki-pisi*, bigger, more fearsome, and able to walk and talk like a human. To signify this change, leopard becomes Leopard. All other animals are spelled with a lower-case letter except when their names have been similarly altered in Haya. *Eki-nyonyi* is a bird and appears as this in several tales. But in one there is an *olu-nyonyi* who is a tall, thin, strange Bird indeed (*It Was Haste That Killed Her*). The connotation "tall, thin" is carried by the prefix.

The connotation "little, pretty, cute" is carried by the prefix *ka-*, so that *mu-bembe*, a leper, becomes *ka-bembe*, "little leper," in *Little Leper of Munjolobo*. Dog, *em-bwa*, is given a praise name *nya-ka-bwa*, "Good Dog," in *Kyusi, Kyusi, Good Dog!*

The tense system in Haya is extremely complex, and a study

of its subtleties of meaning is beyond the scope of this work. In translating the tales, however, I have tried to render tenses of verbs into English as faithfully as possible, *but especially to retain the shifts that occur between present and past tenses.* This shift is important because a narrator often uses it to mark off segments in the narrative. In general, connective and subordinate information is presented in past tenses; central dramatic action is related in the present.

The tense translated as present is actually a form of the verb used almost exclusively in storytelling. It is the least inflected form, pronominal prefix plus stem, as in *a-genda,* "he or she goes." Hayas would rarely use this form in conversation. Present time is rendered *na-genda,* "he or she is in the process of going at this moment," or, more frequently, *ya-genda,* "he or she has gone a short time ago, is going now, or will shortly go in the future," having the effect that his or her presence is no longer at a given place. The storytelling form *a-genda,* used conversationally, means "it is his or her characteristic state to be going." I believe this tense is used in storytelling because it is the simplest to form rapidly. The same can be said of the present tense in English storytelling.

Certain Haya words used as terms of address, reference, and entitlement also require a brief note. The Haya word for "my father" is *tata.* This is used in addressing and in referring to one's male parent and also as a term of respectful address to any male adult. The word may even be addressed to a child, as a form of praise. *Tata* is translated as "father" in the tales, or as "my father" if the additional specificity is needed. A shortened form of *tata, Ta,* is used as a title, like "Mister" in English. *Ta* may be used with either one's family name or one's given name; thus Haruna Batonde might be addressed or referred to either as *Ta* Haruna or as *Ta* Batonde. I have chosen to retain "Ta" in the translations rather than substitute the English "Mister."

The Haya word for "mother" is *mawe* or *mae* (two syllables). *Mawe* has the same pattern of usage as *tata,* except, of course, it refers to and addresses female adults and sometimes children. Its shortened form, *Ma,* is used as a title placed in front of women's names; *Ma* has been left untranslated in the tales.

Baba is a term of address for which there is no English equivalent. It implies familiarity, the way "father" and "mother" imply respect. *Baba* is said to derive from *iba,* "husband," and is used by a wife to address her husband familiarly and intimately. A man might also address his wife this way, or another woman with whom he is on familiar terms, a woman of his own village, for example. *Baba* appears to be used most often by women, however, and among women one to another, to express their solidarity. It remains untranslated in the tales.

Bojo is a term of address that derives from *mwojo*, "male child." It can be used to address a child of either sex or an adult, usually of lower status than the speaker. *Bojo* is used as praise and in situations where the speaker tries to cajole the addressee into a certain action or belief. "Child" as it appears in southern United States English might be used to translate *bojo*, but "child" would not fit all the situations *bojo* does and might cause confusion if the reader tries to understand one pattern of usage in terms of another. *Bojo* is therefore left untranslated. When the word "child" appears in tales, it translates the more frequently used Haya *mwana*.

Mwana wa mawe, "child of my mother," is a term of address or reference for the speaker's full sibling, but can also be used to address unrelated people. It connotes the highest degree of intimacy and solidarity. "Child of my mother" appears in English in the tales.

Waitu, "my lord," is a term of address that is based upon the traditional social structure of Hayaland. *Waitu* was used to address members of the ruling clans—those related to the chiefs. The speaker might be a member of either a ruling or a nonruling clan. The pattern of usage has been extended to all male adults and sometimes to women. "My lord" is used by a narrator to address collectively the members of his or her audience, regardless of sex.

Exclamations in storytelling performance often signify a kind of confoundment or astonishment. These have been included in the tales and left untranslated. There appear to be two principal types: exclamations spoken by the dramatis personae themselves and exclamations that appear to be spoken in the authorial voice. The former are expressions of a particular character's predicament; the latter appear to comment on the course of events in the tale as a whole.

Most common among the exclamations spoken by dramatis personae themselves is "Eh?" which has a length of almost two syllables and a high or mid-falling intonation pattern that might be represented linearly as ⌐╲ (high-falling) or ⌐╲ (mid-falling). "Eh?" is said with the lips open. An alternate form, with the same intonation pattern and meaning, is "Mh?" It is said with the lips closed. Both exclamations are reactions to unexplainable or unex-

pected events and can be taken to have the approximate meaning,
"How can this be?" or "What's this?" In a sense they are quasi
confoundments, suggestions of or references to that state without
the more formal declaration that a verbalized description entails
(see p. 23).

More emphatic forms of "Eh?" and "Mh?" are, in ascending
order of emotional intensity: "Iy?" said with a high-falling intonation ⌐\ ; "Iyo!" three syllables long, a high-falling-high intonation ⌐\/ ; and "Iyo-o-o," a high, trailing off intonation ⌐\ .

Two exclamations appear to remark on the speaker's own position vis-à-vis an unexpected or unexplainable event. "Hii!", high-
steady intonation or trailing off at the end, ⎯ or ⌐\ is an
expression of surprise and self-pity at an unhappy turn of events.
An exclamation that seems to be related to this is "Ha!" or "Ha-
ah!", middle-steady or falling intonation, ⎯ or ⌐\ . With this
a character seems to say to himself, "Look at where I now am" or
"Consider me in my present circumstances"; the circumstances
may be either fortunate or unfortunate.

"Mh!" and its open-lipped variant "Eh!" appear to be expressions of concern or of sympathy. They are one syllable long, said
with a low intonation. They may be repeated several times, as in
"Mh! mh! mh!", an expression that seems to mean, as it does in
English, "That's too bad."

Other nonverbal utterances appear frequently, but are not exclamations. They are expressions of assent and dissent. "E-e-h" has
a short e sound as in the English "bet." It is held for a length of two
or three syllables in a middle-steady intonation ⎯⎯⎯. "Mm" is
the same sound (with the same meaning) uttered with the lips
closed. "Uh-uh," signifying dissent, sounds the same as it does in
English: middle-steady intonation with a glottal stop halfway
through. "M-m" is the same utterance sounded with the lips closed.

One nonverbal utterance may answer or follow upon another.
The sequence "Eh?" "Mm!" could result from the following situation: person A makes a statement surprising or dismaying to person
B. "Eh?" B reacts (how can this be?); "Mm!" A affirms (it is so!).
The same sequence might be articulated: "Mh?" "E-e-h!" Or a
character who is surprised by something dangerous to him may
react and then reflect "Mh? . . . Ha-ah!" ("What's this? . . . Now
see where I've gotten myself!")

Utterances of assent and dissent occur frequently in conversational speech as well as in formal narrations. The others, "Eh?",

"Mh?", "Iy?", "Iyo!", "Iyo-o-o!", "Hii!", "Ha!", and "Ha-ah!" are used less frequently in conversation; their appearance depends on the emotional and theatrical level of the conversational discourse. The following two exclamations do not appear in conversation, but are found in the tales more frequently than any others. They are spoken in the authorial voice, rather than in the voice of particular dramatis personae.

"Eh-Eh!" and its closed-lipped variant "Mh-Mh!" are said with a glottal stop midway, like the negatives "Uh-uh" and "M-m." But their intonation pattern rises in the middle and falls at the end, like $\wedge$; or, if it is a more emphatic "Eh-Eh!" rising and falling become lengthened into glides or swoops $\frown$, glottal stop and highest level of tone coming at the same (mid-) point.

The expressions seem to link segments of the narrative. They comment on the significance and intensity of an action just completed at the same time that they introduce another action that adds to the affective energy of the plot. Their meaning might be expressed lexically as something like, "And then look what happened!"

"Eh-Eh!" and "Mh-Mh!" seem to evoke a lyric quality in the tales, connecting a string of similarly structured events that build in energy to a climax. These and other nonlexical utterances are "phatic" in nature—they speak to the feelings rather than to the intellect. They open affective channels of communication. In storytelling, this brings the situation described in the tale affectively closer to the situation of the actual storytelling performance. Through these phatic utterances, the narrator coaxes greater emotional participation from herself and the audience. The fullest examples of this are several of the tales of Kelezensia Kahamba and *Greens of the Cow Pasture* by Erika Manuel.

NARRATIVE STYLE

Tedlock's system of notation makes several things possible when presenting narrative style. First, it invites and enables a reader to participate in the re-creation of a traditional tale. Contributing to the enactment of storytelling events enables one to see them vividly and with deeper insight.

Second, the system represents a narrator's discourse more accurately than conventional paragraph notation would. The minimal unit of an utterance bounded by pauses (that is, a line) requires the translation to convey information in the order, at the rhythm, and in the quantum units which are dictated by the narrator's own speech. In these translations, the storyteller determines the pace at which events unfold, the relative emphasis placed on words, phrases, or whole incidents, and the division of the tale into dramatic acts.[7]

Finally, this system of transcription enables us to see differences in style among the narrators. We see Benjamin Kahamba begin his tale (*Open and Let Them Come In*) slowly, ploddingly, careful to place each detail in proper order under the watchful eye of his mother, Ma Kelezensia Kahamba. This labored pace, which can be characterized as "X does a. After he has done a, he does b. Now after he has done b he does c," is resorted to by all narrators at one time or another to confirm the order of events and to give themselves time to plan subsequent action. Benjamin moves into a more fluid style as he develops his tale.

Benjamin's mother is one of the four or five premier storytellers whose performances appear in this collection. Ma Kelezensia Kahamba's style of narration tends toward the lyrical. The scenes she depicts are symmetrically balanced. She focuses on a telling detail that affects listeners with its immediacy or intimate poignancy. She builds her tales from successions of similarly structured episodes.

See, for example, her portrayal of the stepmother's decision to kill her stepdaughter so her own daughter will be the beautiful one. The balance and rhythmic swing of the stepmother's deliberation sets the story on its sentimentally beautiful, if somewhat terrible, course (lines 9–12 of *Nchume*). Similarly, the scene in which bride, bird, and half-naked mother arrive at the chief's court mixes beautiful, terrible, and poignant elements of song: pleas by courtiers to the chief to "stop killing people"; the girl's tears flowing in four pathways from her face; and a sing-song compilation of details of the little cowbird's triumph (*Teaser*, lines 89–127).

But my favorite example of Ma Kelezensia Kahamba's lyricism is her treatment of how dog brought the dawn by refusing to turn around and see a pretty sight. The first messenger sent for the dawn hears a maidservant's song, turns, and fails:

(the maidservant sings:)
      "You, man! You, man!
      Look back and see what Lugeye does!

He sings with his arms, he sings with his legs,
He wears beads like 'dancing maidens.'
It goes 'cheku,' it goes 'waah.'
It goes 'cheku,' it goes—" THE MESSENGER TURNS
AROUND. "MH?"
(Hands clap!)
     (Fingers snap!)
        The dawn is gone.

o

He's traveling along in darkness again.
He goes to the chief and says, "My lord, it has beaten me."
      (*Look Back and See What Lugeye Does!*, lines 28–31.)

The Tedlock notation allows at least some of the charm and rhythmic elegance of the Haya original to find expression in English print.

Ma Winifred Kisiraga's style in the tales included here is more cerebral. She focuses her descriptive sights on a character's flow of internal thoughts. Interactions between protagonists are played out as strategic encounters or choreographed sequences of action, speech, and intent. See, for example, a bride's gradual surrender to desire in *I Ate Minnows, Little Minnows* (lines 20–33), or the conversational deception between husband and wife in *Satisfaction* (lines 17–40). The victimization of the foolish girl in *The Glistening One* is danced in rhythms of fast and slow, in utterances loud and soft, in intonations rising and falling:

WHEN DAWN CAME ON THE PLANNED DAY,
THEY DRESS FOR A JOURNEY.
THEY SAY, "WHEN WE GO INTO THE FOREST . . . "
they say, "no one should have her eyes open.
                       Everyone should
   shut them."
THEY SAY, "AFTER EACH PERSON SHUTS THEM . . .
then she'll cut a walking stick.
              BUT WHOEVER CUTS A
DEFORMED STICK . . .
             cannot stay with us."

o

So, now that one, the poor thing, was foolish. They go, and
   when they arrived in the forest,

"HAVE YOU ALL SHUT YOUR EYES?" "We've shut them."
    "HAVE YOU ALL SHUT YOUR EYES?" "We've shut
    them."
She closes her eyes.
The other children keep theirs open.
They go and look for a good walking stick. Each person cuts one.
"ARE YOU ALL FINISHED?"
                              They say, "We've finished."
"LET'S LEAVE."
              "Let's leave."
They go outside the forest.
"OPEN YOUR EYES."
"We're opening them." The children open them. (narrator and
    audience laugh)
Now the foolish one returns.
THEN THEY JUDGE THE WALKING STICKS. "PUT
    THE WALKING STICKS DOWN." THEY PUT THEM
    THERE.
WHEN THEY COME TO LOOK AT HERS,
LOOK,
it's as twisted as an eight.
They say, "We can't stay with you any more."

Ma Kisiraga's vision of events in this tale is a clockwork of wills and
designs. Although it is not always seen by all, the hidden movement sometimes appears in a song whose symbolic meaning is
opaque to Leopard or in a stick that is twisted like an 8.
    Another narrator whose distinctive style warrants particular
attention is Ma Laulelia Mukajuna. Ma Laulelia's style is epic. The
images she paints and the rhythms she creates impel her stories
forward with a dramatic force unequalled in the collection. Examples could be drawn from any of her tales included here. *The Legend
of Ikimba* moves from the mysterious interior of a water jar, with its
echoing, descriptive "inside" (the Haya particle *mu*, lines 1–5); to a
loud, roaring, swirling scene of an overflowing lake, a wizardlike
mother-in-law trying to turn back the flood, and a fleeing bride
(lines 27 and 28); to a slow and somber rising, rising, falling intone-
ment of the women's fate (lines 29–31). *Blocking the Wind* is also a
virtuoso performance, replete with furious action (lines 22–24),
outrageous onomatopoeia (line 65), and a highly charged legal re-
buttal in which the speaker pulls out all the rhetorical stops (lines

108–122). There is little chance to linger on a poignant detail in Ma Laulelia's performances. They are continually impelled forward by the force of the unfolding drama.

Ma Laulelia Mukajuna's details increase dramatic tension and move the tale toward resolution. In *Crested Crane and Dove*, for example, the conflict is between a beautiful, long-necked glutton, crested crane, and a homely, short, self-controlled gray dove. The narrator depicts their characteristic movements as they gather grasshoppers in a field:

Now when the (grasshoppers) have fallen . . .
the dove goes with her basket.
She strikes and PUTS them in, strikes and PUTS them in, strikes
    and PUTS them in. CRESTED CRANE
SHOOS THEM OUT SH———— and swallows them.
Sh———— and swallows them.
Sh———— and swallows them.

The busily bobbing dove stores the food. The slowly swooping crane gluttonously devours it. Rhythm, emphasis, and onomatopoeia create a fusion of sound and sense, embody the dramatic conflict, and push the action forward to confrontation and resolution. *Kibwana*, the narrator's premier work, is composed of many such stylistic enactments that inexorably impel the tale and the character from misfortune to misfortune to eventual redemption. Chapter 7 is composed entirely of Ma Laulelia Mukajuna's tales and interpretations of them.

Other distinctive narrative styles can be found in the collection. An index of storytellers is provided to facilitate comparisons of oral narrative styles. Readers merely need remind themselves that the printed texts are recorded speech. One can "hear" the performances by applying the few simple rules of the Tedlock system of notation.

RECORDING AND PERFORMANCE CONTEXT

All performances were tape recorded by Sheila Dauer from 1968 to 1970, except those of Ma Winifred Kisiraga and Ta Elias Kaishula, which were made in contexts (c) and (d) below, and those by Ta Haruna Batonde, which were recorded in later trips. Haya audiences for storytelling were as follows. (a) Most tales were performed before relatively small groups of family and neighbors: all tales of Ma Kelezensia Kahamba and her son, Benjamin; the tales by the Bake family; tales by Ta Keremensi Lutabanzibwa and those of his wife, Ma Laulelia Mukajuna, except *Kibwana*. (b) At my prompting the local chapter of *Umoja wa Wanawake wa Tanzania*, "Tanzanian Women's Unity," met twice for storytelling and refreshments. Only adult women and their small children were present. At the first session the following tales were told (in this order, but not necessarily contiguously): *The Glistening One, The Serpent of Kamushalanga, Magezi, Child of the Valley*, and *Lusimbagila Bestows on All*. The second session was composed of the following four tales: *Give-Him-Sweetness-If-He-Cries, The Woman "Full Moons," Greens of the Cow Pasture*, and *Kibwana*. (c) From sessions at which Sheila Dauer, Ma Winifred Kisiraga, Ta Elias Kaishula, and I were present, three tales are included: the two by Ta Elias and *Satisfaction*. (d) Ma Winifred Kisiraga performed *I Ate Minnows, Little Minnows* for her children with Ta Elias Kaishula, Sheila Dauer, and me present. (e) Ta Haruna Batonde told the two tales included here in his house in the company of a male neighbor and me.

3

Tales of Parents and Children

The four tales in this chapter are presented together because all turn upon a central concern with the parent-child relationship. As a group, they make several, related, narrative observations on the nature of this complex and enduring bond between the generations in a family. They are stories that can be told to children, teaching stories, stories that analyze and comprehend the parent-child relationship by seeing it from several different perspectives.

Two themes emerge in the tales: first, the marked importance of filial duty properly enacted by a son for his father and, second, the pervasive, sustaining nurture that characterizes a mother's relationship with her offspring. The first and last tales in the chapter embody the latter female theme. Note that in these tales the children's sex is unmarked, unnoticed, unimportant to a Haya listener or narrator. What is important is that the characters are mothers and children. The English language makes it difficult to convey this non-specificity, so the translation of the child's name in the first tale is Give-him-sweetness-if-he-cries, but the Haya text does not mark the child as male. The two middle tales, which are about filial duty, specify that the protagonist is a male child. The issues involved in those tales, revenge and inheritance, are features of traditional male kinship obligation.

The final tale in the chapter, *I Shall Be Drinking from Them*, portrays a conflict between male and female principles—between duty and nurture—over some preternatural calabashes. Calabash gourds are grown in many shapes and sizes in Hayaland. With their insides hollowed out, the calabash containers serve a variety of pur-

poses, from ladles to bottles to butter churns. Sometimes calabashes are used to hold fermenting beer; in this case, they are
placed near the hearth, where the fire's warmth will increase the
rate of fermentation. A similar development occurs in *I Shall Be
Drinking from Them*; in this tale, however, the calabashes contain
growing children rather than beer.

Give-Him-Sweetness-If-He-Cries

AS TOLD BY MA KELEZENSIA KONSTANTIN

Now then, my lord, I went and saw for you.
Audience: See so that we may see.
I see a woman bears a child
                              who was crippled.
o
Now when he had become crippled . . .
"That child, my kings, what can we do with him? That child
    who cannot walk?"
She took him to h-e-a-l-e-r-s.
                         But at the healers, everything
        they tried failed.
She went out. She sat down and said, "I'll abandon
    the child . . .
As the Lord has impelled me, I have done."
o
Now while she was there . . .
10 a woman suddenly appears to her.
She says, "You," she says, "that child of yours,"
she says, "if you would take him,
over there to Katóma,"
she says, "there's an old woman,"
she says, "a healer."
                    She says, "She can cure him."

She replies, "Mother, where did you say she is?"
She says, "She's at Katóma."
She says, "Now,"
 she says, "she has Leopards. Her house is full
  with them. And animals of every kind," she says,
  "are also in there."
She says, "But if she would see the child . . . "
20 she says, "she could cure it."
She replies, "Yes, mother, I understand."
She says, "But when you go to travel,"
she says, "find little oranges."
 She says, "Find
  little bananas."
 She says, "Find little lemons."
 She says, "Find
  little sugar cane stalks."
 She says, "Find . . . "
 she says,
"FIND EVERY LITTLE THING THAT'S EDIBLE."
She says, "Fill your basket with them."
 ○
She says, "Then go over
 to the man's house, Ta Katatílwa's . . . "
she says, "and order a little drum to be made for you."
She says, "Whenever the leopards stop and question you,"
she says, "always play the little drum."
 She says, "And the little
  bananas, and the little bits of foods," she says,
  "take some out each time and hand them some
  and let them eat."
 ○
Now the woman goes.
 ○
30 She goes and finds all those little things. She gathers them up
  and puts them in her basket.
Her child . . .
 she throws upon her back
and she goes.
 ○
Now when she had reached to about Kamulengéra
  right over here . . .

○

she is stopped there . . .
                              by Leopard.
○ (Leopard speaks in a deep voice; the woman speaks in a
      high voice.)
"YOU, WOMAN, WHERE ARE YOU GOING?"
"Father, I'm going to Katóma there,
      where they've directed me . . .
                                    to the healer."
"IY? WHAT'S THAT YOU'RE CARRYING ON YOUR BACK?"
"Father, it's my child."
40 "WELL, HOW IS HE?"
"He became crippled."
"TAKE HIM OUT. LET'S SEE."
She takes him off her back.
He looks.
"MH!
        MOTHER
              THEY WILL CURE HIM.
MH! MH! MH! MH!
              THEY'LL SOON CURE HIM. GO AHEAD.
                                    BUT NOW,
        WHAT ARE THOSE LITTLE ONES IN YOUR BASKET?"
"Father, they're little things of Give-him-sweetness."
It says, "COULDN'T YOU GIVE ME A BIT TO EAT?"
She takes out a little lemon,
                    she gives it one and it eats.
                                    "NOW
        THEN, WHAT'S THAT LITTLE THING?"
50 She says, "That's a drum."
"BUT WHAT'S IT FOR?"
She says, "To play, father."
"PLAY IT FOR ME A BIT. LET'S SEE."
        ○

Well, then she did it there!
      Ĭn dín-dĭ-lĭn-dĭn dín-dĭ-lĭn-dĭn dín-dĭ-lĭn-dĭn ń
      Ĭn dín-dĭ-lĭn-dĭn dín-dĭ-lĭn-dĭn
"AND WHAT'S THAT? AND THAT?"
                    "That's a sweet banana for Give-him-
                          sweetness-if-he-cries.
                    I'll use it here to ward off danger."

"DO IT. LET'S SEE."

        Ǐn dín-dǐ-lǐn-dǐn dín-dǐ-lǐn-dǐn dín-dǐ-lǐn-dǐn ń

        Ǐn dín-dǐ-lǐn-dǐn dín-dǐ-lǐn-dǐn

"MH!

    GO ON, MOTHER.

        GO ON, THEY'LL CURE HIM FOR YOU."

That's how she went. When she reached Mbále . . .

                            she

    is stopped by another one.

"YOU, WOMAN, WHERE ARE YOU GOING?"

60 "I'm going that way, father, to the healers. I've been directed
    to an old woman there.

They say she will heal my child's legs."

"IY?

NOW WHAT'S THAT LITTLE THING YOU'VE PUT UNDER YOUR ARM?"

"That's a little drum, father, to play for this child of mine."

"PLAY A BIT. LET'S SEE."

        Ǐn dín-dǐ-liǹ-dǐn dín-dǐ-lǐn-dǐn dín-dǐ-lǐn-dǐn ń

        Ǐn dín-dǐ-lǐn-dǐn dín-dǐ-lǐn-dǐn

"WHAT'S THAT? AND THAT?"

        "That's a little drum for Give-him-
            sweetness-if-he-cries.

        I'll use it here to ward off danger."

"DO IT. LET'S SEE."

        Ǐn dín-dǐ-lǐn-dǐn dín-dǐ-lǐn-dǐn dín-dǐ-lǐn-dǐn ń

        Ǐn dín-dǐ-lǐn-dǐn dín-dǐ-lǐn-dǐn dí

Now, then she goes.

   o

She goes. When she arrives there, the old woman
    is in . . .

        She enters . . .

70 Now, then, she welcomes her . . .

                She greets her . . .

She says, "How is everything?" And the woman replies,
    "It is well.

Mother, I have brought this child of mine.

My child has become crippled in the legs. Now please
    look at him for me."

The old woman holds him and examines him.

Eh-Eh! She says . . .

        "Let me go and gather medicine [herbs].

But these things in your basket, mother, what are they?"
She says, "The little foods of my child, mother.
Now if he cries I give him something to eat."
"Iy?" she says, "Couldn't you give some to my children?"
80 She answers, "Mother, I can give them some."
Now . . .
She calls to them.
                    "My children, my children,
leave what you're doing and come eat the little things
        this woman has brought you."
Out jump Leopards.
Some jump up wooly,
                    some are horned,
                                and some have
        wide, staring eyes.
The woman says, "Ha-ah!
                    Today I live driven
        from place to place.
Now see the danger that giving birth has thrown me into!
        Do I die here or do these things save me?"
    o
Now, then, she takes things out and gives to them. She
        gives to them.
They eat.
90 Now the old woman says,
                        "You, mother, little-girl-whom-I-
        have-borne-well,
What is this little thing?"
She says, "That's the drum of Give-him-sweetness."
"Is it to play?"
"Yes, mother, to play."
She says, "Play it a bit. Let's see."
                        Ĭn dín-dĭ-lĭn-dĭn dín-dĭ-lĭn-dĭn dín-dĭ-lĭn-dĭn ń
                        Ĭn dín-dĭ-lĭn-dĭn dín-dĭ-lĭn-dĭn
"And what's this? And this?"
                        "That's a little *ishasha* for Give-him-
                            sweetness-if-he-cries.
                    I'll use it here to ward off danger."
"Do it. Let's see."
                        Ĭn dín-dĭ-lĭn-dĭn dín-dĭ-lĭn-dĭn dín-dĭ-lĭn-dĭn ń
                        Ĭn dín-dĭ-lĭn-dĭn dín-dĭ-lĭn-dĭn dí -

"Now, mother . . . "
　　　　　　"Yes," she says.
　　　　　　　　　　"I will cure him."
The old woman . . .
　　　　　　　takes out some medicine and spreads it
　　on the child.
　　　　　　She rubs it in.
100　*After two days the child stands by himself.*
　　　　　　　　　He walks.
That's why when a child is ill they say,
　　　　　　　　"Rush him
　　to the old women."
That's just the way I saw it for you.

The Water of Ikongora

AS TOLD BY TA KEREMENSI LUTABANZIBWA

A man
o
fathered children of his own.
o
They were many.
o
He fathered his children and their number grew.
Now it happened that he became ill.
o
He suffered with an open sore on his leg.
He searched for medicines.
They applied them.
Nothing happened.
　　　　　　They tried others—the same.
10　Now there came a certain person . . .
who knew of a certain hole in the ground . . .
In that hole was a thing . . .
What it was no one knew.
o

He said, "Go there and draw water from the spring . . .
in the hole, inside there . . .
Then let them apply it to your leg and it will heal."
o
The eldest child
            says, "Am I not the one who will bring you
      the medicine?"
They give him a small calabash.
"But when you come to enter into the hole . . .
20 go and say . . .
how your father is afflicted."
o
Now he begins from far off:
(sings)   "Father has fallen ill.
                He needs the water of Ikongóra.
                Ikongóra cannot be reached, they say.
                It is reached by the resolute in heart, like me."
Now the thing itself begins there:
(It chants in   "I'll kill you—I'll take you in payment.
a deep voice.) Just as I killed father–I took him in payment.
                Just as I killed mother—I took her in payment.
                Just as I killed father—I took him in payment."
"Mh?
Ha!
That's something that could kill me."
                                      He returns
                               and says, "It
      cannot be done."
That one takes up the calabash. (The narrator's wife interrupts.
      "The second child," she specifies.)
He says, "I'll go."
He goes.
                "Father has fallen ill.
                He's fallen ill with a sore.
                The sore that makes him ill
                Needs the water of Ikongóra.
                Ikongóra cannot be reached, they say.
                It is reached by the resolute in heart, like me."

(It chants in   "I'll kill you—I'll take you in payment.
a deep voice.) And father I killed him—I took him in payment.

And mother I killed her—I took her in payment.
And baba I killed him—I took him in payment."

30 "Mh?
Not me," he says.

o

He turns back.

o

They go.
Each and every one . . .
                              does just the same.
                                        Each
     and every one . . .
                              does just the same.
                                        Each
     and every one . . .
                              does just the same
                                        until only
     the youngest child was left.
He's the "last of his father's fertility."

o

He says, "Father, I'm leaving to bring back the water that will
     make you well."
He replies, "You?
It was too much for your elders
How can you do it?"

40 "I am bringing it," he says, "and if it will kill me, let it kill me.
Just so you recover from your constant illness."

o

He left the house
with the small calabash.
                    "Father has fallen ill.
                    He needs the water of Ikongóra.
                    Ikongóra cannot be reached, they say.
                    It is reached by the resolute in heart, like me."
The thing begins:
(It chants in   "I'll kill you—I'll take you in payment.
a deep voice.) Just as I killed mother—I took her in payment.
                    Just as I killed father—I took him in payment.
                    And baba, I killed him—I took him in payment."

                    "Father has fallen ill.
                    He needs the water of Ikongóra.

Ikongóra cannot be reached, they say.
It is reached by the resolute in heart, like me."
"I'M DOING IT!"
o

Now the child
is drawing closer.
He's drawing closer.
He's drawing closer.
50   "I'm doing it!"
Now when he approaches very close,
like about from here to there, among dense trees [which surround
    a water hole]

(He sings in   "Father has fallen ill.
a high, child-   He needs the water of Ikongóra.
like voice.)   Ikongóra cannot be reached, they say.
                 It is reached by the resolute in heart, like me."

(It chants in   "I'll kill you—I'll take you in payment.
a deep voice.)   Just as I killed father—I took him in payment.
                 Just as I killed mother–I took her in payment.
                 And baba I killed him–I took him in payment."

(He sings in   "Father has fallen ill.
a high, child-   He needs the water of Ikongóra.
like voice.)   Ikongóra cannot be reached, they say.
                 It is reached by the resolute in heart, like me."

The child . . .
                is doing it.
At that place he's dipping . . .
water from the well.
He's doing it there . . .
                He's dipping water from the well.
Going to look,
he finds a ring-necked dove, the thing that lives there, in a tree.
Now he draws out the water
60   and brings it.
They pour it over his father's leg
                and they wash him with it.
The leg heals.
Well now . . .
It's this way when a man
comes to die:

he leaves his house to his youngest son.
The man who leaves an inheritance . . .
leaves it to his first-born.
But the last-born does not depart from . . .
70 his father's house.
o
That's the story.

Lusimbagila Bestows on All

AS TOLD BY MA ERIKA MANUEL

Now, mother, I went and I saw.
Audience: See so that we may see.
I see . . .
o
a woman
is married into her husband's house.
o
Now in those days it used to be that when a person did
  something wrong . . .
they would take him to the chief and execute him.
The husband of that woman leaves her in bed one day.
o
He goes to the chief and he maligns someone.
                                        THEY
    EXECUTE HIM.
10 The woman dwells there doubled over in grief. And where
      can she go to accuse anyone?
o
The sun did not rise and set many times
                            before a child is born.
    It's a boy.
    He dwells there,
              he dwells there,
                        he dwells there.

                                                  They play
          in the forecourt. Other small children, his friends, say,
          "We're going to our father."
He continues growing.
He questions his mother. He says, "Mother, in the
          house there . . .
whenever we go to a neighbor's . . .
                                        and eat . . .
When we go to the home of Ta So-and-so and we're eating there,
          he portions out the food to the children. But, how is it
          that only we live here, just you and me?"
She says, "My child, don't remind me of my sorrow.
                                                  Your father,
          the chief . . .
killed him."
20   "Eh?"
he says, "The chief killed him and that is why
          I have no father?"
                              She says, "That is why you
          have no father."
     o
The child dwells there. He grows, day after day, day after day.
     o
"Eh?" The child thinks about it. He's confounded.
     o
He says, "Mother, which chief was it?"
                                        She says, "The chief
          in this land who people will say rules over them."
                                                  She says,
          "He is the one who killed him."
The child strings his bow.
Eh-Eh!
          He cuts his arrows and binds them.
He takes to the road and goes.
     o
Now on his way he meets Ma Miria. [a member of the audience]
She is there chopping weeds away from the cassava.
30   "IY?"
          she says, "You, child,
where are you going?"
Mh-Mh! The child sings:

"Mother, let me be.
I'm going to Lusímbagila.
Lusímbagila killed my father.
Today I'll be killing him."
"IY?" SHE SAYS, "WHAT? YOU, CHILD?
KILLING
A CHIEF?"
(child sings) "No, mother, you heard badly.
You, mother, didn't you ask me,
'You, child, where are you going?'
I said, 'I'm going to Lusímbagila.
Lusímbagila bestows on all.
Today he'll bestow on me.'"
"IY?" SHE SAYS, "GO AHEAD, BIG MAN." (audience laughs)
SHE SAYS, "AND HERE'S SOME CASSAVA
FOR YOU TO EAT."
She pulls it up and gives it to him.
Eh-Eh! SHE SAYS,
"LET ME WRAP UP ANOTHER FOR YOU."
(pleading voice, as a child) *"Wrap it up for me, mother.*
I'm traveling to have wealth bestowed on me."

o

He leaves that place. He travels along and meets children playing.
[a mother of one of the children says]
"IY? YOU, CHILD! WHERE ARE YOU GOING TO,
LOOKING LIKE YOU DO?" [that is, small]
He says: "Mother, let me be.
My misfortune makes me wander.
I'm going to Lusímbagila.
Lusímbagila killed my father.
Today I'll be killing him."
[a man says]
40 "IYO! YOU, CHILD, TO KILL THE CHIEF? WHO TOLD
YOU THIS?"
"Father, listen to me.
You know, father, what you asked me.
You said, 'You, child, where are you going?'
I said, 'I'm going to Lusímbagila.
Lusímbagila bestows on all.
Today he'll bestow on me.'"
"Iy?" he says, "Go on!"

"Ha!" he says, "If my ears could be removed!
The child sings me a pretty little song . . .
and now look, I was close to killing him . . .
                                        Did I think
    you're going to kill the chief? GO ON,
    FATHER, GO ON.
YOU CHILDREN, if you're eating plantains, give him
    some to eat."

    ○

He goes. He rolls along, that little one, to Kyábagenzi,
    where the Arabs live. [They have a grocery store.]
"IY? THE WAY THAT CHILD PUSHES ON
    YOU'D THINK HE WAS A LITTLE GROWN MAN.
    BOWS ARE SHOULDERED BY GROWN MEN.
WHERE IS HE GOING?
YOU, CHILD, WHERE ARE YOU GOING?"
50 "I'm going to kill the chief."

    ○

"You, child, to kill the chief?"
"What is it you say, father?
                I said, 'I'm going to Lusímbagila.
                Lusímbagila bestows on all.
                Today he'll bestow on me.'"
"Repeat that so we can listen carefully."
                "This is what you asked me, father.
                You said, 'You, child, where are you going?'
                I said, 'I'm going to Lusímbagila.
                Lusímbagila bestows on all.
                Today he'll bestow on me.'"
"IY? GO ON AND MAY HE BESTOW WEALTH
    ON YOU.
                FOR I KNOW HOW LUSÍMBAGILA
    BESTOWS WEALTH. (audience laughs)
Ha-ah!
These ears?
The child has a song, and he makes it sweet. He's journeying
    to have wealth bestowed on him by the chief. Now, but I,
DID I THINK HE'S GOING TO KILL THE CHIEF?"
At Harub's [store]
    he says, "Here are some loaves of bread."
60 He says, "Go on, little child, little-maker-of-such-beauty."

He wraps them up and goes.
When he had gone—let me not delay you—
he arrives near the chief's palace.
They say it is the place.
He's going along, singing like that, singing like that.
When he arrived there
                    at Katóngo
○
he reaches Masúd's [store].
                    "YOU, CHILD, WHAT IS IT?
         AND THERE ARE CARS ON THE ROAD!"
                    "I'm going, father.
         I'm going to Lusímbagila.
         Lusímbagila killed my father.
         Today I'll be killing him."
They say, "Grab the little one!" They say, "Tie him up!"
                    "No, father don't tie me.
         Listen to me well.
         You know, father, this is what you asked me.
         You said, 'You, child, where are you going?'
         I said, 'I'm going to Lusímbagila.
         Lusímbagila bestows on all.
         Today he'll bestow on me.'"
"The poor child!
70   NOW LISTEN TO WHAT THE CHILD SINGS. NOW WE
         WERE ABOUT TO KILL HIM. DID WE THINK
         HE'S GOING TO KILL THE CHIEF?"
They take out some candy. They take out some sweet rolls.
         They give them to him there, near the palace.
He flies along and finally arrives.
He climbs into a *mushalázi* tree.
Whoever comes to pick an *enshalázi* fruit . . .
Eh-Eh! You've got it! [You've been hit by an arrow!]
You've got it!
People lie strewn about . . .
Others go to the palace . . .
They say, "Lord provider . . . "
80   they say, "WHAT WE HAVE SEEN IN THE *MUSHALÁZI*
         TREE," THEY SAY, "WE HAVE NEVER SEEN
         ITS LIKE BEFORE!"
THEY SAY, "IF YOU SEE SOME FRUIT HAS FALLEN
         AND YOU GO TO PICK IT UP,"

THEY SAY, "YOU FEEL . . .
A BULLET CATCHES YOU, A SPEAR CATCHES YOU,
    AN ARROW."
                    THEY SAY, "WE ARE CONFOUNDED."
The chief sends his police.
                    They go.
They look up in the tree.
EH-EH! YOU'VE GOT A BULLET!
YOU'VE G-O-T . . .
AN ARROW!
YOU'VE GOT A SPEAR!
90 THEY FALL. THEY LIE STREWN ABOUT.
THEY SAY, "PROVIDER," THEY SAY, "THOSE
    THAT MARCHED OUT AS RIFLEMEN
    HAVE NOW COME BACK AS CASUALTIES."
They say, "Perhaps, Lord, you yourself should go there."
The chief equips himself . . .
and when he had gone . . .
Eh-Eh! the retinue mills about. They say, "The chief," they say,
    "we've brought him there." They say,
"WHATEVER WAS KILLING PEOPLE,
                              NOW WE'LL SEE
    WHAT IT IS."
Now the child sees that the chief has equipped himself
    with a shield. He sees his followers honor him
    as the sun . . .
When he let fly a spear . . .
Eh-Eh!
        It catches the chief . . .
100 When they went to give the chief aid . . .
the child leaps . . .
and lands on the ground . . .
and goes along jumping for joy . . .
He avenges his dead father.
WHEN I HAD SEEN THIS
I said "Let me go and relate these things to them."
Audience: Congratulations on your journey.

I Shall Be
Drinking from Them

AS TOLD BY MA KELEZENSIA KAHAMBA

Now a woman . . .
was about to give birth to offspring.
She became pregnant . . .
The foetus grew . . .
o
She bore offspring . . .
two of them.
When she came to give birth, she bore little calabashes.
o
NOW THE FATHER STOOD THERE AND SAID ,
    "WE SHOULD BREAK THOSE CALABASHES."
THE MOTHER SAYS, "NO,
10 Those are my CALABASHES . . .
                      I'll take them
    and STORE them.
I shall be drinking from them."
She takes the little calabashes . . .
the woman does . . .
She stores her calabashes . . .
              She hides them in the
    middle room.
          THEY SIT THERE.
T-H-E-Y S-I-T T-H-E-R-E
FOR ABOUT EIGHT MONTHS.
o
AND THEN THEY CONTINUE FOR ABOUT ANOTHER
    EIGHT . . .
          THEY MATURE.
o
Now they all go out to cultivate, and when they leave . . .
out come the children.
20 This one comes out
           and that one comes out
                    from inside
    the calabash.

The little ones go out to the front yard.
THEY PLAY.
This one sits down over here.
                              That one sits down.
Over there he begins:
(sings)   "Father says, 'Break them!'
                 Mother says, 'Let my calabashes be.
                 I shall be drinking from them.
                 I shall be drinking from them.'"
The little ones go into the middle room where their mother
    had stored them and eat a bit of plantains.
They finish eating.
    o

The little ones hurry. They return
        to their calabashes
                        and are quiet.
Now when the father would come . . .
he looks and finds this little one has defecated over here,
                                        that one
        has defecated.
30 Over there he finds they've eaten plantains.
    o

He's confounded.
                 "But in our house we have no children!
Now whatever it is that's eating plantains and defecating
    in the front yard—where does it come from?"
The mother says the same.
The next day
they appear.
                 "Father says, 'Break them!'
                 Mother says, 'Let my calabashes be.
                 I shall be drinking from them.
                 I shall be drinking from them.'"
They're jumping about.
They're jumping about.
    o

But they watch for them.
    o

Now . . .
        their mother watches for them.

40 When they had watched for them
      the little ones appear and go
  into the front yard.
THEY TAKE OUT THE COOKED PLANTAINS,
THOSE THAT THEIR MOTHER HAD STORED
  BECAUSE SHE COULDN'T FINISH
  EATING THEM.
      They eat.
THEY'RE DONE EATING.
      They sit down in the front yard.
    "Father says, 'Break them!'
    Mother says, 'Let my calabashes be.
    I shall be drinking from them.'"
They jump up and grab hold of the little ones.
They cut their hair in the style of a weaned child . . .
Eh-Eh!
They rub them with oil . . .
They clothe them . . .
They become children there . . .
50 That's how a child causes a mother pain.
∞
It pains the father also, but only a little.
      A child causes
  a mother pain.
That is the story. When I saw them dressing the little ones . . .
and making them pretty . . .
Eh-Eh! I came quickly saying, "Let me go and report
  to the people of our house."
      The story is finished.

COMMENTARY

As a group, the four tales in this section contrast motherly values with fatherly values. This opposition between masculine and feminine principles is embodied in dramatic conflicts situated in a Haya landscape, whose places and dimensions invest activities with cultural significance. We will first look, therefore, at the geography of the tales and then proceed to what they say about male and female values.

The direction of dramatic action in the four tales is an overall movement from inside to outside. In *Give-Him-Sweetness-If-He-*

Cries, a mother carries her child from her own village, outward through a wilderness of leopards, to the home of a healer. There she enters inside. The youngest son in *The Water of Ikongora* also leaves his village and pushes further and further outward into the wilderness, until he comes upon a healing spring. The male child in *Lusimbagila Bestows on All* travels outward from his own home toward the chief's palace. In *I Shall Be Drinking from Them*, preternatural children emerge from calabashes located inside the house near the cooking hearth and go outside to play in the front yard.

Within the overall framework of outward movement, there are several other noteworthy insides and outsides. The mother in *Give-Him-Sweetness-If-He Cries* carries her child on her back, as all Haya mothers do, supported and covered by a cloth. The infant is thus inside, as the woman fends off leopards by singing and by giving them bits of food. This is an interesting transformation—that is, a recombination of elements—of a scene in *The Glistening One*, where a child in a sack on Leopard's back sings to women in the fields who then give Leopard food for his "singing sack's" performance. A child is inside in both tales. The child's mother controls the boundary between inside and outside in *Give-Him-Sweetness-If-He-Cries*. Leopard controls it in *The Glistening One*. Women provide food in both tales, and Leopard, the glutton, takes food.

Inside/outside occurs in *The Water of Ikongora* as the distinction between appearance and reality. The youngest son is outwardly the least likely to brave the dangers of the wilderness. But inwardly the little one is "resolute in heart" and succeeds where his elder brothers have failed. The outward aspect of the creature that guards the spring is a terrifying, threatening voice. When the child arrives inside the copse of trees where the well is located, however, he finds only a ring-necked dove. What was apparently strong was in reality a powerless bird. Ring-necked doves do have a booming, rhythmic, contralto call that could be interpreted as sung or chanted speech. Comparing the youngest son to the ring-necked dove, we see that the former was apparently weak but proved to be strong, and the latter was apparently strong but proved to be weak. Taking into account the geography of the observed strengths and weaknesses, we may note that what was weak outside when inside the village was strong inside when outside in the wilderness—that is, the youngest child. What was strong outside when outside in the wilderness was weak inside when inside at the well—that is, the ring-necked dove. This same set of elements, strong/weak and apparent/real as functions of different internal and external settings, appears in *The Strong One*.

The little boy in *Lusimbagila Bestows on All*, like his comrade in *The Water of Ikongora*, is apparently weak, but inwardly strong—strong enough here to avenge his father's death. But as he travels along the road, another contrast between outside and inside becomes evident: the difference between his outwardly stated goal of having a chief bestow wealth on him and his true inward intention of killing the chief. The child first announces his inward purpose to whomever he meets (perhaps, like the central character in *Greens of the Cow Pasture*, he simply cannot keep it in). When people are shocked to hear about his regicidal intent, he quickly covers up, telling them they heard badly: what he *really* said was that he is visiting the chief to have wealth bestowed on him.

The boy's song first uncovers his purpose and then masks it. In a sense, the singing controls the boundary of the boy's intent, at first opening it to view, then closing it. Songs in the tales often control the boundaries between inside and outside—*Give-Him-Sweetness-If-He-Cries* is one example, *Open and Let Them Come In* and *Child of the Valley* are others.

In addition to illustrating inside/outside movement, all four tales in this section attest to the high value Hayas place on perseverance. The principal protagonist in each tale personifies this perseverance. The mother of Give-him-sweetness-if-he-cries (a child's name) fends off leopard after leopard as she makes her way through the wilderness to the house of a healer, there to undergo still another test of her internal resolve. The youngest son in *The Water of Ikongora* proves himself to be one of the "resolute in heart" who succeed where others fail. The little child in *Lusimbagila Bestows on All* surprises all who see him with his determination to push on like an adult. And finally, the mother who vows, "I shall be drinking from them," perseveres for sixteen months against the will of her husband, protects her calabashes, and receives her reward.

A central feature of the female principle in Haya society is embodied in the mother's actions in *Give-Him-Sweetness-If-He-Cries*. In this mother's hands, a woman's nurture becomes a powerful defensive weapon as she keeps the hungry leopards from her child and herself. Dedication and love for the child she has borne motivate her to perform brave deeds in dangerous situations. As she says, " . . . see the danger that giving birth has thrown me into!" (line 87). The mother receives no formal rewards for her devotion, only the love of her child and the general approbation given one who continues the existence of family, clan, and society.

This contrasts with the traditional father-son relationship, in which there are economic consequences—the inheritance of rights to land, livestock, and other capital goods. The father-son relationship is therefore a more formal one, less intimate than mother-child. A son has duties to perform for his father. He owes him respect, and he can expect rewards. In a sense, a boy's father is the same sort of figure as are the elders of his clan or the chief himself. He is an embodiment of the moral, political, and economic structure of Haya society.

We can assume that the sons in *The Water of Ikongora* act out of a sense of duty to their father. There may be some personal concern for the father's feelings in the youngest son's motivation, but in general each son tries to demonstrate that he is a brave and worthy successor to his father. The one who succeeds proves himself man enough. He is unafraid of paying the price, even if the price is his own life. The voice booms, "I'll kill you—I'll take you in payment," but the youngest son strengthens his resolve and presses forward. The "payment" refers to the money or goods given in exchange for medicine. In tales, this may involve a human life—as in *Kibwana* and *Magezi*. His willingness to stand firm and meet all dangers, known and unknown, on his father's behalf, justifies, in Keremensi Mukajuna's telling of the tale, the youngest son's inheritance of his father's house.

The Haya father's position as embodiment of political and moral values is even more strongly stated in *Lusimbagila Bestows on All*. Here there is no question of the father's physical well-being, for he is already dead when the son begins his quest. There is no ghost or spirit to goad the son into action (as in *Hamlet*); nor is there a memory that could motivate the child. He acts purely on behalf of the ideal father-son relationship, and avenges his unknown father's death.

But he kills a chief. This presents a problem for our interpretation: how can the boy act on behalf of the male principle in society—his father—by killing a chief? The answer would seem to lie in the principle of "segmentation" which has been widely observed among African and other societies. According to the segmentation principle, a given standard—usually loyalty—may be applied in different political contexts so as to define larger or smaller groups. Me and my tribe against other tribes, the example usually runs, me and my clan against other clans, me and my brothers against my cousins, me and my descendants against my brother and his descendants.

Lusimbagila Bestows on All clearly focuses on the household group. In fact, the boy first learns that he lacks a father because male household roles are unfulfilled (lines 13–17). It is logical, then, that one may honor the male principle within the family by killing someone outside of it, even the chief. Conflict between chiefs and commoners was not unknown, although in such cases, the commoner would have to flee the chiefdom to avoid execution. Killing a chief may not have been a frequent occurrence, but killing one to avenge a dead father makes sense in a woman's tale, which is centered on the social group that shares a hearth.

The final tale of this section, *I Shall Be Drinking from Them*, is in many ways the most intriguing. It is also, I feel, the most richly expressive of Haya concepts of male and female parentage as seen from a woman's point of view. A western reader meets a problem with this tale, however, because its symbolism is somewhat difficult to grasp. Most other tales in the collection, particularly the other three tales in this section, make sense to a western reader almost without explication. For we share with Hayas beliefs that mothers are nurturing and will meet any danger on behalf of their children, that the youngest son may triumph where his elders failed (especially in fairy tales), and that dead kin need revenge. The expression of these cultural ideas in Haya folktales is direct. The symbols are familiar—or not too unfamiliar—and easily apprehended.

In *I Shall Be Drinking from Them*, on the other hand, a woman gives birth to calabashes, children come out from them secretly and sing, and this, the narrator tells us, shows how children hurt their mother more than their father. The tale is told by a fine storyteller. It makes sense to Hayas. Let us let it make sense to us.

To begin with, male and female principles are present and in conflict. But, contrary to the direct representations in the previous three tales, they appear here in a transformed manner. The principles remain; the form of their expression has been changed.

In a sense, we are seeing the obverse side of them. In *The Water of Ikongora* and *Lusimbagila Bestows on All*, the young child saves his father's life and avenges his death. In *I Shall Be Drinking from Them*, the father demands that the calabashes be broken—that is, that the children be put to death. Although these acts appear to be in op-

position to one another—children aid father, father kills children—
they are actually alternate expressions of the same male principle.
That principle is duty. Just as the boys reaffirm the male social
order by serving their fathers, the father acts to protect that social
order by removing the threat posed by the monstrous birth of calabashes. In Haya terms, the birth of the calabashes is an *eihano*, "an
unnatural wonder," evidence of an unbalance in nature that may
threaten society and must therefore be excluded. The father acts
on society's behalf and with the warrant of its principle. Other instances of this can be found in the tales: a father kills his incestuous
children (*Child of the Valley*), and a chief banishes a woman who has
created havoc in the natural order (*She's Killed One. We've All of Us
Come*).

The expression of the female principle in *I Shall be Drinking
from Them* is also transformed. Other tales portray mothers and
grown women nourishing children. Here the mother says, "I shall
be drinking from them": the woman will be nourished by her children. Her statement refers literally to calabashes, which are used
as drinking vessels. It refers metaphorically to the children contained within them.[1]

She will "drink from them" in the sense that they will refresh
her, as drinking the cool contents of a calabash refreshes one. Children are an important gratification in a woman's life. They help
elevate her to a position of relative prestige in her husband's clan;
they provide for her in her old age; and their affection is one of her
strongest emotional supports. Life with her husband and his kin is
not always easy. A loving relationship with her children can refresh
her: it can soften the hardness in her life, cool the heat, water the
dryness.

The figurative reversal of her role as nourisher is emphasized
by the fact that she does not nurse or otherwise feed the preternatural children—they feed themselves. This otherwise inconsequential detail is included in another version of the same Haya tale (not
in this collection), in which the children come out of the calabashes,
cook for themselves, eat, and also sing their mother's refrain, "I
shall be drinking from them."

A mother nourishes her children, and she is "nourished" by
them. This is a concrete expression of the diffuse, enduring relationship between mother and child. In a general sense, that relationship is what we have been calling the female principle in society.

Male and female principles are in conflict in the tale. "Father says, 'Break them!'/Mother says, 'Let my calabashes be.'" The mother is pained by the conflict because she must defend her position alone, unsupported by anyone. Her actions are motivated by a strong desire for children which is embodied in her determination to wait and see what will develop. The father's attack on the calabashes is motivated by the social imperative that the anomaly be cast out. He acts in defense of the social order, while she acts in defense of the objects of her maternal love. The tale suggests that a man's allegiance is split between society and his children, between duty and love, but a woman's is not.

This is why the story illustrates, as the narrator points out, that a child pains a mother more than a father. A mother is devoted solely to the children; she sees her welfare as identical with theirs. She depends upon them as a source of her happiness and well-being to a greater degree than does a father, who participates in wider political and economic institutions traditionally closed to women. She is therefore more vulnerable to a hurt from her child than a father is, for he identifies his welfare not only with his children, but also with the wider structures of society. The strange birth of calabashes evokes the divergence between male and female values. It also evokes for the narrator the pain, as well as the "refreshment," that children bring.

That Haya children cause their mothers pain is proverbial. *Ekyohyir'omunda nikishasa*, as Hayas say, "That which you take from inside causes pain." The *ishasha* fruit (a wild fig) that concludes the series of sweet things in *Give-Him-Sweetness-If-He-Cries* may be a punning reference to the word *oku-shasa* or *oku-shasha*, "to cause pain." Some of this pain may be at the hands of children who are more insolent with her than they would dare to be with their father. Perhaps this is how Teaser, the girl in the tale with that title, got her name. But I believe the deeper, more systemic reasons for a woman's vulnerability lie in the degree to which her prestige and happiness depend on her children. This same theme underlies the logic of *Blocking the Wind* and the irony of its reversal in *Kibwana*.

Give-Him-Sweetness-If-He-Cries takes its title from the name the mother gives to her child. Sweetness is the food of people who do not eat as discriminately as grown men do. It is therefore a fit food for children and, in tales, for leopards, who are gluttonous. Note the greetings between the mother and the healer (lines 69–72).

They follow the correct Haya etiquette: first the guest enters; the host welcomes the guest as she is entering; (both sit); they greet one another; they ask after the welfare of each other; and finally the business at hand is introduced. The epithet on line 90, "little-girl-whom-I-have-borne-well," is a praise name given to the mother by the healer. She sees how the mother bravely feeds the leopards and praises her by figuratively taking her as her own child.

Lusimbagila Bestows on All also has a praise name (line 60), given to the child because of his beautiful song. He is called "little-maker-of-such-beauty." The chief's followers honor the chief as the sun (line 97) with the traditional greeting given to the chief, *Habuka eizoba*, literally, "Appear, sun."

Note the point of view this story takes. It centers on womanly concerns, beginning with the wife's bereavement and ending with the child's safety. The line, "He avenges his father's death" resolves the tension created by the immediately preceding intonation pattern at the same time that it resolves the dramatic tension generated at the beginning of the tale. A line like this can be called an *enko-melo*, "that which ties up" the story.

In *I Shall Be Drinking from Them*, the children's parents and the narrator herself are not moved to disgust by the children's feces. Their indiscriminate placement is looked upon rather as an essential property of children as opposed to older human beings. Each infant's feces are ritually buried near a banana plant in the grove surrounding the house—girls' near a plant to the left of the house, boys' near a plant to the right.

Different hair styles (line 45) were traditionally used to mark transitions in an individual's life. This practice seems to be declining in recent years. The present emphasis appears to be on more decorative, less meaningful hair styles. Traditional styles that are still widely practiced are the "crested crane" hair style of a bride—resembling what is called an Afro in the U.S.—and the complete shaving of one's head as a sign of bereavement.

4

Tales of Sisters and Brothers

Tales in this section treat aspects of relationships among siblings. They typify the relationship among sisters as a loving one, among brothers as rivalrous, and between brother and sister as affectionate. The first two tales speak of sibling affection and loyalty which can overcome great obstacles. Like the parents and children in the previous chapter, siblings in the first two stories can perform brave deeds motivated by their attachment to a blood kinsman. A character's perseverance and resolve overcome fear and opposition by others, be they animal or human.

The remaining two tales in the section speak of resolve and self-control as well, but evoke them through portrayal of their opposite. Specifically, the tales speak of two appetites that should be suppressed among siblings and about the conditions that can cause them to escape control. These two tales, *Three Brothers* and *Child of the Valley*, are in a sense tragedies of siblinghood, for they portray flaws in the relationship among brothers and between brother and sister that can, if unchecked, cause the ruin of family life.

The omnipresent principle of inside and outside appears in the first two tales in an overt, physical manner. In both, a sister inside (a house, a leopard, a marsh) is the center of dramatic movement. The second pair of tales is structured by the principle in more subtle ways: inward appetites emerge in outlying locales and complex symmetries are formed from entities that are put in or taken out.

Open and Let Them Come In

AS TOLD BY BENJAMIN KAHAMBA

I give you a story.
Audience: I give you another.
It's done.
Audience: The news of long ago.
I came and I saw.
Audience: See so that we may see.
Now long ago
there was a man . . .
He married a wife.
10 They give birth to . . .
a child,
a son, the first born.
When they had had the first born son . . .
then they have a girl.
When they had borne the girl,
they dwell there . . .
                    with their mother
                              and their father.

o

Now in a short while . . .
                    the boy grows
and the girl grows.
They reach the age of adolescence.
o
20 Now then, when they had lived there for a while . . .
                                        their
        mother dies.
Now when their mother dies . . .
their father . . .
marries another woman
who is called the "husband's wife" [stepmother] . . .
of the children,
o
the wife of their father.
Now then, they dwell there.

When they had dwelled there . . .
                             that woman continually gives
them no rest.
She gives them no rest
           no rest
               no rest.
30 Now the young man . . .
               leaves when he had grown up.
He goes.
He goes to a far-off land and settles there.
Now when he had settled there . . .
                    he goes among the people.
He goes among them proposing . . .
                  "Give me your cattle and
I'll take them to pasture for you."
o
Now then, he builds a house
and lives in it.
One gives him cattle and another gives him goats.
He pastures them for the people and lives well.
Now when he had succeeded doing this . . .
40 he says, "My sister . . .
still lives in adversity.
Now because she's in trouble . . .
I'll go and find her
and we'll live together,
for our stepmother . . .
gives her no rest."
Now then, he leaves there . . .
He goes . . .
He speaks with his sister . . .
50 He takes her away with him . . .
They come together and live in his house.
Now in the place where he brought her . . .
the youth . . .
had cattle that he had sought from people to take to pasture.
Now he told her,
                 "Whenever I bring the cattle home . . .
at night,
you'll hear this little song I'll be singing:

'Good water they have drunk.
Open and let them come in.
Good grass they have eaten.
Open and let them come in.'"
So
   now he told her . . .
"LISTEN FOR IT.
60 Now every time I return,
I'll be doing just that. Every day."
So
now the youth . . .
                    leaves and takes the cattle to pasture.
When he had finished feeding them . . .
                         he comes in the evening
    and sings:
          "Good water they have drunk.
          Open and let them come in.
          Good grass they have eaten.
          Open and let them come in."
So
now in the past there were things like Leopard . . .
It had been wanting to eat that girl.
It goes to an old woman, a healer.
So
   it says,
       "I've seen a little bit of food for me in that
     place over there.
Now I'd like to eat it.
70 Now since I'd like to eat it . . .
find me some medicine . . .
so I can go and eat it."
Now she told him,
"Now when you go inside there to where it is,
if you go in the evening,
the brother
         of the girl will not have come.
Sing just as he does.
But while you're traveling on the road . . .
don't eat anything at all."
80 Now when it had reached the road . . .
the girl . . .
is at home.

Now when Leopard approached the door,
it sings with a low voice:
(an octave lower than the boy)
> "Good water they have drunk.
> Open and let them come in.
> Good grass they have eaten.
> Open and let them come in."

So
now the girl . . .
> refuses to open.

Now the brother comes.
He sings:
> "Good grass they have eaten.
> Open and let them come in.
> Good water they have drunk.
> Open and let them come in."

So
90   now the girl opens up.
Now she tells her brother . . .
> "SOMETHING CAME HERE.

TOMORROW YOU'LL FIND LEOPARD'S FOOTPRINTS.
THAT'S WHAT CAME AND SANG IN A LOW VOICE,
    BUT I REFUSED TO OPEN."
So
now then
   o
the next day the brother takes the cattle to pasture.
So
NOW LEOPARD GOES AGAIN TO THE OLD WOMAN.
IT SAYS, "NOW
100   THAT LITTLE MORSEL HAS CAUSED MY DEFEAT.
WHEN I TRAVELED ON THE ROAD I SAW AN ANT.
    HUNGER WAS KILLING ME.
I ATE IT."
So
now then
the old woman says,
> "NOW WHEN YOU GO,
>   CLOSE YOUR EYES AND DON'T EAT A THING."

So
now when Leopard went,

he goes without eating a thing. He goes
with closed eyes to the house of the young man.
He finds the girl is in and sings:
"Good water they have drunk.
Open and let them come in.
Good grass they have eaten.
Open and let them come in."
So

110   now
the girl opens up.
When she had opened up . . .
Leopard leaps and grabs her . . .
It eats her . . .
The girl dies.
Now when the young man comes . . .
he begins to sing:
"Good water they have drunk.
Open and let them come in.
Good grass they have eaten.
Open and let them come in."
HE LISTENS — NOTHING:
HE HEARS NO ONE.
HE OPENS THE HOUSE AND WHEN HE WENT
TO LOOK . . .
HE FINDS THAT LEOPARD HAS EATEN HER.

120   THE GIRL IS NOT THERE.
SO NOW HE KNOWS THAT LEOPARD . . .
is what ate her . . .
his sister.
So,
now the youth . . .
GRABBED ALL KINDS OF WEAPONS
RIFLE
SPEAR
MACHETE
EH-EH!
HUNTING
KNIFE
FISHING SPEAR
AND STONES
AND STICKS AND STAFFS to go to kill that Leopard.

Now when he had gone to Leopard's home,
he meets a child.

130 HE SAYS, "WHERE HAS YOUR FATHER GONE?"
IT SAYS, "HE HAS GONE TO CULTIVATE."
HE SAYS, "WHERE HAS YOUR GRANDMOTHER
      GONE?"
             IT SAYS, "SHE
HAS GONE TO CULTIVATE."
                         "HAS YOUR
PATERNAL AUNT GONE?"
                    IT SAYS,
"SHE'S GONE."
              HE SAYS, "BEGIN BY CALLING
YOUR AUNT."
NOW THE CHILD BEGINS TO CALL:
(sings)   "Auntie, Auntie,
          The brother of the partridge has come,
          The one we ate at night
          And we finished off the crumbs."
Eh-Eh!
      THE PATERNAL AUNT COMES.
WHEN SHE ARRIVED,
              THE YOUTH HAS THE THINGS
HE BROUGHT WITH HIM.
A SPEAR,
      HE LETS FLY A SPEAR!
It leaps.
It impales . . .
that Leopard,
140 the paternal aunt Leopard.
Eh-Eh!
The Leopard child calls again:
          "Mother, Mother,
          The brother of the partridge has come,
          The one we ate at night
          And we finished off the crumbs."
Eh-Eh!
IT COMES.
THE MOTHER COMES.
EH-EH!
      HE SPEARS IT.

HE SAYS, "CALL YOUR SISTER."
IT CALLS:

> "Sister, Sister,
> The brother of the partridge has come,
> The one we ate at night
> And we finished off the crumbs."

EH-EH!
      WHEN THE SISTER HAD COME . . .
150 HE LETS FLY A STONE THAT STRIKES
      HER RIGHT IN THE FACE.
SHE WRITHES.
SHE DIES.
EH-EH!
      HE SAYS, "CALL YOUR FATHER."
    NOW THEN, HE HAD FINALLY REACHED HIM.
IT CALLS:

> "Father, Father,
> The brother of the partridge has come,
> The one we ate at night
> And we finished off the crumbs."

THE FATHER COMES.
WHEN IT REACHES THE FRONT YARD, IT SEES THE
      OTHERS WHO DIED,
IT SAYS TO HIM, "MY MASTER, DO NOT KILL ME."
    IT SAYS, "I AM THE ONE WHO ATE
    YOUR SISTER."
IT SAYS, "NOW CUT MY LITTLE FINGER.
THIS ONE,
        CUT IT,
             AND YOU WILL TAKE OUT FROM
    THERE — YOUR SISTER
160 AND ALL THE CHIEFS I ATE."
So
the youth
GRABS THE LITTLE FINGER AND CUTS IT OFF.
HE TAKES OUT HIS SISTER
AND ALL THOSE CHIEFS IT HAD EATEN.
EH-EH!
HE GRABS LEOPARD AGAIN AND KILLS IT.
When he had killed it . . .
he hurried to tell me about it,
170 and I said, "Let me go and report to the guests in my house."

*Nchume**

AS TOLD BY MA KELEZENSIA KAHAMBA

My story is done . . .
Audience: The news of long ago.
A man married a woman.
She gave birth to a girl . . .
And when the child was about two . . .
                           her mother died.
The man marries again.
o

This woman becomes pregnant . . .
                        She bears
    a child [a daughter].
SHE DWELLS THERE.
o

SHE LOOKS AT HER THIS WAY AND SAYS,
    "[MY STEP-] CHILD IS REALLY BEAUTIFUL."
o

10 SHE LOOKS AT HER THAT WAY AND SAYS,
    "THAT CHILD IS REALLY BEAUTIFUL.
                       HII!
    WHY CAN'T MY OWN BE THAT BEAUTIFUL?"
She says, "Now, I'll just kill that child.
Since she's so pretty . . .
                I'll kill her.
                     Then my child will
    be the pretty one."
o

Now when she came to do it, SHE SEES HOW MUCH
    THEY LOVE ONE ANOTHER. EVERY TIME
    ONE GOES FOR WATER, THE ONE WHO DOESN'T
    GO FOR WATER stays at home and cries.
Now when she came to do it, she takes this one,
                      her own,
and sends her to about Kitáhya.
o

---

* Pronounced N-chóo-may

She takes . . .
                    her stepchild
and sends her to Nshékasheke, close by.
                                        She says, "But the one
        who comes back first
is the one
                    I'll give plantains first to eat."
They go.
                    Her child goes running.
20   Her stepchild goes running, too.
It's close by. She's sent her close by.
                                        She easily comes back first.
Now when the stepchild had come . . .
the woman says, "Come, let's go to fetch water,
                                            since you've
        already come,
so you can meet your sister when she returns. Then
        you'll eat together."
They go.
            THERE ARE PAPYRUS PLANTS LIKE
        THIS (indicates length with hands)
TALL ONES.
She goes in there.
She cuts a hole like this
and pushes her down into it.
30   She brings papyrus and packs it down on top.
SHE PACKS IT DOWN! MORE AND MORE AND MORE
        AND MORE.
                        SHE TIGHTENS IT.
She leaves.
She returns.
with her water.
Now when she returned, she finds her own child
        has already come.
Now she asks her, "Mother . . .
Now then, Nchume . . .
has she come?" She says, "She hasn't come yet.
You both left the same time. I haven't seen her yet. And look,
        as I was waiting for a long time, I said, 'I'll just go
        and bring some water.'"

        o

40 She stays there, the girl.
She's confounded.
Again she says, "Well, now, mother . . .
                                        Nchume . . .
where did she go?"
She says, "I've told you. She hasn't come yet."
                                        She falls silent.
They sleep that night.
Next day the father comes.
                        "Now then, where did my child go?"
The wife says, "Wherever she went, she'll return."
Now the next day the child picks up her water calabash
                                        and goes
    to fetch water.
She reaches the path.
(sings)   "I go for water, Nchume,
                I go with baba, Nchume.
                I go for firewood, Nchume,
                I go with baba, Nchume.
                I go for long grass, Nchume,
                I go with baba, Nchume."
50 She comes to the river and draws water.
    o
Now the other begins O-V-E-R T-H-E-R-E
                                        where she
    pushed her down in the reedy marsh:
(Nchume   "Happy-one, happy-one, child-of-my-mother,
    sings)   Leave me.
                Your father and your mother killed me, saying,
                    'Kanshánda
                Will grow.'
                I'm dead on the left side,
                In the right side there's life."
"Mh?" She listens.
    o
"Now that voice is like my sister's!" SHE RETURNS HOME.
SHE SPILLS OUT THE WATER QUICKLY.
SHE SAYS, "I'M GOING BACK FOR WATER."
She goes outside
and when she comes to about the road . . .

       "I go for water, Nchume,
       I go with baba, Nchume.
       I go for firewood, Nchume,
       I go with baba, Nchume.
       I go for water, Nchume,
       I go with baba, Nchume."
She begins there
       and now she comes to the river.
The other one begins there, in the reedy marsh:
       "Happy-one, happy-one, child-of-my-mother,
       Leave me.
       Your father and your mother killed me, saying,
         'Kanshánda
       Will grow.'"
60   She goes home.
She sleeps. Dawn comes.
Again she spills out the water.
She returns there.
When she gets outside, at about the front gate, she begins:
       "I go for water, Nchume,
       I go with baba, Nchume.
       I go for firewood, Nchume,
       I go with baba, Nchume.
       I go for long grass, Nchume,
       I go with baba, Nchume."
She reaches the river.
The other begins over there:
       "Happy-one, happy-one, child-of-my-mother,
       Leave me.
       Your father and your mother killed me, saying,
         'Kanshánda
       Will grow.'
       I'm dead on the left side,
       In the right side there's life."
   o
Now when she had gone about four times . . .
               she comes
     and tells her father.
She says, "Truly, father,"
she says, "in the marsh."
70   She says, "That's where it comes from. A voice speaking.
     It sounds like Nchume's."

She says, "When I go to the water, you come and follow me."
She spills out the water. Her sister possesses her.
o

For all those days, she hasn't seen her.
o

She goes again.
>"I go for water, Nchume,
>I go with baba, Nchume."

Now her father follows. She was going and talking
   with her father.
>>She's going along and he's going along . . .

She reaches the river.
She draws water.
The other begins there:
>"Happy-one, happy-one, child-of-my-mother,
>Leave me.
>Your father and your mother killed me, saying,
> 'Kanshánda
>Will grow.'
>I'm dead on the left side,
>In the right side there's life."

Now her father goes. He goes with her, cutting a path with a
   machete, cutting a path.

80 He goes and reaches her. He uncovers her and when he does,
   he finds her rotted on one side . . .
the left one . . .
>The right side was still whole . . .
>>>He

  takes her out . . .
He brings his child . . .
>When he had come, he banishes
his wife . . .
o

Now, this is to say, when a woman marries and finds a child
   of her husband already in the house, she doesn't
   consent to raise the child well.
She wants it to die . . .
>so her own . . .

will be the one to grow.
o

My story is finished.
It ends here.

When I saw the child beginning to recover,
                                        I said,
"Let me go and report to the people at home."

Three Brothers

AS TOLD BY TA KEREMENSI LUTABANZIBWA

There was once a man
one.
o
That man
had gone on a journey
o
WITH HIS BROTHERS.
o
So when he journeyed with his brothers . . .
o
IN THE WILDERNESS
o
now, they go and stay the night at a certain man's.
o
[The traveler's] brothers
                    were two in number.
o
10   So they were two . . .
He was the third.
So while they were in the wilderness . . .
                                    they stop and stay
            the night in a man's house.
Now . . .
            they scheme
                    at night.
The man was rich.
Now they conspire to steal this many thousands . . . (holds up
      three fingers)

o

three.

o

Now they travel on and trade their things at the place
    where they were going.

o

Now when they arrived [back] there [at the rich man's place]
the people had gone to sleep . . .

20   They go and steal the three thousand.

o

THEY ARISE IN THE NIGHT
and go.

o

Now when they had gone . . .

o

IN THE WILDERNESS THEY SPEND ALL DAY
    G-O-I-N-G
              and when it
    got to be about this time of day [late afternoon],
now they make camp.

o

They remember THEY HAVE NOT EATEN.

o

When they remembered they had not eaten,
now two of them leave . . .
and go to get food.

o

30   Something to eat.
So when they had left to get something to eat . . .
one remained behind.
So he remained there
to bring water and to cut firewood.

o

Now when the two had gotten some distance away . . .
they said,
        "Now, that one, shall we kill him?
Won't one take a thousand-five and the other a thousand-five?"

o

Now when they left . . .
the other one SCHEMES.

40   "If I kill them,
won't those three thousands be mine?"

o
Now he runs.
He goes to someone's house.
He finds them preparing . . .
                                    sweet juice for banana beer.
Now they give him some. He drinks.
He takes some with him
saying, "I'll take it to my brothers."
Now he puts in POISON.
o

After he puts the poison in . . .
50   he comes and sits with it at the camp.
Now THEY COME BACK.
o

Now all peel [plantains] and cook.
(softly) Now they seize and throttle him.
o

When they had seized him and throttled him and
     wrung his neck . . .
now, they throw him out [like trash].
o

AFTER THEY THREW HIM OUT,
AFTER THEY KILLED HIM,
now they seize that unfermented juice and drink.
(softly) They share with each other
60   AND THEY DIE
o

just as the other one died.
o

NOW THAT RICH MAN . . .
WHEN HE GOT UP IN THE MORNING . .
o

he sees that his money is gone.
He takes to the road
o

on his horse.
Now he's coming to spend the night at Kyábagenzi.
It's here they have fallen dead.
o

Now dawn comes.
70   He's about to arrive right about here . . .
"Look, someone has died!"

o

"Eh? Let me go look around."
He sees they are dead when he comes to find his money.

o

He returns.

o

Now this story
is to make it known:
three people CANNOT DO ONE THING.

Child of the Valley

AS TOLD BY MA KOKUBELWA ISHABAKAKI

Now then, I go and I see.
                    I see a woman
bears children of her own,
                    a boy and a girl . . .
two children . . .
Now those two children take goats to pasture . . .
While pasturing the goats . . .
they lie with one another.
When you come to see the girl, look, a belly.
You children, what have you done? They had a big rock there.
    They had looked it over and said, "When the child is born,
    we'll put him in there."
The child was carried
                    and when it was born, it was born
        in the fields, and they kept it there.
10   Now the rock
                    rose up, and below there was a hole.
They cut grass for the infant, and whatever else [it needed]
        they did for it.
They put it in there.

o

Now they come home.

They find their mother has already cooked. The food was ready,
    they ate, and they finished.
When they had finished eating,
when they had finished eating,
they wrap up some food in a package and take it along —
    the food of their parents— to eat in the fields.
They say, "Now the goats don't return at lunchtime. They stay
    the whole day."
"Yes, they stay the whole day."
    o
20   The girl stands by the rock.
(sings)   "Little mountain, little mountain, child of
                    the valley,
                Of anthills that are spotted,
                Of termite hills that are red,
                Come and see, little milk-fed one, little father.
                Come and see, little one of the valley."
                "E-e-eh [child's cry]
                E-e-eh"
She picks up the things she covered the infant with, takes it out,
    and gives it her breast.
It nurses.
She goes.
One day. In the morning she returns.
And whenever she comes, she stands by the rock and calls
    the same way. In the morning they come and call.
    In the morning they nurse it.
                                    Now
one day an old woman comes cutting grass [for the floor
    of a house] . . .
Now, they . . .
    o
come . . .
to take goats to pasture.
30   The old woman stoops in the grass. Now they stand there.
    The old woman's back is bent as she ties up
    her bundles of grass.
Now the girl stands by the rock.
                "Little mountain, little mountain, child of
                    the valley,
                Of anthills that are spotted,

> Of termite hills that are red,
> Come and see, little milk-fed one, little father.
> Come and see, little one of the valley."
> "E-e-eh
> E-e-eh"

The old woman cocks her ear like this.
She keeps quiet.
The girl takes out the rock
                        and picks up what she used to
    cover the infant. She goes inside and nurses her child.
    She finishes.

o

They round up the goats and they take them here and there.
They judge the hour
to go to nurse.
The old woman says, "I'd better spread my grass to dry
and look more closely at what I saw."

o

40 They return and stand at their rock. They call.
They nurse and finish nursing. The old woman ties up her grass
    and goes home.

o

When she comes to their mother, she says, "Bojo,"
she says, "what I saw . . . "

o

She says, "Tomorrow we'll go to cut grass."

o

The mother says, "Mh?" Then she says, "E-e-h." [first she
    questions, then she agrees] She says, "But what
    will I wear?" [so as not to be recognized] She says,
    "I'll give you my leather skirt."
She gives her the leather skirt.
[The next day] she leaves while everyone is still at home.
Before they had gotten up, and while the children are going
    to untie the goats,
                        the woman is the first one out there.
Among the rocks she cuts and cuts grass. The old woman
    also cuts and cuts.

50 Now when they came and stood by the rock,
                    "Little mountain, little mountain, child of
                        the valley,

Of anthills that are spotted,
Of termite hills that are red,
Come and see, little milk-fed one, little father.
Come and see, little one of the valley."
"E-e-h
    E-e-h"
"IY"
       THE WOMAN SAYS, "WHAT'S THIS?
WHILE IN THIS PLACE, HAVE THEY BORNE A CHILD
    AND HIDDEN IT AWAY?
SO THAT'S WHY I SEE HER BREASTS BECOME
    HEAVY.
            SHE HAS A CHILD HERE!"
She goes home . . .
She hits her husband with the news . . .
The husband comes and stands at the rocks. They come
    and call . . .
The child cries . . .
When they open it, look, a child.
    ○

The parents stay there and wait. The children round up
    the goats and take them.
60 The father asks, "Whose child is that?"
"The girl
and her brother."
They go and find a watery place among the papyrus stalks.
in a reedy swamp like the one at Kyábagenzi.
    ○

It was the final act. [Literally, "You did not see the danger."
    The girl, her brother, and their child were drowned
    in the swamp.]
When I had seen these things . . .
I said, "Let me go and report to them." It's finished. What
    is it you say, "The news of long ago"?

COMMENTARY

The love between brother and sister is often presented as the
ideal cross-sex relationship. Its intimacy, mutual devotion and sharing are said to be unequalled, even by the love between husband
and wife. (This sentiment is expressed directly in *Kulili Your Brother*

of Only One Mother on line 81). Sibling love is the motivating force in *Open and Let Them Come In;* it is the reason that the sister is inside the brother's house in the first place, and the reason that he embarks on his dangerous mission to kill Leopard. To be sure, the story entails more than this theme in the exuberant performance by seventeen-year-old Benjamin Kahamba, son of Ma Kelezensia Kahamba. But sibling loyalty is the major motivation.

An interesting version of *Open and Let Them Come In* was published in *Kiziba Land Und Leute,* by Hermann Rehse. It is essentially the same as the one here, except for the detail of the mechanism that allows Leopard to deceive the sister. In the Kiziba version, Leopard goes to ironsmiths who forge him a small voice box. He is instructed not to swallow anything before singing, but—as in Benjamin Kahamba's version—he does and has to return again.

Note the symmetry of the tale. The singing Leopard tries and tries to get inside; he finally does and kills the sister. In revenge, the brother brings the Leopards inside one by one through a song and kills them, finally removing his sister from the dead father Leopard. Leopard sings, gets inside and kills, is sung to, lured inside, and killed.

The inside nature of character motivations and the manner in which they emerge are central themes in the final three tales of the chapter. In the tale of *Nchume,* the title character's half-sister Kanshanda is motivated in her quest for the entrapped Nchume by an uncontrollable desire to see her beloved sibling. Even before this, one could see "how much they love one another. Every time this one goes for water, the one who doesn't go for water stays at home crying" (line 12). The love between sisters is so great that, when Nchume is missing for several days, the narrator says of Kanshanda (line 71), "her sister possesses her." This is a metaphorical statement. The desire to see her sister is like a spirit that has gone inside Kanshanda, taken possession of her, and caused her to act in an extreme manner. The statement is metaphorical because it is love for her sister that possesses her, not a real spirit; Nchume is not dead.

Nchume's sister seems to begin singing nearer and nearer the house as she goes out to fetch water. She begins sooner each time, I believe, as a sign of her increasing anxiety about her sister's fate and her growing excitement about her discovery in the swamp.

The lines in Nchume's song, "I'm dead on the left side,/In the right side there's life," might be interpreted as a metaphorical ref-

erence to Nchume's parents' situation: her mother has died, but her
father still lives. This would be another statement of the male:
female::right:left analogy we found in the previous section (p. 72).
Left/right is very important in Western moral and political symbolism, and it has been noted in several societies in eastern Africa.[1]
But it does not seem to appear in Haya culture with the same frequency or importance. Moreover, Ma Winifred Kisiraga insists that
the meaning of the song is literal, and the narrator seems to agree
by supplying the necessary details (lines 79 and 80).

The love between brother and sister must undergo a transformation at marriage. Sex and reproduction are not a part of the sibling love relationship, nor do they ideally figure at all in the lives of
young people. As the Haya proverb states, "A woman loves her
brother but does not marry him." Marriage of one or both siblings
introduces potentially disruptive elements into the brother-sister
relationship (as in the tales *Blocking the Wind, Kulili Your Brother of
Only One Mother*, and *Who Was the One Who Ate It?*).

Given this norm, we may ask what went wrong in the case of
the incestuous pair in *Child of the Valley*. A Haya explanation is
something like the following. The love between brother and sister
must not be allowed to develop a sexual component. Sex is an appetite that grows as an individual matures. The sexual appetites of
brother and sister must be controlled so that they do not emerge.
What happened to the brother and sister in *Child of the Valley* was
that they found themselves in a setting where restraints were ab-
sent, and sexual appetite, combined with their love for one another,
emerged. The setting for their loss of control thus is a significant
element in explaining their behavior.

The siblings in *Child of the Valley* regularly pasture the goats.
This task is usually performed by young boys. There is supposed
to be a good deal of verbal by-play at this time, much of it about
sex. Pasturing goats is proverbially the scene for learning the verbal
arts of repartee and double-entendre. A *woman* who is adept at
witty retorts, for example, might be put down by one of her female
peers with, "Did you used to take the goats to pasture?" Outside,
then, among the rocks where the goats are taken, is a place where
sexual themes emerge. What the children have kept inside themselves while they are inside their parents' house gets out when they
go to pasture the goats.

In *Child of the Valley* the narrator gives considerable emphasis
to the fact that the children eat their parents' food after they have

borne a child (lines 14–17). To my knowledge, Hayas make no formal symbolic statements regarding the separation of parents' food from children's in relation to incest, as has been reported elsewhere in Africa.[2] But sharing food does define a household group, and the narrator's descriptive emphasis seems to increase the dissonance of the children's behavior outside in the fields. Sharing the food inside strongly marks them as a household group. Their incestuous behavior outside is made more terrible by the contrast.

The same connection between inside desire and outside setting occurs in the dark tale of *Three Brothers*. The inclination that brothers often have is not directly named in this version of the tale, but happens to be in another: it is *obushuma*, the desire to take what belongs to someone else. It is portrayed hyperbolically in the tale, as brothers kill one another to get a larger share. In the West we name this motivation sibling rivalry. It can be seen as the tendency in Haya society and other societies toward segmentation (see p. 70).

While brothers are at home, in an environment of control by family and clan, *obushuma* is kept inside. When they journey into the wilderness, the constraints are relaxed; and, when there is wealth to be fought over, *obushuma* emerges. As with the love between brother and sister in *Child of the Valley*, the *obushuma* between brothers is kept inside when siblings are inside their parents' dwelling, but comes out when they move outside societal and parental control.

5

Tales of Suitors and Maidens

Tales in this section represent aspects of courtship as it is experienced by maidens and their suitors in Hayaland. A proper Haya courtship is a long series of meetings, negotiations, rituals, and celebrations. The particular suitor and maiden involved may initiate the courtship, but the process itself involves both families, each of which traditionally holds the prerogative to dictate terms to its child.

The tales speak more to the experience of courtship, the underlying motivations, concerns, and feelings of the boy and girl, and less to the politics of the ritual process. Specifically, the tales speak of adolescent girls' appetites for making things pleasing (*okushemeza*), a motivation that indicates their growing readiness and unconscious desire for marriage. Tales also speak of the necessity for a groom to demonstrate to his prospective in-laws a virtuous character; here, a capacity for self-control. This virtue in a husband increases the likelihood that the bride will find domestic happiness, and also that the bride's parents will not have to become involved in their daughter's marital disputes.

In four of the five tales in the section, the principal dramatic action involves preternatural beings: a talking bird who is the agent of a chief, a singing serpent, a magical ram, and a monster composed of excrement. To claim that the tales represent aspects of the experience of courtship is to assert that the tales speak in an indirect, symbolic mode. Moreover, the motivation involved in the two tales about reluctant maidens is an unconscious one—unconscious, not in the strict Freudian sense of emanating from the deepest level of human mental function, but in a more general sense that an act may be governed by rules of symbolic association beyond the conscious understanding of the actor.

The two tales about reluctant maidens, *Teaser* and *Little Leper of Munjolobo*, portray girls being lured into marriage through their desire "to make things pleasing." As we have noted, this verb may refer directly to a variety of acts: sewing, crocheting, fine basket work, and serving out food properly. As a form of speaking politely (*oku-tesa*), the word can refer to dining, such as when a host informs his guest that dinner is about to be served: "Come, let us make things pleasing" (*Ija tushemeze*); that is, "Come, let us dine." "To make things pleasing" may refer in more allusive speech to sexual intercourse. There the word would be used as a praise name (*eki-shambagizo*) for the act. *205143*

In each reluctant maiden tale, a messenger of the chief comes and snatches away something a girl would use "to make things pleasing." The bird in *Teaser* grabs a basket used for serving food, while the Little Leper makes off with the girl's *empindwi*, an iron tool five or six inches long which resembles a needle and is used in decorative basket work. By holding the object just out of the girl's reach and jerking it away when she tries to get it, the messenger leads the girl onward to her marriage. In a third tale, recorded but not included here, a leper requests a roasted banana from a reluctant maiden, but refuses to take it when it is offered. The maiden tries to give it to him, and off they go to the chief's palace, singing back and forth as in *Little Leper of Munjolobo*. The song is quoted below. The three items differ in kind—basket, *empindwi*, banana— but they all involve "to make things pleasing."

The girls' desires enable them to be lured in the same way that a desire for food allows Leopard to be lured by women in *The Glistening One* (the desire for food also enables a bird to entice a young bride to her death in *The Bride's Relish*). The reluctant maidens' entrapments will result in marriage and initiation into sex, fitting rewards for those so interested in "making things pleasing." In a sense, running down the road uncontrolledly and exposing her desires for public view are the girl's punishment. The haughty girl who refused so many suitors is seen to be governed by her desire "to make things pleasing" and all that this implies. Her public exposure is mirrored in *Blocking the Wind*, where a husband's desire for his new bride causes him to run about uncontrolledly in the fields.

Teaser

AS TOLD BY MA KELEZENSIA KAHAMBA

I give you a story.
Audience: I give you another.
I came and I saw.
Audience: See so that we may see.
∞
N-o-w
        A man had fathered a child of his own.
o
This one was b-e-a-u-t-i-f-u-l.
o
She was really beautiful.
Men c-o-u-r-t-e-d her but she refused.
o
The chief courted.
o
10   He sent his men there.
                        He sent one man . . .
He went. Nothing doing.
Eh-Eh! He had another man rubbed down and *dressed in
    b-e-a-u-t-i-f-u-l fabrics and leathers.*
He went to arrange a marriage.
She refused.
Again he sent a man, the second.
He tried to arrange a marriage.
She refused.
He sent another, the third.
He tried to arrange a marriage.
20   She refused.
o
Now a little bird, a little cowbird comes forward and says,
    "My Lord . . .
o
I will go to court her for you." They say, "You, bird!
MEN HAVE FAILED . . .
o
AND THEY ARE PEOPLE . . .
HOW CAN YOU, BIRD, GO AND GET THE GIRL OUT?"

o

He says, "I am going."
The chief takes out l-e-a-t-h-e-r-s . . .

$\qquad$ *has him d-r-e-s-s-e-d*

$\qquad\qquad$ *and he goes.*

At the home of the girl,
the old woman was preparing a meal by grinding millet . . .
30 Her grinding basket was full and so she stuck it by the
$\qquad$ hearth stones where water was boiling.
SHE MAKES PORRIDGE.
NOW WHEN SHE GOES TO LOOK, SHE SEES
$\qquad$ THAT OVER ON THE SIDE THERE IS NO
$\qquad$ SERVING BASKET.

$\qquad$ "EH!" SHE SAYS, "MY CHILD,
GO NEXT DOOR TO THOMASI'S HOUSE . . .
Go find for me . . .

$\qquad$ my serving basket so I can serve out the
$\qquad$ food."
The child goes.

o

They hand her the serving basket.
She comes with it.
The bird eyes the tree at the front gate . . .

$\qquad$ PA!

$\qquad$ [It alights there.]
It stands straight up.
40 When the child was near the tree at the front gate . . .

$\qquad$ It

$\qquad$ pounces!
Mh!
It snatches the serving basket away from her.

o

Eh-Eh!
The old woman looks.
"TEASER, TEASER,
BRING ME THE SERVING BASKET SO I CAN
$\qquad$ SERVE OUT THE FOOD.

o

TEASER, TEASER,
BRING ME THE SERVING BASKET SO I CAN
$\qquad$ SERVE OUT THE FOOD."

She says,
(sings)   "Mother, how can I bring the basket? I have
                            a little bird that turns to show its spots.
                        It teases like an itch."
50 The bird then begins,
(sings)   "Lubángo, I've been sent by Muyánge.
                        Lubángo, I've been sent by Muyánge."
EH-EH! THE OLD WOMAN RUNS OUT OF THE
  HOUSE WITH HER MIXING SPOON.
THEN THEY DASH THROUGH THE FRONT GATE
WITH HER S-P-O-O-N
                        AND WITH HER WORK SKIRT AND
HER LEATHER T-I-E-D THERE SO HER BREASTS
WERE UP A-B-O-V-E.
(sings)   "Teaser, Teaser,
                        Bring me the serving basket so I can serve out
                            the food."
                        She says, "Mother, how can I bring the basket?
                            I have a little bird that turns to show
                            its spots.
                        It teases like an itch."
(sings)   "Lubángo, I've been sent by Muyánge.
                        Lugángo, I've been sent by Muyánge."
EH-EH!
            THEY DASH DOWN THE ROAD.
EH-EH!
            THE OLD WOMAN IS AT THE FRONT GATE
  OF THOMASI'S HOUSE
WITH HER BREASTS UP ABOVE AND HER SPOON IN
  HER HAND.
THE BIRD HAS THE SERVING BASKET.
EH-EH!
(sings)   "Teaser, Teaser."
That's the old woman.
(sings)   "Bring me the serving basket so I can
                            serve out the food."
60 The girl:
(sings)   "Mother, how can I bring you the serving basket?
                            I have a little bird that turns to show
                            its spots.
                        It teases like an itch."

The bird itself:
(sings)   "Lubángo, I've been sent by Muyánge.
              Lubángo, I've been sent by Muyánge."
Eh-Eh! They're on the road.

o

Well, then, they are going to Kanázi.
That's where the palace is.
EH-EH!
THE OLD WOMAN . . .
WEARS HER LEATHER WRAP SO SHE'S NAKED
    ABOVE AND IN HER HAND
    IS HER MIXING SPOON.
        "Teaser, Teaser,
        Bring me the serving basket so I can serve
           out the food."
        She says, "Mother, how can I bring it? I have
           a little bird that turns to show its spots.
        It teases like an itch."
        "Lubángo, I've been sent by Muyánge.
        Lugángo, I've been sent by Muyánge."
Eh-Eh!
They're at Nyakimbímbili.
70 Then the old woman descends on the road and comes to
      the river.
        "Teaser, Teaser,
        Bring me the serving basket so I can serve
           out the food."
        She says, "Mother, how can I bring you the
           serving basket? I have a little bird that turns
           to show its spots.
        It teases like an itch"
        "Lubángo, I've been sent by Muyánge.
        Lubángo, I've been sent by Muyánge."
Eh-Eh! They climb at Lugéle.
        "Teaser, Teaser,
        Bring me the serving basket so I can serve
           out the food."
        She says, "Mother, how can I bring it? I have
           a little bird that turns to show its spots.
        It teases like an itch."
EH-EH!

When they open their eyes, they find they're in Kashéngi.
The old woman is there a-t
Kagáye.
>   "Teaser, Teaser."
The porridge is still near the hearth.
The dollop she had on her spoon
never got back to the rest. [It's still on the spoon.]
>> "Teaser, Teaser,
>> Bring me the serving basket so I can serve
>>> out the food."
>> She says, "Mother, how can I bring it? I have
>>> a little bird that turns to show its spots.
>> It teases like an itch."
>> "Lubángo, I've been sent by Muyánge.
>> Lubángo, I've been sent by Muyánge."

EH-EH! THEY'RE AT KALÉBE . . .

80   THE OLD WOMAN REACHES KIGÁTA.
MH-MH!
THEN SHE CALLS LOUDLY,
>> "Teaser, Teaser,
>> Bring me the serving basket so I can serve
>>> out the food."
>> She says, "Mother, how can I bring it? I have
>>> a little bird that turns to show its spots.
>> It teases like an itch."
>> "Lubángo, I've been sent by Muyánge.
>> Lubángo, I've been sent by Muyánge."

Eh-Eh!
They reach the top of the hill
up there at Hatabíke.
>> She's reached Kalébe.

THE OLD WOMAN STILL HAS THE SPOON
> IN HER HAND.
>> "Teaser, Teaser,
>> Bring me the serving basket so I can serve
>>> out the food."
>> She says, "Mother, how can I bring it? I have
>>> a little bird that turns to show its spots.
>> It teases like an itch."
>> "Lubángo, I've been sent by Muyánge.
>> Lubángo, I've been sent by Muyánge."

They're at Musa's house.

○

The old woman is following them behind there
>wherever she is.

"Teaser, Teaser,
Bring me the serving basket so I can serve
out the food."
She says, "Mother, how can I bring it? I have
a little bird that turns to show its spots.
It teases like an itch."
"Lubángo, I've been sent by Muyánge.
Lubángo, I've been sent by Muyánge."

EH-EH! THE FIRST ONE WHO GOES OUTSIDE
THE PALACE
90 SAYS, "MY LORD PROVIDER,
>THE BIRD HAS
BROUGHT THE WOMAN."
EH-EH! HE SAYS, "TAKE THAT ONE AND KILL HIM.
I HAVE SENT MEN WHO ARE MEN AND THEY
FAILED TO BRING THE WOMAN.
YOU COME TO TELL ME
A BIRD?"
THEY TAKE THAT ONE TO EXECUTE HIM.
THEY STRIKE HIM WITH AN AXE
AT THE SHOULDERS [cut off his head].
EH-EH!
THE THIRD ONE TO GO OUT
SAYS, "MY LORD PROVIDER, STOP KILLING PEOPLE.
THE BIRD HAS BROUGHT HER."
>EH! "AND
THAT ONE TOO, TIE HIM UP."
EH-EH!
>AT THE PALACE GATE
100 THEY GRAB HIM AND TIE HIM UP WITH ROPE.
MH-MH!
The old woman calls,
"Teaser, Teaser,
Bring me the serving basket so I can serve
out the food."
She says, "Mother, how can I bring it? I have
a little bird that turns to show its spots.
It teases like an itch."

The bird sees that he's come to the palace. He's jumping up
and down.
> "Lubángo, I've been sent by Muyánge.
> Lubángo, I've been sent by Muyánge."

EH-EH!
THE ONES WHO HEAR SAY, "MY LORD PROVIDER,
STOP KILLING PEOPLE.
THE BIRD HAS BROUGHT HER."
They jump up and run out of the p-a-l-a-c-e.
They take out a l-e-a-t-h-e-r c-a-p-e.
> *They take out a s-e-c-o-n-d c-a-p-e.*

Eh-Eh! They take out a s-e-d-a-n c-h-a-i-r.
110   THEY FIND THE GIRL CRYING FOUR PATHWAYS OF
TEARS.
Now, t-h-e-n,
> *they put the girl in a s-e-d-a-n c-h-a-i-r.*

They bring her inside the p-a-l-a-c-e.
And the old w-o-m-a-n . . .
They pick her up and c-a-r-r-y h-e-r.
They take out c-a-t-t-l-e.
They take out m-a-i-d-s-e-r-v-a-n-t-s.
They give them to her . . .
The old woman . . .
they return to her home.
120   *The bride goes to be married in the palace.*
The b-i-r-d . . .
That's why you see they don't kill the cowbird when he eats
> *on the cattle.*
> > THERE IS NO MAN WHO KILLS IT . . .

THE COWBIRD.
AND IF YOU HIT IT AND KILL IT . . .
Its curse kills you.
> My lord, my story is done.

When I saw the bride was married and hadn't yet come out
I said, "Let me go to report."
o

At your mother's brother's is a little basket of ashes and
> a half-measure of skin eruptions.
> > So,
> > > at our house,

> at my mother's brother's, the bananas grow fatter and fatter.
My story finishes there.

Little Leper of Munjolobo

AS TOLD BY MA KELEZENSIA KAHAMBA

N-o-w
    there was a girl.
THE GIRL WAS B-E-A-U-T-I-F-U-L.
SHE WAS BEAUTIFUL.
Now men continually come to court her, but
    she refuses . . .
                They come to court.
    She refuses . . .
                They come to court. She refuses . . .
Eh-Eh! The chief s-a-y-s,
                "I'll go and court her myself."
   o

The chief chooses and chooses men
                and sends them.
   o

They go, but she says, "No."
EH! HE PICKS OUT ONE HANDSOME MAN, HAS HIM
    RUBBED WITH BUTTERFAT, DRESSES HIM
    IN BEAUTIFUL CLOTHES OF GOLD. NO!
He goes to arrange a marriage and she refuses.
   o

10   Then there volunteered a short man who was LEPROUS.
He had contracted leprosy.
THE LITTLE ONE HAD BECOME ALL DRY
    AND HARD.
He says, "I'm going to search for her."
They say, "You, Little Leper, you?
You go and bring the girl?"
He says, "I'll bring her."
   o

Mh! He takes out a leather cape. He takes out butterfat and
    he annoints himself. He dresses.
Just like that.
            He goes.
   o

He goes and finds the g-i-r-l.

10   She's there in the entrance to her h-o-u-s-e.
      She's weaving a basket.
          o

      He says to her,
      "The chief has sent me to you."
                                      She says, "You?
      To you, to you I say never."
          o

      As she's weaving the basket,
                          he jumps up and snatches her
          empindwi.
      She's using it to weave the basket.
          o

      He runs and reaches the courtyard.
      "Little Leper, Little Leper of Munjolóbo,
      give me my *empindwi.*"
30   He says,
      (sings)   "Beautiful soft grass of the palace,
                       Here, take your *empindwi.*
                       Beautiful young calf of the palace,
                       Here, take your *empindwi.*"
        o (Narrator's aside: Look at the cooking pot, Benja.)
                       "Beautiful young calf of the palace,
                       Here take your *empindwi.*"
      (sings)   "Little Leper, Little Leper of Munjoló-"
      That's the girl.
      (sings)   "Little Leper, Little Leper of Munjolóbo,
                       You don't give me my *empindwi.*"
                       "Mother, fertile piece of land,
                       Here, take your *empindwi.*
                       Beautiful soft grass of the palace,
                       Here, take your *empindwi.*"
                       "Little Leper, Little Leper of Munjolóbo,
                       You don't give me-"
      NOW, THEN
                  THEY LEAVE THERE
      and go for about two hours.
          o
      THE GIRL . . .
                     followed the Little Leper.
                                      HE TOOK

HER *EMPINDWI*
AND IS RUNNING
to take her to the chief.

o

EH-Eh!
They're moving along.
They go for about six hours.
40 THEN THE GIRL . . .
                              doesn't know the way back.
NOW THAT LITTLE LEPER . . .
is running on the way to the palace
to take her to the chief.
                    AND THE *EMPINDWI*,
he's taken it.
Eh-Eh! They move along. They go and stop, stop and go,
    bit by bit.
THEN THE GIRL . . .
has begun to cry.
She tries again:
            "Little Leper, Little Leper of Munjolóbo,
            You don't give me my *empindwi*."
            "Beautiful farmland of the palace,
            Here, take your *empindwi*.
            Beautiful young calf of the palace,
            Here, take your *empindwi*."
EH-EH!
50 THEY MOVE ALONG. They go on for about nine hours.
    o

THEN THE GIRL . . .
                        has begun to cry.
All that's left is a j-o-u-r-n-e-y . . .
                                of about half an hour
to reach the palace.
Then the palace residents . . .
                        go outside.
                            They say, "Chief,"
                                            they

    s-a-y,
"The Little Leper has brought the woman."
                            Eh-Eh!
The one who said this first,
the chief cuts him down.

He takes out a machete
AND CUTS HIM DOWN.
60   EH-EH!
THE SECOND ONE SAYS,
"MY LORD,
          DON'T KILL PEOPLE.
THE LITTLE LEPER HAS BROUGHT THE WOMAN."
     o

EH-EH! HE SAYS, "KILL HIM ALSO."
THEY CUT HIM DOWN TOO,
WITH A MACHETE.
MH-MH!
     o

THEN THE TWO OF THEM
                              go and stop, stop and go, bit
     by bit. There's only a half hour to go.
WHEN THEY APPROACHED CLOSE BY THE PALACE,
70   THEN THE GIRL BEGAN TO CRY . . .
THAT LITTLE LEPER
                    was running ahead with her *empindwi*,
JUMPING UP AND RUNNING AHEAD,
JUMPING UP
AND RUNNING AHEAD.
EH-EH!
     *The one who raced out of the palace this time was a royal
     adviser, a favorite of the chief.*
He says, "I'll go and tell the chief."
He says, "My Lord,
stop killing people."
He says, "THE LITTLE LEPER HAS BROUGHT
     THE WOMAN."
80   Eh-Eh! They leave the house.
They take our beautiful clothes of GOLD . . .
THEY GO AND DRESS HER . . .
THEY PICK HER UP . . .
THEY PUT HER ON THEIR SHOULDERS . . .
AUTOMOBILES . . .
BUSES . . .
THE KING'S DRUMS SOUND . . .
CANNON . . .
They bring her into the house.

90 As for the Little Leper . . .
the chief gives him cattle.
He presents him with a maidservant.
He presents him with a manservant.
When I saw them giving him a manservant,
                                        giving him
    a maidservant,
                    and he himself eating plantains,

o

I left there . . .

o

I said, "Let me go and report."

o

It's done.

The Serpent
of Kamushalanga

AS TOLD BY MA KELEZENSIA KONSTANTIN

I went and saw for you my lords.
(Aside: Let me fumble about and see if I can do this.)
Five girls arise and go to cut grass [for the house]
at Kamulengéra.
Now when they went into the fields,
they cut. They cut. They cut. They cut.
Mh-Mh!
They straighten up to rest.

o

They say, "Bojo, come, let's go have a chat."
                                        "Okay."
10 They go.
Now this one begins,
                "Bojo,
where will you marry?"
She says, "Me?"
                "Mm!"

o
"I'm to marry the nobleman, Ta Manuel."
"Eh?"
        "Mm!"
"And who are you to marry?"
"I'm to marry the nobleman, Ta Alphonse from over there."
"Eh?"
"And who will you marry?"
20   "Perhaps I'll marry the nobleman, What's-his-
        name, from Kishogo."
"Okay."
"And you,"
            (Audience: We won't take anything to her
        kalaile kata)
            "Where will you marry?"
"I don't know where I'll marry."
"MAKE HER SAY, THAT TROUBLE-AT-SUNDOWN!
YOU WON'T TELL WHERE YOU'LL MARRY?
                                        WE'VE
        CHOSEN NOBLEMEN.
YOU REFUSE TO CHOOSE A NOBLEMAN?"
Now they leave that place.
They go.
            "BUT SINCE YOU'VE REFUSED TO CHOOSE
        THE MAN WHO'LL MARRY YOU,
A NOBLEMAN,
                A RICH ONE,
30   EH?
Go on—you'll be married into poverty!"
And she says, "Mother, I don't know who will marry me."
o

Then they went and put their bundles of grass up on
        their heads.
They went home . . .
Mh-Mh!
They went back in to their mother.
                            "Eh? HAVE YOU COME
        ALREADY, MY CHILDREN?" "Yes,
yes, we've come. See what we've done. See what we've done."
        "E-e-h" [the mother acknowledges their work].
Now the sun did not rise and set many times before . . .
Eh-Eh!

40 the nobleman made the first girl truly happy . . .
He marries her.

   o

Eh-Eh!
But when I went to take a look . . .
I see it's her misfortune to live in houses all
     run down and strewn about.
ALL OF THEM WERE MARRIED.
Now that foolish one
              is left there.

   o

Now she says, "Now what shall I do?
All my comrades have married.
Mh?

   o

50 Ha-ah!"
She says, "I'll leave."

   o

She grinds a little millet for herself.
She makes it into porridge.
She finishes it.
She wraps it.
She finishes wrapping . . .
She goes and forges for herself nine arrowheads.
She ties them up.

   o

She carries her bundle.
60 She goes INTO A GREAT W-I-L-D-E-R-N-E-S-S.
Now in the place she went . . .
the rain falls.
She says, "I'll go seek shelter."
Now there were many boulders with great caves among them.
She goes inside.
When she enters she finds an ADDER in there.
NOT A SMALL ONE.
Eh-Eh! She says, "This ADDER, but what shall I do with it?
In the place I've come for shelter from the RAIN,
                          now I've
     found this adder. What shall I do?"

   o

70 She remains there

and after she thought about it, her heart
says, "No!
Take out your arrows.
Aim to impale . . .
the serpent.
          See if you will kill it."
She takes out one arrow.
She arms her bow.
She lets fly.
(sings)   She says, "I impale, I impale, I impale the
                     Serpent of Kamushalánga,
                 With whitened teeth like chalk, with reddened
                     eyes like blood."
                 It says, "Mm———m."
                 It says, "Maiden, Darts-of-iron, Iron-darts-
                     in-the-valley,
                 Go on, go on and do it, Iron-darts-in-the-valley.
                 Tomorrow, come and let us fight, Iron-darts-in-
                     the-valley."
                 She says, "I impale, I impale, I impale the
                     Serpent of Kamushalánga,
                 With whitened teeth like chalk, with reddened
                     eyes like blood."
                 It says, "Mm———m."
                 It says, "Maiden, Darts-of-iron, Iron-darts-
                     in-the-valley,
                 Go on, go on and do it, Iron-darts-in-the-valley.
                 Tomorrow, come and let us fight, Iron-darts-in-
                     the-valley."
Then she hurls an arrow.
Again she takes out her little bit of millet.
She eats.
80   She finishes and lies down.
When the sun rose in the morning . . .
she takes out another arrow.
                 She says, "I impale, I impale, I impale the
                     Serpent of Kamushalánga,
                 With whitened teeth like chalk, with reddened
                     eyes like blood."
                 It says, "Mm———m."
                 It says, "Maiden, Darts-of-iron, Iron-darts-
                     in-the-valley,

Go on, go on and do it, Iron-darts-in-the-valley.
Tomorrow, come and let us fight, Iron-darts-in-
    the-valley."
She says, "I impale, I impale, I impale the
    Serpent of Kamushalánga,
With whitened teeth like chalk, with reddened
    eyes like blood "
It says, "Mm————m."
It says, "Maiden, Darts-of-iron, Iron-darts-
    in-the-valley,
Go on, go on and do it, Iron-darts-in-the-valley.
Tomorrow, come and let us fight, Iron-darts-in-
    the-valley."
She says, "I impale, I impale, I impale the
    Serpent of Kamushalánga,
With whitened teeth like chalk, with reddened
    eyes like blood."
It says, "Mm————m."
It says, "Maiden, Darts-of-iron, Iron-darts-
    in-the-valley,
Go on, go on and do it, Iron-darts-in-the-valley.
Tomorrow, come and let us fight, Iron-darts-in-
    the-valley."
Then, my lords—let me not delay you—
THE ARROWS SHE IMPALES IT WITH . . .
are used up,
but it hasn't yet died.
    o
Now when she realized they were used up . . .
she says, "What will I do with this serpent?
I'll rest again
90 AND TOMORROW AT DAWN . . .
I'll go again to search for other arrows to impale it."
The girl lies down.
She falls asleep.
When she woke up,
she finds . . .
        SHE HAS LAIN WITH A HANDSOME
    YOUTH . . .
SHE FINDS SHE'S ON A VONO BED [trade name for a
    steel bed] . . .

SHE FINDS MAIDSERVANTS PASSING HERE
   AND THERE . . .
SHE FINDS THEY'RE BRINGING HER MILK . . .
SHE FINDS SHE'S IN THE "HIGH BRIDGE
   OF UGANDA" [a bed?].
100 THAT'S HOW I SAW IT FOR YOU, MY LORDS,
WHEN YOU GIRLS ARE IN THE FIELDS GATHERING
   GRASS,
          SPEAKING YOUR MINDS,
BOASTING, "I'LL BE MARRIED AT SUCH-AND-
   SUCH A PLACE." AND "I'LL BE MARRIED
   OVER THERE."
THAT'S JUST HOW I SAW IT FOR YOU. AT
   YOUR FATHER'S SISTER'S AND AT YOUR
   MOTHER'S BROTHER'S, THEY'RE EATING
   BEER BANANAS AND BEAN LEAVES.
Audience: AT YOUR HOME THE BANANAS GROW
   FATTER AND FATTER.
AT OUR HOME THE BANANAS GROW FATTER AND
   FATTER.

Squeezer

AS TOLD BY TA ELIAS KAISHULA

I give you a story.
Audience: I give you another.
It's done.
Audience: The news of long ago.
MY LORD, I WENT AND SAW.
Audience: See so that we may see.
I see a man marries a woman.
Now after he married . . .
the woman . . .
10   he left her while she was still a bride . . .
He goes to seek fortune.
When he went to seek fortune
                    all that he brought WAS A LOSS.

HE GOT NOTHING.
NOW WHEN HE REACHED THE ROAD . . .

he meets

a man selling a ram.
He bargains back and forth for it.
They agree on a price.
He buys it.
with the ten shillings that he had, poor man.

o

My lord, he brings the ram and puts it in his house.
20   *He tells his wife his troubles,*
how he went to seek fortune and nothing was to be gotten.
The woman says, "That's okay.

We'll be getting other things."

o

Now the woman . . .
bears a female child . . .
And then . . .

she bears a male child.

o

Now . . .

o

They would take it to pasture and bring it home,

take the ram to

pasture and bring it home.
Now when the girl had grown until . . .

o

she was desirable
30   now the sheep . . .
from where it was tied on a tether in the house
now it calls to the girl.
Her father and mother have already gone to cultivate.

o

It says,

"YOU, GIRL!

YOU GIRL!

COME AND LET ME SQUEEZE YOU.

COME

AND LET ME SQUEEZE YOU."
She replies (high voice),
"If I wasn't holding my mother's nursing infant,

I would

come
     and you squeeze me
          and you squeeze me."
Hii! (narrator laughs)
Now then, my lord,
         the child looks and she's confounded.
WHEN HER PARENTS RETURNED
                FROM WORK,
40   she comes to tell them, "What I saw here I have never seen
    before, nor has anyone else."
SHE SAYS, "THAT SHEEP YOU TIED ON A TETHER
    ROPE . . . "
She says, "WHEN IT THINKS YOU HAVE GONE
                    it says,
'YOU, GIRL!
      YOU, GIRL!
         COME AND LET ME SQUEEZE YOU.
                 COME
AND LET ME SQUEEZE YOU.'"
She says, "And I replied, (high voice) 'If I wasn't holding
    my mother's nursing infant,
I would come
       and you squeeze me
and you squeeze me.'"
  o
"Mh?"
They say, "Let's hide ourselves and lie in wait for it."
My lord . . .
      the sun set.
         It rose.
50   They say, "We're going to cultivate."
They go into their banana grove
         and hide themselves.
AS IT STANDS THERE IT STARTS TO BELLOW.
"YOU, GIRL!
     YOU, GIRL!
        COME AND LET ME SQUEEZE YOU.
             COME
AND LET ME SQUEEZE YOU."
She says, (high voice) "If I wasn't holding my mother's
    nursing infant,

           I would come and you squeeze me

                                     and

you squeeze me."

   o

HII!

When the parents came back, THEY CAME
       WITHOUT ASKING ANY QUESTIONS.
THEY UNTIE IT.
THEY TAKE IT OUT INTO THE BANANA GROVE . . .
THEY SLAUGHTER IT.

60   They finish slaughtering it and begin to roast the meat . . .
When they finished roasting it they take the bones and
       throw them away . . .
Now when they had thrown away the bones, one bone comes
       back again.
It comes and speaks as before.
Eh-Eh! They grab the bones and throw them
       into the place where the cattle-fumigating fire is made.
The man picks up a burning stick and THROWS IT
       IN THERE.
He sets the bones on fire like this . . . (gestures)
And when he set the bones on fire . . .
the smoke that erupted . . .
billows up and up INTO THE SKY.

70   IT BECAME A MOUNTAIN.
   o

HII!
They look and are confounded.
   o

Now they dwell there for a while and the children would play.
Now when they were playing, they said, "Can anyone go and
       climb that mountain?"
They try and fail.
           They try and fail.
                   The girl climbs up.
When she climbed, she didn't turn back.
"Turn back!" No answer.
Climb
    climb
       climb

climb
        climb
                climb.
They look and cry out in alarm, "Everyone see!" "Turn back,
    girl!" No answer.
                    "Do this!" No answer.
                                    "Be thus!"
            No answer.
80 She disappears into the sky.
    She goes and finds the smoke there, the sheep.
    The smoke that went up there . . .
    is of the sheep.
    He became a chief there.
    My lord . . .
        o

    they dwell in the sky. The girl,
        o

    who "Squeezer" wanted to squeeze and marry,
    HE GOES AND HE TRULY MARRIES HER.
        o

    In the home she left, the people mourn.
90 They finish.
                For the person who was lost . . .
                                they shave
        their heads.
                They dwell there.
    They complete a year and the girl bears a child.
    They complete another year and the girl bears a child.
    They complete another year and the girl bears a child.
    When they had reached . . .
    about four children . . .
    My lord, the husband says, "She has emerged from her
        bridal seclusion."
    He takes to the road saying, "Let me take you to your
        father and mother.
    They wanted to kill me, but I always loved you. A person
        who loves another,
    my lord, sends gifts."
100 He delivers . . .
    cattle,
    a herd of them.

He delivers goats . . .
                    a herd of them.
He gives . . .
            ALL GOOD THINGS THAT CAN
    BE GIVEN.
AND MAIDSERVANTS AND MANSERVANTS,
my lord, he brings them too.
He comes with them to the home of Ta Pita.
There was a feast and a holiday declared.
And when I saw these things I said, "Let me go and tell
    Ma Wini."
110 I leave off.

Mutele, You've Left Me, You've Gone

AS TOLD BY TA JOELI BAKE

I give you a story.
Audience: I give you another.
It's done.
I am Joeli Bake,
Bugengéle Village,
Ibwéra township.
I went and I saw.
(Audience: But you didn't mention the county.)
I went and I saw.
10 I saw a man . . .
was going to court a woman . . .
And when he would go on the road . . .
whenever he was taken by a great need . . .
he begins to relieve himself [defecate].
        o

Now when he had relieved himself during all that time . . .
down to the days approaching the wedding . . .
he goes . . .

with beer . . .
to make a feast . . .
20   It's "*Kaláile Káta*."
      ○

When he approached . . .
their place . . .
                  now at that time he would go and relieve himself
         in the thickets . . .
the turds form . . .
a "committee" . . .
                  They say, "Let us go and spoil his courtship."
   ○
Well now . . .
            They begin to gather . . .
                              those that he dropped
         as he was traveling along . . .
                              and those that he dropped at
         the very beginning . . .
                        Now
                  they gather themselves
         together . . .
to go and spoil the courtship.
   ○
On the road [the body of gathered turds] begins to sing.
      Its song . . .
The man's name was Mutéle.
It begins to speak:
(sings)   "Mutéle, Mutéle, Mutéle,
                 You've left me, you've gone, Mutéle.
                 Mutéle, Mutéle, Mutéle,
                 You've left me, you've gone, Mutéle.
                 Pluck the string! Beat the drum!
                 I follow Mutéle into his courtship."
30   THEN THE MAN . . .
stops and listens.
"What's that behind me?
What are these things that are singing?
                        Let me listen to whatever
         is calling my name."
                  He listens.
(sings)   "Mutéle, Mutéle, Mutéle,
                 You've left me, you've gone.

Pluck the string! Beat the drum!
I follow Mutéle into his courtship."
My lord, the man . . .
          knows that it's his name . . .
He goes back . . .
with his walking stick . . .
HE HITS IT . . .
HE SCATTERS IT ABOUT.
HE THROWS BITS OF IT HERE, HE THROWS BITS
    THERE, OTHERS HE THROWS THERE.
40 He says, "It won't come again."
HE CONTINUES HIS JOURNEY. EH-EH!
    IT'S GATHERING ITSELF TOGETHER. SLOWLY.
    SLOWLY. IT COMES.
IT BEGINS TO SING
AND IT PUTS IN CLAPPING [*].
          "*MUTÉLE *MUTÉLE *MUTÉLE,*
          YOU'VE* LEFT ME,* YOU'VE *GONE,
          PLUCK* THE STRING. *BEAT
                    THE* DRUM.
          I FOLLOW* MUTÉLE INTO HIS
                    COURTSHIP."
HE LISTENS.
          He says, "But . . .
                    what shall I do?"
                              The man
    shrugs it off.
          But he feels shame.
o
He enters the house where he's courting . . .
                              They put out
    a woven mat for him and he sits.
Now when he had sat . . .
                    IT COMES.
At the time everything was complete . . .
                              They'd agreed on
    the amount of beer . . .
                    They'd agreed to give the
    woman to him . . .
Now when they look at the front gate . . .
it comes singing.

"Mutéle, Mutéle,
You've left me, you've gone.
Pluck the string! Beat the drum!
I follow Mutéle into his courtship."

50   "EH?"
        They say, "What are these?"
When the people in the house go to look, they grab
    their noses, they do this (turn away). Some are nauseated
    to see it.
            Others begin vomiting.
                            "Eeh," they say, "You,
Mutéle . . .
            all of that shit— it's you it's followed.
Both the fresh and the dried have followed you!"
                                            And he
answers,
            "My lord, I don't know where it
came from.
            My lord . . . "
They say, "Let it enter the house so we can see what it will do."
    It comes into the MIDDLE OF THE ROOM. IT SINGS.
    IT JUMPS FOR JOY . . .
IT COMES TO THE WOVEN MAT AND SITS.
Now,
    they say to the man,
                        "You who go and shit . . .
turds upon the road . . .
                    We know that when a person
is courting he does not travel and do bad things
on the road.
            Look— What you dropped at your
neighbor's fence . . .
                        as well as what you dropped on
the road you regularly travel . . .
                            now look— that is
what has come here and made such a stink.
                                            Now
the courtship is finished.
                        The woman is no longer yours."
My lord, when I had seen this . . .
I said, "Let me go and tell them."
When a person goes to court
he doesn't go and defecate.

Defecate at your own house, go where
you're going, and return.
60 That's how shit ruined a courtship.

○

Believe it.

COMMENTARY

The action of *Teaser* is placed geographically and temporally
by the progress of the characters from the vicinity of the Kaham-
bas' house (where the story is being told) to the chief's palace at
Kanazi. The participants at the storytelling session visualize the
villages that the bird, girl, and mother pass through as the narrator
names them. In *Teaser* the succession of places is more complex than
in other tales of this kind because the girl's mother is always a distance behind the bird and the maiden. Each repeated singing by
the characters therefore encompasses two places: one from which
the mother calls and the other from which the girl answers and the
bird coaxes her on. It is a difficult feat in storytelling to visualize
this and to tell about it.

The underlying sexual component of the young girl's behavior
in *Teaser* and *Little Leper of Munjolobo* can be seen in the songs sung
back and forth by the protagonists. The young girl in *Teaser* sings
to her mother that the little bird "teases like an itch." This sort of
description is applied to sexual desire in Haya epic poetry. In *Little
Leper of Munjolobo*, the title character moves a little closer to the
point when he poetically addresses the girl as "beautiful soft grass
of the palace" (something that one may lie down on), "beautiful
farmland of the palace," and "fertile piece of land." But the leper,
in a tale recorded but not included in this collection, makes the
most direct statement of all. Recall that he asked the girl for a
roasted banana and then refused to take it. Their song goes:

"Leprous One, Leprous One, sorcerer that you are,
Here take your banana and let me go home.
Mother and Father are asking, 'Where's the plump one that
fills our house?'"
[he replies:] "Come, mother, come. The one who lies with you
hates to see the sunrise.
He lies and rocks you back and forth until dawn.
He drinks water late at night like a bird.
He lies between banana leaves like the bundles of grass to be
kept moist."

Kelezensia Kahamba, who, on separate occasions, narrated both *Teaser* and *Little Leper of Munjolobo*, tells the stories to her children as examples of how little characters can accomplish great things if they persevere. The tales surely illustrate that lesson, but when one questions the motivation of the reluctant maiden, a broader picture emerges. The version quoted above was narrated by Kelezensia Bake. It is almost exactly the same as *Little Leper of Munjolobo*, except for the song.

The song in *Teaser* includes one phrase whose meaning is hard to determine. The bird is described as *ke'nkinga magabo. Oku-kinga* means either "to close" (as a door) or "to turn around." *Magabo* are either spots or shields. I have translated the phrase "that turns to show its spots," but can fathom no meaning, symbolic or otherwise, in it. In another version of the same tale, a different phrase appears, equally ambiguous. Unlike words in a narrative, which must make coherent sense, particular words in a song may lose their coherent interpretation, but continue to be sung for metrical reasons. They seem to have no bearing on the main action of the tale.

The four pathways of Teaser's tears (line 110) refer to two pathways down one's cheeks plus two pathways out the corners of one's eyes. To cry in all four pathways means one is crying a lot. *Muyange* in the song in *Teaser* is the name of the chief whom the bird serves.

The Serpent of Kamushalanga and *Squeezer* are representative of a body of Haya tales in which mates emerge from animal or plant form. In other tales, a bride emerges from a wooden pole that was to be used as a column in a traditional Haya house; another bride emerges from a hollow reed, where she had enclosed herself because of a dispute with her sister; and a groom emerges from a tree trunk. There appears to be a logical connection between the container and the person contained. In times past, the spirits of ancestral chiefs were said to inhabit certain snakes, although these were pythons, not adders as in *The Serpent of Kamushalanga*. That a libidinous groom would inhabit the body of a ram would make sense in western symbolism. Rams and billy goats are metaphors for our sexual appetites. However, I have not found rams used as metaphors for libido in other examples of Haya oral literature.

That a bride should emerge from a wooden column or a hollow reed is consistent with one of the Haya ideals of young feminine beauty—a tall, erect, and willowy build. The ideal also appears in the praise name given the reluctant maiden, Teaser, by the little bird. *Lubango*, he calls her, "straight staff," a long, evenly-shaped shaft of a spear or walking stick. This ideal of beauty becomes the basis of dramatic and domestic conflict in *Crested Crane and Dove*.

"Trouble-at-sundown" is an abuse aimed at the central character in *The Serpent of Kamushalanga* (line 24). A problem that comes late in the day must usually be endured the whole night before remedy can be sought by daylight.

The protagonist in *Mutele, You've Left Me, You've Gone* is on his way to a celebration given just a day before the actual wedding ceremony (line 20). It is called *kalaile kata*, "how did (the bride) sleep?" a form of the traditional morning greeting *Ma' / tata olail' ota*, "Mother/Father, how did you sleep?" It is a large celebration to which neighbors, friends, and relations are invited; refreshments are served. Although a *kalaile kata* is a red-letter occasion in the social calendar, one of the wise-cracking ladies in the audience of *The Serpent of Kamushalanga* says they will probably not go to the one in Kishogo (lines 20–22) because the village is too far away.

Mutele, You've Left Me, You've Gone presents the Rabelaisian dilemma of a man being joyfully pursued into his courtship by a monster made of his own excrement. The monster persists even after being broken apart and scattered about. The tale seems to be widespread in Africa; one version appears in a collection of Limba tales from Sierra Leone.[1] The interpretation to be developed here, of course, is meant to pertain only to the Haya version.

Excrement, as we have seen, can be a sign of the presence of children (*I Shall Be Drinking from Them*). It can also be a symbol for a substantive problem that requires remedial action. A Haya proverb states, "What is defecated by a child is cleaned up by an adult," meaning that problems created by junior members of a clan or other organization must be dealt with by the senior members as well. Other Haya proverbs also use this symbol.[2]

The suitor's unrestrained and unrestrainable excrement in *Mutele, You've Left Me, You've Gone* spoils his courtship. The central character, Mutele, did not defecate where he was supposed to: in his own banana grove. The monstrous results of this prove to his prospective in-laws that he is unfit for marriage. The logic of this conclusion depends on the cultural fact that excrement is figuratively like domestic problems between spouses in that it must be kept inside—the person, the banana grove—and properly disposed of; otherwise it can get out and bring trouble and shame. Thus, a man who cannot restrain his own excrement cannot hope to control a domestic enclave. His weakness means trouble, not only for the wife, but also for her parents, principally her father, to whom she will come running with problems that should have been kept inside the marriage.

The same symbolism is present in another Haya tale from a previously published collection.[3] The story begins, "A man had a daughter. People come (to court). He says, 'Let the man who will marry my child come and dwell here for six days without defecating. When he completes those days, he'll marry her.'" Everyone who hears the conditions is afraid and leaves without trying. But one day Hare comes, and, by employing a ruse, he wins the girl. He digs several holes out in the front yard, requests that the people of the house come outside and point out to him the local villages, and, as they are doing so, he sits over the holes and defecates.

For Hare, preternatural control of defecation is the criterion for qualification as a husband. For Mutele, its opposite—monstrous noncontrol—is the criterion for disqualification. Both tales are informed by the same symbolism, which metaphorically equates marital problems with excrement—things to be controlled and disposed of properly inside, not to be let loose where they will bring humiliation and breaches of the peace.

Mutele's monster shares a significant feature with Squeezer, the ram in the fourth tale in this section, namely, the indestructibility of their desires. No matter what is done to them, they come back and say what they want. This feature appears in another Haya tale, recorded but not included here. It concerns a tree stump that attaches itself to a maiden, sings about how it wants to marry her, and refuses to leave her. People chop it up and throw it into a river, but it comes back, sings again, and refuses to leave. Eventually, the girl goes off with it, and out of the stump comes a young chief.

To my knowledge, Haya tales that include this motif are all tales about courtship. Squeezer's (and the stump's) indestructible desires seem to be metaphoric evocations of a lover's yearning to marry his or her chosen mate, whether or not the families involved approve the match. In real life, of course, a lover's desire may not be so invincible in the face of family opposition. In *Mutele, You've Left Me, You've Gone*, the unsuccessful suitor is betrayed by a parody of that indestructible desire. Ruth Finnegan gives this latter interpretation to the excremental monster in the Limba folktale cited above.

6

Tales of the New Bride

A newly married woman, still properly called a bride (*mugole*) until she emerges from her bridal seclusion, is the central character in many Haya tales. A Haya bride experiences a significant and potentially painful transformation in her entire living situation: she leaves the family of her birth and goes to live with the family into which she has married. The transition from womanly daughter to young wife can be a difficult one. The time a bride spends "inside," doing no work, having few social contacts except her husband's family, and, ideally, becoming pregnant, can be looked upon as the term of her initiation into the world of an adult married woman.

The bride must learn to adjust her behavior to a new social framework. Before her change of residence and status, she lived among the members of her own clan as an economically productive maiden who was sought after in marriage. In her bridal seclusion, she dwells among people not of her own clan as an economically dependent young woman whose dutifulness and responsibility as a family member are yet to be proved. Imagine the haughty maiden, Teaser, or her counterpart in *Little Leper of Munjolobo*, who refuses an army of suitors but will then have to adjust to a new family situation under the watchful eye of her mother-in-law.

To help the bride behave properly, members of her own family instruct her on the night before she will move to her husband's home. This ceremony is called *oku-hana omugole*, "to warn the bride," that is, to tell her what she should not do in her new situation. Warnings include admonitions not to behave disrespectfully

and not to put on airs—Hayas say, "to take a name for oneself."
Several tales in this section can be read as this kind of negative
cautionary statement.

The bride's antagonist in four of the six tales in this section,
her mother-in-law, is well suited to be a demanding mistress of
initiation. Not of her husband's or her son's clan, she herself came
to dwell among the members of that clan as a young bride. Having
undergone the same initiation about two decades earlier, the
mother-in-law can demonstrate how difficult it is to become a func-
tioning member of her new family, and how well she herself has
succeeded in making the family's interests her own.

The principal motive force in these tales is the circumstance of
bridal seclusion itself. The setting here—like the wilderness in
Three Brothers and the goat pasture in *Child of the Valley*—enables
certain appetites to emerge. Surrounded by the family's food reserves, left alone all day, and having no work to occupy her, a bride
may not be able to restrain an overwhelming appetite for food. Her
uncontrolled eating, in itself, is not the problem; she is, in fact,
encouraged to grow plump and pregnant. It is rather the control of
family resources that is at issue. When a bride's appetite emerges,
it may violate the basic premise of her new existence: that the property which surrounds her is not owned by her or by her clan as it
was when she lived in her parents' home. The resources belong to
her husband's clan members, and she must ask them, in the person
of her mother-in-law, for permission to use or to consume them.

The category of food called relish (*omukubi*) usually consists of
some form of protein eaten as a sauce with the staple food, plantains, millet, or cassava. Together, the two make a proper Haya
meal—plantains and fish stew, plantains and beef, plantains and
cooked sour milk. Sometimes plantains are eaten with only salt as
the relish.

The Bride's Relish is an unusual one—Hayas would not normally
eat a small bird. The mother-in-law's relish in *I Ate Minnows, Little
Minnows*, cooked flies, is similarly an unusual one. Hayas would
not eat flies, but two or three kinds of insects are eaten. The tale
Crested Crane and Dove revolves around the seasonal appearance of
the species of grasshopper called *ensenene*, a tasty relish. A Haya
bride would thus react to finding that her in-laws eat cooked flies
not with horror, as we would, but with something more akin to
surprise, as we would on learning that someone eats small birds.

The Legend of Ikimba

AS TOLD BY MA LAULELIA MUKAJUNA

Now
     an old woman
had caught that lake, Ikimba . . .
She had closed it up inside.
In a water jar, inside there.
There were fish inside.
  o
Now, she would take them out . . .
and cook.
She reaches in like this, takes out fish with her hand, and cooks.
  o
Now eventually her son came to wed . . .
  o
10 a bride.
  o
Now
the bride . . .
her family escorts her to her new home . . .
The old woman, the mother-in-law, drew out fish and cooked
     for them . . .
She didn't give anything for the bride's mother to take home.
  o
She didn't give anything for the bride's mother to take home.
  o
Now, then . . .
the bride became angry.
She thought,
     "Even though she cooked for my people, and
    they ate . . .
20 she could have taken out a few more fish . . .
                       so I could wrap
    them up . . .
         and send them for my mother."
  o
Now when the old woman went out around back to the
     banana plants . . .

she said, "Just let me reach in there.
I'll draw out fish to send my mother."
o

She reached in.
o

When she had reached all the way inside . . .
                                                    the water
        boiled over . . .
She had nothing to stop it up.
o

IT POURED OUT OF THE JAR A LAKE, WO WO WO.
    BRIDE! RUN! RUN! RUN! WO WO WO.
    THE MOTHER-IN-LAW,
    FROM WHERE SHE STANDS, SEES THE BRIDE.
    THE WATER HAS ALREADY DRIVEN HER AWAY.
    "HELP! HELP! HELP!"
(draws breath)
THE OLD WOMAN RAISED HER HOE TO THE WATER.
    "IKIMBA, IKIMBA, KILL ONE VILLAGE,
    BUT LEAVE ANOTHER. KILL ONE VILLAGE,
    BUT LEAVE ANOTHER." ON THE LAKE,
    WEH WEH WEH WEH WEH.
o

Bride . . .
30 and mother-in-law . . .
the water swallowed them.
o

The place . . .
where they fell . . .
it's there the lake subsided.
o

That's why it doesn't resemble the other one— The Great White
    Lake [Victoria/Nyanza].
It stayed a little marsh.
o

Now, what does this matter point out to us?
It points out to us . . .
Myself, if [my son] Lauliáni would marry . . .
40 I would have a bride in the inner room . . .
I wouldn't refuse to send gifts to her people.
o

I'd wrap up a gift for her to send to her mother . . .
That's when
        she'd be happy.

  o

That little lake points out to us: . . .
                don't refuse your son's
    wife . . .
        something to send her people.

The Bride's Relish

AS TOLD BY MA KELEMENTINA BAKE

I went and I saw.
I saw a girl.
The girl married.
Now in her marriage, in bed there, she comes to desire . . .
Whenever she would go to the bathing enclosure . . .
                        she sees
    a small bird.
Every time she would go . . .
              she sees a small bird.
                      Now
    she comes to desire it.
Now desiring it she says,
        "I can't go to my mother- in-law.
She won't agree to do it for me.
But now . . .
10 who shall I tell?"
The bird alighted there . . .
She catches it . . .
Members of the household are out cultivating . . .
When she caught it . . .
  o

she plucked and plucked its feathers . . .
She put it in a little packet and tied it up . . .
Eh-eh! She peeled plantains . . .

She put the packet on top of them . . .

  °

And after she put it on top there . . .

  °

20 The food was done . . .
Eh-eh!
      She serves out the plantains . . .
She washes her hands . . .
When she comes to open the packet . . .
                 the bird . . .

FLIES AWAY.

  °

EH?
AND THE BRIDE . . .
THROWS OFF HER BARKCLOTH.
SHE RUNS AFTER IT.
(bride sings)   "My little bird, my little bird,
            Why have you gone before I've eaten you?
            My little bird, my little bird,
            Why have you gone before I've eaten you?"
            Pulili-chwai. [sound of wings]
(bird sings)   "Here's relish, the bride's relish.
            Bride, bride, bride, come hurry. I'll
               throw you where the water's full.
            Bride, bride, bride, come hurry. I'll
               throw you where the water's full."
            Pulili-chwai.
            "Here's relish, the bride's relish."
THEY GO ON!

  °

30 EH?
When her mother-in-law returned,
                    "Where has the bride
   gone?
      Where has the bride gone?"

  °

She runs.
(bride sings)   "My little bird, my little bird,
            Where have you gone before I've eaten you?
            My little bird, my little bird,

Where have you gone before I've eaten you?"
Pulili-chwai.

(bird sings)   "Here's relish, the bride's relish.
Bride, bride, bride, come hurry. I'll
     throw you where the water's full.
Bride, bride, bride, come hurry. I'll
     throw you where the water's full."
Pulili-chwai.
"Here's relish, the bride's relish."

THEN

○

WHEN THEY HAD GOTTEN TO A DEEP PART
   OF THE LAKE . . .
THE BRIDE . . .
TUMBLED HERSELF IN . . .
WHEN IT SAW HER DISAPPEAR . . .

○

IT COMES FLAPPING ITS WINGS.
(high voice) "DIDN'T I TELL YOU SO?
                        DIDN'T I TELL
   YOU SO?"
40 IT COMES TO THE BATHING ENCLOSURE.
IT TELLS THEM.
IT SAYS, "I'VE THROWN THE BRIDE WHERE
   THE WATER'S FULL."
IT SAYS, "SHE HAD COME TO KILL ME,
BUT I KILLED HER."
"HII?"
When they go to the water near the ferry . . .
they find the bride stretched out . . .

∞

Now . . .
      when they find she has died . . .
they leave that place.
50 Now, my lord, that's why you see the bride . . .
Whatever she wants . . .
she tells the people of the house.
She doesn't get it for herself.
And when I had seen how the bride was killed . . .
because of desire,
          I said, "Let me go and tell them about it."

Kyusi, Kyusi, Good Dog!

AS TOLD BY GRACE BAKE

I came and I saw.
I see a man
married a woman.
Now he kills a goat.
When he had killed the goat, he sets aside the head to
    have it later.
He says, "I'll go," he says, "I'll go to buy some tasty meat
    for you, my wife,
                since you cannot eat
a goat's head."
Now when he had left,
                now there was a dog in there . . .
They call him Kyusi.
10 Now when he had left . . .
the woman takes the goat's head and she eats it.
When she'd begun to eat it, it catches on her cheek.
She calls the dog.
She says, "Kyusi, Kyusi
          (w-h-i-s-t-l-e-s)."
The dog jumps up and lands in the yard.
He says,
(sings)   "Come and look at the bride.
          A goat's head has caught her cheek.
          She says, 'Kyusi, Kyusi, Kyusi.'
          But you never ever call me. Now you say,
            'Kyusi, Kyusi, good dog.'
          But you never ever call me. Now you say,
            'Kyusi, Kyusi, good dog.'"
She says, "Kyusi, Kyusi (w-h-i-s-t-l-e-s)."
  o
He jumps up and reaches the gate.
He says,
(sings)   "Come and look at the bride.
          A goat's head has caught her cheek.

She says, 'Kyusi, Kyusi, Kyusi.'
But you never ever call me. Now you say,
    'Kyusi, Kyusi, good dog.'
But you never ever call me. Now you say,
    'Kyusi, Kyusi, good dog.'"

20 Now then . . .
when her husband had reached the gate
she calls again, "Kyusi, Kyusi, Kyusi
(w-h-i-s-t-l-e-s)."
He says,
(sings)   "Come and look at the bride.
          A goat's head has caught her cheek.
          She says, 'Kyusi, Kyusi, Kyusi.'
          But you never ever call me. Now you say,
             'Kyusi, Kyusi, good dog.'"
When her husband had come . . .
that's when the head came off.
It shamed her, and she got nothing.
When I had seen these things for you, I said, "Let me go and
    report to them."

I Ate Minnows,
Little Minnows

AS TOLD BY MA WINIFRED KISIRAGA

I give you a story.
Audience: I give you another.
It's done.
Audience: The news of long ago.
I came and I saw.
Audience: See so that we may see.
There was once . . .

∞

a man . . .
He comes to marry a bride.

10   Now . . .
     when she comes to dwell in the house, the bride meets her
        mother-in-law.
     Now when she had met her mother-in-law . . .
        o
     she finds in that house they eat flies.
        o
     Now, they cook some for her.
        o
     The bride says, "My mother,"
                              she says, "I— the flies," she says,
        "I don't eat those little things."
     Now they dwell there.
     Now the husband of the bride . . .
                              leaves to seek fortune.
     When he had gone to seek fortune . . .
                              her mother- in-law goes
        to cultivate.
     She had collected m-a-n-y flies, put them in a pot, and
        cooked them.
20   Now THE BRIDE thinks about it.
     She is four months pregnant.
     She thinks but is confounded.
     "Now," she says, "What will I do?"
     She says, "I'll just go to the smoke-curing net over the
        cooking fire and take out . . .
     a few flies that have dried."
                              She says, "I'll taste a bit."
     She goes to the net and finds some dried flies.
                              She tastes.
                                          WHEN
        SHE TASTES
                    she finds they taste good.
     "Eh?" She returns and takes a few more.
     She returns to the bed and lies down. She gets up again.
     She goes,
              saying, "I'll take just a few more. Then I'll stop."
30   She takes a few more.
     She eats the ones in the net. She devours them.
     Eh-eh! She goes to the cooking pot and eats those as well.
     Now when she had devoured the ones in the cooking pot . . .
     her mother-in-law leaves work.

She finds her there.

               "Bride!"

She answers, "My lady?"

She s-a-y-s, "Where did my flies go?"

She replies, "I don't know where they are."

  o

She says, "You don't know where they are?"

40 She says, "That's right."

She says, "But who took them?"

                            She says, "I don't know."

                                        "Was

    there someone who came here?"

                              She says, "I don't know."

Then the woman . . .

becomes angry.

She goes to an officer of the chief.

She tells him, "They robbed me." She says, "They

    stole . . .

                 my relish from the pot."

Now the chief says, "Sound the drums."

He says, "Go and tie a piece of twine over the lake . . . "

He says, "The person who has eaten the flies," he says, "cannot

    cross over on it."

He says, "Whoever hasn't eaten them . . . "

50 he says, "will cross over."

Now they go and bring twine and tie it over the lake.

Now every person who comes passes over . . .

passes over singing,

                "I ate minnows, little minnows,

                A string of little minnows.

                Snap twine, let me go

                Fall into the water—snap!"

He crosses over.

And the second comes.

                "I ate minnows, little minnows,

                A string of little minnows.

                Snap twine, let me go

                Fall into the water—snap!"

He passes over.

NOW

    everyone comes and does it.

                    Everyone comes and does it.

o
Now . . .
then the bride
60 is the one they arrive at.
She comes.
               "I ate minnows, little minnows,
               A string of little minnows.
               Snap twine, let me go
               Fall into the water—SNAP!"
It snaps.
She falls into the water.
Now all the people . . .
leave that place. They go.
Now when she had fallen into the water . . .
her husband was away seeking fortune . . .
When he returns, they say, "Your wife is lost."
Now . . .
70 when she fell into the water . . .
she went inside . . .
   o
She gives birth to a child.
When she bore a child,
The child grows.
Now . . .
her husband goes.
He goes to a spirit medium.
The medium divines.
Now when he had divined . . .
80 the medium tells him . . .
                   "Go . . ."
he says . . .
           "to your mother . . ."
He says, "Coax her . . .
so she will go to the lake, throw in coffee beans, and say she
    has no blame in the matter . . ."
he says, "so your wife will come out."
Now the youth goes and coaxes his mother.
He gives her money.
His mother agrees.
   o
She goes to the lake . . .
She throws in the coffee beans . . .

90 She says she has no blame in the matter . . .
The bride comes out. She's come with two children.
Now I've finished a story for you. I've finished another . . .
At someone's mother's brother's they're eating beer bananas
　　　and bean leaves.
When I had seen this for you
　　　　　　　　　　I said, "Let me go and report
　　　to them."
　o
Now this story . . .
teaches us that
whenever they ask you what you did,
tell the truth.
Now if the bride had told the truth
　　　　　　　　　　at first, when she tasted
　　　and ate the flies,
100 she would not have fallen in the water.
Or when they asked her who ate them, she would not
　　　have fallen in the water.
Now this story shows us that
to tell the truth is good. To say something you shouldn't
　　　say brings danger.

Woman-of-People-Forbidden-Horn

AS TOLD BY MA KELEZENSIA KAHAMBA

Now then . . .
I came and I saw.
Audience: See so that we may see.
My story . . .
　oo
Now when a man had come to marry a wife of his own . .
he went to seek fortune.
He left his wife with his father . . .
and his mother.

    o

He went on a journey of trade for about two months.

10   Now when he had left, they abuse her verbally.

    o

Uh-uh! [no]
They give her no rest.
When she got up one morning
                          she says, "I'll go and
    hang myself."

    o

There was a lake there, a B-I-G one.

    o

There was a tree that stood on the shore of that lake.
She goes and climbs.
                  Up in the tree she sits.
Now her mother-in-law comes home . . .
"BRIDE?"
        NOTHING.
"YOU, BRIDE!"
        NOTHING.

20   "Eh? My children! Where has the bride gone?"
She s-e-a-r-c-h-e-s.
When she goes to look,
               she sees the bride has climbed a tree
    that's near the lake. But it's not in the middle of the lake.
"Hii! My child, Woman-of-people-forbidden-horn,
now then, what made you hang youself in the tree?"
She says,
(sings)   "Listen to my mother finding fault.
           She says, 'Woman-of-people-finding-fault.'
           Little tree, shake yourself. Let us to
                the spirits and possess."
"HII?" THE TREE JUMPS UP FROM THE BEACH,
    MOVES AWAY AND DROPS
    DOWN IN THE WATER.
"Hii?" The old woman looks. She is confounded.
She runs and calls her husband.
That's the girl's father-in-law.
               She says, "Come and see what
    the child has done."

30   The old man comes running.

"My child, Woman-of-people-forbidden-horn,
now, then, what brought you to the tree to climb it?"
She says,
(sings)   "Listen to my father finding fault.
                    He says, 'Woman-of-people-finding-fault.'
                    Little tree, shake yourself. Let us to
                        the spirits and possess."
"Hii?
My chiefs!"
THEN THE TREE PULLS ITSELF UP BY THE ROOTS.
    IT GOES FURTHER ON THE LAKE WITH HER
    THERE WHERE SHE CLIMBED UP.
EH-EH! "RUN AND CALL THE NEIGHBORS."
"Come and see what's happened to the bride."
THOSE WHO COME RUN ALL THE WAY.
40   "BRIDE, WOMAN-OF-PEOPLE-FORBIDDEN-HORN.
WHY DON'T YOU COME BACK, MY CHILD?
NOW WHAT HAS TAKEN YOU?"
                    "Listen to the people talking.
                    They say, 'Woman-of-people-finding-fault.'
                    They say they'll make amends, Woman-of-
                        people-finding-fault.
                    Little tree, shake yourself. Let us to
                        the spirits and possess."
"EH?" THEY SAY, "RUN TO HER HOME."
HER HOME WAS NOT FAR OFF. IT WAS
    IN NSHÉKASHEKE.
THEY CALL HER FATHER.
                              THEY CALL
    HER MOTHER.
                        HER BROTHERS.
THEY COME.
"MY CHILD.
BETTER TO RETURN AND LET THEM MAKE
    AMENDS.
BUT, W-E-L-L,
            STOP GOING FURTHER IN THE TREE
    AND TRYING TO KILL YOURSELF."
50   She says,
                    "Listen to my mother finding fault.
                    She says, 'Woman-of-people-finding-fault.

Eight cows, Woman-of-people-finding-fault.
Return and let them make amends,
           Woman-of-people-finding-fault.'
Little tree, shake yourself. Let us to
           the spirits and possess."
THEN THE TREE
           MEASURES ITS STRIDE.
IT GOES FROM THERE LIKE ALL THE WAY
TO K-Y-A-B-A-J-W-A.
THEY COULD NO LONGER SEE HER. THEY SEE HER
    AS AN ANT.

o

EH-EH! They say, "Go to the palace and report this."
They go and tell the chief.
Eh-Eh! The chief sends cattle and gifts. He says, "My chiefs,
if the child's husband comes, what will they do?
MY CHIEFS,
           WOMAN-OF-PEOPLE-FORBIDDEN-HORN,"
HE SAYS, "RETURN
AND LET THEM MAKE AMENDS."
HE SAYS, "EIGHT COWS."
She begins there,
           "He says, 'Let them find fault,
           Woman-of-people-finding-fault.'
           He says, 'Eight cows, Woman-of-people-finding-
                fault.'
           Little tree, shake yourself.
           Let us to the spirits and possess."
"Hii?"

o

60 SHE DISAPPEARS FROM VIEW.
THEY CAN NO LONGER SEE HER.

o

NOW FINALLY THEY SEARCH FOR HER SISTER-IN-
    LAW. THEY FOLLOW AFTER HER. LIKE THEY
    FOLLOW AFTER HER TO
                      K-A-N-Á-Z-I.
She's her husband's next younger sister.

o

They bring her.

o

Now when she had come to the water . . .
o
she speaks.
She says, "Bojo, child-of-my-mother," she s-a-y-s,
"My sister-
in-law,"
she says, "Woman-of-people-forbidden-horn,"
She says, "better to return and let me make amends, Woman-of-
people-forbidden-horn."
She says,
"Nine cows and nine maidservants, Woman-of-people-
forbidden-horn."
o
70 She begins there,
"Listen to my sister-in-law speaking.
She says, 'Woman-of-people-forbidden-horn.'
She says, 'Eight cows, Woman-of-people-
forbidden-horn.'
She says, 'Nine maidservants, Woman-of-people-
forbidden-horn.'
Little tree, shake yourself. Let us from
the spirits now return.
Little tree, shake yourself. Let us from
the spirits now return."
EH-EH!
THEY SAY, "SPEAK TO HER AGAIN."
SHE GOES OUT FURTHER ON THE WATER,
    THAT SISTER-IN-LAW.
SHE SPEAKS AGAIN AND THE OTHER ANSWERS.
"Little tree, shake yourself. Let us from
the spirits now return.
Little tree, shake yourself. Let us from
the spirits now return."
o
Now then, the bride . . .
returns . . .
She comes with her sister-in-law . . .
She gives her maidservants . . .
nine of them.
She gives her eight cows.
80 That's why you see when a bride gets married . . .

her sister-in-law . . .
if she has one . . .
is the one who knows everything . . .
She's given a knife . . .
She's given an *empindwi* . . .
She's given a food-storing net . . .
SHE'S GIVEN EVERY LITTLE THING.

 ○

When a boy has married and has a sister . . .
they give many things. And she's the one who knows all
      her secrets.

 ○

90   Here my story is finished. It's done.

It Was Haste
That Killed Her

AS TOLD BY MA KELEZENSIA KAHAMBA

Now once there was a bride . . .
She came to be married as a young maiden . . .
Now at the place that she was married, there was her
      mother-in-law . . .
                         there was her father-in-law, there was
      her husband . . .
                  who married her . . .
Now she was still a bride.
When she's been there about three months . . .
                                            she
      becomes pregnant.
In the house there are cattle.
When they all have gone to cultivate—
her mother-in-law goes to cultivate;
her father-in-law goes to prune the banana plants—
10   now there comes a strange Bird.
Bird comes . . .

He takes out manure . . .
He drinks milk . . .
and goes.
   He tells the bride,
      "Bride,
if you speak of me . . .
and say, 'Bird is the one who drank the milk and took out
  the manure,'
I'll come and peck you
and take from you two children."
The bride is silent.
20 Now her mother-in-law returns.
She comes from work.
She says to her, "My child,
      what was it that took out
  the manure?"
    She is silent.
"What was it that drank the milk?"
       She is silent.

o

The next day they go to cultivate again.
He comes again.
He takes out manure.
He brings it outside and disposes of it.
Again he drinks milk.
Now, then, her mother-in-law comes.
      "My child, what is it
  that does this?"
30 The bride says, "What takes out the manure,"
      she says, "what
  drinks milk,"
    she says, "is a Bird."
They say, "Let's wait for him."
The next day they wait for him.
     He doesn't come.
       The next day
  they wait for him.
    He doesn't come.
The next day they don't wait for him. They go to cultivate.
When they had left . . .
Bird comes. He takes out manure. He drinks milk. He says,
  "You, bride,
what did you say about me?"

o

He cuts and cuts, he cuts and cuts her belly and takes out
    two children.
Twins.
        He takes them.
                        He goes and cares for them for about
        three years.
                The children grow.
Now the children ask one another, "But, now,
                                    that bird,
                                            is that
        what bore us?
40 NO!
That's not what bore us!
The place where we were born,
our home, is f-a-r away. Very far. A journey of about one year, maybe."
Now they begin to make plans together.
Bird says, "Go, go out and search for food."
He tells the children
and the children go to search for food.
                            Now while
        traveling on the road, they devise a clever plan.
They say, "We'll go singing,
                Our home is Kyandéle,
                Kyandéle in Endéle.
                The Endéle plant dances for joy
                But lacks something to welcome.
                Father is Kalyagáma and the Dog-of-the-Hunters.
                Mother is Nyamutíndilyo. It was haste
                    that killed her."
EH!-EH! Again they go.
50 They make a journey of about two hours.
Again they begin,
                "Our home is Kyandéle,
                Kyandéle in Endéle.
                The Endéle plant dances for joy
                But lacks something to welcome.
                Father is Kalyagáma and the Dog-of-the-Hunters.
                Mother is Nyamutíndilyo. It was haste
                    that killed her."
*Then they go. They rest about noon and continue resting
    until about two o'clock.*

Now they approach their village
>where their mother died.

o

Those who were cultivating see them. They say,
>"These children . . .
are of the hunter's family,
>these children."
EH-EH!
Those who were cultivating . . .
They welcome them . . .
They pick them up in their arms . . .
60 They take them to the home of their mother's brother . . .

o

They are happy . . .
They sprinkle them with millet . . .
and ashes . . .
And so, when I left, they were cooking plantains for them
>to eat . . .
I came quickly. I said, "Let me go and report to the guests
>who come from far away and those of our home."
My story is finished . . .
At your mother's brother's there's a basket of ashes.
At our home the bananas are growing fatter and fatter.
My lord, this story of mine finishes here.

COMMENTARY

A bride must ask permission to use or to consume the resources she finds when she comes to live with her husband. This
principle is directly stated in the lesson the narrator culls from the
tale, *The Bride's Relish* (lines 50–53): "Now, my lord, that's why you
see the bride . . . Whatever she wants . . . she tells the people of
the house. She doesn't get it for herself." This tale is a very strong
statement of the principle: even if the desired object does not apparently belong to the clan, permission must still be requested.
The same statement, in varying forms, is made in *The Legend of
Ikimba, Kyusi, Kyusi, Good Dog!*, and *I Ate Minnows, Little Minnows*.

The Legend of Ikimba relates how the small lake (see p. 4) came
to be. A young bride usurps the right of her mother-in-law to draw
fish magically from a water jar. She thereby unleashes a flood that
drowns both women. In this version of the legend, the bride
wanted the fish, not for her own consumption, but to send to her

mother as a gift. She violated the moral injunction not to appropriate clan property, but she was not a glutton in her own right, as
several other brides in this section are.

Ma Laulelia Mukajuna's elegant telling of this legend appears
to be somewhat at variance with the common interpretation. Other
versions see the bride as solely at fault. One telling of the legend by
Ta Jakobu, Kelezensia Kahamba's husband, imputes to the bride a
motivation of desiring what belongs to someone else (*obushma*; as in
Three Brothers). In an earlier version that appears in French translation, the raconteur, in a knowing aside, attributes the bride's motivation to curiosity (the appetite at the center of *Look Back and See
What Lugeye Does!*).[1]

Ma Mukajuna sees the tale from the point of view of a mother-
in-law who knows that a son's wife needs objective demonstrations
of her worth and her acceptance into the new family. A gift to the
bride's mother would signal the mother-in-law's positive feelings
about her. As Ma Mukajuna says, "I'd wrap up a gift for her to
send to her mother. That's when she'd be happy. That little lake
points out to us: don't refuse your son's wife something to send to
her people."

The mother-in-law's use of a hoe in her attempt to halt the
waters of Lake Ikimba (line 28) is consistent with another symbolic
use. In a heavy rainstorm, a woman may raise her hoe and drive it
into the ground to halt the wind that threatens crops.

The bride's garb that she throws off in her gluttonous, uncontrolled pursuit of the bird in *The Bride's Relish* (line 27) is a barkcloth.
An artisan makes this from the bark of a certain tree by pounding
it on a flat surface with a wooden mallet. The beaten bark grows
thinner and thinner until it becomes cloth.

The bride in *Kyusi, Kyusi, Good Dog!* is also an uncontrolled
consumer who transgresses the boundaries of proper behavior. Not
only does she expropriate property that is not rightfully hers, the
goat's head that she unsuccessfully tries to eat is, moreover, a food
traditionally forbidden to women. She calls the dog, Kyusi, to
come and take the head which has fastened itself on her cheek. She
wants the dog to take both the head and the blame for eating it.
Dog's reputation as glutton would make him a believable perpetra-
tor. But this dog is too clever for the bride and, in addition, he can
sing. The narrator, Grace Bake, was fifteen years old at the time of
this performance.

The action of the goat's head in *Kyusi, Kyusi, Good Dog!* is analogous to that of a lungfish in the tale that accounts for why women are forbidden to eat them. Once, as a lungfish was being prepared for cooking, although apparently dead, it bit a woman on the breast. As noted before, there is a complex of associations involving lungfish, breasts, milk, and women.

The bride in *I Ate Minnows, Little Minnows* is outwardly a simple glutton, as in *The Bride's Relish* and *Kyusi, Kyusi, Good Dog!* But there is a complicating element: her pregnancy. A pregnant woman is subject to strong cravings that must be satisfied, lest her baby miscarry. The mother-in-law thus shares some blame for the bride's apparent death in the lake. Given the bride's delicate condition, she should have been more understanding. Everything is set aright by the husband's return and the bride's subsequent resurrection, an episode added by the narrator herself (by her own assertion). Brides may appear gluttonous, but mothers-in-law are sometimes ill-natured as well.

The coffee beans used in the ritual of appeasement in *I Ate Minnows, Little Minnows* (line 89) come from coffee plants of the *robusta* variety indigenous to Hayaland. The minnows that everyone claims to have eaten are the kind that are dried, strung on banana bast, and sold by the string. This tale was performed by Ma Winifred Kisiraga for her own children. This accounts, I believe, for the lesson culled from the tale—"tell the truth."

Two Haya concepts appear in *I Ate Minnows, Little Minnows* that are worthy of special note. Both reveal a part of a Haya ideology about the social significance of speaking. The lesson of the tale is translated, "To tell the truth is good. To say something you shouldn't say brings danger." The words that are translated, "to say something you shouldn't say," are *oku-gamba ebishuba*, which in some contexts mean "to speak lies." A synonym for this Haya phrase is *oku-beiya*. These words describe an utterance that asserts something not empirically true *or* an utterance that reveals information that should be concealed for personal, familial, or social reasons. Thus, "to lie" is only a part of its meaning. By joining the two concepts under a single category, Hayas classify an act of speech according to a single criterion, namely, the effect the utterance has on relationships among people.

The same social criterion is evident in the second concept of note: the kind of statement the mother-in-law makes in order to bring the bride back from the lake. This is translated, "she says she has no blame in the matter." The Haya verb here is *okw-etongolola*, which can refer to statements made to deny that one committed a misdeed *or* to statements that explain the extenuating circumstances surrounding the misdeed one, in fact, committed. The intended result of either of these kinds of statements is the restoration of a peaceful relationship between the speaker and the person to whom he or she addresses the statement. The criterion that groups these kinds of statements together is, thus, the same one noted above, namely, the effect a given utterance has on relationships among people. As with the concept of "saying what should not be said," the concept of "saying one has no blame" does not necessarily involve the criterion of empirical truth.

Obviously, Hayas can see a difference between empirical truth and social truth. They also know the distinction between something empirically correct, on one hand, and socially correct, on the other. They appreciate the confoundment that can be created when empirical and social realities conflict, when what is empirically correct is socially wrong, and vice versa. This is the situation in the two tales narrated by Ta Haruna Batonde and the nature of the paradox embodied in their central questions *Who Was the One Who Ate It?* and *What Was It That Killed Koro?*

In *Woman-of-People-Forbidden-Horn*, the ill will of her new family, rather than her own gluttony, drives the bride out of her seclusion and almost to her death. Because they give her no rest, the bride attempts suicide by climbing up into a tree to hang herself. The reason and the method of suicide are characteristically Haya. Although it appears to be uncommon, a woman might take her life because her living situation has become unbearable. More likely, though, she would leave. A man, on the other hand, commits suicide when he can no longer face the rest of male society because his honor has been shattered (compare Koro's suicide in *What Was It That Killed Koro?*).

Woman-of-people-forbidden-horn's threat to become a spirit and possess is based on the belief that unsatisfied or vengeful spirits sometimes may possess several members of a clan, making them ill. Such spirits must be mollified through ritual sacrifices.

There is no clan in Hayaland, to my knowledge, whose forbidden thing is horn. The bride thus comes from a mythical, generalized clan. It might be any clan, and she might be any bride.

In the final tale, *It Was Haste That Killed Her*, an appearance of gluttony rather than gluttony itself leads to the bride's death. After her mother-in-law compels the bride to divulge the dangerous secret of a milk-drinking Bird, the family lies in ambush for only two days. On the third day they leave, assuming that the bride herself drinks the milk. Given the usual characterization of brides, like the ones in *The Legend of Ikimba*; *The Bride's Relish*; *Kyusi, Kyusi, Good Dog!*; *I Ate Minnows, Little Minnows*; and *Blocking the Wind*, the assumption of the bride's guilt is reasonable, if incorrect.

Bird returns, kills the woman and takes two children from her womb. Subsequently, the children sing a song that blames their father's kin for her death: "It was haste that killed her" is the refrain. That is, it was the in-laws' hasty decision to discount her story about Bird that killed the twins' mother. The family should have been more believing in her. But, after all, we can say from outside the situation, the real culprit is the setting itself: it makes gluttony a ready presumption. Nevertheless, the in-laws are at fault for their disbelief, and when the children return home, they go to live with their mother's clan, not with their father's, as would be the customary practice in the case of a mother's death. Their father's family has proved itself unworthy of them.

In *It Was Haste That Killed Her*, cattle are kept inside the house, as in *Open and Let Them Come In*. If the bride had taken the manure outside, as the family surmised, she would have been working when she should not have been. The song sung by the returning twins is designed by them to broadcast their identities, in the hope that someone will recognize them and help them reach home. The song in *The Glistening One* serves a similar purpose. The millet and ashes sprinkled over the twins' heads (lines 62–63) are a way of giving thanks to the unseen spirits for the children's return.

7

Domestic Comedy

Haya married life is evoked symbolically in the tales of this
section through the abstract behavior of fanciful protagonists, who
include a new bride, a pair of birdy cowives, a sister-brother-sister-
in-law trio, a handsome Haya prince, a German chief named Kaiser, and his daughter, Whitelady. The tales are comedy in that all
end happily. All but the first contain elements of humor. Haya
marital affairs are playfully observed in these tales, as characters
find themselves in dramatic situations that foreground aspects of
domestic life. Protagonists reveal their priorities and their appetites
by choosing among dramatic alternatives.

Two of the tales, *Blocking the Wind* and *Kibwana*, form complex
aesthetic symmetries on a number of levels ranging from tit-for-tat
reciprocity to underlying logical complementarities. These give rise
to moments of high dramatic irony and precise poetic justice. Humor in the tales is also significant of their overall meaning, especially two outbursts of hearty laughter that occur in somewhat unexpected places.

All four tales were told by Laulelia Mukajuna. Ma Laulelia
performs well on other subjects, but her storytelling métier is
clearly the world of domestic relationships. Ma Laulelia on marriage begins with a tale about a character we have met before, the
new bride. As in the previous chapter, she is a woman of strong
desires. Here, however, her yearning is not for the material things
of her husband's family. The object of her longing is the husband
himself, who has gone away to seek trade and has become lost. She
sets out without knowing what will befall her. "If he is to be lost

forever, let me perish there," she vows, "If I am to see him, there let me come." She is motivated by an almost siblinglike love for him. Just like Nchume's sister, the bride is "possessed" by the person lost to her: "He's forbidden me my rest," she sings to the people she meets. She travels a long way, finds him, and they return. It is the simplest of tales about a basic and undifferentiated emotion that infuses the ideal Haya marriage.

With *Blocking the Wind*, outlines in the picture of domesticity become more hard-edged. It becomes clear that marriage is more than a fulfillment of deeply-felt affections. In fact, it is the fundamental societal cell that sustains and reproduces lineages, clans, and chiefdoms. The domestic unit produces food and children, necessary ingredients of society, and the respective concerns of the two episodes in *Blocking the Wind*.

The instrument used to block the wind is a wicker screen (*ekisiika*), the partition between inner and outer rooms that is used to conceal the privacy of the family's hearth, sleeping area, and the place where a bride is "hidden." It is supposed to shield domestic matters from public view; in this tale, it uncovers them.

The events of *Blocking the Wind* take place towards the end of the long dry season, in August or September. This can be a time of hunger, as in the tale, and also a time of gusty winds. The following season is that of the light rains. A few weeks into the rains, the *ensenene* come. This is the setting for *Crested Crane and Dove*. *Ensenene* are a type of grasshopper that flies over Hayaland from somewhere on the other shores of Lake Victoria and drop down in large numbers. Women capture them, often finding it necessary first to shoo them from their perches in thick grass or thorny plants. The *ensenene* are stored in baskets. After they are brought home, they are "peeled" (wings and legs removed), boiled, and then fried. This may be served as a relish with a main meal or as a bit of food to share with a guest. Because of the latter use, *ensenene* are sometimes called "the laughter (that is, the happiness) of guests." An alternate mode of preparation is to smoke them over a fire after boiling, instead of frying them. This allows the food to be stored for a longer time, and is the method used in *Crested Crane and Dove*. Grown women are traditionally forbidden to eat *ensenene*.

Papyrus stems, which mark a high point in the action of the tale, are split into many milk-white strands that resemble woolen yarn. They are traditionally used in bunches to mark calabashes of beer destined for the chief, to wrap extra special gifts like household vessels for a bride, and to make a miniature fly whisk or broom about three or four inches in length that is presented to an honored person about to dine. The honored one ceremonially rubs the papyrus napkin between his palms to prepare his hands for eating (every meal begins and ends with a ritualized washing of the hands with soap and water). The milky whiteness of the strands makes them an apt symbol for joy as "to be white" and "to be joyful" are the same word, *okw-era*. A papyrus napkin is dove's crowning domestic touch to the meal of *ensenene* she serves her husband.

The conflict between the cowives, crested crane and dove, entails weighing the relative marital values of external beauty and of inward determination and knowledge. Crested crane is outwardly beautiful—long-necked, with a slow, graceful stride, and a tufted coiffure like a bride—but inwardly she is a glutton. The little gray dove—short-necked and squat, with a quick, bobbing gait—is outwardly plain, but inwardly controlled and competent in the affairs of marriage. She defeats her overly elegant adversary and wins sole possession of the husband.

Dove's triumph over crested crane is a victory of heart over beauty. But it also shows how one ideal of physical form overcomes a different ideal. The ideal types are significant because they represent the stereotyped physical builds of Haya ruling and nonruling clans (*balangila* and *bailu*, respectively). Hayas are members of the same group of societies as the Tutsi and Hutu of Rwanda and Burundi (Inter-Lacustrine Bantu). The clans who formerly ruled Hayaland, like Tutsis, are said to be of a tall and thin physical type. The rulers and their kin were cattle owners. The nonruling clans, like the Hutu, did agricultural labor. Their physical stereotype reflects this—relatively short and muscular. There was conflict between the two groups, and it appears in their folklore.

Crested crane embodies the ideal beauty of the former Haya ruling group: tall, slender, and moving with a slow, regal pace. Dove, on the other hand, represents the nonruling clans: short, muscularly compact, and moving briskly about at work. Dove is thus a determined class heroine in addition to a knowing Haya wife.

Note that the narrator changes dove's species from the larger ring-necked variety (that appears in *The Water of Ikongora*) to the smaller gray dove (in Haya, *ekiiba* to *akaiba*). Ma Laulelia Mukajuna does this because the latter is a punning reference to *eikaiba*, the name for the jealousy between cowives.

A pleasing exterior does not belong only to crested crane and other females. The Haya prince, Kibwana, suffers an almost continuous series of misfortunes because of his beauty. As you will see, each calamity that befalls the poor man occurs when certain people, thinking only of his outward beauty, want him as chief, as husband, and as begetter of children. But inwardly, in reality, he is incapable of filling these roles, as he is either too young, too dutiful, or physically incapacitated.

The name Kibwana seems to derive from Swahili. *Bwana*, a word that translates as "mister," is placed in the *ki-* noun class signifying, perhaps, that he has a fault, that something is missing, like the Swahili words *kipara*, "a bald person," and *kipofu*, "a blind person." Each Bantu noun class has a number of semantic connotations, so that it is difficult to draw exact conclusions, but this one seems apt.

The Kaiser's daughter's appellation, Whitelady, is a translation of the narrator's *mamisabu*, a word that comes from *memsab* in Swahili or *memsahib*, the term of extreme deference used by Africans to address any white or East Indian woman. The word is no longer common in Swahili, *bibi* and its male counterpart, *bwana*, being used to address all nationalities. As a term of address, *memsab*, *mamisabu*, *mausap*, or a number of other varieties still can be found in Hayaland, but it is much less common than the Haya *Ma* plus the first name. In the tale *Kibwana*, "Whitelady" (the translation that seems most appropriate) is used, as is "Kaiser," both as the name of a social status and as a proper name.

The German chief's daughter wants to marry the handsome prince, Kibwana, so that others will say, "That's the husband of Whitelady." The desire to possess a beautiful spouse or to be ruled by a beautiful chief is an expression of a more general desire or appetite, which can be called wanting "to be seen with (a person of high social prestige)," in Haya, *oku-boneka hamoi*, "to appear together."

In sum, then, facets of Haya marriage treated in this section are love, food, sex, beauty, and knowledge of domestic matters.

Have You Not Seen Luhundu?

<small>AS TOLD BY MA LAULELIA MUKAJUNA</small>

W-e-l-l n-o-w
        I went and I saw for you.
o
Long ago . . .
o
there was a man . . .
o
He m-a-r-r-i-e-d . . .
a woman.
o
Now when he had married and lived with her three months,
o
now then,
        three months,
                he left her and traveled to seek fortune.
o
He left her still a bride.
o
He didn't even say to her,
                "I'm going to trade
10 in this land . . .
           or in that . . . "
He just went.
o
He came to be delayed there three years.
o
H-i-s w-i-f-e w-a-i-t-e-d but the husband was lost.
o
Now she loved her husband very much.
                    She thought, "I'll follow
      him. I'll go and search for him."
                  But she goes without
      knowing where . . .
the realm he was in.
o

So she just went, saying,
        "If he is to be lost forever . . .
                                   there
   let me perish.
If I am to see him . . .
        let me come there."
  o

She threw herself into the journey.
  o

The first one she met was a man.
  o

20 Now, she asked him by singing.
  o

She sang thus:
  o

           "You, man! You, man, who's traveling,
           Have you not seen Luhúndu?
           So dear to me and handsome,
           Adorned with beads in hundreds,
           Kalimpíta na kalánga, bojo, he's forbidden
              me my rest."
The man said, "I have never seen him."
  o

She HITS the road.
She travels a LONG way,
in miles something like FOUR hundred.
  o

She meets a woman there.
  o

And she sings to her.
  o

           "You, woman! You, woman, who's traveling,
           Have you not seen Luhúndu?
           So dear to me and handsome,
           Adorned with beads in hundreds,
           Kalimpíta na kalánga, bojo, he's forbidden
              me my rest."
"No," she said.
  o

She g-o-e-s a long way, about two hundred miles.
  o

30   She comes upon a child
     like this one.
     She asks him,

               "You, young man who's traveling,
               Have you not seen Luhúndu?
               So dear to me and handsome,
               Adorned with beads in hundreds,
               Kalimpíta na kalánga, bojo, he's forbidden
                    me my rest."

     ○

     THE CHILD SAYS, "I HAVE SEEN HIM. I KNOW
          LUHÚNDWA.

     ○

     Let's go. I'll take you."

     ○

     He takes her from THERE and brings her a distance like
          to Mwánza.

     ○

     They go and reach . . .
     her husband.
     EH! EH! EH! SHE IS HAPPY TO BE WITH HER
          HUSBAND. HE IS HAPPY TO SEE HIS WIFE COME.

     ○

     The two remain there. There are celebrations. There's a new
          wedding.

     ○

40   They pack their things and come home.

     ○

     When his parents HAD SEEN THEIR CHILD WHO HAD
          BEEN GONE THREE YEARS . . .
     they were very happy . . .
     To the young woman they give cattle . . .
     They give goats . . .
     People of the village collect money . . .
     They give it to them . . .
     They are wealthy . . .
     They build a house . . .
     They bear children . . .
50   And never again . . .
     does the husband depart and leave her.

     ○

They are wealthy and they dwell there.
o

Now I finish for you a story, I finish another.
The news of long ago.
I'm done.

Blocking the Wind

AS TOLD BY MA LAULELIA MUKAJUNA

Well, now, my lord, long ago I saw for you that there came
    a season of hunger.
∞

Now at the time that the hunger came . . .
an unmarried girl had a brother . . .
but the brother had a wife.
Now the girl had cultivated millet . . .
                                  A LOT OF IT.
Now the hunger GREW G-R-E-A-T-E-R.
The girl takes up . . .
Three děbě's of millet . . . [a five gallon measure]
She brings them . . .
10   to her people. [the brother and his wife].
o

Now . . .
The sister-in-law would grind the millet . . .
stir it into porridge, and they would eat.
She grinds,
           she stirs and she eats with her husband.
Now when she saw that only a little remained . . .
                                about one
    and a half děbě's . . .
She devised a plan to deprive her husband.
o

She said, "The wind has become great . . . "
She said, "Go and block the wind . . .
                        so I can grind
    the millet . . .

The millet is blowing away."
20 The man picked up a wicker screen
and went into the fields
                                to block wind.

    o

HE BLOCKS IT
LOOK OUT, IT'S GETTING THROUGH THERE!
                                                    LOOK
    OUT, IT'S GETTING THROUGH
    THERE!
                    LOOK OUT, IT'S GETTING THROUGH
    THERE!
                    LOOK OUT, IT'S GETTING THROUGH
    THERE!
                    LOOK OUT, IT'S GETTING THROUGH
    THERE!
                    LOOK OUT, IT'S GETTING THROUGH
    THERE!
AT HOME THE WOMAN GROUND GROUND
    GROUND THE MILLET . . .
SHE STIRRED,
        SHE ATE
                                and for her husband, she left a little.
(tired voice) He came home weak from exertion.
                                                    She said,
    "You blocked the wind badly.
WHILE YOU BLOCKED AT LYAMAHÓRO . . .
                                                    WIND
    WAS COMING FROM KAMULENGÉRA.
NOW WHAT HAVE YOU ACCOMPLISHED?
LOOK, THE LITTLE THAT'S LEFT IS THIS. YOU
    EAT IT.
30 I'll do without."
    o

THE DAY DAWNED.
She said, "Run and block the wind."
Now he went to Kamulengéra where she had told him to go.
OUT IN THE FIELDS
                                WITH THE WICKER
    SCREEN
                    LOOK OUT, IT'S GETTING THROUGH
    THERE!

LOOK OUT, IT'S GETTING THROUGH
THERE!
THE WOMAN ground and ground the millet,
she stirred it.

o

SHE ATE IT.
She left a little.
Her husband came
                    and she gave it to him.

o

She said,
40 "All of the millet is gone, taken by the wind.
                              I told you,
        'BLOCK THERE . . .
AT LYAMAHÓRO,' BUT YOU BLOCKED
        OVER THERE.
                    Now the millet is ruined.
                                    Look at the little
        that's left. I'll go hungry."

o

SHE RAN HIM ALL OVER THE PLACE . . .
THEY CALLED THE YOUNG MAN CRAZY . . .
                                    THOSE
        WHO SAW HIM IN THE FIELDS
        BLOCKING WIND . . .
BLOCKING NOTHING AT ALL WITH A WICKER
        SCREEN . . .
They said he was crazy.
NOW THE SISTER WHO WAS CULTIVATING MILLET
        THERE . . .
                    CAME TO HEAR OF THESE THINGS.
What the sister-in-law had done . . .

o

to her brother.

o

SHE KEPT STILL. SHE DIDN'T SHOUT
        ACCUSATIONS.

o

50 She waited for the season of hunger to pass.

o

Now that sister-in-law had not borne a child.

                                        She had not yet
been pregnant.
The sister went and prepared a small calabash
                                        about this big [3-
        inch diameter].
She stopped it up and brought it along.
        o

When she had come
she told the sister-in-law,
                        "The hunger is over now, but"
she said,
                "this little calabash . . .
I've been to a diviner . . .
I've come to give you a fertility medicine, and if you
        are to bear a child . . .
you must regularly deposit into it—farts.
60   WHEN IT'S FULL . . .
I'll come to give you other medicine."
        o

The girl put the calabash near the cooking fire.
        o

Whenever one comes upon her, she unstops the calabash and
        sh——sh——sh——
                                she farts into it.
SHE STOPS IT UP!
Whenever one comes upon her in the banana grove, SHE
        RUNS BACK WITH A TIGHTENED ASSHOLE
        MMH-MMH-MMH TILL SHE REACHES
        THE CALABASH SH——SH——SH——
SHE FARTS! (audience laughing)
        o

Shen she had done this for about four months . . .
        ∞

unstopping the calabash and looking inside, she finds
        it's as white as white can be— there's not a thing in there.
        o

"Hii!"
70   She says, "Well now, in there
the calabash, I could fill it for five years,
ten years,
and there wouldn't be a thing inside."

She is confounded.
When she felt confounded, she said, "I'll go and tell
      my mother about this."

      o

She doesn't ask anyone. She just gets dressed and goes home.

      o

She goes and lays the matters before her father and mother.
"EH YEH! YEH! YEH! YEH!"
THEY ARE DUMBFOUNDED! THEY SAY, "THAT
      WOMAN IS A SORCERER."
80   THEY SAY, "IT MUST BE SHE WHO KEEPS YOU
      FROM BEARING CHILDREN."
THEY SAY, "FARTS ARE WIND.
IF SHE HAD TOLD YOU URINE.
                              IF SHE HAD TOLD
      YOU TURDS.
BUT SHE SAYS
            FARTS!
                  WHO HAS EVER SEEN A FART?
SURELY WE SMELL THE ODOR AND HEAR THE
      NOISE 'BWI!'—IT'S NOTHING!
ARE THEY SOMETHING TO PREPARE A CALABASH
      FOR?
            Let her come here."

      o

The husband goes to ask why his wife was there.
                              They say,
      "You have a case on your hands."
"What kind of case?
Since the woman came to live with me, we've never fought."
They say, "She fought with your sibling.
                              Go and bring
      your sister."

      o

90   He goes and tells the sister.
            The sister says, "Sit yourself down.
      It's a small matter.
Just wind and wind."

      o

THEY INVITE . . .
THE WOMAN AND THE MAN . . .
THEY FILL THE HOUSE COMPLETELY.

THEY'VE COME TO LAUGH [derisively] AT THE
    WOMAN . . .
at how she caused their child to fart those farts.

    o

She comes and enters the house. They welcome her and
    greet her.
                    Now,
they open the case.

    o

That sister-in-law begins . . .
100 How this sister-in-law brought a small calabash . . .
and said, "You should fill it with farts . . .
Then I'll have some medicine made so you can bear a child."

    o

She continues . . .
"NOW I REGULARLY FARTED IN THERE, FARTED IN
    THERE TILL A MONTH PASSED.
                            THE SECOND
    PASSED.
              THE THIRD PASSED.
                            THE FOURTH . . .
THERE WAS NOT EVEN ONE SMALL FART IN THERE.
    I UNSTOPPED IT AND FOUND THE CALABASH
    AS WHITE AS WHEN SHE BROUGHT IT.
THAT IS WHAT CONFOUNDED ME AND BROUGHT
    ME HERE, RESPECTED ONES.

    o

That's my case."
Now this sister-in-law begins her side.
She says, "I, my lord, saw the season of hunger coming."
110 She says, "The hunger struck." She says, "I cultivated
    my millet." She says, "It ripened." She says,
    "I brought them my děbě's,
four of them.
I said, 'It's yours to grind and eat.
The hunger will be finished.'"
She says, "She made my mother's child crazy."
She says, "She made him block the wind." She says, "You,
    do you block wind when you grind millet?
Do you set up at the chair and put a wicker screen
    over there?
                    Or do you go to block in the wilderness?

IS MILLET GROUND HERE . . .

                                 AND THE WIND

   BLOCKED AT LYAMAHÓRO?

IS MILLET GROUND HERE . . .

                                 AND THE WIND

   BLOCKED AT KAMULENGÉRA?

WELL, MY OWN MOTHER'S CHILD RAN ABOUT

   IN THE FIELDS AND

   BECAME A CRAZY ONE.

                         LOOK OUT,

   IT'S GETTING THROUGH THERE!

                                 LOOK OUT,

   IT'S GETTING THROUGH

   THERE!

          AND ALTHOUGH SHE WAS MAKING HIM

   BLOCK WIND— HAD SHE CULTIVATED

   THE MILLET?

120   I CULTIVATED MY FOOD TO FEED MY MOTHER'S

   CHILD AND SHE GOES

   AND MAKES HIM BLOCK WIND.

AND THAT IS WHY I MADE HER BLOCK THE WIND

   OF THE ANUS.

AND LET HER BLOCK IT, IF WINDS CAN BE

   BLOCKED!"

o

The people, my lord, let out a great cry of laughter.

                                   They

   laughed at that woman.

They observed, "ARE THESE THE MATTERS THAT

   BROUGHT YOU HERE BEFORE US?

   TO COME AND BRING US SHAME?"

"YOU, MISTER, WHAT MADE YOU CRAZY?"

"FOR THAT MATTER, I SAW HIM TOO."

                                AND

   ANOTHER SAYS, "I SAW

   HIM. I CAME UPON HIM IN THE FIELDS

   AT SUCH-AND-SUCH A PLACE

   WHILE HE WAS BLOCKING." AND ANOTHER

   SAYS, "AND I SAW HIM TOO."

The wife was defeated . . .

She had to pay . . .

for the millet of her sister-in-law

130   A WHOLE COW on the hoof.
        o
I finished you a story.
                    I finished you another.
                              At your mother's
brother's they're eating beer bananas and bean leaves. At my
mother's brother's the bananas are growing fatter and fatter.

Crested Crane and Dove

AS TOLD BY MA LAULELIA MUKAJUNA

Now . . .
            long ago,
a man had married. His wives are two,
o

a crested crane . . .
o

and a ring-necked dove.
o

Now you've seen that little short one.
      (a long interruption here, after which the story is
   oo
         resumed)
Now his wives are two,
both crested crane . . .
and gray dove.
o

Now they dwell and they dwell and they dwell there.
10   The man leaves . . .
and goes to seek fortune.
o

When he left . . .
the *ensénene* fall.
o

Now when they have fallen . . .
the dove goes with her basket.

She strikes and PUTS them in, strikes and PUTS them in,
    strikes and PUTS them in. CRESTED CRANE
SHOOS THEM OUT Sh————— and swallows them.
Sh————— and swallows them.
Sh————— and swallows them.
  o

20   The dove brings her *ensénene*, cooks them and dries them.
                                                She
    wraps them up.
                   She stores them.
Now their husband returns from his journey.
  o

"Welcome, welcome, welcome." They bring him inside, they
    salute him, they prepare food for him.
  o

The dove . . .
                brings out the *ensénene*, she cuts open a packet
    of them . . .
she sets down a plate . . .
                    she sets down a banana leaf . . .
                                            she
    sets down papyrus strands . . .
  o

before her husband.
  o

Crested crane casts down its eyes. (the women laugh)
It looks into its little beard [of feathers].
  o

"Crested crane . . .
and where are yours?
  o

30   and YOURS?"
  oo

When the sun arose, the crane has already gotten up
    there . . .
            In the fields,
                    there aren't any. They
    have stopped falling.
  o

It shoos them sh————— nothing.
  o

It shoos them sh——— nothing.

o

Now that dove, the little bobbing one . . .
exults in her triumph over the crane. She was speaking thus,
(tight gloating voice) "The short one is the wife.

                         The short

      one is the wife.

             The short one is the wife."

That tall crane with the long neck

                  now looks like a slow dimwit

    out in the fields.

It sh———

        it sh———

             it sh———

and till today has not returned.

40   The short one dwelled where she was wed.
Now then, this is to say,
A BEAUTIFUL APPEARANCE

                  is not the same as heart.

Wasn't the dove, so homely . . .
the crested crane, so beautiful . . . ?
But the dove surpassed her in the art of marriage.

o

IT'S DONE!

Kibwana

AS TOLD BY MA LAULELIA MUKAJUNA

Well, now, child-of-my-mother, I came and I saw for you.
Audience: See so that we may see.
I saw for you a man fathers a child.
AND THAT MAN WAS A CHIEF.
AND THAT MAN IS KAHÍGI WHO RULES BUGÁBO.

∞

Uh-uh, oh no
Lwakyendéla [was his name].

∞
Now, that Lwakyendéla was ugly.
He was ugly . . .
10   as Laulelía.
               Just as you see Laulelía,
                                        that's what Lwakyendéla
               looked like.
o
Now, then, he goes and fathers a child.
BEAUTIFUL!
Shya! [as beautiful as can be]
A BEAUTIFUL MALE CHILD . . .
Among us, now, who might I compare him to?
Maybe to the European woman [Sheila Dauer]. (laughter)
o
But no, among us, there's none.
o
Well sir, that child of his
nurses
          is weaned
                    r-e-a-c-h-e-s
                              the third grade in school.
o
20   Now my lord, the chief's retinue would look at
          him . . .
                    "Ha-ah!" (softly) they say, "If only the chief
          would die,
(softly) the child could rule us—Kibwana.
                                   And even though he's
          small, we could teach him.
                         But then
                                   we'd be ruled by a chief
          about whom others looking at him would say, 'Is that chief
          not beautiful?'"
o
Everyone wanted it so
                    wanted it so
                              wanted it so
                                        wanted it so.
o
Now
the chief,
          word of this finally reaches him.

He thinks, "My own retinue—look, it's about to kill me . . .
so this child might rule.
Now the child must go.
                    I'll hide him far away where they won't
    see him.
Let him dwell over there."
    o

My lord, he took him from the palace at Kaléma.
30 He went and concealed him at Lubáfu.
    o

LUBÁFU ON THE WATER AT THE VERY END OF OUR
    CHIEFDOM.
    oo

Now sir, the child dwells there.
He grows, is given a wife, marries and fathers three children
    of his own,
two boys . . .
                    and one girl.
    oo

Now the chief . . .
                    again turns to courting.
He marries another woman, a young bride.
    o

Now her little maidservants who fetch water and
    peel plantains . . .
say to her, "Even though you're here [in the palace], bride . . .
Ha-ah!"
            They say, "You've found misfortune.
40 If only you had married the child of the chief, Kibwana,
    Kibwana, Kibwana whom he has concealed at Lubáfu . . .
Is he not beautiful . . . ?
                    He is the sun rising from the lake."
    o

The bride lives there racking and racking her brain for
    a way . . .
            to see Kibwana.
                    For he's been forbidden to
    set foot in the palace . . .
But his father did not disinherit him. He said,
"When I die . . .
            leave Lubáfu. Come here and claim
    the Royal Drum.

But for now, you can't stay here with the people always looking
   to you."
∞

Now . . .
            the bride continually racks and racks her brain. She
      searches for Kibwana. He doesn't appear.
Now while she was going on like that . . .
his youthful companions . . .
plan a trip. They say, "Let's visit Nyakáto."
   o

50   Now Nyakáto,
            you know, he comes to pass by Kaléma [where
      the palace is].
   o

Now he passes by on the road to K-a-y-ú-n-g-w-e
to reach Nyakáto.
Now his comrades say, "Let's pass by here . . .
The chief isn't in the palace.
Now we'll only pass by.
                  We'll take the short cut to Nyakáto."
And he . . .
            agrees.
   o

He says, "O.K. Let's go, as long as the chief isn't in."
   o

Now, as he's passing the palace . . .
the little maidservants see him.
60   They run to the bride and say, "Baba,"
they say, "The child of the chief we told you about— It's he,
      it's he, it's he, it's he at the front gate.
He's passing to go to Nyakáto."
The bride paces in her room. She racks and racks her brain and
      says, "Baba," she says, "help me. Summon that young man
      to me so I can see him with my own eyes."
   o

They go and tell him. He says, "No, no, no, no. It's forbidden.
The chief has forbidden me the palace.
                  Go and tell the
      bride, 'The chief HAS FORBIDDEN HIM.
Perhaps nevermore
                  will he be able to enter.'"

o

They go and tell the bride. She racks and racks her brain.
    She goes to the chief's deputy and says, "Father, my ruler,"
    she says, "HELP me!
Ha-ah! Wealth is beauty, bojo,
                     and beauty is beauty.
                                     That's how
    it is."

o

She says, "Help me."
            She says, "Summon Kibwana to me."
                                     She
    says,
70 "Let him enter inside there."
                     She says, "I'll see him for a
    short while and then he'll go," she says,
                        "so the chief's unborn
    child will not miscarry."

o

The chief's deputy didn't ask any questions. He goes to Kibwana
    and says,
               "Go. Enter the house, so the bride can
    see you.
              Then take the road and go."
He replies, "But, my lord, what if they speak of me to the chief,
    saying, 'Kibwana entered inside?'"
He says, "There is none who will speak. Surely you know I am
    the guardian of the palace when the chief is not here.
Can someone pass without my knowledge? Who could say such
    a thing?"

o

Now the chief . . .
              had bought for his son
a walking stick
like the one carried by President Nyerere . . .
                          You should know
    that, in that land, no one has one like it.
And that child had the walking stick.

o

You should know that the bride
                    said she would give the deputy
    cattle,

80   seven of them . . .
and four maidservants . . .
and six manservants.
o

Now the desire for WEALTH
                              motivates . . .
                                        the deputy to go
        and call . . .
                        the child of the chief to come and
        enter the house.
Now when he was spoken to by the deputy
                                he thought, "I'll go
        inside. There's nothing to worry about. Where
        could the person come from who might say
        what he shouldn't?"
He goes and enters.
The bride brings out the chair the chief sits on.
                                        She puts it
        out there so . . .
Kibwana can be the one who sits on it.
                                He says, "Stop it, baba!"
(sighs) He says, "It is forbidden."
EH-EH!
        She brings the glass the chief drinks from
                                        so that . . .
90   Kibwana can drink from it.
                        Kibwana says, "Stop it!
o

I cannot drink from there."
o

After a short time . . .
o

Kibwana . . .
says, "You've seen me.
The child of the chief cannot miscarry now. I'm going."
"Iyo!" she says,
                "Take me with you
                        to where you live.
                                        Don't
        leave me here."
HE SAYS, "IT IS FORBIDDEN!
                        IS THIS WHY YOU
        SUMMONED ME?

HAVE I COME
HERE TO CARRY YOU AWAY?
I'm leaving you here."
∞

The bride leaps up and falls about Kibwana's middle.
100 "Take me!" "I'm not taking you!"
                              "Take me!" "I'm not taking
       you!"
                   She grabs the walking stick.
       o

While she was grappling with him over that walking stick
       of his,
              he hears the horns announce the chief's return.
He let go of the walking stick . . .
                           to flee for his life.
∞

When he had left, the bride
puts on the way you all know Hayas do.
She picks up her bridal gift pole . . .
the one you see them taking outside
                              when its owner dies.
                                              SHE
              HURLS IT into the courtyard.
SHE PICKS UP a chair . . .
                   and HURLS IT into the
       courtyard.
                   She picks up things . . .
                           and hurls them
       into the courtyard.
       o

When the chief returns, he finds the palace in ruins. "What
       sort of thing is this, baba?
                           What is it? Where was
       the deputy?
Have them summon him at once. He's the one . . .
                                              they'll
       execute right now."
       o

110 The deputy said, "I didn't see who did this, baba.
       o

Maybe I was in the court when they made things look like this."
       o

The chief said, "In the inner room is the bride. Let them
     summon the bride and let the bride be the one they ask.
But where has the bride gone?
o

Come here, bride.
Who did these things?"
She says, "Kibwana did them."
o

"Kibwana?"
o

She says, "Kibwana."
               "KIBWANA WHO DOES NOT
    SET FOOT IN HERE?"
She says, "Kibwana."
              "You accuse him falsely."
120 She says, "If I accuse him falsely, whose walking stick is this?"
  ∞ (member of the audience gasps)
Eh!
They saw it was so.
             In these parts there's no other who carries
    one.
        It's carried by Kibwana.
"It's true. He's the one who did it."
"Go immediately, palace guards. Abashasha, run and bring
    Kibwana to die."
o

In a moment they marched straight away. In a moment
    they got to Kibwana.
            His hands, mh!
                  They tied them up.
They brought him dragging kululu kululu kululu kululu kululu
    before his father.
o

HE HAD NOT SAID ONE WORD NOR HAD HE MADE
    ACCUSATION, when they said, "Take him to the place
    of execution,
and execute him."
All of the retinue that wanted him to be chief because of his
    beauty . . .
130 They pleaded
          on Kibwana's behalf.
o

The chief said, "What made him enter inside was desire. Now,
    undress him, cut off his penis and testicles, and
        throw them away.
And that's the end of it."
        ∞

They made a quick pass with the knife and cut them completely.
They carried Kibwana on a stretcher tebe tebe tebe [gently]
        to his home. They set him down there.
He lies sick. He recovers.
                              His wound grows smooth.
He's not a boy . . .
                    not a girl . . .
                          He's shattered . . .
                                            with
        all his beauty.
    ○

HOW HIS WIFE TREATS HIM!
When she went visiting at nine o'clock in the morning . . .
                                                      she
        didn't return until nine o'clock at night.
"What is it, baba? Where did you go?"
140 She answers, "'What is it, baba?' Did I take something from
        the house?
Have you been hurt on my account?"
    ○

"IY!" he says, "What hurts me, bojo, is that you are my wife.
    I have three children with you." SHE SAYS, "LEAVE OFF
    THE MATTER OF THE CHILDREN, BABA. PUT IT
    DOWN.
    ○

The thing that doesn't eat bananas— (laugh)
what do you think it eats?" (Audience: The thing that doesn't
    eat bananas, what do they give it?)
    ∞
"MH?
        Bojo. My wife, is this how you are?"
                                    She says, "That's
        how I am!"
    ○
"Then let me give you room.
    ○

It's better I go.
o

Mh!
     Rather than killing you in the end . . .
stay here with your children. I'm going."
150 He cooks some small cakes for himself and he wraps them.
                                       He
     ties them on his motorcycle and off he goes.
o

He drives hard, Kibwana.
HE DRIVES F-A-S-T.
When he passed through his father's chiefdom . . .
and then a second chiefdom . . .
he arrives at a town like Nyakáto . . .
That town
belongs to a whitelady like her [Sheila Dauer].
o

That whitelady is the daughter of . . . (Narrator tries to recall the
     name. Member of the audience: Mr. European?)
oo

Mh-Mh [no]. She is the daughter of . . .
oo

160 Kaiser.
Kaiser
     has a daughter . . .
She's alone. He has no other child.
And that daughter is the reason he built that town. It
     grew about as large as you see Nyakáto . . .
He searched the world over for a man who could marry her,
     but such a one does not appear.
o

She lived there like that.
All the men she sees, she sees as trash.
                         All the men she sees, she
     sees as trash.
               All the men she sees, she sees as trash.
o

Now Kibwana, on that day
               when he went to the town,
                        took a rest
     to eat those cakes of his.

o

Now while he sat down to rest, Whitelady stood at her
    window . . .
SHE LOOKED AT KIBWANA . . .
                                    "THAT'S HIM!
    The man I'm searching for is the one I see!"
170 She says, "Hurry! Run and call that man to me."
    o

They went and approached him.
(soft voice) He says, "Me, in that place I will not go,
Who summons me there?"
                        They say, "It's Whitelady."
                                                He says,
    "Whitelady? Forget it!
If I had been called by Bwana—okay.
BUT A WOMAN IS TABOO FOR ME.
    o

It was such a one that took me from our kingdom
                                        and
    brought me low," he says.
"Now I don't want Whitelady to appear . . .
                            before me."
    o

They go and tell Whitelady. She says, "What is this?
The one I see is the one I've been searching for. How can
    he pass me by?
180 I'll go myself."
She quickly put on her little shoes and a short skirt. (laugh)
Dyai [sound of high heels]
                        dyai
                            dyai
                                dyai
                                    dyai, she approaches him.
She says, "You, mister, I'd like you inside my house."
He says, "Stop it, baba.
THAT VERY THING IS MY TABOO. IT'S TABOO. IT'S
    TABOO.
                I'VE BEEN DRIVEN OUT FROM OUR
LAND BY WOMEN LIKE YOU.
    o

My father's wife gravely wounded me . . .
Now my wife did the same . . .
Now I have no need to meet a woman again."

She says, "You are about to meet me.
Me myself. Those who drove you out . . .
                                        had an ulterior
      motive.
                My motive is appearance
                              alone.
○

You see there is no man in my house.
I am alone in there.
My father is the one who rules this land. ALL OF IT
                                        and he had
        only me.
Me alone.
Now because he had only me, I received all of these things.
I lacked someone to live with,
                        but now I'll live with you."
He says, "ME?
              What can I do for you?
I am a woman, a comrade of yours.
                        But I am not a woman
      as you are,
              I am half a woman.
Now if I would go to live with you, what could I do for you?"
She says, "What do you mean?"
"Look,
      see how I am."
She says, "I have never tasted these things since I was born.
How can one be troubled by a thing one has not tasted?
I AM TROUBLED BY YOUR APPEARANCE
                                    AND
      WHENEVER YOU GO OUTSIDE THEY'LL
      SAY, 'THAT'S THE HUSBAND OF WHITELADY.'"
○

He was ready now to go inside the house.
(Narrator's aside: Baba, when I didn't heat the water,
      who do you think heated it? Shah!)
The youth had already washed,
                        he was
all ready!
WHITELADY SAYS, "COME HERE AND I'LL HUG
      YOU." SHE HOLDS HIM A BIT.
Something to do her with—he has nothing. (laugh)

o

He snaps his fingers in frustration. What you have tasted,
     she had not yet tasted. It doesn't pain her. But he,
     who had already tasted it, is pained.

∞

He's miserable.
They dwelled there, my mother—let me not delay you—
     the first month, the second, the third, the fourth . . .
They announced . . .
to Kaiser that . . .
the man who married Whitelady hasn't a thing.
He's a woman, a companion of hers, that stranger.

                                             And does he
     speak their language?
"He hasn't a thing!"
o

At that place there was a GREAT BIG river.

o

220   Now Kaiser plans a trip. He says . . .
                              "Tomorrow . . .
                                             I will go
     to the river and all of you from the town will bathe there.
And while bathing you will be naked, naked, naked, naked."
o

Whitelady did not delay. There was an old woman there
     like me
               who was all dried out
                              with ashen hair.
                                        She says,
     "My mother," she says, "what will I do?" she says.
     "They've come to kill my husband. My father has decreed
     they will bathe."
She replies, "Are these not matters I look after?"
She fashions balls of clay, like this, (shows fists) (laugh)
she fashions a long clay thing like this, (shows forearm) and
     ties them to a strap.
                         He puts them on. (laugh)
o

They go swimming in underwear.
Kaiser says, "These people,"
                         he says, "They have been put
     to shame, baba."

He says, "Is that not it?
Baba, what do they want from him?" (laughter)
He returns. "The man," he says,
                    "has one." (laughter)

o

230 DEATH DID NOT WAIT FOR THE OLD WOMAN WHO
        KNEW THINGS, LIKE ME . . .
It struck her in the act of brewing beer.
                              She dies!
They return to him and say, "My lord . . .

o

THAT MAN HAS THINGS THAT HE WAS WEARING.
    AND THEY WERE SHAPED FROM CLAY BY AN
    OLD WOMAN. AND NOW THE OLD WOMAN
    has died.
Go and make them bathe. See if he will show them now."

oo

He says,
        "Next month . . .
                        in the middle of January I'll call all
    of you to bathe."
Kibwana says, "Bojo, I'm leaving.
                        Haven't you heard your father
    has ordered us to bathe?
What will I wear to go bathing? Mh!"
She says, 'All right, go, but I'll die. Look, I'm hanging a
    rope for myself in the rafters.
When I leave there I'll be nothing but bare bones."

240 He says, "Be bare bones. (laugh)
    I . . .
        I once pulled my life out of our own kingdom. Again I'm
        taking it and making a run for it."
                        She says, "Be off.
                                        But
    I'll die. Look where I'm hanging a rope for myself.
                                        And who
    will speak of me?"

o

She climbs up.
Kibwana takes up his motorcycle.

o

He drives it.

He drives it.
He passes through that chiefdom and when he had arrived in a
    second chiefdom, he comes to a tree.
(exhausted voice) He says, "Even if I had stayed there, Kaiser
    would have killed me.
Now how will I end this journey, Kibwana?
Whew!"
    o

250   He heaved a great sigh.
The tree says, "What is it? What's wrong, baba?"
    oo

He says, "Father, you see what I have become.
                                            Look,
what am I?
AS OTHER MEN ARE, AM I ALSO?" (laugh)
The tree says, "No." (laugh)
He says, "That's what's killing me.
I continue to flee, but although I travel in this direction,
    I DON'T KNOW WHERE I'M GOING OR
    WHAT PLACE I'LL LEAVE BEHIND."
"How did you become like this?" He tells it the news.
He recounts it from about where I began.

260   The tree says, "Make your bed and lie down here. When night
    lifts you'll find you have your things."
    oo   [comes the dawn]
(Narrator holds a section of her skirt in front with two hands to
    simulate a penis. General uproarious laughter
    throughout this scene.)
"Iyo!
A miracle!
    o
Iy!
    o
They don't come off!
Iyo!
Am I really holding them?
    o
Iy!
They're okay."
    oo
He drives it.

o

270   He jumps on his motorcycle.

o

He goes back.
Eh-eh!
   At Whitelady's place it's about to happen.
(soft voice) He finds she's hung a rope for herself.
THOSE WHO'VE STOOD THERE SAY, "WHITELADY,"
  THEY SAY, "KIBWANA HAS COME."
             SHE SAYS,
  "STOP IT. WHO SPEAKS THAT WORD?"
HE SAYS, "I DO. COME HERE."
She drops down.
All ready.
(They converse softly.) She says, "Is it you?"
            He says, "It's
 me."
   She says, "Have you returned?"
            He says, "I've come."
She says, "Now . . .
      how did you get it?"
            He says, "You make
 the bed."
THEY IMMEDIATELY FELL INTO BED WITH
  A THUMP.

o

280   He says, "Let that little girl come closer."
HE DID IT THERE. (laughter)
HE DID HIS WORK.(Member of audience: There's trouble.)

o

Now matters were pleasing.
My chief!
The girl did not delay. She immediately became pregnant.

o

She gave birth to a big boy child.
The grandfather—how happy do you think he was?
HE THINKS, "THOSE PEOPLE ARE SORCERERS.
They were slandering the man, saying he hasn't a thing.
290   Now where did he get a child from, baba?
And I'll give the child my own name. HE'LL BE 'KAISER.'"

o

He grows.

He reaches to here. (indicates height with hand)
He reaches to here.
             He reaches to here.
When he began to be beautiful, he had grown to here . . .
and his BEAUTY is that of Kibwana himself.
o

That tree made him promise that when he would have the first
    child, he would bring him to it— TO EAT.
o

Now Kibwana finds the child so sweet, he thinks, "I can't take
    him to the tree to be eaten.
                  Better it should take
    its things back."
But the girl, who now has tasted them says, "If they are
    given back, what will I do?"
She says, "Go and see my father, now, this very day."
When Kibwana had gone, "KAISER . . .
300 COME HERE."
As soon as he had come, she lay the knife across his throat.
o

She tosses him into a pot.
(Narrator's aside: These are things you would refuse to do,
    to cook him so the famine will end. That's why he
    was cooked—laughter)
SHE STEWS HIM UP AND THE CURRY POWDER
    DROPS IN THERE.
                THE ONIONS
DROP IN.
          SHE BOILS IT. IT'S DONE. SHE
FINISHES.
SHE POURS IT INTO A DISH.
                 SHE WRAPS IT
                        IN
A CLOTH.
        SHE CARRIES IT AND
    SETS IT DOWN . . .
IN THE AUTOMOBILE.
o

Her husband returns.
o

"KAISER?

KAIS—" HE SAYS, "WHERE'S KAISER?"
                                                    "I'VE ALREADY
    COOKED HIM,
310 I'VE COOKED HIM, ME MYSELF.
    TAKE HIM TO THAT TREE AND LET IT EAT
    SO MY THING WON'T LEAVE ME."
        (Audience member: Mh! Baba!)
    o

    THE MAN DIDN'T ASK AGAIN.
    ∞ (general laughter, including narrator)
    HE DIDN'T ASK.
    HE DROVE, FOR NOW, COULD HE REFUSE HER?
        WHAT WILL HE DO WITH PIECES OF MEAT?
    He drove hard.
    o

    At the tree
    he meets it.
    He uncovers the dish.
320 It takes out a piece and bites into it.
    It says, "Okay,
                    you've cooked it okay."
                                    He replies, "Yes, my lord."
    The second piece.
    o

    "EH! ALL RIGHT!"
    o

    It says, "Set it here.
                    Lie down.
                            When night lifts you'll find
        your child. Take him.
    The matter is finished. Go and lie together with your
        wife again."
    ∞

    He goes to sleep.
    o

    WHEN NIGHT LIFTS, AT DAWN HE HEARS KAISER,
        "WHERE'S MY FATHER? (laughter) FATHER?"
    o

    WELL, WASN'T HE LOOKING GOOD? SINCE HE WAS
        INFUSED BY ONIONS, BABA, AND CURRY,
        AND OIL,
    he was even more beautiful than before.

330   He takes up his own little child and tosses him
              onto his shoulders.
        He gets into his auto.
        BACK HOME THE RUMORMONGERS APPROACHED
              KAISER.—
        THEY SAY, "FATHER, THE STRANGER WHO
              MARRIED WHITELADY— THEY COOKED THE
              CHILD AND ATE HIM. IT'S A HORROR!" (laugh)
        "HA!"
                 he says, "Wait for the dawn."
        HE SAYS, "WAIT FOR THE DAWN. TOMORROW I'LL
              GO AND IF I FIND MY KAISER IS NOT THERE,
              THE PERSON WHO INFORMED ME WILL BE HEIR
              TO MY CHIEFDOM. I FATHERED A GIRL AND
              NOW HAVE BEEN BLESSED BY HER BEARING
              A SON WHO WILL RULE AFTER ME.
        IF I FIND THEY HAVE EATEN HIM, I'LL HAVE BOTH
              OF THEM SHOT DOWN WITH RIFLES.
        Let them die."
              o
        That very day Kibwana returns.
        The day his father-in-law planned to come was when Kibwana
              arrived with his son.
              o
340   All ready. It was the child himself to the very fingers and
              fingernails.
        The car of HIS FATHER-IN-LAW PULLS UP. NOW . . .
                                                                    he
              himself has arrived long ago.
        WHEN HE STOOD THERE AND CALLED,
              "KAISER?"
                         "Y-E-S . . . ?" (laughter)
              o
        He had been ready to welcome his grandfather for quite
              a while, now.
        "Eh?"
              Kaiser thinks, "What kind of people are they, baba?
        What will they do next . . . ?
                         What can I do . . . ?
                                         A while ago
              they say he hasn't a thing . . .

A child was born . . .
                                                          Now
they say they've eaten him . . .
                                 Now here
he is . . .
            WHAT KIND OF
PEOPLE HAVE THEY BECOME . . . ?
IYO!
WHAT SORT OF STRANGE EVENTS ARE THESE? MY
    CHILDREN, LEAVE THIS PLACE."
THAT DAY HE BREAKS OPEN THE SECRET.
HE SAYS, "THEY CAME AND TOLD ME THAT THE
    MAN WHO MARRIED YOU HASN'T A THING."
350 HE SAYS, "WHEN THE CHILD WAS BORN, THAT'S
    WHEN I KNEW WHAT TO BELIEVE."
HE SAYS, "NOW THEY SAY YOU'VE EATEN THE
    CHILD
          AND NOW HERE HE IS."
HE SAYS, "WHAT WILL THEY DO NEXT?
                                  WHAT SORT
    OF STRANGENESS?"
                      HE SAYS, "LEAVE THIS
    PLACE, MY CHILDREN, MOVE TO ANOTHER.
BUT NOW, I CAN'T LEAVE KAISER HERE.
HE'S GOING WITH ME. HE'S GOING WITH ME."
He puts him in his car.
They thought, "Take him or don't: when we cooked him
    were we to have seen him again?"
"Take him."
    o
They dwelled there in peace.
They had another, a boy.
                      They had another, a girl.
                                        When they
    got to where THEIR CHILDREN
    NUMBERED FOUR . . .
360 at that other place his father dies, Lwakyendéla.
    o
They say, "EVEN THOUGH HE CUT HIS THINGS OFF,
    LET US GO AND BRING KIBWANA TO RULE,
    SO OTHERS WILL SEE US
    WITH HIM."

o

They wanted it so. (Audience member: There's a problem!)

o

They walk with their little calabashes, chewing
    c-a-s-s-a-v-a
          kolocho-o-o kolocho-o-o searching for
    the place he w-e-n-t.
              They were starving on the r-o-a-d.

o

Now they arrive at the town here . . .
They sit down to drink water and inquire.
Others say, "He's in there.
Don't lose heart."
They enter and meet Whitelady.
They say, (beseeching voice) "MOTHER,

370   LIVE FOREVER
WITH THAT WHICH BROUGHT YOU FROM YOUR
    HOME IN EUROPE!
SHOW US OUR CHILD KIBWANA, IF IT IS HE WHOM
    YOU HAVE."

o

She says, "Is it not he?"
              "YES, IT'S TRULY HE.
IT'S TRULY HE.
COME, FATHER, YOUR FATHER HAS DIED. COME
    AND TAKE THE ROYAL DRUM."

o

Well, they had been on foot, but he tossed them into his
    car
        along with his wife.
Off they go.
Bugábo [his home chiefdom].

o

He went and found his father's wife still there, the one
    who threw . . .

380   the milk vessels outside.
What do you think he did?
They would light a fire . . .
and bind her close by thus. (shows her hands palms out, as
    though they were raised to a fire)
She d-r-i-e-s o-u-t until morning.

When night would lift, they would take her and stretch her
    in the sun, there. (indicates sunny spot outside)
She d-r-i-e-s o-u-t until sunset.
At sunset they would take her and put her near the fire.
At last she died.
                They were roasting her like a piece of meat.
Kibwana rules.

   o

390 The matter is finished, baba, it is completely erased. That
    young man lives there well. He finds those children
    of his are there. He finds that wife of his is there.
(draws a breath) Things are good. He assumes the chieftaincy.
    There is nothing he needs. His children are those that he
    fathered. His thing is that which he bought.
That's how I saw it for you . . .
I came to tell you about it. At your mother's brother's there are
    beer bananas and bean leaves. At my mother's brother's
    they're getting FATTER AND FATTER.
Audience: Congratulations on your journey!

COMMENTARY

Food and Sex

Food and sex (as reproduction) are explicitly the topics of conflict in *Blocking the Wind*. In *Kibwana*, the explicit topic is sex (in several senses), but food is frequently joined to it, for example, Kibwana's first wife's explanation to him of her infidelity caused by his lack, phrased, "the thing that doesn't eat bananas—what do you think it eats?"; or Whitelady's cooking her own child into food so she can retain Kibwana's newly-found sex.

Haya ways of speaking about food and sex shed light on the two topics in the tales. Part of this system of ideas has been previously described, for it is relevant to other tales as well. An appetite for food motivates many dramatis personae, from Leopards to brides. The three-part ideology of food—1. ownership of land, 2. cultivation and preparation, and 3. consumption—has been described above, as has the central importance of the principle expressed in the aphorism, "The one who feeds you is the one who rules you," and its connection with the traditional feudal land-tenure system of *nyarubanja* (pp. 12–13). Certain symbolic meanings attached to food have already been noted, principally those connected with the kinds and amounts of food one consumes and the cooking and sharing of a meal as symbolic reaffirmations of the unity of the household group.

Food and sex are metaphorically equated in the symbolism of many societies. They are linked in Haya symbolism through analogies drawn between the three categories of food (providing, preparing, consuming) and similar categories of sexual reproduction. These can also be thought of as three in number: bearing a child, giving one's spouse sex, and enjoying the sensual pleasure of the act. One spouse gives sex to the other, satisfying the partner's appetite; this can describe the act in Haya terms. The act provides sensual pleasure, *obunula*, "sweetness," and may also lead to a pregnancy. Food and sex are analogous in the following way:

a) providing food   is like   bearing a child
b) preparing food   is like   giving sex
c) eating food   is like   enjoying sex

The sensual similarity (c) is recognized by many cultures. It can be found in Haya metaphorical descriptions of sex that employ sweet foods such as *mulamba*, ripe banana mash, drunk as is or brewed into beer. Literary metaphors of this kind appear in Haya epic poetry.

To serve or to give food is metaphorically equated with giving sex (b). This is the base for the interpretation of Kibwana's first wife's rhetorical question, "That thing that doesn't eat bananas—what do you think it eats?" That is, she needs someone who can satisfy her sexual appetite. The same metaphorical base is employed in a form of joking. The traditional Haya farewell, *Mpaho*, which in other contexts means, "give me a little," usually referring to food, can be punned on in the right leave-taking circumstances to refer to sex. A similar idea is expressed in the narrator's description of Kibwana's amorous return to the Kaiser's daughter, where the generalized "working" replaces the more specified "serving food": "They immediately fell into bed with a thump . . . He did it there. He did his work."[1]

Preparing food is woman's work. During pregnancy, however, giving "food" in the domain of sex is man's work: in traditional belief, continued intercourse is needed to "feed" semen to the unborn child so that it will develop normally.[2]

Providing food is like bearing a child, component (a), in that together they represent the basis of society—the economic structure and the means to reproduce it. A Haya mother is said to "feed" her husband's clan by bearing children. She is fed by the clan (in that they own the land she cultivates), and she fulfills her reciprocal obligation to "feed" them.

The principle expressed in "the one who feeds you is the one who rules you" also can be applied to sex: traditionally, the desires or cravings of a pregnant mother, who is in the process of feeding her husband's clan, must be obeyed lest the unborn child miscarry. (Kibwana's father's wife makes use of this to lure Kibwana where he should not go, line 70.) The principle also applies to reproduction, in that bearing and raising children is a woman's road to prestige within her husband's clan; by "feeding" clan members, she is accorded a limited right to "rule" them. The aphorism, "the one who feeds you is the one who rules you," applied literally, to food, refers to a man's ability to control others' behavior because he provides the land that feeds them. Applied figuratively, to sex, the proverb refers to a woman's ability to exert control over others' behavior because she provides children that "feed" the clan.

Proper and improper evaluation of various aspects of marriage are recurrent themes in *Blocking the Wind* and *Kibwana*. Things seem to get placed in hierarchical orders quite frequently in traditional Haya society. Evaluation of another person's social standing, for example, is a calculation that begins most social encounters. Status must be evaluated so that proper verbal greeting forms may be exchanged, thereby creating a framework within which the ensuing interaction can take place.[3] To give a person a greeting of less status than he or she deserves is *oku-gaya*, "to treat (someone or something) as of lower status." To give someone a greeting of greater status than he deserves is *okw-etohya*, "to make oneself small (in relation to the status of the other)." The occasions for status evaluations are not limited to greeting; nor are the objects of evaluation limited to people. Cultural artifacts, mythical beings, and abstract ideas can be placed in rank orders by Hayas, not unambiguously to be sure, but each one reflecting the hierarchical structures of the traditional Haya chiefdom.

To accord to each thing its proper value, neither to undervalue it nor to overvalue it, is a virtue in the Haya ideology of behavior equal to self-control. Both of these traits are characteristic of one kind of Haya ideal person, a *mwemanyo*, literally "one who knows himself."

The motivational force inside a person that can overturn both judgment and self-control is, of course, appetite. When this occurs in tales, it is not necessarily a tragic failing and may even be the subject of humor.

Blocking the Wind

The bride in *Blocking the Wind* is a glutton. The force of her appetite pushes food consumption to a place in her order of values far in excess of what it should be, displacing other more wifely ones, such as dutifulness and the proper handling of family resources. The bride overvalues food consumption. In the second episode of the tale, the bride shows that she undervalues the process of sexual reproduction, because she believes that so worthy a product as a child can be produced from something as worthless and as inconsequential as a fart. "If she had told you urine. If she had told you turds," her parents say, for both of these substances are employed in some Haya rituals of conception and infant care, as farts definitely are not. Just as she overvalues consumption in food, the bride undervalues production in sex.

The brother, the bride's husband, is also affected by a strong appetite that makes him overturn the proper order of things. Contrary to the principle of, "the one who feeds you is the one who rules you," he does not rule his wife. He is ruled by her, even though his clan holds rights to the land that produced the food, even though his own sister grew and harvested it, and even though the wife only prepared it. These conditions clearly give him the right to rule. But instead, at her whim, he goes out to block the wind with a wicker screen. In the domain of sex, the brother might justly be ruled by his wife if she "fed" or was in the process of "feeding" his clan with children. But the tale states explicitly that the woman had not yet conceived. The appetite that makes him act so strangely is not overtly stated in the tale; we shall name it after we note the tale's logical symmetries.

In *Blocking the Wind* the plot itself turns on an outrageously precise and poetic justice: as the brother was made to block wind to no avail, so was the bride. Symmetry extends as well to the level of motivation.

We have seen that the bride overvalues food consumption, undervalues sex production (thinks a child can come from farts); she is moved by an overweening appetite for food. The brother, on the other hand, undervalues food production—he is ruled by someone who does not feed him. This leads to the question, "What appetite made the brother behave as strangely as he did?" or as the text itself

asks, "What made him crazy?" (line 125). The tale does not explicitly answer this question, but points to the importance of the
brother's craziness by noting it no fewer than five times (lines 43,
45, 114, 119, and 125).

What made the brother crazy is that he was driven by an uncontrollable appetite for sex. The evidence for this assertion is as
follows. First, there must be a strong appetite that makes him behave in an unconventional way. Every other character in every
other tale who behaves in a marked way is so motivated. On explicit evidence internal to the tale, his desire could be either for
food or for sex. The brother might have acted out of hunger, but
protagonists with a craving for food almost always take more direct
action to obtain it. Moreover, a motivation of hunger would seem
to obviate the humor in the trial observer's pointed question, "You,
Mister, what made you crazy?" It seems clear that *Blocking the Wind*
is a funnier story if the brother is led around by his desire for sex.

A second reason to impute this motive is the nature of the
newly-wed state, a time of strong appetites. It is not only a bride
who suddenly finds herself in a context where an appetite—for
food—can be satisfied in an extraordinary degree. The desire for
sex, which, previous to marriage, had no proper means of gratification, may be indulged to satisfaction by newly-weds. Like a "hidden" bride who does no work but is encouraged to grow plump and
pregnant as she reclines all day surrounded by food, a new groom
(or bride, for that matter) suddenly finds himself in a situation
where fulfillment of sexual desire is not only not forbidden; it is
encouraged so as to produce new clan members. It is a case of the
proverbial poor man (or woman) set in a palace of riches. This feature of the newly-wed condition used to be the subject of humor in
our own society before the advent of the mass-produced automobile, the Pill, and other social formations.

The evidence for the brother's motivation is circumstantial.
We have shown that he had to have been motivated by some appetite and that he had the opportunity for a sexual motivation, but
direct evidence is lacking. I think Ma Laulelia Mukajuna, the narrator, prefers to remain silent on this matter, pointing with rhetorical questions (What made him crazy?) to the most logical conclusion—the brother was ruled by a woman who merely satisfied his
appetite. Just as in the domain of food, where he was ruled by a
woman who prepared, but did not produce it, so in the domain of
sex he was ruled by a woman who provided satisfaction, but had

not produced a child. As he undervalued food production and the traditional right it gives to rule, he overvalued sex consumption, and was ruled by someone who did not "feed" him or his clan.

Here, then, is the symmetry that underlies the windy justice. In food, the bride overvalues consumption and the brother undervalues production. In sex, the bride undervalues production and the brother overvalues consumption. The symmetry of motives in simple tabular form is:

	motivated by appetite for	overvalues	undervalues
bride	food	food consumption	sex production
brother	sex	sex consumption	food production

The brother's "craziness" and the bride's stupidity in believing a child can come from farts, for which both are publicly shamed, result ultimately from the power of appetite to overturn a proper priority of values. The sister set them straight. The sister, coolly self-controlled and in control, stands above the heated food-sex reciprocities of the newly-weds.

The intriguing symmetries of *Blocking the Wind*, its food/sex metaphors and its appetites, have led the interpretation on a merry chase all around the principal theme of the tale, which is the sister's control. At the center of the plot is an affinal triangle composed of two appetite-driven newly-weds and a knowing sister, who not only successfully defends the integrity of her clan, but also restores equilibrium to her brother's marriage. She does nothing less than hold together a domestic unity against the chaos of unleashed appetite. Her Chaucerian choice of instrument should not obscure the fact that she stands, mutatis mutandis, like the proverbial Dutch boy with his finger in a dike.

Consider the situation from her point of view. Before her brother's marriage, she enjoyed a sibling comradeship with him that is the ideal of intimate peer relationships. The incoming bride is inserted like a wedge between them. This is implicit in the "but" of the opening description, "an unmarried girl had a brother . . . but the brother had a wife" (lines 3–4).

An economically productive, domestically responsible and generous woman, she gives three five-gallon measures of millet to the couple—only to see the gluttonous bride make a crazy fool of her brother. When she found out that her sister-in-law was avariciously gobbling the food while her own brother was running uncontrolledly through the fields, what did she do? "SHE KEPT STILL. SHE DIDN'T SHOUT ACCUSATIONS. She waited for the season of hunger to pass." The narrator's long, rhythmic pauses reinforce the character's calm, quiet self-control. To have exposed the bride's gluttony immediately would have redressed the insult to her clan, but would also have led to the dissolution of her brother's marriage. Her patient control enabled her to achieve positive outcomes in both areas.

When the bride, totally confounded by the sister's strategem, has run back to her parents (who, hearing what has transpired, are titanically outraged), the brother, having sought his beloved wife in vain, returns to the sister, she is again calm, telling her distraught sibling, "Sit yourself down. It's a small matter. Just wind and wind." In contrast to all around her who are in a churning uproar, she is coolly in charge of herself and of the situation. She awaits a forum she knows must come where logic, not unrestrained passions, will prevail. The sister thus meets the most difficult of challenges: she solves the contradiction between the demands of blood relationships and those of marital ties; that is, she gains revenge for her clan and at the same time preserves her brother's marriage.

Seeing the tale from the sister's point of view, one can appreciate the aptness of the symbol of farts. In the perspective of the sister's calm, confident control, the bride's gluttony appears as a marital problem, to be sure, but nothing that cannot be easily dispatched. In marked contrast, Mutele's excremental monster (*Mutele, You've Left Me, You've Gone*), the symbol of marital problems run amok, proves substantial enough to undo the ties of marriage. To the sister, however, the bride's gluttony and the brother's craziness are nothing over which to break up a marriage; they are problems, but they are without real substance for one who can exercise control. Less substantial than Mutele's gross incontinence, but from the same motivational source, they are not excrement, merely farts. They do not require a radical restructuring of relationships, merely that the air be cleared. In a multileveled ironic logic that seems to be the mark of a well-wrought traditional composition, wind, by nature uncontrollable, stands as the symbol for a controllable problem arising from uncontrolled—but controllable—appetites.

Kibwana

The tale of *Kibwana* can be read as a series of events that embody one questionable evaluation after another. Added complications arise from Kibwana's beauty and the theme of appearance versus reality. Of course, the tale cannot be reduced to this, but here is the skeleton. The retinue of an ugly chief wish he would die so that his beautiful son might rule; they value "being seen together" over the proper order of chiefly succession. The chief's new wife wants her husband's son, Kibwana, to be her mate. The text is not explicit, but it seems clear she desires sex with the beautiful one. She values the enjoyment of sex over proper wifely behavior. Rejected, she accuses Kibwana of entering in where he should not. Kibwana's father mistakes appearance for reality and judges his son to be guilty.

Kibwana's wife, unable to obtain satisfaction for her sexual appetite at home, begins to find it elsewhere. Kibwana appeals to her in the name of their children to stay at home, but she chooses the satisfaction of her appetite over the values of the hearth. Kibwana then meets Kaiser's daughter, who wants to marry him for his beauty. She wants only "to be seen with" him, disregarding sex and the other aspects of marriage out of ignorance. Kaiser, however, has children in mind, for he lacks a male heir. Through some clever technical manipulation of appearances, Kibwana manages to convince Kaiser that he is capable of producing his succession. But eventually appearances fail and he must flee. A tree magically restores his penis, but requires his first-born child in return. Faced with the choice between sex and a child, Kibwana chooses to relinquish his sex. But Whitelady, no longer ignorant in these matters and possessed of a newly-whetted appetite, kills her child and cooks him up into a stew. Given the same options as Kibwana, she takes sex. The tree restores the child, other circumstances fall into place, and almost all live happily ever after. The separate components of married life, which, one by one, were the subjects of difficult and questionable decisions, in the end exist together in Kibwana's marriage, as they do in most Haya marriages.

Kibwana abounds in structural symmetries and logical complementarities. It appears to have existed in oral tradition for a long time: versions of it have been reported to me from Ethiopia on one side and from Angola on the other. Collective linguistic creativity has apparently been long at work on this tale and has left its mark. Moreover, I believe Ma Laulelia Mukajuna regards this as the most impressive tale in her repertoire; she performed it for a sizeable female audience of her peers.

One fairly obvious symmetry is the poetic justice meted out to the woman responsible for Kibwana's emasculation. She was dried out before a fire and in the sun until she died. Women and women's sexuality are associated with water. Menstrual flow and feminine fluids of copulation are ritually and poetically invoked symbols of the female principle. Note also how many times water appears in the tales of new brides. Drying out the Jezebel-like woman removed the essence of her female sex, just as she caused Kibwana to be deprived of the essence of his male sex.

She is turned into a kind of food: "They were roasting her like a piece of meat," the narrator says. She thus makes an interesting contrast to Kaiser's grandson, who is also turned into food. Her punishment, a slow death and a permanent one, kills an adult female who was the cause of Kibwana's losing his penis; it turns her into dry food and removes her essential fluid. The grandson's sacrifice, on the other hand, a quick death and a temporary one, kills a male child who was the result of Kibwana's regaining his penis; it turns him into wet food and increases his essential beauty (line 329).

Note also that the evil, young, sexually desirous woman destroys things to cause Kibwana to fall afoul of the Haya chief, while a beneficent, old, dried-up woman creates things to save Kibwana from the judgment of the German chief. The Haya chief is fooled into thinking Kibwana is sexually desirous; Kibwana loses his real penis and is exiled. The German chief is fooled into thinking Kibwana is sexually capable; Kibwana has an artificial penis and remains. Kibwana unwillingly loses his penis because of an imaginary foetus (line 95); after it is regained, he would willingly return it for a real child. There are more homologies to be found. The formation and appreciation of aesthetic structures are entertainments of humankind and have both universal and particular dimensions.

Two Punchlines
There is much humor in these tales, and audience laughter is indicated in the transcriptions. I would judge the most uncontrolled outburst to occur when Ma Laulelia enacts before an all-female audience Kibwana's waking up to discover his newly-attached genitalia. Holding a length of her skirt in front as a stage

prop penis, the narrator shows the changes the man goes through upon waking—from surprise and wonderment to momentary uncertainty of what he sees and feels, to his unbounded joy that appearance and reality are identical. The audience cannot contain its laughter. The broad humor in this scene, and in another in *Blocking the Wind* (lines 62–66), where we see the bride trying to fill her calabash, is easily appreciated by non-Hayas.

But on two other occasions the laughter seems more explosive. It erupts at a particular moment brought about by a well-timed punchline. This seems to be the kind of laugh—and a loud one at that—that pops out at the appreciation of a logical twist, rather than, as above, the rollicking laughter of seeing a human comedy enacted.

One such explosion occurs in *Kibwana* after the descriptive line, "The man didn't ask again" (line 313). To appreciate why this is funny, we must understand the significance of the situation at this point in the tale. Whitelady, a European woman, but first and foremost a woman, has completely overturned her husband's culturally-sanctioned domination. She has tricked him, murdered and stewed his child, boldly claimed full responsibility for this deed, and finally, has staked a claim of ownership over his "thing." She overthrows his sexual domination. She is now the one who owns the maleness. But what will Kibwana do in return? Does he have some retaliatory move, as men certainly have? What will he say? The narrator tells us, "The man didn't ask again." The audience breaks up in laughter. Utter defeat: she rules.

The Swahili language itself plays a direct role in portraying this. Some of the dialogue between Kibwana and Whitelady and a bit between the magical tree and Kibwana is in Swahili (in all, lines 300, 309–12, 321, 323, 327, and 342). But the most dramatic use of Swahili is when Whitelady wrests the role of maleness from her husband. She is not only domineering, expropriating, and anti-sentimental; she expresses herself in the language introduced into Hayaland under German and British colonial domination. She speaks imperiously, in the simplified, ungrammatical, and loud Swahili of a colonial boss. The narrator uses the shift in language to twist the male/female, dominant/dominated irony to another level.

A similar outburst of laughter occurs in *Crested Crane and Dove* with the line, "Crested crane casts down its eyes" (line 26). A similar revolution has taken place. Gray dove, the little homely one, has just surpassed her cowife, the beautiful crested crane, as the wife who is most pleasing to her husband. Dove has prepared, step by step, a succulent dish. Given the same opportunity, crested crane ate the food herself and saved none. Now dove serves the dish with domestic flourish: out comes the food, out comes a plate, then a banana-leaf tablecloth/placemat, and finally, honorific-of-honorifics, the snow-white strands of papyrus, symbol of royalty and happiness. What will crested crane do? Surely a beautiful wife will have some pleasing wiles to work on her husband, some kind of explanation to return her to his good graces? No, Ma Laulelia says, "Crested crane casts down its eyes. It looks into its little beard [of feathers]." Total victory: the quick turnabout releases laughter.

Both instances of humor result from the sudden overthrow of a commonplace cultural hierarchy. They both seem to embody the same formal sequence: first, a character performs a series of unanswered acts, which together make a claim on a particular social status, which happens to be occupied by another character; second, the narrator pauses to look for a reply from the previously-dominant character now under attack; third, there is no reply, but instead, the description of a silent act that signals utter defeat.

The tales in this section are in no sense fully interpreted by these few pages of text. I have tried to indicate what appear to be the major themes and structures, the principal symbols and their most immediate meanings. Further insight into the tales comes by reflecting on them in relation to other tales in the collection as a whole. Projecting one tale onto another may deepen the reader's understanding of both. The importance of male succession in *Kibwana*, for example, is enriched by *Lusimbagila Bestows on All*. The significance of Whitelady's turning her child into food is intensified by *Give-Him-Sweetness-If-He-Cries*, as the irony of *Blocking the Wind* is by *I Shall Be Drinking from Them*. A knowing Haya audience has heard many tales, and meanings of one listened to resonate silently with meanings of those already known.

Additional Notes on Kibwana

In *Kibwana*, Ma Laulelia makes a mistake on the name she wants to give the prince's father. She begins by calling him Kahigi, a chief of Kihanja, the area in which she was living; but then she corrects herself. Lwakyendela, she wants to call him, a chief of the former chiefdom on Bugabo, where her family is from. In the flow of seeing the imagined events, however, she reverts back to calling

Kibwana's father Kahigi. I have changed these all to Lwakyendela as this is consistent with her stated wish.

The bridal gift pole (line 105) is a wooden staff, about 1½ inches in diameter and 7 feet in length, which is covered completely in white papyrus strands. From it are hung papyrus-wrapped, newly-carved, wooden milk vessels. This festive gift collage accompanies the bride to her new home among her husband's people. Nowadays, people wrap china tea sets as well.

The palace guards are called *abashasha* (line 124), the name of a particular clan. They were, at least in Ma Laulelia Mukajuna's telling, the clan delegated by the chief to fulfill this function. It is difficult to obtain unambiguous information about the clan that performed a particular function at the court of a particular chief. Ma Laulelia is herself of the *abashasha* and she may have added this detail to inject her own identity, as she does in asides (lines 205 and 303) and comparisons (lines 10, 222, and 230). Ma Winifred Kisiraga makes her own clan a part of her telling of *The Glistening One* (Chapter 9).

The old woman who is knowledgeable in many matters dies "in the act of brewing beer" (line 230). This is a way of saying that she died suddenly, apparently a relatively good death like that of Kaiser's grandchild, unlike that of Kibwana's father's wife.

Ma Laulelia's aside (line 303) playfully chides the women in the audience for being unwilling to make ritual sacrifices to end a famine and to produce a successful harvest. She draws a parallel between sacrificing to produce food and satisfy hunger, on one hand, and sacrificing to retain Kibwana's sex and satisfy desire, on the other.

When Kaiser's grandchild reappears, he is the same person "to the very fingers and fingernails" (line 340). This expression might be used to welcome a person who has been away for a long time. "It's you," someone would say taking the traveler's hand, "to the very fingers and fingernails."

8

Tales of Gluttony and Separation

Tales in this section assert the positive link between sharing and "familyhood" by portraying its negative opposite, the nonsharing of food that is gluttony, and its ruinous result that is separation. Sharing food literally and symbolically reaffirms the circle of familyhood that unites members of a household. The principal meal is prepared so as to be eaten in the evening, after the equatorial sun sets around 6:30 or so. Family members gather in the flickering light inside a house now shut against the night. They pass the time waiting for the food to cook with conversation, riddles, and tales. Just before the meal, they ceremonially wash their hands, one helping another with the water or one child serving all. The woman deftly turns a pot of cooked plantains into a steaming mound in the middle of a colorful enamel tray or broad green banana leaf. Each member of the household will eat from the side of the mound that faces him or her. The meal's relish, for example, meat, fish, vegetable stew, is usually served in separate portions. After mealtime grace (if the family is Muslim or Christian) they begin. At the outset, one person may pass a part of his portion of the relish—usually a piece of meat or fish—to another person as a sign of caring. It can be a time of peaceful, quiet conversation over food, or of high-spirited talk interspersed with laughter. Hayas compare the latter mealtime situation to a nest of weaverbirds, who cheerily converse with joyful commotion.

So strong is the assertion that the opposite of such sharing leads to the destruction of family unity that the entire dramatic structure of the tales turns on this theme. When murder occurs, revenge is not a central issue; the murder is left unavenged. The tales focus instead on the gluttony that motivated the killing and the separation that resulted from it. Murder invests gluttony with a high seriousness that can meet a just punishment only in separation.

Gluttony threatens the structure of a society in which the universe of goods is accurately perceived to be limited. To such a society, taking more than one's share upsets the natural order of things. A person who does this (and a tendency for it exists in everyone) cannot be included within the circle of familyhood. There are degrees of seriousness in gluttonous behavior, of course, but the contradiction is always present.

The Woman "Full Moons"

AS TOLD BY MA CHRISTINA DOMISSIAN

I see a famine coming,
                                a time when old women . . .
are pleased and a time when sons-in-law are angered.
The famine grows and grows,
"The-Bringer-of-Shame" that killed a boy's mother while a girl's
        mother thrived well.
  o
At that time, when the famine had already come, an old woman
        was visiting the home of her son-in-law . . .

                                                coming and
        cultivating with her daughter . . .

                                bringing her little things
        to eat . . .
                        bringing her little things to eat . . .
                                                        They
        would cook together and the old woman would eat . . .
NOW HER SON-IN-LAW LOOKS AT HER AND SAYS
        "THAT LITTLE OLD WOMAN . . . "
  o

HE SAYS, "IF ONLY WE COULD EAT AND BE
        SATISFIED.

BUT WITH THOSE PLANTAINS SHE EATS
   EVERY DAY WHEN SHE COMES HERE . . .
SHE CAUSES A LOSS."
    o

10 When the daughter saw it was time, she cooks plantains
      and eats.
           She finishes eating and at two o'clock
    she accompanies her mother for a short distance
    on her way home.
It's as though she were leaving here and going to about Kitáhya
    [approximately 2 miles].
She reaches a spot like Nyaiyánga.
She calls to her departing mother, "MOTHER, MOTHER,
    GREET THEM AT HOME FOR ME.
                       "I WILL. AND
YOU DWELL IN PEACE. I'M GOING."
                            "WHEN WILL
YOU COME AGAIN?"
"WHENEVER THE TIME SEEMS RIGHT, I'LL COME TO
    LOOK IN ON YOU."
The old woman goes.
The son-in-law . . .
had chosen a spot in the sandy place
                  and had sat down to wait.
    o

He is there when the old woman appears with her staff
    moving slowly, slowly, slowly.
He picks up a knife.
    o

20 He slashes her.
           She falls dead.
He turns back.
He comes home.
    o

"Iy! Baba, where were you?"
           "Eh! I was visiting around close by.
I was strolling about in Nyakimbímbili."
                "Iy! Did you meet
my mother?"
        "Mh-mh [no], I haven't seen her. Perhaps she
passed by a different way."

"M-m-m." [Yes, I see.]
The next day the daughter picks up a hoe and goes to cultivate.
There, where she bends over her work, a small bird appears
    to her.
It comes.
  o
(sings)   "Little bird, kempúnda buchéke.
                Little bird, the woman 'Full Moons.'
                Little bird, kempúnda buchéke.
                Little bird, she's in the white place.
                Little bird, kempúnda buchéke.
                Little bird, she moves in trepidation.
                Little bird, kempúnda buchéke.
                Little bird, they killed her.
                Little bird, kempúnda buchéke."
"Eh?" The daughter looks at it.
"Eh?
    What is that little bird doing?" She raises up her hoe
    and chops.
          She raises it and chops.
30 She finishes working.
             She goes and cooks.
She eats.
      They lie down in there. The day dawns.
She picks up her hoe and returns to work.
  o
The little one comes again.
            "Little bird, kempúnda buchéke.
            Little bird, the woman 'Full Moons.'
            Little bird, kempúnda buchéke.
            Little bird, she's in the white place.
            Little bird, kempúnda buchéke.
            Little bird, they killed her.
            Little bird, kempúnda buchéke.
            Little bird, she's in the white place.
            Little bird, kempúnda buchéke."
"Iy?"
    she says. "That little bird,
                what does it say?
                    Yesterday it
    spoke to me and now it speaks to me again."
A WEEK PASSES.

EVERY TIME SHE CULTIVATES
the little bird comes.

EVERY TIME SHE CULTIVATES
the little bird comes.

> "Little bird, kempúnda buchéke.
> Little bird, the woman 'Full Moons.'
> Little bird, kempúnda buchéke.
> Little bird, she's in the white place.
> Little bird, kempúnda buchéke.
> Little bird, she moves in trepidation.
> Little bird, kempúnda buchéke."

"Iy?"

A WEEK PASSES.

THE SECOND.

40 THE LITTLE BIRD DOES NOT FAIL.

o

It meets her there and speaks.

"Iy?
Now my mother said she would come here this Sunday . . .
Now why doesn't she come?
Mh-mh. [No! She comes to a decision.]
> I'll go and have a look at my mother. She
> may be ill."

o

The girl takes to the road . . .
As she goes and goes into the sandy place . . .
she comes upon her m-o-t-h-e-r . . .
Both b-l-a-c-k

a-n-t-s . . .
and r-e-d a-n-t-s . . .
HAVE

ALREADY EATEN.

o

THEY HAVE ALREADY FINISHED.

∞

THE GIRL CRIES OUT A LAMENT. SHE CRIES OUT
> FOR HERSELF . . .

o

50 SHE SCREAMS . . .

THOSE WHO HAVE SEEN HER . . .

SAY, "YOU MIGHT

AS WELL NOT SCREAM."
    o
They say, "It is your husband.
He came and left your mother dead. We tried to find a way that
    we could say these things, but they confounded us.
Don't trouble yourself [trying to find the killer]."
    o
My lord, I give you a story, I give you another, of the reasons
    that sons-in-law do not like old women.
Audience: Congratulations on your journey!

Kulili Your Brother
of Only One Mother

AS TOLD BY TA ELIAS KAISHULA

I give you a story.
Audience: I give you another.
It's done.
Audience: The news of long ago.
My lord, I came and saw.
Audience: See so that we may see.
I see a time of hunger really became a time of hunger.
    o
My lord, while we were there that way . . .
    o
a man goes and marries a woman.
10   Now when he marries a woman . . .
that woman had a brother.
    o
She leaves him AT HOME.
Now the time of hunger STRIKES.
When the hunger had struck . . .
the hunger grows greater.

Now the young man says,
                    "I think I'll follow my sister . . .
I'll go to where she was married.   COULDN'T I GO
     AND FIND A BIT OF FOOD THERE?"
My lord, he takes to the r-o-a-d.
                         He goes to his s-i-s-t-e-r's place.
The s-i-s-t-e-r
          welcomes him.
20 And the brother-in-law is there, too . . .
They all dwell together . . .
They're there for about a month.
    o
The husband . . .
               feels overburdened.
He says, "THAT ONE
               HAS FOLLOWED HIS SISTER
     AND COME TO LIVE WITH ME.
     BUT HOW CAN I FEED THEM?"
Now, then, he thought about how he would kill him.
When the young man had been there for one month . . .
he said, "Father, I'm going . . .
I'll go home to have a look at what's happening there.
Then I'll return a second time to see you."
30 She
       says, "E-e-eh [agreement]."
Now when he had planned the trip, he said,
"In the afternoon, I'll take to the road and travel."
The husband of the sister
went ahead.
He left home saying good-bye. "Dwell in peace. I'm
     going visiting." He answers, "E-e-eh." The husband goes
     with a knife,
a machete.
HE GOES AND CHOOSES A PLACE LIKE KITÁHYA
     AMONG THE LONG GRASSES . . .
                              THERE'S
     A COPSE OF TREES . . .
where he sits beside the path.
He says, "He'll come!
    o

40 The man has eaten plantains at my house.
                                    I've been searching for
      food until I'm exhausted.
NOW HE'S SAID HE'LL GO AND THEN RETURN
      AGAIN."
      o

My lord, he lies in wait.
The young man says farewell to his sister.
He takes to the road and goes.
WHEN HE GETS OUT THERE, LIKE TO
      NYAKIMBÍMBILI IN THE COPSE OF TREES . . .
HE FINDS THE ONE WHO HAS LAIN IN WAIT
      FOR HIM.
HE HITS HIM ON THE NECK.
HE BREAKS IT!
      o

He hits him "a bend in the neck."
                                    HE KILLS HIM!
      o

50 ON THE PATH . . .
                        WHERE HE WAS TRAVELING, HE
      KNEW THAT BEFORE HIM AND BEHIND
      THERE WAS NO ONE.
But with him there was a small bird.
Now, my lord, he takes to the road, the young man—
      the killer . . .
the one who married the sister . . .
He returns home.
      o

Now there was a little bird there.
IT GOES.
            IT GOES QUICKLY.
IT GOES AND TELLS THE S-I-S-T-E-R.
      o

The wife of that young man.
It says,

                  "Kulili your brother of only one mother,
                  Kulili your husband has killed him.
                  Kulili and his pretty eyes,
                  Kulili and his pretty teeth,

Kulili and his pouch of charmed things,
Kulili and his ram's horn on the head,
Kulili he's put them in a covered basket.
Kulili he says, 'They're property of the chief.
Don't you touch them. Don't you touch them.'"
60 "IY?"
    THE WOMAN LISTENS AND SAYS, "WHAT?
WHY DOES THE LITTLE BIRD COME HERE TALKING
    LIKE THAT?

o

HII?" She falls silent.
The next day it comes again.
    "Kulili your brother of only one mother,
    Kulili your husband has killed him.
    Kulili and his nice eyes,
    Kulili and his nice teeth,
    Kulili and his pouch of charmed things,
    Kulili and his ram's horn on the head,
    Kulili he's put them in a covered basket.
    Kulili he says, 'They're property of the chief.
    Don't you touch them. Don't you touch them.'"
My lord, the woman . . .
looks and is confounded. She says, "No! [She's made
    up her mind.]
These words the little bird speaks . . .
I'll go and have a look at my brother
to see if he has arrived."
She takes to the road and goes.
70 THAT LITTLE ONE WENT BEFORE HER.
WHEN IT HAD REACHED THE PLACE,
IT SPEAKS TO HER AS PEOPLE DO.
                  IT SAYS, "HERE.
    IS IT NOT HERE?"
                WHEN SHE TURNED
    A CORNER
          she finds the body already decomposed.

o

My lord, I won't delay you . . .
Famine is a bad thing . . .
That was when she went running . . .
She cried out a lament . . .

She cried out. She cried it for herself . . .
She calls the people . . .
They arrive there . . .
80   The woman and the man separate.
   o

The woman and the man there
                              that was when they were not
      siblings.
People may dwell where they are married even when
      the marriage is without love.
                              If love turns bad . . .
   o

everything else turns bad, even if it is a religious marriage.
My lord, when I saw these things, I said, "Let me go
      and narrate them a bit."

Satisfaction

AS TOLD BY MA WINIFRED KISIRAGA

I came and I saw for you.
Audience: See so that we may see.
Now I come and see a time of hunger comes.
Now when it had come . . .
a man had . . .
                  already married a wife.
   o
Now . . .
         the man has a mother.
And the woman . . .
has a mother.
                  THEY ARE ALL IN ONE HOUSE.
Now they dwell there, they dwell there and the hunger
         GROWS GREATER.
10   Now when it HAD GROWN . . .
   o
Now

the man says, "Look," he says, "my wife,"
HE SAYS, "THIS FOOD . . . "
he says, "it's causing me a lot of trouble."
HE SAYS, "NOW WHAT WE SHOULD DO,"
o
he says, "WE SHOULD KILL THOSE OLD WOMEN."
o
HE SAYS, "FIRST WE'LL KILL YOUR MOTHER."
He says, "Then we'll kill my mother."
o
SHE SAYS, "YES,"
                  SHE SAYS, "BUT . . . "
20 SHE SAYS, "NOW
                  WE MIGHT BEGIN WITH YOUR
    MOTHER."
The woman continues.
She says, "Then we'll kill my mother."
THE MAN SAYS, "NO."
HE SAYS, "WE'LL BEGIN WITH YOUR MOTHER."
o
"EH?"
        The woman says, "Yes." She says, "My mother.
    We'll begin with her."
(whispers) Now the girl thought to herself, "Now what
    shall I do?"
SHE SAYS, "YOU'LL FIND I'VE ALREADY KILLED MY
    MOTHER." SHE SAYS, "WHEN YOU
    RETURN FROM SEARCHING FOR FOOD," she says,
    "you'll find I've already killed her."
o
The girl . . .
GOES
        AND DIGS A HOLE INSIDE THE HOUSE.
o
30 There, near the hearth she goes and puts her mother in.
                                She tells
    her, "DON'T MOVE AT ALL."
SHE SAYS, "BOTH FOR RELIEVING YOURSELF," SHE
    SAYS, "RELIEVE YOURSELF THERE." SHE SAYS,
    "AND FOR URINATING," SHE SAYS, "I WILL BE

COMING FROM TIME TO TIME TO TAKE IT OUT."
SHE SAYS, "BUT DON'T MOVE AT ALL!"
She says, "Okay."
After the young man had come, she came
saying, "I HAVE FINISHED MY MOTHER."
HE SAYS, "YOU'VE FINISHED?"

                  She says, "E-e-eh." [yes]
She says, "Now how about you and your mother?
I'VE KILLED MY MOTHER.
                  IS YOUR MOTHER
    STILL LIVING?"
The young man thought to himself.
"Now my wife has killed her mother . . .
40   If I don't kill my mother will she not come to hate me?"
HE GRABS A KNIFE.
He cuts his mother at one stroke.
RIGHT AFTER HE CUTS HER
she dies.
   o
Now . . .
they dwell there.
The young man . . .
brings m-i-l-l-e-t.
The woman brings m-i-l-l-e-t.
50   They make it into porridge and eat. And when they would make
      it into porridge
                  the daughter
would put one cooking-spoon-full in a basket
                       and carry it
    to the hole.
NOW SATISFACTION IS ALSO A BAD THING.
   o
SHE, WHOM SHE TAKES THE MILLET TO,
                        EATS.
SHE IS SATISFIED.
WHEN SHE BECAME SATISFIED . . .
it began to make her come out from her cover.
   o
Now . . .
they leave home.
They go to search for food.

60 THERE, WHERE THE WOMAN WAS IN THE HOLE . . .
    she looked at herself.
    "Eh!"
        she says, "I've become fat."
    She says, "LOOK AT THIS."
    SHE SAYS, "MY SON-IN-
        LAW WAS ABOUT TO KILL ME."
        SHE SAYS, "I MIGHT HAVE DIED AND LEFT
        THIS FOOD." SHE SAYS,
        "LOOK HOW I'VE BECOME . . . "
    SHE SAYS, "I'M BETTER OFF NOW THAN WHEN I
        COOKED FOR MYSELF."
    Eh-eh!
    She leaves the hole.
    Then she comes
    out into the middle of the inner room.
70 She begins:
    (sings)   "A grain of millet, baba, a grain of millet.
                     It killed the mother of a boy while the
                         mother of a girl thrived well.
                     Look at the Arm!
                     Look at the Leg!
                     Look at the Buttock!
                     Look at the Head!
    Eh?
    Ha-ah!"
            Again she looks at herself saying, "But don't I really
        look good?"
                    Again she runs and returns to the hole.
    One day.
        o
    Now . . .
    the young man . . .
    dwells there.
    They eat. They eat.
    "Eh?"
        he says, "Now . . . "
                    he says, "truly
    we knew what we were doing."
80 He says, "Now wouldn't the famine have killed us . . . "
    he says, "if we hadn't gotten rid of those old women?"

The woman says, "Yes,"
she says, "it surely would have killed us."
They make the millet into porridge.
Again she takes . . .
more millet . . .
and puts it in the hole . . .
She brings it to her mother and her mother eats . . .
NOW SATISFACTION DID HER BAD.

        o

90   WHEN SHE HAD BECOME SATISFIED . . .
     SHE WAS ALMOST TOO BIG FOR THE HOLE. SHE
         COMES OUT.
     She begins to do herself harm out in the open there.
     The grandchildren saw her.
     They saw her when they were in the front yard . . .
     She comes out.
                    "A grain of millet, baba, a grain of millet.
                    It killed the mother of a boy while the mother
                        of a girl thrived well.
                    Look at the Arm!
                    Look at the Leg!
                    Look at the Buttock!
                    Look at the Head!
                    Look at the Cheek!"
     "IY?"
             The grandchildren . . .
     run away from there.
        o
     They've gotten a look at her.
     Now after a while, they say, "But father,"
100 they say, "when you leave . . . "
     they say, "a woman comes . . . "
     they say, "BEAUTIFUL," THEY SAY, "AND FAT."
     They say, "She sings for us."
        o
     The man says, "A woman?"
                            They say, "Yes, my lord."
     He says, "You children are telling me a lie."
                            They say, "That's
         not so!"

Now . . .
        when they have arisen the next day . . .
the young man plans to himself.
He says, "That woman has fooled me." He says, "I KILLED
        MY MOTHER . . . "
HE SAYS, "AND LOOK HER MOTHER IS
        STILL HERE . . . "
110 He sharpens that knife of his.
        ○
Now he says to the children, "Go. Run and play." They go.
                                                                        And
        he says, "I'm going." He says, "I'll come back
        in the evening."
                        They say, "Okay."
The girl goes to cultivate.
Now the young man . . .
goes into the house. He lies in wait.
When he had lain in wait . . .
satisfaction makes her come out from her cover. She leaves
        the hole.
        ○
She looks this way. She looks that way. She finds no one. She
        goes to the threshold—no one.
She goes outside under the thatch that's over the door.
                "A grain of millet, baba, a grain of millet.
                It killed the mother of a boy while the mother
                        of a girl thrived well.
                Look at the Arm!
                Look at the Leg!
                Look at the Head!
                Look at the Cheek!"
"Eh?"
        The young man . . .
120 looks.
        ○
Now . . .
WHEN SHE STARTED TO COME INSIDE,
she was met by the young man.
HE CUTS HER!
And when he had cut her . . .
he drags her.

HE PUTS HER INTO THE HOLE . . .
HE WIPES UP THE BLOOD . . .
o
He keeps silent.

130   Now . . .
the daughter comes.
o
When she had come,
"YOU'VE ALREADY RETURNED."
                      He says, "I'VE
    ALREADY RETURNED."
"HII!" SHE SAYS, "I THOUGHT YOU WERE
    PLANNING TO COME BACK IN THE
    AFTERNOON."
                   HE S-A-Y-S,
                         "NO," HE SAYS, "AS I
WAS GOING ON THE PATH," HE SAYS, "THEY
TOLD ME, 'WHERE YOU'RE GOING, THEY'RE NOT
AT HOME.' SO I RETURNED." "I see." They cook.
When they cook the food
it's getting done.
It's completely done and they serve it out.
When they were about to eat, the daughter takes out a bit.
She goes to the hole.
                  (whispers) "Mother, mother.
140   (whispers) You, mother."
o
(whispers) Silence.
             "You, mother. You, mother."
(whispers) Nothing.
(whispers) "Here's the food. Have you fallen asleep?"
(whispers) Nothing.
"Hii!
What kind of sleep is this?"
When she puts in her hand . . .
SHE FINDS HER MOTHER HAS GROWN COLD, COLD,
    COLD. "IYO-O!"
SHE SAYS, "THE MAN HAS KILLED MY MOTHER FOR
    ME."
150   Now . . .
then the girl cries out a lament . . .

People arrive there . . .
She tells how her husband told her they should kill her mother,
    how she concealed her mother . . .
She says, "Now . . .
I find he has killed my mother."
"Eh?"
Everyone looks and is confounded.
The woman packs up and goes . . .
Now that's how I saw it for you . . .
160   Hunger brings the-killing-of-one-another among people . . .
Hunger does not bring siblingship . . .
I also saw satisfaction for you . . .
how it makes a person have no shame, and how it killed
    an old woman.
Had she not gotten satisfaction and left the hole, she
    would not have died.
When I had seen these things for you I said, "Let me go and
    report to them."

She's Killed One.
We've All of Us Come

AS TOLD BY TA KEREMENSI LUTABANZIBWA

A woman would go to work in the fields.
o
Whenever she went . . .
she would go with plantains.
o
She eats them there . . .
cooking on a fire in the fields.
o
She deprives her husband.
o
When she would return . . .

o

her husband says to her, "My, but you're late."
She says, "I didn't spend the day eating dirt, baba. [She spent it
    working.]
10   That's how I am."

o

Now
where she would cook the plantains . . .
there were WILD ANIMALS.

o

They come and take out food and carry it away.

o

While they were carrying it away . . .

o

now, one day . . .
the woman . . .
comes and sees the animals taking her plantains off the fire,

o

carrying them away to eat.

o

20   She picks up a hoe . . .

o

She strikes an animal and kills it.

o

WHEN IT CRIED OUT . . .

o

ALL THE ANIMALS GATHER TOGETHER.

o

They come.

o

(sings)   "SHE'S KILLED ONE. WE'VE ALL OF US
                       COME.
                   SHE'S KILLED ONE. WE'VE ALL OF US
                       COME.
                   SHE'S KILLED ONE. WE'VE ALL OF US
                       COME."
The woman runs.

o

She goes to her husband.
She says, "Baba,"
she says, "the animals . . .
she says, "have come to kill me!"

30 And he says, "Where did they come from?"
She says, "They took a plantain from among the
    hearth stones . . .
from in the cooking fire."
She says, "Now I came and killed it."
She says, "The animals have come to kill me!"
The husband says, "Sit down here. I'll go kill them."
As he stood there . . .
                  they suddenly appear to him.

  o

           "SHE'S KILLED ONE. WE'VE ALL OF US
               COME.
           SHE'S KILLED ONE. WE'VE ALL OF US
               COME."
HE SEES . . .
the land is in an uproar.

  o

He says, "I'm telling you,
40 I've been telling you . . .
'Child of mine, stop coming home at sunset,'
and you say, 'I didn't eat dirt.'
                  Now those plantains
    that you're always eating, will they help you?"

  o

The woman runs.

  o

She goes to a relative of the chief.
She presents her case,
how the animals came to kill her . . .
and she told her husband . . .
When her husband saw them, he feared them . . .
The royal one says, "Stay here."

  o

50 As the royal one stood there, they suddenly appear.
THE DUST BILLOWS UP IN CLOUDS.
They all sing together:
           "SHE'S KILLED ONE. WE'VE ALL OF US
               COME.
           SHE'S KILLED ONE. WE'VE ALL OF US
               COME."
Well, now . . .
the royal one himself fears them.

o

The woman runs . . .
She goes to the chief.

o

When she has reached the chief . . .
she tells him everything.

o

The chief asks,
60   "The husband fears them?"
She says, "E-e-eh [yes]."
"And the royal one fears them?"
She says, "E-e-eh."
He says, "Stay here."

o

A man leaves the presence of the chief and stands outside
      in the palace courtyard . . .
He sees dust has covered the sun.
They sing as they pass one another here and there, milling about
      and advancing.
They all sing together, "She's killed one. We've all of us come."
                    "SHE'S KILLED ONE. WE'VE ALL OF US
                          COME.
                    SHE'S KILLED ONE—"
THEY SAY, "MY LORD . . . "
70   THEY SAY, "WHAT WE HAVE SEEN AT THE PALACE
      GATE . . . "
THEY SAY, "IT CANNOT BE EXPRESSED."

o

Another leaves.
He goes to have a look.
AND HE COMES RUNNING
and tells the chief.

o

The chief says, "I want nothing to do with you!
GET OUT."
He banishes that woman.
The woman says, "I'll go.
80   Where I will fall is where my strength fails."
After she left the presence of the chief . . .
she traveled about three miles.

o

She's met by bees.
o

The bees . . .
o

say, "Woman . . .
what makes you run?"
o

She stops
       and tells them.
She says, "I am driven out by the animals."
She says, "Animals . . .
              ate my plantains.
90 When I killed them . . .
all the others straightaway came to kill me.
I ran to my husband . . .
When they came he feared them.
I ran . . .
I went to a relative of the chief . . .
HE FEARED THEM.
I WENT TO THE CHIEF . . .
HE FEARED THE ANIMALS.
Now I must be off . . .
100 Where I stay too long is where I will die."
The bees say, "Sit down and rest."
She sits down.
They say, "Wipe the sweat from your face."
She wipes her face.
o

She stays there.
While she was there, they suddenly appear.
THEY HAD FOLLOWED HER THROUGH EVERY
    PLACE SHE PASSED.
o

              "SHE'S KILLED ONE. WE'VE ALL OF US
                   COME.
              SHE'S KILLED ONE. WE'VE ALL OF US
                   COME.
              SHE'S KILLED ONE. WE'VE ALL OF US
                   COME.
              SHE'S KILLED ONE—"
∞ (short interruption)

Well now those bees . . .

o

sting those animals.

o

110 THEY STING EVERY ANIMAL.
Now some animals flee . . .
Some have already reached your land . . .
Some are in Kyamutwála [a chiefdom] . . .
Some are in Tanzania . . .
                              Some are in Rwanda . . .

o

The bees rescue the woman.

o

FROM THAT TIME . . .
AND IN THE PRESENT . . .
A PERSON CALLED A WOMAN . . .
DOES NOT "CUT" BEES [open the hives to get honey].

o

120 It's done.

COMMENTARY

The little bird that reveals the murders is probably an *enyonza*, a species of thrush in whose call Hayas can sometimes discern words. This kind of bird tells whatever it sees although it does not always correctly interpret the significance of observed events. "He's taken out his knife and is stabbing her," it might say, describing the outward appearance of two lovers who secretly meet and intimately embrace in a copse of trees. The name of the *enyonza* bird is proverbially applied to the kind of person who is not afraid to express thoughts that other people, who share them, are too bound by social convention to say. For example, if visitors to a house have stayed for a while and have not received any food to eat, the *enyonza* person might say out loud, "It certainly has been a long time since we have eaten."

The little bird in *The Woman "Full Moons"* plays this role. It comes and tells the woman what others could not tell her. After she has learned the worst, the villagers say, "We tried to find a way that we could say these things, but they confounded us" (line 53). They were confounded because they could not resolve the paradox of murder within a marriage. They were under two contradictory injunctions. On one side, the domestic group must be preserved; no one wants to be the wrecker who breaks it apart. On the other side, the murder must be brought to light so that the social imbalance it created can be redressed. The villagers are bound by this confounding paradox. The little bird apparently is not.

"Little bird, *kempunda bucheke*," in the song of *The Woman "Full Moons"* means literally, "little bird of the decorator (of) little-things-inside-a-rattle." *Cheke cheke* is the sound made by a gourd rattle, and *bucheke* are the little things inside that make that sound. I have not been able to determine the meaning of this, other than its possible reference to the bird's spotted plumage, but *kempunda bucheke* is the kind of almost intelligible things that birds sing in tales.

These lines in the song from *Kulili Your Brother of Only One Mother* are also only partly intelligible: " . . . and his pouch of charmed things . . . and his ram's horn on the head . . . he's put them in a covered basket . . . he says, 'They're property of the chief. Don't you touch them.'" Neither the narrator himself nor anyone I asked could interpret the meaning in light of the events of the tale. They probably refer to circumstances that were part of the tale at one time but have become lost. *Kulili* is the sound of a bird's trilling call. A "brother of only one mother" is a brother who comes from the same mother's womb. A brother-sister relationship of this kind can be most intimate.

In both *Kulili Your Brother of Only One Mother* and *Satisfaction*, a contrast is drawn between siblings and spouses. The former are more sharing and more unified in mutual concern. The reason for this disparity is the traditional clan structure, which divides the interests of spouses, who are of different clans, and unifies the interests of siblings. A man and wife could live as siblings, except that the land that produces food is owned by the husband's family—the wife traditionally has no rights in the land she works—and the couple's children belong to the husband's clan, which has the ultimate right to dispose of them in marriage as they choose. In contrast, unmarried siblings work the land their common clan holds rights to and produce no children. These two basic problems thus do not come between them.

The aphoristic description of famine, "that killed a boy's mother while a girl's mother thrived well" (*The Woman "Full Moons,"* line 4), appears again in the repeated song from *Satisfaction*: "a grain of millet . . . killed a boy's mother while a girl's mother thrived well." The idea that a husband's mother starves while a wife's

mother thrives comes from the fact that a wife prepares and apportions the food of a family's meal. She is thus in a position to secretly
send larger portions of food to her own mother, depriving her husband's mother of food she might have sent her. Should this happen,
it is, as Hayas say, "a matter of shame," as are all of the famine-
caused acts described in these tales. The famine itself is given a
name in *The Woman "Full Moons"* (line 4): "The-Bringer-of-Shame,"
because hunger can make people do shameful things.

If hunger brings shame, its opposite, satisfaction, can cause a
person to have no shame, as the narrator of *Satisfaction* points out
in line 163. A shameful act can cause consternation among those
who witness it; conversely, a shameless act is committed with little
regard for who may witness it. The men who commit shameful
acts threaten the existence of a social group, but the woman with
no shame endangers only herself.

The woman's mother's shameless behavior in *Satisfaction* is a
direct parallel to the chief's adopted mother's follies in *Greens of the
Cow Pasture*. In the former, the action is tragic: the issues involved
have life and death significance for Haya women. In the latter, the
same action is played as broad comedy: the issues there are merely
wealth and prestige.

Satisfaction is a version of a widespread African folktale that is
usually told as an animal fable involving Hare and Hyena. It also
appears in Haya tradition as Hare and Leopard.[1] In that version,
the animals play the roles that the wife and the husband play, respectively, in *Satisfaction*. The episode in which the mother gives
away her existence through her loss of shame does not appear in
the animal versions.

The husband's role is clearly leopardlike. He is a glutton. He
is also easily deceived, not being able to penetrate appearances to
the underlying reality of the wife's deception. And he is danger-
ously powerful and murderous. Like Hare, the woman's character
is defined in opposition to her antagonist. Where he is gluttonous,
she is nurturing. Where he is stupid, she is crafty. Where he is
murderous, she is preserving of life.

Women are nurturing in the two other tales of murder as well.
Note the ever present hoe in *The Woman "Full Moons."* A woman's
hoe is her essential tool; it is to her what a spear is to a warrior. She
is the custodian of the hoe's food-producing, life-sustaining energy.
Recall how the old woman invokes the hoe's power in *The Legend of
Ikimba* (line 28). In *She's Killed One. We've All of Us Come*, however,

the woman is a glutton; she perverts the life-giving power of the hoe by killing an animal, and the land revolts.

A lament is cried out when women hear of the death of a relative. It is a loud ululation that announces the discovery to the village. When someone has died and relatives gather, each one of a designated group of relatives cries out a lament as she approaches the place of the funeral. In the tales, it is specified that she laments for herself (lines 49, 76, and 77), because she is not only bereaved; she must also endure the dissolution of her domestic life.

The theme of separation can be seen as another expression of the inside/outside principle. The relevant boundary and the domains it divides are here social or kin-based rather than physical in nature. In this incarnation, inside/outside might be called "together/apart," and all four tales in this section turn on the problem of inclusion in and exclusion from various kinds of groups. All the tales begin with husband and wife together. The inclusion of another person who is not usually a member of a husband-and-wife household (a wife's brother or mother) draws attention to the boundaries of the domestic group. The first three tales in the section are about defining this group, literally and symbolically, through the sharing of food: in each case, the selfish husband denies food to the tenuous or ambiguous member of the household. The portrayal of events leading to the murder and the subsequent discovery of that unfortunate kinsman or kinswoman confirm the narrative principle that in most tales action is on the boundaries. The tales in this section conclude with the separation of the husband and wife, except for the last tale, which almost concludes that way.

This final tale, *She's Killed One. We've All of Us Come*, elaborates on the theme of together/apart. Symmetrical variations on this theme point with inescapable dramatic power to the central importance of inclusion within a group. Events in the tale portray the expulsive consequences of unrestrained appetite.

The woman gluttonously deprives her husband of food by cooking on a hearth she has misplaced outside in the fields where she works. In addition to the location of the hearth, she had to have removed the plantains from home, where they grow in the grove that surrounds the house.

When the tale begins, all the animals live together outside in the wilderness. At the end, they live apart in different lands. The woman, who was driven out of society by the disorder her gluttony created, is returned to society, put back together with her people, by the bees. In return she never splits apart their hive to get the sweet honey. She may not drive the bees out of their home because they saved her from being driven out of hers. She may not split apart their family because the bees split apart the animals' family in order to put her back together with hers. The tale, told by a hunter, Ma Laulelia Mukajuna's husband, Ta Keremensi Lutaban-zibwa, evokes a wondrous picture of the animals coming as one clan to seek revenge. They are a powerful metaphor for the threat to social existence that gluttony can set in motion.

9

Tales of Knowing and Unknowing

The tales of this section portray clever protagonists and stupid ones, smart ones and outsmarted ones, characters who know how to keep certain information private and one who does not. The events portrayed focus on various aspects of knowing and knowledge: questions of perception and judgment, curiosity, the social construction of reality, and the proper handling of confidential information.

A clever person (*omugezi*, from *amagezi*, "cleverness," the name of the central character in the tale of that title) is able to manipulate social conditions to his own benefit. The clever person can construct an external false reality that induces others, who are deceived by it or entrapped in it, to act in ways that serve his own ends. A knowing person (*omumanyi*) is one who can see inside outward appearances and penetrate to the underlying realities. The object of a knower's understanding may be a person, a situation, a word or phrase. The opposite of a knower is a nonknower (*mutamanya*) to whom people, situations, and words are opaque. Leopard is the incarnation of a nonknower.

Leopard cannot fathom the meaning of the girl's song in *The Glistening One*. He does not realize that its words reveal, to one who can interpret their meaning, the plight of the trapped girl and her identity. She sings:

> " . . . I meet the Incarnation-of-ripe-bananas in
>   the Glistening One.
> He jumps and catches me in the Glistening One.

He throws me in a sack in the Glistening One.
Our home is Kikonjwa
In the Glistening One, my clan is the
        Apportioner and the Cattle-Hater."

The Incarnation-of-ripe-bananas is leopard; he has yellow skin
with black spots—bananalike. The Glistening One is a forest,
whose trees shimmer in the wetness after a rain. Apportioner and
Cattle-Hater refer to the clan sibling (*mulumuna*, see p. 10) of the
Mukulwa clan, which is the rat. Members of the Mukulwa clan
were preparers of food at the court of certain chiefs. They shared
with their clan sibling the distinction of touching and tasting the
chief's food before he himself did. Thus, the rat is called Apportioner (of food). He is called Cattle-Hater because he eats the cow-
hide that has been cured and stored. Poetic allusions to clan siblings
usually appear in poems of self-praise (*eby'ebugo*) recited by warriors
and other men.

But one does not always need esoteric allusions to keep the
leopard outside in ignorance. As a sheep chews its cud, the leopard
asks, "What are you eating?" "I am eating Unknowing," sheep replies. "Well give me a bit," the gluttonous one demands, thinking
he has heard the name of a food he has not yet tried (*Salute Leopard,
Who's Living in the Past*, lines 103–104).

The paradigmatic action in the latter tale is an exchange of
greetings that leopard participates in as he travels along the road
with sheep. Leopard has wrapped sheep's child in a package and is
taking it as a brideprice payment to where he has arranged a marriage. Sheep meets leopard on the road and carries his package for
him, without knowing what is inside. As they go, the people they
meet call out a hunter's salute to leopard: "Shwaga, leopard."

Greetings, perhaps better named as salutations, form a highly
elaborate system in Haya society.[1] Selection among alternatives is
made according to criteria such as age, sex, social status, previous
acquaintance, kin relationship, time of day, and speaker's intent (to
honor or insult). The salutation called to a hunter as one sees him
returning from the hunt is "Shwaga."

When people see leopard traveling along with a package, even
though it is carried by sheep, they assume he has been out on a
hunt because of his reputation as a hunter. "Shwaga," they call out
to him. Leopard, his dim intelligence aglow because he is putting

one over on sheep, answers, "Salute sheep who has taken up something it doesn't know." Sheep later turns the tables.

Salutations and answers can have hidden meanings in Hayaland. The traditional greeting between an adult male of the ruling clans and his counterpart in the nonruling clans is: (lower status male to upper status male) "*Shumalamu waitu*"—(upper status male to lower status male) "*Osingile*." Lower status always speaks first.[2] The meaning of these words is opaque to many Haya speakers, but the following is a story of their origin.

One day a relative of a chief saw the goat of a man from a nonruling clan. He took it, although the owner was watching. The owner said nothing, but the following day went to the chief's court and made an accusation. "*Oshumalamu, waitu*," he said, "there is thievery in you, my lord" (from *obushuma*, "the desire to possess what is not one's own"). "*Osingile*," the lord replied, "you just stood there doing nothing" (from *oku-singa*, "to continue what one is doing"). The chief's relative won the case, and from that time on, the status-affirming greeting exchange has been *shumalamu—osingile*. Hidden inside those words is a kernel of knowledge about social dominance.

Sometimes churlish Haya lads, during the windy dry season, may call to a woman working in the fields a travesty of the usual salutation, "*Mahyo, mawe!*" ("Work [you're doing], mother!"). "*Mana, mawe!*" ("Vagina, mother!") they call out, and she, her hearing impaired by the blustery wind, never knows.

Magezi, the boy whose name means "cleverness," in the tale with that title, plays a similar linguistic trick. When called by name, a person of lower status, like a child, must never answer, "Hm?" or other such non-articulated ways of saying, "I am here. What do you want?" The lower status person should answer with a word. "*Kaboneke?*" is the most common, literally meaning, "let it appear." When his parents call "*Magezi!*" (cleverness), instead of "*Kaboneke*," he answers, "*galibalya*," literally, "It (cleverness) will eat (that is, finish) you." He expresses his determination to survive and foreshadows his ultimate victory. This kind of antagonistic verbal by-play is said to have occurred between royal women at the chief's court and their female servants, who were known for their linguistic abilities.

The final example of the inside meaning of words comes from the tale *Who Was the One Who Ate It?* That question is called from a

distance into the house of a brother-in-law by the central protagonist of the tale. He and his wife approach the house and call out
before they enter. It is customary to make an announcement of
one's presence in the vicinity of another's house. Called *oku-kaguza*,
it usually goes something like this: "*Mulimu?*" answered by "*Tuliho.
Nyegera*"—"Are you inside?" "We are here. Welcome." By substi-
tuting the question "who was the one who ate it?" for "are you in?"
the husband neutralizes the brother-in-law's hold on him. The logic
of this escape is explicated in the commentary.

The Glistening One

AS TOLD BY MA WINIFRED KISIRAGA

I give you a story.
Audience: I give you another.
It's done.
Audience: The news of long ago.
I went and I saw.
Audience: See so that we may see.
I see young g-i-r-l-s . . .
                                    nine of them.
They were in a group.
Now they were spending time together playing.
NOW AMONG THE NINE, there was one comrade
        whom they didn't like.
She was a foolish one.
She was of our clan, a Mukulwa.

NOW ONE DAY THEY DECIDE. "BOJO,"
                                    THEY SAY,
        "LET'S GO CUT WALKING STICKS."
THEY PLAN THE TRIP.
WHEN DAWN CAME ON THE PLANNED DAY, THEY
        DRESS FOR A JOURNEY.
THEY SAY, "WHEN WE GO INTO THE FOREST . . . "
they say, "no one should have her eyes open.

                                                        Everyone should

shut them."
THEY SAY, "AFTER EACH PERSON SHUTS THEM . . .
then she'll cut a walking stick.   BUT WHOEVER CUTS

    A DEFORMED STICK . . .

                                cannot stay with us."

     o

20   So, now that one, the poor thing, was foolish. They go, and
         when they arrived in the forest,
     "HAVE YOU ALL SHUT YOUR EYES?" "We've shut them."
     "HAVE YOU ALL SHUT YOUR EYES?"
     "We've shut them."
     She closes her eyes.
     The other children keep theirs open.
     They go and look for a good walking stick. Each person
         cuts one.
     "ARE YOU ALL FINISHED?"
                                They say, "We've finished."

     "LET'S LEAVE."
                        "Let's leave."
     They go outside the forest.
     "OPEN YOUR EYES."
     "We're opening them." The children open them. (Narrator and
         audience laugh)
30   Now the foolish one returns.
     THEN THEY JUDGE THE WALKING STICKS. "PUT
         THE WALKING STICKS DOWN." THEY PUT
         THEM THERE.
     WHEN THEY COME TO LOOK AT HERS,
     LOOK,
     it's as twisted as an eight.
     They say, "We can't stay with you any more."
     "BOJO, TAKE ME THERE AGAIN." They say, "But why
         should we go back?"
     "BOJO, TAKE ME." They say, "Not us.
     If you didn't cut a good walking stick, you have no right
         to go with us."
     She says, "I'm going back."
40   She turns back.

234

They go on.
When she had gone . . .
and entered the forest . . .
she meets in there—a leopard.
o

The leopard says, "What are you searching for?"
She says, "I've
come to cut a walking stick."
He says, "Where have your comrades gone?"
"They left."
Leopard grabs her.
After it grabbed her, it puts her into a big sack that it had.
It goes along.
o

It leaves from about here, and when it arrived in about
Lyamahóro, it meets women harvesting groundnuts.
IT SAYS, "MOTHER," IT SAYS, "GIVE ME A FEW
GROUNDNUTS.
I'll sing for you."
They give it groundnuts.
Some
it eats. Others it puts in its sack.
(whispers) "Sing! Or I'll kill you."
[The child sings from inside the sack.]
"I was going to take a walking stick in
the Glistening One.
I meet the Incarnation-of-ripe-bananas in
the Glistening One.
He jumps and catches me in the Glistening One.
He throws me in a sack in the Glistening One.
Our home is Kikónjwa.
In the Glistening One, my clan is the
Apportioner and the Cattle-Hater."
"EH?"
They say, "The Leopard is singing. It has a singing sack."
THEY SAY, "BRING MORE GROUNDNUTS." THEY SAY,
"BRING GROUNDNUTS AND GIVE IT SOME."
o

So
Now then, they call to one another from afar.

50

60 "YOU, YOU WHO ARE CULTIVATING IN
  NYAKIMBÍMBILI! DON'T LET THAT LEOPARD
  PASS YOU BY WITHOUT GIVING IT SOME
  GROUNDNUTS."
When it arrived there . . .
about Nyakimbímbili . . .
it meets women.

o

Now then. THE CHILD,

∞

her home is like Kafúnjo.
It travels along.
Nyakimbímbili.
They give it groundnuts.
It sings for them.
70 It travels along and arrives in Lushénye.
  WHEN IT ARRIVED IN LUSHÉNYE . . .

o

it meets someone like Wini [the narrator].
"Eh?"
She says, "That VOICE,
doesn't it seem like our own child?
The one who is lost."
SHE SAYS, "LET ME GIVE YOU SOME MORE
  GROUNDNUTS."
SHE SAYS, "BRING A BASKET." SHE SAYS, "I'LL GIVE
  THEM A SPECIAL MEASURE." SHE SAYS, "I'LL
  MEASURE FOR THEM WITH MY OWN BASKET."
She gives it to Leopard. It's pleased.
80 It eats.
Again it puts some in the sack.
(whispers) "Sing! Or I'll kill you."
               "I was going to take a walking stick in
                   the Glistening One.
               I meet the Incarnation-of-ripe-bananas in
                   the Glistening One.
               He jumps and catches me in the Glistening One.
               He jumps and catches me, baba, and throws
                   me in a sack in the Glistening One.
               Our home is Kikónjwa.

In the Glistening One, my clan is the
Apportioner and the Cattle-Hater."
"Eh?"
The woman listens and her hair stands on end.
NOW SHE SAYS, "YOU SHOULD GO . . . "
SHE SAYS, "AND WHEN YOU REACH TO ABOUT THE
MIDDLE OF KITÁHYA THERE . . . "
SHE SAYS, "YOU'LL FIND OTHER WOMEN." SHE
SAYS,
"THEY'RE HARVESTING
GROUNDNUTS."
SHE SAYS, "DON'T
PASS THEM BY."
IT GOES ALONG PRAISING ITSELF AND FEELING
THE WEIGHT OF THE SACK.
It goes and arrives there.
90   It speaks to the women.
They give it groundnuts.
It puts them in the sack.
The child sings again.
Now then, her father's sister was there.
"EH?"
SHE SAYS, "MY! YOUR SACK SINGS VERY WELL."
SHE
SAYS, "NOW COME WITH ME. I'LL SHOW
YOU THE WAY.
I'LL TAKE YOU TO SOME OTHER WOMEN, MY
COMRADES."
SHE SAYS, "AND THEY WILL NOT JUST GIVE YOU
GROUNDNUTS." SHE SAYS, "THERE ARE WOMEN
WASHING SWEET POTATOES," SHE SAYS,
"THEY'LL ALSO GIVE TO YOU."
It says, "Okay."
They go.
When they arrived at the Kemísha stream . . .
100   they meet some women washing sweet potatoes and others
with groundnuts . . .
They give it groundnuts.
Now the child's mother was there . . .
and people from her home . . .
They put out more groundnuts for him.

THEY SAY, "NOW
LET'S GO HOME."
THEY SAY, "WE'LL GO AND GIVE YOU NICE THINGS,"
THEY SAY, "SO YOU'LL SING FOR US THERE."
o
It goes,
           and when they reached home . . .
they say, "Now we'll give you other things . . .
We'll also give you some meat."
They say,
           "But first, please fetch us some water.
110 WHEN YOU ARE THROUGH FETCHING WATER . . .
COME AND CARRY AWAY YOUR THINGS." It says,
      "Okay."
They give it a wide-weave basket.
It goes to the river.
o (audience laughs)
IT SCOOPS UP.
The water won't stay in.
                    IT SCOOPS UP.
The water splashes out.
                    IT SCOOPS UP.
The water splashes out.
IT GETS SOME MUD.
IT SPREADS IT ON.
120 BUT THE WIDE-WEAVE BASKET WON'T WORK.
"EH?"
IT'S CONFOUNDED.
NOW THE PEOPLE, WHEN IT LEFT THE HOUSE . . .
take out the child.
They bring stones.
               They bring stumps of banana plants.
                                        They
      bring all sorts of things. They put them in the sack and
      close it up. They take the child and hide her
      and then they hurry off.
AFTER IT HAD SCOOPED AND THE WATER
      RUN OUT,
               it says, "I'm leaving here and going."
IT COMES.
WHEN IT ARRIVED, IT FINDS THEY ARE NOT IN.

"EH?" IT SAYS, "I'M REALLY LUCKY
                                        THEY'RE NOT
HERE IN THE HOUSE." [because it had failed
   to perform the required task]
IT GRABS ITS SACK.
130   "EH? IT'S HEAVY."
It says, "I'm going."
It throws down that no-good wide-weave basket.
   (audience laughs)
WHEN IT ARRIVED . . .
TO WHERE ITS HOME WAS . . .
it invites its leopard friends.
It says, "We'll have a feast."
It says, "I have some meat . . .
that will taste really good."
IT SAYS, "YOU ALL COME, AND GATHER LOTS
   OF FIREWOOD,"
140   it says, "so we can eat the meat."
They all work hard. The leopards cut wood, bring it and
   pile it up there.
Now
they light the fire.
                  They bring the sack and put it on.
      o

POOH! [sound of something steaming and bursting in a fire]
"There's an eye."
POOH!
"There's the head."
POOH!
"THERE'S THE BELLY."
150   POOH!
"EH?"
THEY SAY, "WE PUT IT ON THE FIRE LONG AGO.
   THOSE THINGS HAVE ALREADY BURST.
   IT MUST BE DONE IN THERE.
Now all there is to do
is unwrap it and eat."
They unwrap it.
WHEN THEY UNWRAP IT,
LOOK AT THE STONES!

"IYO!"
THEY SAY, "WHEN WE GATHERED FIREWOOD YOU
    TRICKED US. YOU'VE EATEN THE MEAT
    AND WRAPPED THE STONES FOR US!"
160   They grab Leopard . . .
They eat it.
   o

Now then . . .
When they had eaten it . . .
               the girl was at home recovering . . .

Now from that day . . .
they say, "If you are among people . . .
               first open your eyes and

    see what the people are doing.
STOP SAYING, 'WHATEVER THEY DO . . .
WE'LL DO,'
          BEFORE YOU'VE UNDERSTOOD."
NOW SAYING, "WE'LL DO,"
             ALMOST killed the girl, but
    her kinfolk saved her.
               When I had seen this for you, I said,
    "Let me go and report to them."

The Strong One

AS TOLD BY TA KEREMENSI LUTABANZIBWA

A man set out to go hunting.
   o
When he went hunting . . .
he journeyed in the wilderness.
   o
And in the wilderness . . .
he went and captured . . .
             a cat.

The cat . . .
had been protecting a lion.
        o

The lion was its blood brother.
At the time when the lion was its blood brother . . .
10   it said to the cat, "Blood brother of mine . . .
stand watch for me against strong beasts.
        o

I myself . . .
am a STRONG ONE.
Therefore watch out only for strong ones."
        o

Now . . .
                as the cat stood there . . .
a gazelle suddenly appeared.
The cat hurried off.
        o

It calls to the lion.
(softly) It says, "My blood brother,
20   (softly) a strong one has come."
(softly) The lion gets up.
(softly) It looks.
                (softly) It sees the gazelle.
                                It says, "No, that's not
        a strong one.
Protect me from a strong one."
        o

Now . . .
the lion stays there.
                It falls asleep.
As the cat stood there . . .
look, a buffalo.
It sees him WITH THE HORNS.
(softly) It says, "My blood brother, my blood brother,"
                                                it says,
        "the strong one is that one there."
30   The lion raises himself up.
        o

"Eh?" he says, "That's not a strong one.
        o

For me, you protect me from a strong one."
Again he goes to sleep.

o

As the cat stood there, an elephant suddenly appears,

o

BEARING TUSKS.
It runs and says, "Look, a strong one!"
The lion says, "That's not a strong one.
Protect me from a strong one."
He goes to sleep.
As the cat stood there . . .

o

40 all of the other animals come.
The lion rejects them.
Now . . .
the cat stays there. It sits down. It's confounded.
As it sat there, it sees a man.

o

He approaches.

o

When he kept getting closer . . .

o

the cat thought, "No,
I won't wake him. He said . . .
'Protect me from a strong one.'
That one . . .
is soft and weak . . .
His arms wobble to and fro . . .
50 He has nothing . . .
Well, there's nothing to do."

o

(softly) He comes slowly. He steals up, he steals up, he steals up.
(softly) He reaches the lion and spears it.

o

WHEN HE S-P-E-A-R-E-D IT, THE LION
BOLTED AWAKE. "PULUBULU." [falsetto cry of pain]
IT SAYS, "I TOLD YOU TO GUARD AGAINST
A STRONG ONE. WELL NOW,
A STRONG ONE HAS KILLED ME.
A STRONG ONE HAS KILLED ME.
Eh-eh! It jumps up.
It says,
"I'll kill you!"

o

The lion writhes on the ground.
The lion dies.
60   When it dies . . .
the cat runs and follows the man.
o

Wherever the man goes, it follows. Wherever he goes, it follows.
It comes down the path and asks the man.
                                        It says, "You there!
Now that you've killed my blood brother
what will I do?"
He says, "Come, let's go. We'll live together."
o

The cat comes . . .
slowly . . .
As it keeps getting closer . . .
70   it comes and sees . . .
the man has entered the house.
When it sees the man has entered the house . . .
∞   (short interruption)
He takes the spear . . .
He hands it to the woman . . .
He takes the dagger . . .
He hands it to the woman . . .
He takes the machete . . .
He hands it to the woman . . .
o

The woman takes them.
80   She places them near the bed.
∞   (short interruption)
When she took them and placed them near the bed . . .
the cat looks.
"Iy!" it says, "And I thought this man was the strong one . . .
Can it be woman is the strong one?
o

The one who stows away those weapons?
Now it follows,
is she not the one who can bring out the weapons that killed
     the lion?
She went and stored them."
o

It runs to the woman and follows after her in the inner room.

     o

90 Now this story is done.
It is the story of cat and human.

Salute Leopard, Who's Living in the Past

AS TOLD BY MA LAULELIA MUKAJUNA

Now, long ago
the leopard
used to live with the sheep.

     o

They're living in one house like that.

     o

Now the sheep had . . .
its own child,
and the leopard had . . .
its own child.
They all live there. They bring them up.

10 Now
the leopard goes to search for food
and leaves the sheep with the children.
Another day the sheep goes to search.
He leaves the leopard with the children.

     o

Now those times he went out,
the leopard was arranging a marriage with a woman.
They required as brideprice . . .
                       a sheep.

     o

Now, he comes.
He takes hold of the sheep's child.

20 He looks for some banana bast.

He WRAPS it up.
He wraps the sheep's child in there.
Mh! He puts it up on his head to carry.
                                    But he hasn't killed it.
It's tied well, here and there.
  o
He says to his own child . . .
                         that one of the leopard,
                                              he
      says,
            "You stay here
until . . .
I come to get you."
He goes.
When he had left . . .
30   that child of the leopard . . .
                              is confounded to be there alone.
  o
It says,
         "I must follow after them."
  o
It follows after.
  o

Well now, when the sheep
finished his search for food, he met the leopard as he was
      carrying a package on his head. The leopard said, "Help me
      here. Walk along with me."
Now those who meet them on the road . . .
call out a hunter's salute to the leopard,
"SHWAGA, leopard!"
They know he's coming from the hunt.
"SHWAGA, leopard!"
40   The leopard s-a-y-s,
                         "Salute sheep, who has taken up something
      he doesn't know."
  o   (audience laughs)
"SHWAGA, sheep!"
  o

They walked and they walked and when they reached a place
      where they came upon a man,
                              "SHWAGA, leopard!"

He said, "Salute sheep, who has taken up something he
   doesn't know."
                  "SHWAGA, sheep!"
o

(Audience member: Why doesn't he peek inside? Narrator: How
   should he peek inside? If he peeks inside at the quick-
   tempered leopard, won't he kill him? Hm?
   Audience member laughs)
Now finally
the leopard says, "Listen. There are people talking."
Here they rested their loads. He says, "Sheep, you wait here . . .
I'm going to hunt up a little beer."
Like this.
o

W-e-l-l
o

50   the sheep stays. The leopard goes.
While the sheep was there, the leopard's child appears.
                                                   It's

   running
          kwi kwi kwi kwi kwi. [the whispered
   sound of a leopard cub running on
   padded paws]
It comes to him.
o

"Where are you going? Where have you left your comrade?"
He says, (pitifully) "FATHER WRAPPED HIM UP INSIDE
   BANANA BAST.
I'VE BEEN ALONE ALL DAY."
The sheep unwraps, unwraps.
                            He looks.
                                    He finds
   his child.
            He takes him out still alive and puts him aside.
He takes the leopard's child . . .
and puts him in there.
                       He says, "Lie down inside. Let's see what
   it's like to be wrapped up as your comrade was."
He wraps, wraps, wraps.
60   He tightens it. He tells his own child, "YOU RUN HOME . . .
   o

Don't leave until I come to meet you there."

o

The leopard comes.
The sheep puts the package up on his head.
They go and go and go and meet someone.
"SHWAGA, leopard!"
                    He says, "Salute sheep, who has taken up
          something he doesn't know."

o

"SHWAGA, sheep!"
He says, "Salute leopard, who's living in the past."

o

They go and go and go and go and go and reach a town
          like Kyábagenzi. They meet someone there.
          "SHWAGA, leopard!"
He says, "Salute sheep, who has taken up . . .
70   something he doesn't know."
"SHWAGA, sheep!" He says, "Salute leopard, who's living in
          the past."

o

The pair of them go along like that.
Finally they arrive at the place where he was bringing
          the things . . .
The leopard sets them down there . . .
at the place where he has been arranging a marriage . . .
He tells them, "When you go to open the package . . .
look over here. This is where the head is.
Mark it r-i-g-h-t here.
                    First STRIKE IT like this.
Then untie it and be careful so that what's inside doesn't
          get away."
     o   (audience laughing)
80   When the sheep saw he had succeeded, he says, "WELL,
          LEOPARD, I'M LEAVING TO GO CHECK ON
          THE CHILDREN."
He says, "Fine, go right ahead."

o

The sheep goes running. It arrives home and meets its child
          there. It says, "HURRY, LET'S GO. IF THE LEOPARD
          FINDS US HERE, WON'T HE KILL US?"
          OFF THEY GO! (woman laughs; narrator draws breath)
Run run run run run run run run.

○

As they were running . . .
they come upon a man.
"WHY ARE YOU RUNNING, SHEEP? WHAT IS IT?"
HE SAYS, "LEOPARD TIED UP THIS CHILD OF MINE
     TO KILL HIM." HE SAYS, "NOW I TIED HIS."
     HE SAYS, "NOW I'M RUNNING.
     YOU DON'T KNOW LEOPARD'S STRENGTH!
     WON'T HE EAT ME?"
He replies, "Let's go. I'll take you."

○

He takes the sheep with him.

○

90   From long ago
               the leopard and the sheep lived together.
                                             Now that
          was the day they split up.
                         Then the sheep lived with us.
People.

○

He brings it home.
He braids a rope.
               He feeds them.
                              He brings them out
     of the house and takes them to pasture.

○

TRULY, the leopard dwells there and searches for the sheep that
     made him kill his own child.

○

Now rain spreads out across the sky.

○

The rain pours down.

○

When it poured, the sheep and its child run to seek shelter
     in a cave among the rocks.

○

Now in that very place where they find shelter, they come upon
     the leopard. He lives inside there. That's his home.

○

He sits there
               and looks at them.

o

100 And the sheep's child says, "I am dead. This day the leopard
        surely eats me!"

o

The sheep stands there chewing its cud, "mnywa mnywa
        mnywa mnywa mnywa mnywa mnywa mnywa."
The leopard says, "What are you EATing?"

o

He says, "I am eating Unknowing."

o

It says, "Well give me a bit."

o

The sheep says, "Let the child go and bring you some."

o

The sheep tells the child in secret, "When you leave, keep going
        and return home."

o

Away the child goes.

o

It runs straightaway mh! mh! mh! mh! mh! mh! all the way
        home. [lamb running on small hooves]

o

It came to tell its owner.

o

110 The sheep is still there. It eats "mnywa mnywa mnywa mnywa."
        The leopard says, "GIVE ME SOME."
"The child hasn't come yet,
the one who went to bring it.
Maybe I should go after him and call."
"Run and call."

o

It scampered off.
"MY BA-A-A-A-ABY,
MY BA-A-A-A-ABY,
MY BA-A-A-A-ABY,
MY BA-A-A-A-ABY."
o   (narrator and audience laugh)
120 It runs and runs and doesn't slow its pace until it sees
        the leopard left behind.

oo

To its owner's house

it comes and reports how the leopard had been about to eat
    them.
   o

He braids rope.
He would take them to pasture on a tether.
He tied them
               with rope . . .
WHEN HE SAW THE RAIN COMING . . .
he would go and put the livestock in his house.
   o

NOW ONE DAY
comes the leopard.
   o

130   It comes right to that place.
   o

It meets them there eating.
It says,
"Why did you trick me, sheep?
   o

You ran away . . .
Now today's the day I eat you!"
It answers, "Eat me. What can I do?"
"But what is that you're eating?
                        Give me some."
   oo

The sheep says . . .
"Go to the trunk of that tree . . .
140   Climb up . . .
Stand there and roar . . .
and I will stand below and bleat . . .
   o

And when Unknowing comes . . .
you can eat it."
   o

The leopard does so.
It climbs up the trunk,
(rasping voice) kwararai kwararai kwararai kwararai kwararai
      kwararai [sound of leopard climbing— claws on tree bark].
And that sheep, "MY BA-A-A-A-ABY,
                     MY BA-A-A-A-ABY,

MY BA-A- A- A-ABY,
        MY BA-A-A-A-ABY."
Their OWNERS . . .
150 COME WITH SHIELDS AND SPEARS.
THEY DRIVE LEOPARD BEFORE THEM. MH! MH! MH!
    MH! MH!
        o

(softly) His heart ceases. They throw him down there.
The sheep go home.
∞
It's finished.

Magezi

AS TOLD BY MA WINIFRED KISIRAGA

I came and I saw.
A man marries a wife of his own.
They dwell there . . .
            but have no children.
Now after they thought about it for a while . . .
                        they say,
    "Leopard
        is the one who has a fertility medicine."
    o
Now they go to the leopard's place.
The man says, "I brought my wife." He says, "Give her fertility
    medicine on my account so she can bear a child."
The leopard says, "MY MEDICINE is difficult.
                        THOSE
        I GIVE MEDICINE . . .
do not finish their debt easily.
    o
NOW IF I GIVE YOU MEDICINE
10 the child you bear first . . .
you will bring to me so I can eat him."
    o

The man says, "So be it."

        "But," the leopard says, "after you
have given me the first-born," he says, "you will come
to bear other children."

        The man says, "E-e-eh." [He agrees.]

Now they go home.

  o

The woman becomes pregnant.
She gives birth to a male child.

  o

Now the boy grows.
The name they give him is Magezi [cleverness].
NOW THAT CHILD WAS BORN BEAUTIFUL.
The man says, "We should take the child."

        The woman says,

"Bojo, let's not take him."

        She says, "My child,"

        she says,

"It's better to bear another. When we have another,
let that be the one we take."

20 They bear a second.
NOW THE LEOPARD COMES.
It says, "But my good friends,

        those things that we promised one
another—

        why haven't you brought them to me yet?"
They say, "We will bring them."
So now they have a third child

        and a fourth and a fifth and
they reach nine.
He is the tenth,

        Magezi.

After it thought about this for a while, the leopard says, "Now
look, you've already borne many children.
Now you should bring me my child

        and let me eat him."

They say, "Yes."
They say, "Now . . ."

30 they say . . .

        "We will send the children to fetch water."
They say, "Now the child who comes . . .
wearing a small leather skin . . ."

they say, "Let him be the one you take to eat."
"Okay."
They wake the children.
                              "Children, go to fetch water,"
                                                      they say.
        "Go for water."
When they were about to go for water, they say to them,
        "Take off your clothes," they say. "But Magezi is the eldest,"
        they say. "You go dressed. You should not go naked."
He says, "Okay."
                    He leaves.
                              When they get outside the village
                                                              he
        says, "Bojo,"
                    he says, "Bojo," he says, "Bojo, let me give
        you all a little piece of this skin so you can wear it."
        He tore it up in small pieces and gave one to each child,
        one to each child. They all go. (audience laughs)
When they got to the river, IT LOOKS AT THEM.
"Eh?" the leopard says, "My kings!
40   Now who can I take?
                        Can I take that one?
                                          Not me."
IT RETURNS [to the parents].
IT SAYS, "BUT I DID NOT SEE THE CHILD YOU SENT
    ME."
THEY SAY, "HE WAS THE ONE WEARING A LEATHER
    SKIN. YOU DIDN'T SEE HIM?"
IT SAYS, "I SAW ALL THE CHILDREN HAD WORN
    LITTLE PIECES OF LEATHER."
"Eh?"
Now they say,
            "This evening at whatever time is right
        for you . . .
go to where the *entula* berries grow.
The one we send to pick *entula* . . .
is the one you should catch."
50   "Magezi!"
He answers their call.
                    They say, "Go and pick *entula*."
EVERY TIME THEY WOULD CALL HIM, "Magezi!"
        [cleverness] he answers, "It will finish you."
        (audience laughs)

o

He goes out and when he reaches the *entula* plant,
                                                    he sees
     the carpenter bee.
It goes, "Juluju."
               He says, "My dear friend carpenter bee,"
                                                        he
     says, "Would you not go and bring for me a few *entula*
     so that father will not beat me?"

o

It goes to the *entula* plant, "Juluju-juluju." It's bringing one
     berry and placing it on a small banana leaf, "juluju-juluju,"
     bringing one berry—THE LEOPARD TRIES TO SEE
     WHAT'S TAKING THE *ENTULA*. It doesn't see a thing.
Magezi returns home and when they saw him, "Magezi,
     you've come?"
He answers, "It will finish you."
                            They say, "You've come?"
                                                    He
     says, "I've come."
He gives them the *entula* berries.
                              "Eh?"
It returns. IT SAYS, "BUT I HAVE NOT YET SEEN MY
     CHILD."
60 They say, "Hasn't he brought us the *entula*?"
                                             It says, "I
     didn't see him."
                 They say, "Now when you see a child has
     come to burn off the dry-season grass . . .
that's the one you should grab."
                           It says, "Okay."
                                        They say,
     "Magezi!"
           He answers, "It will finish you."
                                        They say,
     "Go burn off the dry-season grass."
                                    He says, "Okay."
     They give him a small torch.
He takes his little walking stick,
and when he gets outside the village . . .
he ties the torch to his walking stick and ties this to a longer
     shaft.
          HE HEAVES IT LIKE A SPEAR.

FIRE IGNITES THE GRASS. The leopard looks at it
    burning.
                    He turns back.
"Magezi!"
            He says, "It will finish you."
                                    "Mh?"
Now when these things had confounded them,
now . . .
the father said,
"Now you come at night, leopard,
and the child you find we have rubbed with oil
should be the one you grab and take with you."
                                    It says, "Okay."
They rub it on him and lie down for the night, but after they
    rub the oil and lie down, he himself lies awake.
When the hour grew late . . .
he takes out the container of oil and measures some out for his
    father.
            He rubs it on him. (audience laughs)
HE FINISHES. HE WIPES HIMSELF CLEAN. HE
    FINISHES. HE RUBS HIMSELF WITH
    ASHES.
            He lies down.
When the leopard had come, it feels here and there . . .
                                            It finds
    the father.
It sees he's the slippery one and says, "Isn't this the one?
                                        Bye-
    bye."
Now when they get up in the morning . . .
they arise.
    o
The mother goes to look.
                "Magezi!" He answers, "It will
    finish you."
"Iy?"
When she goes to look in the bed . . .
she finds . . .
her husband is not there.
                    "Iyo!"
SHE SAYS, "A CHILD,"
            SHE SAYS, "A CHILD HAS
    OPENED THE DOOR." SHE SAYS, "THE LEOPARD
    HAS EATEN MY HUSBAND."

They banish the child from their house.
When they had banished him . . .
he goes.
90   Now at the time . . .
when they had been living together,
when the father had not died yet . . .
he had given him a dog.
Now he goes along with that dog of his.
He sics it on, and he hunts . . .
                                    he hunts . . .
Now when he would go into the wilderness . . .
they knew him as a man who hunts a lot . . .
Now after he made a plan . . .
      o
he tells his friend, "Take out my eyes for me."
100   He says, "My friend, take out my eyes for me."
That one replies, "But why should I take out your eyes?"
He says, "TAKE OUT MY EYES FOR ME!"
He takes out his eyes for him.
Magezi says, "Let us go to hunt."
      o
When they had gone to hunt . . .
the spear that he lets fly . . .
brings down an animal. He says, "What have I killed?"
      They say, "You've killed a civet cat."
HE LETS FLY ANOTHER. He says, "What have I killed?"
      They say, "You've killed an antelope."
HE LETS FLY ANOTHER. He says, "What have I killed?"
      They say, "You've killed a leopard."
110   Eh?
They bring a report to the chief about the man who cannot see.
      o
Now they tell the chief,
                    "My lord,"
                                        they say, "there is a man,"
      they say, "and he has no eyes . . . "
They say, "BUT WHEN HE THROWS A SPEAR . . . "
they say, "it does not fall empty."
Eh?
      The chief says, "Now what shall I do?"
He says, "I shall go hunting so I can see the man myself."

Now . . .
>   the chief equips for the journey . . .
>   They sound
>   the drums . . .
They go and take up hunting formation in the elephant grass.
Now they leave the chief in one place with about two
>   other people . . .
120 Now Magezi and his friend—the one who leads him around—
>   go to where the hunters have formed their line.
Now the chief . . .
>   decides, "I'll go . . .
to see how that man hunts."
(This scene is done in a low, secretive voice, almost a whisper.)
When the chief had gone . . .
Now
>   Magezi asks his friend, "Where is the chief?"
He replies . . .
"The chief is close to us right now."
He says, "He is behind us."
He asks, "Who is he with?"
He says, "There is no one."
130 He lets fly a spear.
He impales the chief.
The friend says, "You have killed the ch—" "Stop," he says.
>   "Don't say that."
He says, "Take out the eyes."
He says, "Take out the eyes of the chief."
>   He takes out the eyes
>   of the chief.
>   He puts them in Magezi.
He sees.
>   He says, "Take off his clothes."
He takes off the clothes.
>   He puts them on Magezi, and when he
>   had finished dressing him . . .
they go along with those animals they have killed . . .
∘   (The final scene is narrated in a normal voice.)
Eh-Eh! They say, "That man who cannot see . . .
they say, "he has fallen and impaled himself on a spear . . . "
140 They say, "Now . . .
he is dead.

Let's take the animals we have killed," they say,
"and go home now."

They dragged the body of the chief

and

dumped it in the marsh.
Magezi . . .
and his friend . . .
returned.
Magezi went and ruled in the palace . . .
From that day, "Cleverness will finish you . . . "
And when I had seen this for you, I said, "Let me go and report
to them."

Greens of the Cow Pasture

AS TOLD BY MA ERIKA MANUEL

Well then . . .

I went and I saw.
Audience: See so that we may see.
I see a woman . . .

is born . . .

o

She's a child then, and dwells there . . .

o

Both mother and father, her parents, were living.

o

She grows and becomes a woman . . .
but doesn't bear a child . . .
She's the only one her parents bore, she alone . . .

o

Her parents die.

o

10 She began by burying her father and mourning. She dwells with
her mother, but then she dies. She mourns . . .
SHE LIVES ALONE.
MISFORTUNE HAS FOUND HER.

She hasn't anyone to pinch. She has no brother. The people
     of her uncle, those who bore her mother, were all dead.
     In her home, the place where she had been living . . .
the land was completely destitute.
     o

She wanders about, abandoning one place, sleeping in another.
     o

EH-EH!
               And she has nothing to eat . . .
She walks among the trees . . .
She stops and finds small windfall things. She eats them . . .
She moves on . . .
20 Eh-eh! She says, "What shall I do? Will I die?"
     o

SHE GROWS WEAK!
     o

Now . . .
     o

She goes and the place where she is going . . .
is Amukuzanyána right h-e-r-e
                              where they have a cattle bath . . .
She finds a m-i-l-k-i-n-g w-a-l-l had been e-r-e-c-t-e-d t-h-e-r-e . . .
She finds the place where the cattle-herders used to d-w-e-l-l,
     where the pastoralists herded c-a-t-t-l-e . . .
She finds edible greens g-r-o-w-i-n-g t-h-e-r-e . . .
                                             She finds
     the place where Enoch used to have his corral . . .
                                             She finds
     the greens have t-h-r-i-v-e-d t-h-e-r-e . . .
The woman strips off the raw greens and e-a-t-s t-h-e-m . . .
The woman says, "I am b-l-e-s-s-e-d . . . "
30 *Those greens as plain as plain can be . . .*
Eh-eh! And the luchwámba plants, and who knows what else. She
     eats and eats . . .
                    Now when she happened to look as she was
     eating like that . . .
     o

she sees a chief . . .
     o

When she had seen the chief . . .
and he made a royal appearance . . .

IT WAS NO LONGER GREENS FOR HER.
She goes among royal houses . . .
> She goes among
> > maidservants . . .
She goes among all sorts of things . . .
He sets up a bridal enclosure for her. He builds her a house
> there among the greens in the pasture . . .
SHE DWELLS THERE AS THE QUEEN MOTHER.

o

40   She lives there.

o

She drinks milk. She eats butter . . .
> Eh-eh! She's the queen
> mother. The queen mother dwells there . . .
SHE FORGETS HER POVERTY.
"Ha!" she says, "But it was greens that made my fortune,
> G-R-E-É-N-S.
They made my fortune, L-O-R-D.
How did the greens make me rich?
> The Creator watched over me
> here. He said, 'Your parents will die, but you will find
> things that are greater than your PARENTS.'"

o

When the next day dawned, she goes behind the bathing
> enclosure, inside there . . .
She looks at her arm . . .
"Eh?
> Ha!"
> > She says, "Is it me?"
She turns herself about. She turns an arm about.
> > She looks at
> a breast . . .

o

50   "Eh?
Ha!"
> she says, "My God,
those greens were what gave birth to me, they were . . .
the thing that helped me . . . "
SHE LOOKS HERSELF OVER. SHE LOOKS HERSELF
> OVER. SHE TURNS HERSELF AROUND.
Eh-Eh!

When she looked herself over and turned herself
  around . . .
(whispers) she looks and looks and looks at how she isn't as she
  used to be.
She looks.
Eh-eh! She looks at a leg. She looks at the fingers. THEY'VE
  BECOME SMOOTH AND PLUMP.
She looks and looks. She used to have tendons showing. They're
  gone. She looks.

60 Eh!
One day.
The next day
she looks at the cows they milk, at the things they give
  her . . .
    They bathe the queen mother in heated
  water . . .
      filtered with the right things . . .
Again she goes and looks at herself.
(whispers) "Eh!
    Ah! Baba.
      Iyo?
       Mh!
        Mh! Mh! Mh!
(the woman sings)
    I didn't bear Muyónza [the name of the chief].
    I didn't bear Muyónza.
    I didn't bear Muyónza.
(Audience member: Erika is really telling a story!)
    Greens of the cow pasture.
    Greens of the cow pasture.
    Greens of the cow pasture.
(audience Greens yu-u-u.
laughing) Greens, look at the Arm.
    Greens of the cow pasture.
    Greens of the cow pasture."
Then she looks out at the front gate to make sure they're not
  watching her.
 o

(Narrator jumps up and looks out the door.) Eh!
    "Ye-e-e.
    Greens of the cow pasture.

Greens of the cow pasture.
Greens.
Y-u-u-u.

(audience   Greens of the cow pasture.
laughing)   Greens of the cow pasture.
(whispers) I wonder if they saw me.
(whispers) If they heard, they would say, 'It's not she who bore
    the chief.'
70   (whispers) Enough of this!"
SHE QUIETS HERSELF.
             SHE SITS DOWN.
                     THE NEXT
DAY
SHE EATS AND CONTINUES TO LOOK HERSELF
    OVER.
           EH! SHE FINDS A WATCH PUT ON HER
WRIST LIKE ERIKA'S.
                   SHE HAD NEVER
WORN ONE BEFORE . . .
"HA!
          I DIDN'T BEAR MUYÓNZA.
          I DIDN'T BEAR MUYÓNZA.
          I DIDN'T BEAR MUYÓNZA.
          MY MOTHER!
          GREENS OF THE COW PASTURE.
          GREENS OF THE COW PASTURE.
          GREENS OF THE COW PASTURE.
          GREENS OF THE COW PASTURE.
(whispers) Have they seen me? Have they said, 'She's not
    the one who bore Muyonza'?
          THEY HAVEN'T SEEN ME.
          I DIDN'T BEAR MUYÓNZA.
          I DIDN'T BEAR MUYÓNZA.
          I DIDN'T BEAR MUYÓNZA.
(unvoiced)   Tututu. [expression of inward pleasure]
          I DIDN'T BEAR MUYÓNZA.
          I DIDN'T BEAR MUYÓNZA.
          I DIDN'T BEAR MUYÓNZA.
(whispers) Eh! eh! eh! Do I have a Breast today!
          I DIDN'T BEAR MUYÓNZA.

          I DIDN'T BEAR MUYÓNZA.
          I DIDN'T BEAR MUYÓNZA.
(unvoiced)   Chichichichichichichichi.
          I DIDN'T BEAR MUYÓNZA.
          I DIDN'T BEAR MUYÓNZA."
(women laughing as narrator continually goes to the door to see
    if imagined people outside have heard)
(whispers) "Have they seen me, I wonder? Shhhhuu [sigh from
    running back and forth].
(whispers) If they see me and say, 'She's not the one who bore
    Muyónza,' what will I do?"
(whispers) She shows how good she feels in her joints.
(whispers) She peers out.
          "I DIDN'T BEAR MUYÓNZA.
          I DIDN'T BEAR MUYÓNZA.
          I DIDN'T BEAR MUYÓNZA.
(unvoiced)   Y-u-u-u.
          I DIDN'T BEAR MUYÓNZA.
          I DIDN'T BEAR MUYÓNZA.
          I DIDN'T BEAR MUYÓNZA.
          MY MOTHER!
          GREENS OF THE COW PASTURE.
          GREENS OF THE COW PASTURE.
          GREENS OF THE COW PASTURE.
          GREENS OF THE COW PASTURE.
          GREENS.
          y-u-u-u.
          GREENS OF THE COW PASTURE.
          GREENS OF THE COW PASTURE.
          GREENS OF THE COW PASTURE.
          GREENS OF THE COW PASTURE.
          GREENS OF THE COW PASTURE.
(narrator out of breath, women laughing)
          I DIDN'T BEAR MUYÓNZA.
          I DIDN'T BEAR MUYÓNZA.
          I DIDN'T BEAR MUYÓNZA."
80 Iy? And before she spoke softly.
DOESN'T SHE PLUCK HERSELF ALL OVER?
HASN'T SHE SEEN A BREAST TRULY BECOME A
    BREAST?

HASN'T SHE SEEN A WATCH ON HER WRIST AND
   RINGS ON HER FINGERS?
"I must speak. If they see me, let them see me.
(laughter)
(very loud)   I DIDN'T BEAR MUYÓNZA.
             I DIDN'T BEAR MUYÓNZA.
             I DIDN'T BEAR MUYÓNZA.
             I DIDN'T BEAR MUYÓNZA.
(women   I WAS BORNE HIM BY GREENS OF
broken   THE COW PASTURE.
up in   GREENS OF THE COW PASTURE.
laughter)   GREENS OF THE COW PASTURE.
             MOTHER, THOSE OF THE COW
                PASTURE.
             BABA, THOSE OF THE COW PASTURE.
             MY MOTHER!
(unvoiced)   Y-u-u-u,
(unvoiced)   Y-u-u-u.
             THOSE OF THE COW PASTURE DID
                WELL.
             THOSE OF THE COW PASTURE
                BROUGHT AID.
             THOSE OF THE COW PASTURE
                SAVED ME.
             OF THE COW PASTURE, MOTHER.
             GREENS.
(unvoiced)   Kikikikiki.
(narrator out of breath, the sound of her voice drowned out by
    women's laughter)
               GREENS OF THE COW PASTURE.
               GREENS OF THE COW PASTURE.
               GREENS OF THE COW PASTURE."
(more laughter)
Well, it continued until two Sundays passed. One person
    who went out there saw her. OTHERS SEE HER.
∞

(softly) "We thought she was the queen mother,
(softly) but we see otherwise."
(softly) She goes this way and that showing how good she feels.
Eh-Eh!
After a time they go.

90   The counselors approach the king and say, "Lord, there is
        something that confounds us.

      o

THE QUEEN MOTHER CONFOUNDS US.
                                            APPEAR TO
        US,
PROVIDER, IF YOU WOULD KILL US, KILL US. BUT
    GO AND SEE WHAT THE QUEEN MOTHER
HAS DONE.
                    SHE CONFOUNDS US.
AT FIRST WE KEPT SILENT ABOUT THESE
    THINGS.
                    IF IT IS AN ILLNESS
                                    WE'LL
    FIND MEDICINE FOR HER. AND YOU
    COME, GO SEE HER."
He says, "No!" [he decides]

      o

He says, "Perhaps
she was letting herself be seen among . . .
among her riches."
When he goes to look, he finds her strutting about.
                                            He finds
        she's dressed for a dance.
      o   (laugh)
100 (softly) "Eh!
                    Eh! eh! eh! eh! And this Belly . . .
                                        all of these . . .
I was living like I had already died . . .
Greens have given birth to me. I'm something to see.
                                            I've grown
        fat— the arm I have!
(growing   Look at the breast I have.
in volume)   Look at
        the shoulders.
                    Mother, mother, look at this ear I have . . . "
She's jubilant.
                "GREENS OF THE COW PASTURE.
                GREENS OF THE COW PASTURE.
                GREENS OF THE COW PASTURE.
                I DIDN'T BEAR MUYÓNZA.

                I DIDN'T BEAR MUYÓNZA.
                I DIDN'T BEAR MUYÓNZA.
                I WAS BORNE HIM BY GREENS OF THE
                   COW PASTURE."
When the chief comes to look,
he finds the woman strutting. People attend her there at the
    bridal enclosure. They fill the place.
WHEN HE SAW WHAT SHE WAS DOING . . .
THE OLD WOMAN . . .
EVERYTHING VANISHED . . .
SHE IS LEFT JUST LIKE THAT! ONCE AGAIN
    IN HER POVERTY.
110   THAT'S WHY YOU SEE THEM SAY, "IF YOU GET
        SOMETHING . . .
ALWAYS EXPRESS GRATITUDE IN YOUR HEART.
    DON'T SPEAK LOOSELY
    AND SAY HOW YOU GOT IT."
Audience: M-m-m-m [agreement]
The Lord Creator, who gave it to you,
                         He knows that's the way
it is— just as I've seen for you.

Look Back and See
What Lugeye Does!

AS TOLD BY MA KELEZENSIA KAHAMBA

Now . . .
          there was a chief . . .
and in his chiefdom . . .
dawn does not appear.
o
HE LIVES IN D-A-R-K-N-E-S-S
                 IN D-A-R-K-N-E-S-S
                        IN
D-A-R-K-N-E-S-S ALL THE TIME.

Now when they came to the chief, they told him, "Over there
in the district of Kazínga
                              there is a man.
He's the one who makes it dawn. In his village, dawn comes up
        and the sun shines . . .
Then the sun sets . . .
and it's night."
        o

10 He says, "Now what shall I do?"
He takes one of his men
and says, "Now go . . .
to the man's house, inside there . . .
Go and find the dawn for me."
        o

He takes out a thousand cowries and gives them to him.
        o

The man goes.
He enters inside.
He says, "My lord . . .
                    the chief . . .
                                    has sent me for
        the dawn . . .
At his place it doesn't appear . . .
20 Now, provider . . .
he has sent me with these cowries . . .
                                    Please give me
        the dawn."
He takes out the dawn
        o

and gives it to him.
He says, "Look, here it is.
Take it."
            In his house there is . . .
                                    a little maidservant.
She's sat there like this.
        o

She's there near the door. That's where she stays, under
        the eaves.
        o

The messenger takes hold of the dawn.
                                When he reaches
        the front gate, the little maidservant begins:

(sings)   "You, man! You, man!
Look back and see what Lugéye does!
He sings with his arms, he sings with his legs,
He wears beads like 'dancing maidens.'
It goes 'cheku,' it goes 'waah.'
It goes 'cheku,' it goes —"
                THE MESSENGER
TURNS AROUND. "MH?"
(hands clap!)
        (fingers snap!)
           The dawn is gone.

   o

30 He's traveling along in darkness again.
He goes to the chief and says, "My lord, it has beaten me."
   o

"Iy?" he says, "Now what shall I do?"
EH-EH!
THEN HE TAKES OUT ANOTHER MAN.
HE GOES.
AND THAT ONE GOES WITH TWO THOUSAND
    COWRIES.
He says, "My lord provider . . .
                the chief says that . . .
you should give him the dawn . . .
                  It refuses to appear where
he is." He takes it out there and gives it to him.
   o

He says, "Go on, go on."
             Then the little maidservant squats
    by the door with eyes wide open.
40 She's been sitting and watching him there.
When the messenger got to about where she was . . .
The girl calls to him,
(sings)   "You, man! You, man!
You have taken the dawn of Lugéye!
Look back and see what Lugéye does!
He sings with his arms, he sings with his legs,
He wears beads like 'dancing maidens.'
It goes 'cheku,' it goes 'waah.'
It goes 'cheku,' it goes 'waah.'"

HE LOOKS BACK
TO GET A LOOK AT THOSE BEADS . . .
                                        IT RETURNS
    TO WHERE IT WAS.
HE'S TRAVELING ALONG IN DARKNESS AGAIN.
◦

HE GOES AND REACHES THE CHIEF. HE SAYS,
    "MY LORD . . . "
HE SAYS, "I HAVE FAILED TO BRING THE DAWN.
IT HAS CONFOUNDED ME."
◦

Eh?
50 A dog comes forward and says, "Provider,"
    it says . . .
              "I, my lord, am going now to bring it back."
    ◦

THEN THEY COME FORWARD AND ONE SAYS,
    "A DOG?
WILL A DOG GO AND BRING IT?" THEN ANOTHER
    COMES FORWARD AND SAYS, "A DOG?"
HE SAYS, "WILL A DOG GO AND BRING IT?"
It says, "My lord, I'm going now to bring it."
    ◦

IT DASHES OFF—PYAI!
THE KING SAYS, "A DOG? I DON'T GIVE IT
    A THING.
              Anyway, what do they give a dog?"
IT GOES.
At the man's home, inside there,
60 the dog says, "My lord provider . . .
The chief has sent me.
He says, my lord, that at his place it does not lighten.
He requests, my lord, that you send him the dawn. He says,
    provider, that because darkness falls about us all the time, he
    cannot see."
He takes out the dawn.
He gives it to him.
He says to himself, "And did you think it was going to get
    there?
              He will surely look back. It will look back, beast that
    it is."

o

He hands it to him.

EH-EH! The little maidservant goes out into the forecourt there.

> "Good dog, good dog,
> You have taken the dawn of Lugéye!
> Look back and see what Lugéye does!
> He sings with his arms, he sings with his legs,
> He wears beads like 'dancing maidens.'
> It goes 'cheku,' it goes 'waah.'
> It goes 'cheku'—"
> > EH-EH!
> > IT HOLDS TIGHT.

THERE IT IS ON THE ROAD.

> "Good dog, good dog,
> You have taken the dawn of Lugéye!
> Look back and see what Lugéye does!
> He sings with his arms, he sings with his legs,
> He wears beads like 'dancing maidens."
> It goes 'cheku,' it goes 'waah.'"

70 EH-EH! IT HOLDS TIGHT.

THERE IT IS IN NYAKIMBÍMBILI.

MH-MH! THE LITTLE MAIDSERVANT IS ROLLING
   ALONG.

> "You good dog, good dog,
> You have taken the dawn of Lugéye!
> Look back and see what Lugéye does!
> He sings with his arms, he sings with his legs,
> He wears beads like 'dancing maidens.'
> It goes 'cheku,' it goes 'waah.'
> It goes 'che'—"
> > EH-EH! IT HOLDS TIGHT.

THERE IT IS IN LUKÍNDO.

THAT LITTLE MAIDSERVANT IS BEHIND.

> "Good dog, good dog,
> You have taken the dawn of Lugéye!
> Look back and see what Lugéye does!
> He sings with his arms, he sings with his legs,
> He wears beads like 'dancing maidens.'
> It goes 'cheku,' it goes 'waah.'
> It goes 'cheku,' it goes 'waah.'"

THERE THEY ARE NOW AT KALÉBE. THEY CLIMB UP.

> "Good dog, good dog,
> You have taken the dawn of Lugéye!
> Look back and see what Lugéye does!
> He sings with his arms, he sings with his legs,
> He wears beads like 'dancing maidens.'
> It goes 'cheku,' it goes 'waah.'"

EH-EH! IT DOESN'T LOOK BACK. IT HOLDS TIGHT.
There they are at Kyéma.

> "Good dog, good dog,
> You have taken the dawn of Lugéye!
> Look back and see what Lugéye does!
> He sings with his arms, he sings with his legs,
> He wears beads like 'dancing maidens.'
> It goes 'cheku,' it goes 'waah.'
> It goes 'cheku,' it goes—"
>
> EH-EH!

○

There it is at the palace.
THE KING BEGINS TO SEE.
 HE SEES A LIGHT COMING TOWARDS HIM AS
     WHEN YOU SEE AN AUTOMOBILE . . .
                                        COMING
        TOWARDS YOU IN THE DARKNESS.
80 "IY?"
"MY CHIEFS!"
EH-EH! THE ONE WHO WENT OUT OF THE PALACE
    SAYS, "MY LORD PROVIDER . . .
THE DOG HAS BROUGHT THE
    DAWN."
            EH-EH! "TAKE HIM AND KILL HIM!
MEN HAVE FAILED TO BRING THE DAWN.
DO YOU SAY IT'S A DOG WHO BROUGHT IT?"
EH-EH! IT'S THEM AT THE PALACE GATES.

> "Good dog, good dog,
> You have taken the dawn of Lugéye!
> Look back and see what Lugéye does!
> He sings with his arms, he sings with his legs,
> He wears beads like 'dancing maidens.'
> It goes 'cheku,' it goes 'waah.'"

Then into the palace the dog e-n-t-e-r-s . . .

> *The little maidservant*

> *e-n-t-e-r-s . . .*

The chief s-e-e-s . . .

Sunshine pours d-o-w-n . . .

∞

90 That's why you see a dog . . .
never ceases to dwell at the palace.
Even though a chief might give away all sorts of things, he
    never lacks a dog in there.
My lord, when dawn had appeared . . .
I said, "Let me go and report to the people of my household."
My story ends there.
I leave off.

Who Was the One
Who Ate It?

AS TOLD BY TA HARUNA BATONDE

Now . . .
long ago . . .
o
there were two kinsmen . . .
o
They went . . .
o
on a trading journey
o
a l-o-n-g time ago.
o
THE KINSMAN . . .

> went with his brother-in-law

[wife's brother]
o
and their one dog.

o

One month on the road.

o

10 ABOUT A QUARTER OF THE WAY THROUGH
      THE SECOND . . .

o

they set out one day on foot . . .

o

Twelve o'clock passed . . .
                          one o'clock . . .
                                    three o'clock . . .
                                                      and
        they hadn't gotten food . . .
                            or even water.

o

Now, then . . .

o

THE BROTHER-IN-LAW . . .

o

said to the man,
"Let's slaughter the dog and eat him."

o

And the owner of the dog . .

o

agreed,
"Let's slaughter the dog and eat him."

o

20 They slaughtered the dog.

o

They're laughing
happily.
Their conversation goes back and forth
on sweet, sweet matters.

o

After they finish cutting up the dog,
∞ (The narrator pauses for a sip of beer.)
the brother-in-law . . .
said to him, "I'm going to find some wood

o

so we can put him on skewers,
roast him and eat him.

30 He brought firewood.
THE BROTHER-IN-LAW WAS THE FIRST ONE
to light that fire.
  o

NOW THE KINSMAN . . .
is taking care of other things . . .
  o

He brought the dog . . .
and laid it out on the fire.
oo

THE FIRST SKEWER . . .
He was the one who began to eat it
                          himself.
  o

NOW THE SECOND . . .
40 the brother-in-law refused saying, "Me?
                           Uh uh!
                              I can't eat dog.

And when I get home . . .
have them say I ate dog?
I can't do that.
  o

NOW THE MAN
                  GOT ANGRY THEN.
HE SAYS, "WHY DID YOU SAY, 'LET'S SLAUGHTER
    YOUR DOG
            and eat him'?"
The brother-in-law replies, "Even though . . .
                      you go on and on
    like this,
            it was dog you ate, wasn't it?"
  o (audience and narrator laugh)
Now the man says, "If that's the way you talk,
                      I might hang
    myself."
He says, "You're crazy.
You eat your dog.
50 Now you go to kill yourself. For what?"
  o

Now there the kinsman . . .
                GROWS MORE BITTER.

o
Now then
          this is what he said:
"I'd better throw away these pieces of meat.
I can't eat them."
The brother-in-law . . .
answers him,
"Even though . . .
                    you throw away these pieces of meat, you've
     already eaten dog,
and when we get home, I'll say it!"
o

Now then, they set out,
60   and at about six in the evening . . .
they reached
               an inhabited place,
o

a farming village.
They got food . . .
They got water . . .
o

They're laughing and smiling,
                    but that man says, "Even though
     you're laughing,
you've eaten dog.
And when I get home, I'll tell about you,
how you ate dog."
70   He says, "I won't go home.
                    I'll hang myself
so you won't go and put shame on me
at home
          because I ate dog."
The other says, "My lord,
if I come back alone," he says,
"they might say, 'He murdered him for his money.'
Now therefore . . .
don't kill yourself.
I won't speak of the matter."
o

Now, my lord, one month passed.
                    The second.

80   In the third they bought cattle.
That was the business of long ago.
   o

The business of long ago was cattle or goats.
They drove the cattle along.
   o

They are talking back and forth about their concerns,
     their business,
their troubles.
   o

BUT AT OTHER TIMES . . .
THE KINSMAN says, "When we reach home,
I'll tell how you ate dog." (narrator laughs)
Now, my lord,
90   HERE HIS ANGER GROWS GREATER.
   o

Now, my lord,
       what happened was,
              the man says,
"Rather than having you tell about me at home, I give you all
    my cattle.
Take them,
so you won't tell about me at home."
   o

The man refused the cattle. He says, "I won't take them.
WHEN WE ARRIVE AT HOME
                they might say disturbing
    things,
       like I cheated you."
   o

So, my lord,
THEY CAME.
   o

You know LONG AGO
100   they would always go with a horn.
That is, if they reach like t-o . . .
like to Ibwéra . . . [two miles away]
they sound the horn . . .
so the people here can hear it.
Because our people who traveled would be away for three
    or four months . . .

so their own people would come.
Parents,
          siblings,
                    neighbors from here and there.
They go to welcome and congratulate them.
Now, then,
110 they descend on the road like to NYAKIMBÍMBILI . . .
They meet them.
"MY KINSMEN, WELCOME, WELCOME,
                                        WELCOME,

          WELCOME,
                    WELCOME."
NOW THE KINSMAN WHO ATE DOG . . .
he's angry
          and he's sad.

o

NOW his wife asks him,
"LOVE,
          my, but you seem vexed.
Did you get an illness there?
Did you have a fight with my brother?
What is it?
120 AND
          BESIDES THE MANY THINGS I'M SAYING,
                                        WELL,

          WHERE IS OUR DOG?"
The man answers his wife, (small voice) "The dog, my lady,
          died, my lady."
But he says this to her in sorrow.

o

Now they return
home to their houses.
                    That kinsman goes to his place
                                        and this one
          comes to his.

o

THE WOMAN COOKS FOOD.
THE MAN SITS WITH A BOWED HEAD.
HE REMEMBERS THAT IF THE OTHER ONE
          MENTIONS THAT HE ATE DOG . . .
it would be a great shame.

THE WOMAN S-O-O-T-H-E-D HIM. SHE DID T-H-I-S,
SHE DID T-H-A-T.
The man didn't tell her.

o

130 *They ate their food.*
They finished.
She brought him water.
He bathed.
She rubbed him with oil.

o

Drinks were ready.
But he drinks his beer in tight little sips
like a person who's bereaved.
They lay down.

o

THE WAY THEY WERE LYING THERE . . .
that certain time arrived. (audience laughs)
There's a proverb in Swahili that goes, "Sister-in-law, sister-in-
    law, put out the light."
140 Now the light was put out.
NOW IN THE MIDST OF THINGS . . .
the woman pressed him for an answer.
NOW HE
HAD ALREADY ARRIVED AT THE SPOT THAT
    PINCHES.
He must tell about it.
He says, "My lady, I ate dog,
but your brother refused to eat it.
Now that's why I want to go and hang myself."
The woman says, "You're crazy.
150 This is a great shame?
Dog?
A great shame?
You would go and hang yourself?

o

Who were you with?
Were you not with my brother?
Now then,
why go and hang yourself?
How many people were there?
Were there not just two of you?

Is this not just silly nonsense? Don't go to hang yourself,
    my lord.
Now when the sun rises in the morning . . .
I
 must
    go
      to welcome back
              my brother.
160 Now what we'll do is go together.
You and I.
Don't go and hang yourself.
NOW THEN,
WHEN WE ARRIVE THERE . . .
BEFORE YOU COME TO THE HOUSE,
                      you'll find him
    at home.
    o
You should call to him before you go in.
And don't call him by name.
No, no!"
When they arrived there . . .
170 the people are inside.
he says, "*WHO* WAS THE ONE WHO ATE IT?
WHO WAS THE ONE WHO ATE IT?"
                  In the house
    the brother-in-law was confounded.
He jumped up and said, "OH HO! WHO WAS THE ONE
    WHO ATE IT? WHO WAS THE ONE who ate it?"
And the people in the house tried to ask,
"What kind of thing did they eat?"
"What kind of thing did they eat?"
"What kind of thing did they eat?"
He went inside.
NOW THAT ONE,
180 THE BROTHER-IN-LAW, BECAME MORE
    AND MORE BITTER.
He can't say anything
because he has already preceded him
BY MENTIONING THE MATTER FIRST.
They went inside . . .
They visited politely . . .
They took their leave.

AND IT WAS NEVER KNOWN, WHO WAS THE ONE
    WHO ATE?
              WHO WAS THE ONE
    WHO ATE?
              WHO WAS THE ONE
    WHO ATE?
              WHAT KIND OF THING DID
    THEY EAT?
IT WAS NEVER FIGURED OUT.
That's my story.
190   The matters as I saw them.
And this is the end of the news broadcast.

What Was It
That Killed Koro?

AS TOLD BY TA HARUNA BATONDE

A long time ago . . .
  o
among our forebears . . .
there were . . .
some people who were vassals.
  o
Now those vassals,
              so to speak,
the chiefs
would take people
              and give them cattle
to go and care for.
When they milk the cattle . . .
10 it's taken
        for the chiefs.
  o
They draw blood . . .

and it's taken
for the chiefs.
Now then, there was ONE FELLOW . . .
and he is the vassal
                    of the chief.
AND THAT MAN HAS ANOTHER VASSAL.
He dwells there on his estate.
It's like he's his neighbor, so to speak.
Now then,
            that [second] one had a wife.
20 And his wife is b-e-a-u-t-i-f-u-l,
                                    very much so.
But now that lord
            LOVES THAT WOMAN,
the wife
        of his serving man.
    o
Now then,
            when he milks the cows . . .
he gives it to that serving man of his so he can take it away
to the chief.
                But whenever he goes away . . .
this one goes inside to his wife,
because she's so b-e-a-u-t-i-f-u-l.
Now, and that lord . . .
                    his name is Koro—
the one who is going inside to the wife of his serving man.
    o
30 And that wife of his,
the wife of the serving man,
had a child,
a small child.
Now then, it's like that, day in and day out, day in and day out.
Now then, the neighborhood people told his serving man.
They say, "Sir, whenever you go to take the milk . . .
or the blood . . .
that Koro . . .
                is sleeping in your house with your wife."
    o
Now then . . .
40 When they drew off blood
                        from the cattle,

he gave it to him
and said, "When you go today
                          don't return.
Sleep there.
   o

Finish all the business there
at the chief's court.
Let him give you all the news
                          so you can bring it to me."
So that fellow went.
Now when he went, HE DIDN'T GO THERE!
He hid himself
50 in the forest.
He sat there
                    with the BLOOD.
   o

THAT BLOOD . . . (narrator laughs)
he sat there with it.
Then night fell.
   o

Now that [other] fellow's name was Koro
and he had a beard like mine.
   o

Now around SIX O'CLOCK [at dusk],
the man returned.
He came slowly.
60 He came stealthily and crept between the houses, the kind we
      had in the past, the old style, the *msonge*.
He stood outside.
The other one had already entered—
Bwana Koro.
They're conversing back and forth . . .
Food is being cooked . . .
They're eating . . .
Water . . .
was heated.
                    Feet were bathed. (narrator laughs)
Then they talked for a while.
70 They finished,
and they lay down to sleep.
   o

NOW WHEN THEY LAY DOWN,
IN A SHORT WHILE . . .
                they're asleep.
Now that other fellow came.
You know our custom in the past,
it was [to use] branches like this
                this way in the past.
                        We would
      bend them like this [to lock the front door].
He came little by little until he reached the bed.
He found them asleep.
You know, if you fall asleep like that,
                the sleep that begins
      about 10 o'clock . . .
80   up until around midnight . . .
you can't perceive anything.
             You're completely out.
Now then
he stole the child away from them.
He took out the child
and went with it.
He carried it like to the place of my neighbor, Maksi,
                   up above
      there.
He left the child there.
Then he returned.
He went inside.
90   AND THAT BLOOD,
he's got it.
The blood he had given him to take to the palace.
Now he opened it up
and took out the blood . . .
           He put his hand into the pot
     of blood and spread it on that Bwana Koro,
               in his beard.
He took out some blood
and spread it into his beard.
   o
He finished
       and removed his pot of blood
             and went away.

When he went to that place . . .
where he had left the child . . .
100   he left the thing—in the past we call it an *enyábugyo*
      [a special earthenware pot].
That's what the blood was kept in.
He covered it properly
and then found some stones,
three of them.
He returned with them.
   o

He came and aimed at where the bed was.
   o

STONE!
GWI! [it strikes the thatched house]
He listened.
110   They're asleep.
THE SECOND ONE.
                      GWI!
The woman started awake
                and woke up the lord.
"There's something outside.
Didn't you hear it?" "I didn't hear it." "I heard it."
As they arose,
            "Light the lamp."
WHEN IT WAS LIT
                 AND THE WOMAN LOOKED
     AROUND, SHE SAYS, "WHERE IS THE CHILD?"
NOW THEN,
THE FIRE FLARES UP AND WHEN SHE SEES
     THAT LORD HAS BLOOD ON HIM,
SHE SAYS, "YOU ARE EATING MY CHILD.
   o

120   WHY ARE YOU EATING MY CHILD?"
   o   (audience and narrator laugh)
THERE WAS A GREAT UPROAR.
THE ALARM WAS SOUNDED STRAIGHTAWAY.
PEOPLE!
They came in a crowd.
   o

They found Bwana Koro . . .
Had he eaten a child?

WHEN THEY EXAMINE HIS BEARD . . .
                                        THERE'S
    BLOOD ON IT.
WHY DID HE EAT THE CHILD?
    o
"Where is the woman's husband?"
130 They say, "He sent him away yesterday."
"WHAT? HE SENT HIM SO HE COULD COME
    AND EAT HIS CHILD?"
    o
It became trouble,
            it became trouble,
                        it became trouble.

Now, then
That lord . . .
has a name.
He is well known.
A client of the chief.
To eat a person,
            a whole one,
an enormous shame.
            How can he pass among people?
    o
140 Now, my lord . . .
drums are sounded . . .
The people say, "Let us find that fellow over there . . . "
NOW IN THE MORNING, ABOUT SIX O'CLOCK,
    o
THAT FELLOW KORO
            STOPPED IT FROM GOING ANY
    FURTHER.
THE WAY HE STOPPED IT . . .
He went in among the coffee trees . . .
He tied up a rope . . .
He put in his neck . . .
He died.
150 He committed suicide.
NOW IN THE MORNING . . .
THEY CALL, "KORO!"
            "HE HAS FLED. KORO
    HAS FLED."

They go to search for him.
When they searched for Koro
and went in among the coffee trees,
they found him dead.
   o

Now . . .
they send a message
to the chief:
160   "Your man . . .
           ate a person . . .
                    then he killed himself.
   o

He had sent his own man to you."
The chief said, "That person has not yet come."
   o

Now,
in short . . .
   o

DID THEY NOT PASS A WHOLE NIGHT WITHOUT
   SLEEP?
NOW IN THE EARLY EVENING . . .
they lie down to sleep,
          all of them,
              exhaustedly, because they were
   up the whole night before.
All slept soundly.
Now the fellow comes
170   along with his child.
   o

NOW AT THE LORD'S . . .
THERE ARE PEOPLE,
AND WHERE THE CHILD DIED, there are people.
He comes carefully, carefully, carefully, carefully. HE OPENS
   THE DOOR!
You know about those doors of ours, the traditional ones I've
   already told you about.
   o

He brings in the child and puts him right here.
When he had put him here . . .
   o

he withdrew slowly, slowly, slowly, and when he had left, the
    child now BEGINS TO CRY.
THE PEOPLE IN THE HOUSE WERE
    ASTONISHED
                TO HEAR A CHILD CRYING.
180   "WHAT? WHERE DID THAT CHILD COME FROM?"
When they light the lamp . . .
they find the child crawling around.
"Mh!"
"Allah be praised!"
"The child has been recovered . . .
                Now why should that
    fellow hang himself?"
THE CHILD HAS BEEN RECOVERED. WHY SHOULD
    THE LORD HANG HIMSELF?
  ○ (Audience member: It was a wonder.)
IT WAS A WONDER.
That other fellow went his way.
THE NEXT DAY ABOUT 10 A.M.
               THE FELLOW COMES.
190   He hasn't heard a word.
  ○
They say, "You didn't hear what happened?"
              He says, "I have
    no word.
I hear my child is dead . . .
I hear . . .
Bwana Koro hanged himself . . .
But beyond that I haven't heard."
  ○
Now that's how he returned.
Now, Bwana Pita . . .
this is the place that my story ends . . .
The matter as I understand it,
             that's what I give to you.

COMMENTARY

A knower is able to see into the meaning of situations, that is,
to penetrate below the surface to the underlying reality of events.
He or she does not blindly accept the construction put on events
by others. A knower understands before he acts.

This is the explicit lesson of *The Glistening One* as told by Ma Winifred Kisiraga: "Now from that day they say, 'If you are among people, first open your eyes to see what the people are doing. Stop saying, "Whatever they do, we'll do," before you've understood.' Now saying, 'We'll do' almost killed the girl, but her kinfolk saved her" (lines 165–68). The lesson refers directly to the first episode, in which a group of girls apparently holds a contest by supposedly closing their eyes and choosing walking sticks. In reality, they keep their eyes open and use the game as a device to exclude one of their number, a foolish one, who shuts her eyes and plays along.

A person may think he or she knows the facts of a given situation, but through some oversight—not keeping one's eyes open—the person fails to understand its true nature. One may lack a critical piece of inside information and therefore see only apparent significance. This occurs in several other episodes in *The Glistening One* as well. Leopard does not see through the apparent generosity women show him; they are in reality luring him into their domain, where they trick him further and rescue the girl. At the women's request, Leopard tries to scoop up water in a wide-weave basket, and cannot understand why it doesn't work (one can no more hold water in a wide-weave basket than one can block wind in a calabash). Leopard construes the women's absence when he returns from the river as his own good fortune, since he has "failed" to perform the required task of fetching water. But their absence is in reality a tactical retreat after a successful deceit. Finally, Leopard's friends find the worthless contents of the sack that Leopard said had meat in it. They conclude incorrectly that Leopard has tricked them.

Leopard's distant feline kin, cat (in *The Strong One*) also has difficulty seeing into things. Its desire is to be allied with the strong one, *kikaaka*, the best one, the boss, the first among equals. In Haya terms, cat wants "to be seen with" someone of high social prestige. But cat cannot judge correctly. It perceives only apparent strength, horned and tusked animals in the wilderness, woman in the home. What was inside outside was outside inside: strength.

In *Who Was the One Who Ate It?*, the story of how a shameful secret almost came in from the wilderness, prestige is also the issue. The question here is not who has prestige, but how does one gain it or lose it. The tale turns on a new dimension, before/after, in addition to the ubiquitous inside/outside. Before/after refers primarily to order of occurrence in time but may also describe spatial relationships. The Haya word that names the concept is *okw-ebem-bela*, "to go in front," of someone in temporal or spatial order.

The wife's brother made the husband "go in front" in eating dog, but then the husband himself "goes in front" in revealing part of the secret. The first makes the husband vulnerable, the second removes his vulnerability. Calling out, "Who was the one who ate it?" neutralizes the wife's brother's advantage, since now the husband could easily claim the wife's brother ate the dog. There were no witnesses present when the dog was eaten: who could say it was either one? And the fact that the husband first opens the matter (partially) to public view would be all the more reason to believe that the wife's brother is the guilty one.

The husband's prestige was threatened. The tale makes explicit the fact that his brother-in-law does not want his life or even his wealth. It is prestige he is after. By holding the key to the man's prestige or loss of it, the brother-in-law increases his own prestige, that is, he increases his ability to influence the behavior of another; he augments his power "to rule."

Among Hayas, being the first to speak or to eat has a definite effect on one's prestige, but, as the tale suggests, the nature of the effect varies with the situation. In greeting, to offer a salutation first is to acknowledge one's own lower status. This is dangerous for one's prestige, as the person greeted may respond with a low-status greeting that compounds the first speaker's inferiority. And the one who went first can do nothing about it short of starting a direct argument over relative prestige. If one is concerned with prestige (and who is not?), it is better to wait and see how the other will greet. Ta Haruna, the narrator of *Who Was the One Who Ate It?*, continually advised me not to greet first, for as the Haya proverb says, "He who speaks first does not know what will follow." But one should judge each situation independently—speaking first restored the dog-eating husband's prestige.

To be the first to eat is also potentially beneficial or harmful. Eating first because one cannot hold off one's hunger is a shameful loss of control. The husband is maneuvered into just this kind of act by his brother-in-law. On the other hand, higher-status people may be served food first and they may eat first, not out of hunger, but in accordance with the privilege of their position. There is also the Haya saying that, "He who is first to eat is a bit of food ahead of you." In Haya culture of prestige, as in the tale that derives humor from it, one must understand the particular situation before being the first to eat or to speak.

Prestige is never mentioned directly in the tale itself, although it is the central issue on which the action turns. There is an oblique reference to it when the husband reveals his secret to the wife, " . . . 'I ate dog, but your brother refused to eat it. Now that's why I want to go and hang myself.' The woman says, 'You're crazy. This is a great shame? Dog? A great shame? You would go and hang yourself?'" Here, as in *Blocking the Wind*, the protagonist is pointedly called crazy. And here, as in that other tale, craziness points to a significant principle in motivation. The evidence for his craziness is his expressed desire to commit suicide. The nature of his craziness is that he values social prestige above all else. His fear of losing it drives him to contemplate suicide and blinds his insight into his own situation. The same can be said, mutatis mutandis, for the brother in *Blocking the Wind*.

The husband failed to perceive, as his wife points out, that the significance of the situation lies not in what empirically happened, but in what is publically believed to have happened. And although empirical reality is non-negotiable, social reality is not. The uncertainty involved in reaching a common understanding of what actually occurred when only two people (and a dog) were present is proverbial. As Hayas say, "He who is about to lie says 'I was with my dog' (when we made an agreement)." A dog is hardly an adequate witness. The person who cites its mute testimony about the terms of an agreement is trying to alter those terms. In *Who Was the One Who Ate It?* the significance of the situation lies in its effect on social relationships, not in the empirical question of what really happened (see pp. 199–200).

Concern over prestige made the husband crazy in *Who Was the One Who Ate It?* It also answers the question, *What Was It That Killed Koro?*, for even though Koro knew he was innocent of the cannibal crime he appeared to have committed, his prestige had been so shattered that suicide was his only recourse. Like the dog-eating husband, Koro is bound by a system of social prestige and by his perception of his own place within that system. Unlike the husband, Koro has no loyal, knowing wife whose self-control and outside perspective lead to an insightful plan of escape.

So Koro dies. And when the child whom Koro was supposed to have eaten reappears, everyone asks, "*Omwana yabazokile. Ekyaita Koro kilinkaha?*"—"The child has appeared. What was it that killed Koro?" literally, "That which killed Koro, where is it?" Several versions of the second sentence have become proverbial, "*Ekyaita Koro kiliha?*" and "*Ekyaita Koro kiki?*" They have about the same meaning as the one quoted directly above. The proverb might be used in a situation where people have fought over an issue that appeared to be of paramount importance, but after they have resolved their differences, the issue itself does not seem so significant. To draw a lesson, and to further their reconciliation, a third person might rhetorically ask, "Now what was it that killed Koro?" That is, the issue that seemed to have life and death significance disappears when the situation is viewed in a different light.

Ma Winifred Kisiraga adds that the tale of Koro is like another tale that is the origin of a proverb. Long ago there was a ferryman named Kahaya, who one day decided to require passengers on his ferry to give his dog the highest form of respectful salutation, *shumalamu*, given only to one's social equal or superior (see p. 000). All those who needed to cross the river to go on trading safaris refused to be vis-à-vis a dog what commoners are to royalty and, therefore, had to turn back. Haya people from the chiefdom of Kiziba, however, known for their elaborate salutation forms and their inclination to distinguish even relatively small degrees of difference in computing social prestige, saw where their interests truly lay and freely gave *shumalamu* to the dog, the lowest of the low. From then on, the proverb was established, *Balamya embwa ya kahaya. Abaziba batunda*, "They give the highest salutation to the dog of Kahaya. The people of Kiziba go on a journey of trade."

The lowly dog, the incarnation of indiscriminate eating, the bottom rung of the social ladder, has his day in Ma Kelezensia Kahamba's tale, *Look Back and See What Lugeye Does!* He brings the dawn, a truly heroic feat accomplished by an apparently insignificant being. Unlike Orpheus in the Greek myth, he refuses to turn back and look. He controls his appetite where others have lost control and succeeds where others have failed.

Cowrie shells (line 15) were once used as money in Hayaland. "Dancing maidens" in the maidservant's song refers to a kind of grass that seems to wear beads and to dance in the wind.

The appetite dog controls is curiosity. Hayas say that the desire to see sweet things declines with age, like the desire to eat sweets. Children are indiscriminate eaters and indiscriminate knowers.

Perhaps dog, symbol of indiscriminate eating, becomes here the symbol of discriminate knowing. Dog is the least likely to control his appetite to consume; his resolute act of abstention therefore is the most heroic, coming as it does in the face of his characteristic gluttony. Although his appetite for food is uncontrolled, he controls his appetite for knowledge.

Ma Winifred Kisiraga, however, totally rejects this line of reasoning. She says that if the little maidservant had sung about food, dog would have turned around. The sweet sight of Lugeye's dancing was sweet only to humans, she asserts, and dog's appetite was not attracted to it. Ma Winifred focuses the light of her reason on the nature of appetite, not on the culture of symbolism.

The question of whether or not there is a necessary logical connection between dog and the resisting of temptation to see a sweet sight must remain, for the present, unresolved. Certain overall features of a system of associations can be discerned, but it is difficult to demonstrate the necessity of a particular arrangement of elements, that is, why it is a dog that masters curiosity and perseveres to bring the dawn.

It does, however, seem likely that such a logic exists. Further evidence for it can be found in another version of *Look Back and See What Lugeye Does!* In this version, dog is not the one who brings the dawn. It is the little leper. Recall that little leper brought a reluctant maiden to marry a chief and, compared with the successful messengers of other tales, he had the most sexually suggestive song to sing (see p. 108). A father and his daughter have the dawn, the tale goes, and after a little bird fails to bring it back, little leper volunteers to go. He takes with him two bananas. When he reaches the house where the dawn is kept, he asks the daughter to cook the bananas for him. When she goes to do this, he grabs the dawn and runs. The maiden, like the maidservant in *Look Back and See What Lugeye Does!*, continually tries to make the leper turn around by singing a song:

> "You, little leper! You, little leper!
> Bring back the dawn of my father.
> Turn around! Turn to see how the Creator made me.
> Turn around! Turn to see how the Creator made me."

She tempts the leper to turn by promising him a look at her naked body. He resists and brings the dawn. Here we have a transformation of the situation in which a seductive chief's messenger tempts and lures a maiden to the palace with "making things pleasing" as he sings to her an allusive song about sex. To bring back the dawn, little leper diverts the maiden with "making things pleasing" and then resists her tempting offer of a "sweet sight" of sex.

There is a logic of associations at work here, of dogs, of little lepers, and of food, sex, and knowledge. But whether it is dog who is tempted to see a dancing chief or little leper who is tempted to see a nude maiden, the message is the same: curiosity must be controlled in certain circumstances in order to bring success. The appetite for knowing, for seeing "sweet things," like other appetites, should be indulged in moderation. Sometimes the appetite must be kept in check, even when surroundings tempt it to emerge. As this is so for knowing, it is also true about telling what one knows: the sometimes overpowering desire to reveal a secret must be controlled, must be indulged carefully and in moderation.

An uncontrollable desire to tell what is inside drives the heroine in *Greens of the Cow Pasture* to her downfall and expulsion. As in other tales, events are constructed so as to make the force of temptation almost irresistible and the restraint required almost superhuman. The secret of her sudden elevation from eating raw greens to living as the queen mother completely overwhelms her. Like the girl's mother in *Satisfaction*, the woman begins to come out from her cover. The chief's retinue finally sees her uncontrolled antics, informs the chief, and he expells her.

The narrator enacts the woman's powerful delight in her own prosperity, an ineffable, deep-down feeling of well-being. The unvoiced, or whispered, sounds "tututu," "chichichi," and "kikiki," spoken by a woman as she closes her eyes and slowly shakes her head from side to side, express that pleasure.

This telling of *Greens of the Cow Pasture* was in itself a memorable event. Ma Erika Manuel performed it for her female comrades in a local woman's group. She portrayed the swings of emotion in the queen mother's unfortunate/fortunate plight with such tang and energy that her audience was thoroughly entertained. For weeks afterward, they would sing bits of Ma Erika's song and burst into laughter. The women signal their total agreement with Ma Erika's interpretation of the tale by responding to it with a loud chorus of "Mmmm!"—Yes, indeed!

Appendix

FIVE ORIGINAL TEXTS

Four of the tales included here are in Luhaya. The final tale is in Kiswahili. The latter is included because I felt that a text in noncoastal, nonwritten Kiswahili would be of some interest. Although it differs somewhat from standard literary Kiswahili, its grammatical and expressive qualities are of a high order.

To conserve space, the following notation has been used.

/ signifies a normal pause, marked in the translations by a return to the left-hand margin.

+ signifies a shorter-than-normal pause, marked in the translations by dropping down a line without a return to the left-hand margin.

o and oo indicate the same sorts of pauses they do in the translations.

// marks the beginning and end of a song.

Line numbers are given in parentheses. Translated and original lines may be matched by remembering that only lines that would begin at the left-hand margin are to be counted: in the following texts, this means the initial line of a text, any line thereafter that follows any pause marker except a +, and lines that follow (the second // of) a song. The lines of a song are arbitrarily not counted.

Kabunulila Kalalila

GIVE-HIM-SWEETNESS-IF-HE-CRIES

Mpahosi waitu nkagenda nababonela. / Bona tulole / Mbona omukazi azala omwanawe + alemaile. o Mbwenu olwo yakalemaile / "Omwan' ogusi, bakama bange, tumugile tuta? Omwan'ogu atatambuka?" / Yamutwala omubafumu. + Abafumu byona byayanga. / Yalugayo. Yashuntama ati, "Omwana kamuleke. / Okwo Mungu yansindikile nikwo." o Mbwenu kayabaile aliwo / (10) ayechula omukazi. / Ati, "Iwe," ati, "omwana wawe ogu," / ati, "kawakumutwala, Katoma oku," / ati, "abayo omukaikulu," / ati, "mufumu." + Ati, "Yakumutambila." / Andi ogu, "Mawe, ali lubajuki?" / Ati, "Ali gwa Katoma." / Ati, "Mbwenu," + ati, "agila ebipisi omunju. Bikaijula muno. Na kagunju ka nyakagunju," ahi, "Kaba omwo." / Ahi, "Kyonka kayakumuleba" / (20) ahi, "yakumutambila." / Andi ogu, "Inya, mae, nikwo." / Ahi, "Kyonka kolagya kugenda," / ati, "ohige obuchunkwa." + Ati, "Ohige obunana." + Ati, "ohige otulimu." + Ati,

"Ohige obutenge." + Ati, "Ohige" + ati, "buli kantu kona akalaba kalibwa." / Ati, "Ote omulugega lwawe lwijule." ○ Ati, "Oshube ogende + omw' omushaij' omu Ta Katatilwa," / ati, "obambisemu akagoma kawe." / Ati, "Ebintu ebyo, olata notanganwa nibikubaza," / ahi, "ote notelaho akagoma aka." + Ati, "N' otunana otu, n' otwakulya otu," ahi, "ote noihyaho nobiheleza mbilya." ○ Mbwenu omukazi agenda. ○ (30) Agenda atuhiga otuntu otwo twona. Atugobya. / Ata omulugegalwe. / Omwanawe + amulasha amugongo. / Agenda. ○ Mbwenu kayagobile nka Kamulengera aho ○ atanganwaho + ekipisi. ○ "Iwe mukazi, nogyaha?" / "Tata ningenda Katoma oku, bandagilileyo + omufumu." / "Iy? Eki ekyo ohekile omungongo kiki?" / "Tata, omwana wange." / (40) "Si akabaki?" / "Akalemala" / "Iyayo. Tulebe." / Ahekula / Aleba / "Mh! + Mawe + balamutambila. / Mh! mh! mh! mh! + Mbaija kumutambila. Iloko. + Kyonka mbwenu otu otuli omulugega tuki?" / Tata tuntu twa bunulila." / Ehi, "Tompayo nkalyaho?" / Aiyamu akalimu + akiha kilya + "Si mbwenu, aka kaki?" / (50) Ati, "Aka kagoma." / "Si kaki?" / Ati, "Tata k'okutela." / "Ntelelamu. Tulebe." ○ Mpaho si akakolaho! // In din-di-lin-din din-di-lin-din din-di-lin-din n / In din-di-lin-din din-di-lin-din // "Saaka? Saaka?" // Aka katoke ka bunulila kalalila / Nje nkoleho nyesilikilize // "Kolaho Tulole" // In din-di-lin-din din-di-lin-din din-di-lin-din n / In din-di-lin-din din-di-lin-din // "Mh! + Iloko mawe + iloko, balakutambila." / Nilwo yakagenzile. Kayagile omuli Mbale + atanganwaho ekindi. / "Iwe mukazi, nogya nkaha?" / (60) "Ningenda oku, tata, omubafumu. Bakandagayo omukaikulu. / Ngu alatambila omwana wange ogu amagulu." / "Iy? / Si mbwenu aka kaki akohagatiile?" / "Aka kagoma, tata, k'okutelela omwana wange ogu." / "Telaho tulole // In din-di-lin-din din-di-lin-din din-di-lin-din n / In din-di-lin-din din-di-lin-din // "Saaka? Saaka?" // Aka kagoma kabunulila kulalila / Nje nkoleho nyesilikilize // "Kolaho. Tulole." // In din-di-lin-din din-di-lin-din din-di-lin-din n / In din-di-lin-din din-di-lin-din di- // Mbwenu aho agenda. ○ Agenda. Kagobila nimwo, omukaikulu ali. + Atahamu / (70) Mpaho si, amunyegeza. + Amukeisa. / Ati, "Aliyoki?" Andi ogu, "Halungi. / Mawe, ndesile omwana wange ogu. / Omwana wange akalemala amagulu. Mbwenu omundebele." / Omukakulu amukwata amuleba. / Eh-Eh! Ati, + "Kanyije nyihe omubazi. / Si ebi, mawe, ebili omulgega omu biki?" / Ati "Mae bwakulya bw'omwana wange ogu. / Mbwenu kalata kulila, ninyija nimugabilaho." / "Iy?" ati, "Tiwakuwaho abana bange?" / (80) Andi ogu, "Mawe nakubahaho." / Mbwenu / Abeta + "Bana bange, bana bange, / mulugeyo mwije mulye obuntu obu obwo mukazi ogu yabaletela." / Bilugayo ebipisi / Kulugayo binuuna by'ebishenshe + binuuna bya mahembe + binuuna bigunuile amaisho. / Omukazi ati, "Ha-ah!" + Lelo ntula mbungya. / Lelo mbwenu nagobya oluzalo lwanaga angaga ebi nindalamu mbindokola? ○ Mpaho si, abiyayo. Abiha. Abiha. / Bilya. / (90) Mbwenu omukaikulu + "Iwe mawe kaisiki nzailege. / Aka kaki?" / Ati, "Mawe aka kagoma ka bunulila." / "K'okutela?" / "Inya, mawe, k'okutela" / Ahi, "Telaho tulebe." // In din-di-lin-din din-di-lin-din din-di-lin-din n / In din-di-lin-din din-di-lin-din // "Saaka? Saaka?" // Aka kashaasha kabunulila kalalila /

Ngye nkoleho nyesilikilize // "Kolaho. Tolole." In din-di-lin-din din-di-lin-din din-di-lin-din n / In din-di-lin-din din-di-lin-din li- // "Mbwenu mawe" + Ati, "Ego." + Ndamutambila." / Omukaikulu + aiyayo omubazi. Omwana amusiiga. Amukuuba. / (100) Ebilo bibili omwana ayemelelo. + Atambuka. / Niho obona omwana nalwala bati, "Ilukiza omwana omu'bakaikulu. / Nilwo nababoneile ntyo.

Ndanywelagamuga

I SHALL BE DRINKING FROM THEM

Mbwenu omukazi / akaija yazala abana. / Yatwala enda. / Enda yakula. ○ Yazala abana / babili. / Kayagile kuzala, yazala obushusi. ○ Mbwenu ishe yayema aho ati, "Obushusi obwo tubwaate." / Nyina ati, "Chei, / (10) Obushusi bwange obwo. + Mbutwale mbubike. / Ndabunywelagamuga." / Abutwala obushusi / ogwo n'omukazi. / Obushusibwe abubika. + Abusheleka oku enjulugulu. + Bwikalayo. / Bwikalayo / nke emiezi nka munana. ○ Nke bushuba bwongela emiezi endijo nka munana. + Bukula. ○ Mbwenu bagenda kulima, mbali baluga / alugwamu abana aba. / (20) Aka kalugamu + n'aka kalugamu + omu kashusi. / Bugya omukibuga. / Buzana. / Aka kushuntama aha. + Aka kashuntama. / Aka kemaha: // "Tata ati, 'Bwaate' / Mawe ati, 'Buleke obulele bwange. / Ndanywelagamuga / Ndanywelagamuga'"// Bugenda omunjuluguru oku mbugya mbali nyina abikile, otutoke bulya. / Bumala kulya. ○ Bushuba bwiiluka omu bushusi bwabo, + bwesiza. / Mbwenu ishe kalaija / aleba ashanga aka kanyia aha, + aka kanyia. / (30) Aha ashange bwalya ebitoke. ○ Ashobelwe + "Si mununju titugila bana. / Mbwenu ekilikuta nikilya ebitoke, nikinyia omukibuga, nikilugaha?" / Na nyina kwo atyo aija. / Bukya. / Bujumbakayo. // "Tata ati, 'Bwaate' / Mawe ati, 'Buleke obulele bwange' / Ndanywelagamuga / Ndanywelagamuga // Mbuguruka. / Mbuguruka. ○ Babulinda ○ Mbwenu + nyinabo abulinda. / (40) Olwo yakabulinzile + bugya bujumbukayo bugya omukibuga. / Bwiyayo ebitoke, / ebya nyina abikile ebyamulema. + Bulya. / Bumala kulya. + Bushuntama omukibuga. // "Tata ati, 'Bwaate' / Mawe ati, 'Buleke obulele bwange / Ndanywelagamuga'" // Baguluka babukwata. / Babutega ebishure. / Eh-Eh! / Babusiiga amajuta. / Babujweka emiendo. / Babaho baba bana. / Nikwo omwana ashasia nyina. ○○ Ishe namushasia kyonka kake. + Omwana nashasia nyina. / Olwo lugano. Kanasigile babujweka / babushemeza, / Eh-Eh! Naija nyilukile nti, "Kangende kubalulila abo waitu." + Ogwo mugani gwawa.

Ikimba

THE LEGEND OF IKIMBA

Mbwenu + omukaikulu / akab' akwete enyanja egyo Ikimba. / Agifundikile
omu. / Omu nshuha omu. / Elimu enfulu. ○ Mbwenu, yaiyagamu / nachumba. /
Nakolamu ati n'ebyala naiyamu enfulu nachumba. ○ Mbwenu mwisho yaija
omutabani yashwela ○ (10) omugole ○ Mbwenu / omugole / abowabo bazilima. /
Omukaikulu nyinazala yaiyamu enfulu yabachumbila. / Yamwima ezokutwekela
nyina. ○ Yamwima ezokutwekela nyina. ○ Mbwenu aho / omugole yagila
ekiniga. / Yabona + "Nolwo yachumbila abowaitu bakalya / (20) yakwiilemu
enfulu ezindi + nkoma + ntwekela mae." ○ Mbwenu omukaikulu kayalugileho
akekuba omungemu, / ahi, "Nkanye nkolemu. / Niyemu enfulu ntwekele mae."
○ Yakolamu ○ Olwo yakozilemu + amaizi gayaba. / Yabula okwo alagafundikila
○ Gayaba nyanja wo wo wo. Mugole ! Iruka! Iruka! Iruka! Wo wo wo. Nyinzala
ayem' okwo. Abona mugole. Amaizi gamubingile. "Inywe! inywe! inywe! /
Akaimuka enfuka. "Ikimba, Ikimba, ita akalo, osige akandi. Ita akalo, osige
akandi. Aha nyanja, weh, weh, weh, weh, weh. ○ Omugole / (30) na nyinazala /
amaizi gabalya. ○ Mbali / bagwile / niho enyanja yalekeleile. ○ Nkwo
kutashushana nk'elinye eya lweru. / Kakaikala kali katunga. ○ Mbwenu
ekigambo ekyo nikitwolekyaki? / Nikitwolekya, / Inye, nka Lauleani yakushwela
/ (40) nkagila omugole enjulugu. / Ntamwima byakutwekela abowabo. ○
Mukomele ezawadi eyokutwekela nyina. / Nilwo + alashemelelwa. ○ Akayanja
ako katwolekya + otakwima mukamwana wawe + ebyokutwekela abowabo.

Entuua n'Akaiba

CRESTED CRANE AND DOVE

Mbwenu + eirai / omushaija akaba ashweile. Abakazi baba babili, ○ entuua ○
n'eikiiba ○ Mbwenu nobubona obugufu obu. (long interruption) Mbwenu
abakazibe abo babili / n'entuua / n'akaiba. ○ Mbwenu likala, likala, likala. / (10)
Omushaija alugaho / agya kutunda. ○ Mbali yalugile / ensenene zigwa. ○
Mbwenu olwo zagwile / akaiba kagenda n'omuhi gwako. / Nkaita nkatamu,
nkaita nkatamu, nkaita nkatamu. Entuua / yashuhya s____ nemila / Sh____
nemila. / Sh____ nemila. ○ (20) Akaiba kaleta obusenene bwako, kachumba,
kakala. + Kakoma + kabika. / Mbwenu ibaba yaluga kutunda. ○ "Baba
waihukayo, baba waihukayo, baba waihukayo." Bamunyegeza. Bamushula.
Ebitoke babichumba. ○ Akaiba / azihyaho ensenene. Omutwalogwe ashala. / Ata
aha shahani. / Ata aha olubabi. / Ata aha eisisha ○ omu maisho gaiba. ○ Entuua
ajumika maisho. / Eleba ekileju. ○ Entuua / ezawe ziliha? ○ (30) ezawe? ○○ Olwo
bwakeile bwankya, entuua eimukile aha + omulweya. + Tizikilyo. Zalekeile
kugwa. ○ Eshuya sh____ chei. ○ Eshuya sh____ chei ○ Mbwenu ako akaiba
buchocho / kagilingila entuua egyo. Kata n'kagila kati, / "Omukazi nikalikiile. +

Omukazi nikalikiile. +Omukazi nikalikiile." / Lwonene olutuua olugoto olu + lulashushanile oluchokolo omulweya. / Esh＿＿+ esh＿＿+ esh＿＿."/ Na mwaha tiluka kubukaga. / (40) Kalikiile yaikalaho yashwelwa. / Mbwenu aho, nkwo kugila tuti, / obulungi + tigwo mutima. / Taliba akaiba okwo kali kabi, / entuua okwo eli nungi? / Kyonka akaiba kakagikiza amagezi aha bushweile. o Gwahwa

Aliyokule ile ni nani?
WHO WAS THE ONE WHO ATE IT?

Sasa / wakati wazamani o kuna wajamaa wawili. o Walikwenda o kutafta biashara. o Zamani za kale o Mjamaa + alikwenda na mkwewe o na mbwa yao moja o Mwezi mmoja njiana. o (10) Wa pili, karibu na robo o walianza siku moja kutembea o Mpaka saa sita + mpaka saa saba + mpaka saa tisa + hawajapata chakula + wala maji. o Sasa, basi o yule mkwewe o akamwambia yula bwana / "Tumchinje mbwa tumle." o Na yule mwenye mbwa o akakubali, / "Mbwa tumchinje tumle." o (20) Mbwa wakamchinja. o Wanacheka / kwa furaha. / Wanazungumza / mambo matamu matamu. o Baada ya kumaliza kumchinja yule mbwa oo Yule mkwewe / akamwambia, "Nakwenda kutafta kuni. o Tuje tumbandike / tumchome tumle. " / (30) Kuni akazileta / Yule mkwewe ndiyo wa kwanza / kuoka ule moto. o Sasa yule mjamaa / anashughulika. o Akaleta ile mbwa / akaibandika kwenye moto. / oo Mshkaki wa kwanza / ndiye alianza kutumia + mwenyewe. o Sasa wapili / (40) Mkwewe akakataa, aseme, "Mimi? + Uh uh! + Siwezi kutumia mbwa. / Na nikifika nyumbani / wanasema nilikula mbwa? / Siwezi." o Sasa yule bwana + akakasirika. / Aseme, "Kwa nini unaambia, 'Tumchinje mbwa wako + tumle'?" / Aseme, "Ingawa + ukisema zaidi + lakini mbwa, si unamla?" o Sasa yule bwana aseme "Ukisema hivyo + mimi naweza kujinyonga." / Huyu aseme, "Una wazimu. / Unakula mbwa wako. / (50) Sasa kwa nini unakwenda kujinyonga?" o Sasa hapo yule mjamaa + anazidi uchungu. o Sasa basi + na mwenyewe akasema hivi, / "Afadhali hizi nyama nizitupe. / Siwezi kuzila." / Yule mkwewe / amjibu hivi, / "Ingawa + unatupa hizi nyama, umekwisha kula mbwa. / Tukifika nyumbani nitasema!" o Sasa basi wakaondoka. / (60) Mnamo saa kumi na mbili / wakafika + kwenye watu o kwenye mashamba. / Wakapata chakula. / Wakapata maji. o Wakachekacheka + lakini bwana yule aseme, "Ingawa unacheka, / mbwa umekula. / Na nikifika nyumbani nitakusema, / kama ulikula mbwa." / (70) Huyu aseme, / "Mimi sitakwenda nyumbani. + Nitajinyonga / usiende ukanitoa aibu / nyumbani + kwa kuwa mimi nilikula mbwa." / Huyu aseme, "Bwana, / mimi nikienda peke yangu," aseme, / "wanaweza kusema, 'Alimnyonga kumnyanganya mali.' / Sasa basi iliopo, / usinjinyonge. / Mimi si nitayasema." o Sasa, bwana, wakamaliza mwezi mmoja + wapili. / (80) Wa tatu wakanunua ng'ombe. / Ndiyo ilikuwa biashara ya kizamani. o Biashara ya kizamani ni ng'ombe wala mbuzi. / Wakaswaga. o Wanazungazungumza mambo yao, maneno yao / taabu zao. ○ Lakini saa nyingine / yule mjamaa aseme, "Tukifika nyumbani / nitasema kama ulikula mbwa." / Sasa, bwana / (90) huyu hapo anazidi ukali. ○ Sasa, bwana + yanayotokana + yule bwana aseme, / "Kuliko kunisema nyumbani, mimi nakupa ng'ombe zangu zote. / Uzichukue / kusudi usiniseme nyumbani." ○ Huyu bwana akazikataa zile ng'ombe aseme, "Mimi si nitazichukua. / Tukifika nyumbani + wanaweza kusema matata + kama nilikuibia." ○ Basi, bwana, / wakaja. ○ Unajua zamani / (100) walikuwa wanakwendaga na filimbi (kwa kihaya *enkuli*). Yaani wakifika kama . . . / kama Ibwera / wakipiga filimbi / watu wa hapa wakisikia / kwa kuwa wale watu wetu waliokwenda wanamaliza miezi tatu, miezi minne / ndyo wenyewe wanakuja. / Wazazi + wanandugu + jirani jirani, / Wanakwenda kuwashangilia. / Sasa basi, / (110) wanatelemka kama Nyakimbimbili./ Wanawakutana / "Jameni, poleni poleni + poleni poleni + poleni." / Sasa yule mjamaa aliyokula mbwa / anakasirika + ana huzuni ○ Sasa mkewe anamwuliza, "Jama + mbona unakasirika sana. / Ulipata ugonjwa kuko? / Mligombana na ndugu yangu? / Namna gani? / (120) Lakini + igawa nasema mengi + lakini + mbwa yetu iko wapi?" / Yule bwana amjibu mke wake, aseme, "Mbwa, bwana, ilikufa, bwana." / Lakini anamwambia kwa huzuni. ○ Sasa wanakuja / mpaka numbani. + Yule mjamaa anakwenda kwake + na huyu anakuja kwake ○ Mwanamke anapika chakula. / Yule bwana anainama. / Anakumbuka yule akitamka kwa kuwa alikula mbwa / ni aibu kubwa. / Mwanamke akambembeleza. Akafanya nini. Akafanya nini + Yule bwana hakumwambia ○ (130) Wakala chakula. / Wakamaliza + Akampa maji. Akanawa. / Akampakaa mafuta. ○ Kinywaji tayari. / Lakini anakunywa pombe kwa kinyongekinyonge / kama mtu anayofiwa. / Wakalala. ○ Walivyolala / wakati ukafika. / Panapo hadithi ya mswahili anakuambia, "Shemeji, shemeji zimisha taa." / (140) Sasa taa ikazimwa / Sasa katikati ya maneno / yule mama anamchokoza. / Sasa huyu / kisha fika mahala pa finyo. / Lazima ayaseme. / Aseme, "Bwana, mimi nilikula mbwa, / lakini ndugu yako alikataa. / Sasa iliopo nataka kwenda kujinyonga." / Mwanamke aseme, "Una wazimu. / (150) Hiyo ndiyo aibu kubwa? / Mbwa? + ni aibu kubwa? + Uende ujinyonge? ○ Ulikuwa na nani? / Si ulikuwa na ndugu yangu? / Sasa basi, / kwa nini uende kujinyonga. / Mlikuwa watu wa ngapi? + Si ulikuwa watu wawili? / Hiyo siyo upuuzi mtupu? Usiende kujinyonga, bwana. / Sasa, ukicha asubuhi, / mimi + ni lazima + niende + kumpa pole + ndugu yangu. / (160) Sasa iliopo twende wote. / Wewe na mimi. / Usiende kujinyonga. / Sasa basi / tukifika pale / kabla hujafika nyumbani + utambuta nyumbani. ○ Wewe umwite kabla. / Na usimwite jina. / Hata! / Walivyo fika hapo / (170) na watu wamo, / aseme, "Nani aliyokula ile? / Aliyokula ile ni nani? + na yule nyumbani akashangaa. / Yeye akastuka aseme, "Oho aliyokula ile ni nani? Aliyokula ile ni nani?" / Na watu wa nyumbani wakajaribu kuuliza, / "Walikula kitu gani? / Walikula kitu gani? / Walikula kitu gani?" / Akaingia. / Sasa yule / (180) mkwewe akazidi kupata unchungu zaidi. / Hawezi kuyasema / kwa sababu yule alimtangulia / kutamka kwanza. / Wakaingia ndani. / Wakasabiliana. / Wakajiondokea. / Na haikujulinkana nani aliyokula + nani aliyokula + nani aliyokula + walikula kitu gani? / Haikutambulikana. / Ndiyo hadithi yangu. / Mambo nilivyoyaona / Ndiyo mwisho wa habari.

NOTES

1. The World of the Tales

1. Peter R. Schmidt's recently published work on the archeology and history of Hayaland, *Historical Archeology: A Structural Approach in an African Culture* (Westport and London: Greenwood Press, 1978), has demonstrated the speculative nature of these historical statements. It is sincerely hoped that through the insightful and painstaking work of scholars like Dr. Schmidt even interpreters of literature will in the future be able to evoke the ancient origins of African cultures with some degree of scientific certitude and specificity.

2. A description of the Haya chieftainship may be found in J. Lafontaine and A. I. Richards, "The Haya," in *East African Chiefs*, ed. A. I. Richards (New York: Praeger, 1960), pp. 174–94.

3. This system of land tenure is described in P. C. Reining, "Haya Land Tenure: Landholding and Tenancy," *Anthropological Quarterly* 35 (1962):58–73.

2. Storytelling Performance

1. Sponsored by Research and Fellowship Grants from the National Institutes for Mental Health.

2. Kenneth Burke, *A Rhetoric of Motives* (1950; paperbound ed., Berkeley, Cal.: University of California Press, 1969).

3. V. I. Propp, *Morphology of the Folktale*, 2nd ed. (Austin, Tex.: University of Texas Press, 1968).

4. Much of Lévi-Strauss' work is based upon this methodology. I have found the following three the most helpful: "Four Winnebago Myths: A Structural Sketch," in *Culture in History: Essays in Honor of Paul Radin*, ed. Stanley Diamond (New York: Columbia University Press, 1960); "The Story of Asdiwal," trans. N. Mann, in *The Structural Study of Myth and Totemism*, Edmund Leach (London: Tavistock Publications, 1967); *The Raw and the Cooked*, trans. J. and D. Weightman (New York: Harper and Row, 1969).

5. Supported by the National Science Foundation and the Smithsonian Institution, respectively.

6. Dennis Tedlock, *Finding the Center* (New York: Dial Press, 1972).

7. The reader may demonstrate this fact for himself by noting that shifts in the modalities of storytelling discourse tend to cluster at critical junctures in the narrative. Note, for example, the number of change markers that occur between lines 47 and 50 of *The Glistening One*: a shift in verb tense, a shift from first- to third-person narration, a shift in the loudness of speech, a long pause, and a shift of scene. These mark the transition from the second act, displacement, to the third, attempted mediation. Such clusters also mark junctures that are significant of the narrator's overall purpose. In lines 121–24 of the same tale, the following markers cluster: a shift in verb tense, a shift from first- to third-person narrative, a shift in the loudness of speech, a rising-falling intonation unit (lines 123–24), an

occurrence of the recurrent marker "now" (*mbwenu*), and a shift of scene. This marks a juncture within the successful mediation act at which Leopard's stupidity reaches its zenith and, at the same time, the captive girl is rescued.

3. *Tales of Parents and Children*
1. Students of metaphor will notice that the statement "I shall be drinking from them" entails a double association. Children are metonymically related to calabashes (as container/contained), metaphorically related to calabashes' usual liquid contents. The reversal of the literal "mother nourishes children" is the metaphorical "children refresh mother," thus demonstrating that the converse of Lévi-Strauss' observation that "the transformation of a metaphor is achieved in a metonomy" is also true (*The Savage Mind*, trans. [Chicago: University of Chicago Press, 1966], p. 106).

4. *Tales of Sisters and Brothers*
1. Rodney Needham, ed., *Right and Left: Essays on Dual Symbolic Classification* (Chicago: University of Chicago Press, 1973).
2. J. David Sapir, "Kujaama: Symbolic Separation among the Diola-Fogny," *American Anthropologist* 72 (1970):1330–48.

5. *Tales of Suitors and Maidens*
1. Ruth Finnegan, *Limba Stories and Storytelling* (London: Oxford University Press, 1967), pp. 156–57.
2. Peter Seitel, "Haya Metaphors for Speech," *Language and Society* 3 (1974):51–67.
3. Hermann Rehse, *Kiziba Land und Leute* (Stuttgart: Strecker and Schroeder, 1910), pp. 385–86.

6. *Tales of the New Bride*
1. R. P. Cesard, "Proverbes et Contes Haya," *Anthropos* 24 (1929):579–80.

7. *Domestic Comedy*
1. Perhaps, in the domain of sex, b (giving) and c (enjoying) should be grouped together, for they are both aspects of a description of the sex act, while (a) describes a wholly different situation, the act and consequences of childbearing. This regrouping would not affect any of the interpretations that follow, which do, in fact, tend to view both sex and food as having but two sides: production (a) and consumption (b and c). I retain the three-part division, one, because (b) sees the act as work or service, in contrast to (c), which sees it as pleasure; two, because (b) is primarily a second-person or third-person "other" oriented description of the act, while (c) is primarily a first-person, ego-oriented description; and finally, because the writer is partial to trinary structures, as many native speakers of Indo-European languages appear to be.
2. This cultural fact does not fit into the (a) (b) (c) system of metaphorical equivalences, although it is clearly related. It is rather like a belief in the *vagina dentata*, that is, "a transformation of a metaphor (which) is achieved in a meton-

omy" (Lévi-Strauss, *The Savage Mind*, p. 106). "One spouse 'feeds' another" in sex (part b) becomes the direct, literal, metonymic, "man feeds fetus" during pregnancy. From our vantage point outside Haya culture, we can see that the man's "feeding" during pregnancy functions as a belief that sanctions intercourse for the benefit of the *spouses* and, therefore, something of the connotational meanings in "one spouse 'feeds' another" is carried over (and transformed) into "man feeds fetus" during pregnancy, namely, enjoyment. We have already seen connotational meanings carried over when the transformation moves from metonomy to metaphor: "mother nourishes children" shares affective connotations with its metaphorical reversal, "children 'nourish' mother"; namely, the love that inheres in the mother-child relationship (*I Shall Be Drinking from Them*). This strongly implies that the *vagina dentata* belief, which Lévi-Strauss has shown to be a metonymic transformation of metaphorical expressions of the kind "man 'devours' woman" (in sex), shares connotational meanings with these metaphors, namely, aggressiveness. Hayas, incidentally, have no stories about the *vagina dentata* as far as I know, but do have a proverb, "What saved the penis is that the vagina has no teeth." This is used humorously to explain how one slipped out of a tight situation.

3. An account of Haya greetings is given in Sheila Dauer, "Greetings," in *Haya Grammatical Structure*, ed. E. Byarushengo, A. Duranti, and L. Hyman, Southern California Occasional Papers in Linguistics no. 6 (Los Angeles: University of Southern California, 1977), pp. 189–204.

8. Tales of Gluttony and Separation
1. This version appears in Rehse, *Kiziba Land und Leute*.

9. Tales of Knowing and Unknowing
1. See Dauer, "Greetings."

2. The traditional and modern patterns of usage for these greetings is as follows:

> Traditionally, between equals—B: *Shumalamu, waitu*; A: *Shumalamu, waitu*. Traditionally, between a member of a ruling clan and a member of a nonruling clan—B(nonruling): *Shumalamu, waitu*; A(ruling): *Osingile*. In modern usage, between and among all classes—B: *Shumalamu, waitu*; A: *Shumalamu, waitu*.

INDEX OF NARRATORS

TOPICAL INDEX

Appetite: for knowing, 150, 290–91, 292; for sex, 178; for sex, expressed indirectly, 125, 195; for wealth, 175; kinds represented in tales, 22; need to control, 22; *obushuma* (thievery), 97, 150, 231; of pregnant woman, 151, 174; *oku-shemeza* (to make things pleasing), 98–99; to be seen with a person of prestige, 157, 171, 181, 198, 287

Barkcloth, 150
Before/after: importance of in relation to prestige, 287–89
Bird: *enyonza* (thrush) as speaker, 224–25
Bride: as character in tales, 9
Burke, Kenneth, 33

Calabash: as container of preternatural children, 65; uses, 50, 164
Childbirth: as test of woman's self-control, 7; location of, 7
Children: as nondiscriminating eaters. 15; woman's obligation to bear, 15
Clans: defined, 9–11; double totemic system, 10; subclans in described, 10; things forbidden to contact, 10; women in, 11, 12
—ruling and nonruling: 15, 231; physical stereotypes, 156
—symbolism: clan sibling, 14, 230; forbidden thing, 14; in *eby'ebugo* (self-praise poetry), 10; in tales, 10
Cleverness: as strategic social behavior, 229
Coffee: as cash crop, 2; as conciliator, 151; where grown, 4
Confoundment: as concept in tales, 23–24; empirical versus social truth, 152
Control: as value, 22–23, 98, 196
Craziness (*obulalo*): as character description, 289
Crepitus ventum: as symbol, 197

Dauer, Sheila, 33, 47
Defecation: proper treatment of, 3

Discrimination: as value in eating, 14; as value in food, 14
Dog: as least discriminating eater, 16
Dry season: as setting for tales, 155; social effect of, 17, 18

Economy: sexual division of labor, 13; socialization of young in skills, 7
—agriculture: annual growing cycle, 17; plantains as staple crop, 12
Ensenene (grasshopper): arrival with light rains, 155; preparation as food, 155, 168–69; season for arrival, 168; mentioned, 17
Epic song: quoted, 14
Evaluation: as fixing of status level, 193
Excrement: as sign, 74, 127–28; as symbol, 127, 197

Fancywork: girls' doing as preparation for marriage, 7
Female principle: as anti-structure strongly evidenced in tales, 11; described, 11; in Haya society, 49; nurture, 69–74
Fields: agricultural use of, 4
Finnegan, Ruth, 128
Food: as definer of household group, 96–97, 225–26; as sign of prestige, 18; fish, 15; goat forbidden to women, 150; Haya ideology of feeding and ruling, 12, 13; sweet things, 15, 16, 51; table manners, 18–19
—and sex: metaphors, 191–93; symbolism, 191–93
—*ensenene* (grasshopper), 155; method of preparation, 168–69
—relish: described, 130; *ensenene*, 130; flies and small bird, 130
—symbolism: of cooking, 13–14; of eating, 14–16
Front yard: as activity space, 3

Gluttony: as motivation, 16; destroys family, 203–204; disrupts family, 18, 19
Grasshopper. *See Ensenene*
Greetings: Haya system of, 230; hidden

Propp, V. I., 33
Proverb: "A woman loves her brother but does not marry him," 96; "Blood is thicker than water," 18; "He who is about to lie says 'I was with my dog' (when we made an agreement)," 289; "He who is first to eat is a bit of food ahead of you," 288; "He who speaks first does not know what will follow," 288; "It sickens but does not cause vomiting," 20; "That which you take from inside causes pain," 20, 73; "The one who feeds you is the one who rules you," 12, 193; "They give the highest salutation to the dog of Kahaya. The people of Kiziba go on a journey of trade," 290; "What is defecated by a child is cleaned up by an adult," 127; "What Was It That Killed Koro?" 289–90

Reciprocity: in social relationships, 18; in structure of tales, 18
Riddling: formulas in play, 26–27

Segmentation: as principle in society, 70, 97
Setting: as determinant in motivation, 96–97; 130
Sex and food: metaphors, 191–93; symbolism, 191–93
Shame: revealment and, 226
Shamelessness: and lack of concealment, 226
Siblings: relation between brother and sister, 94–95
Songs: in tales, at boundary crossings, 21
Speaking: as characteristic of palace dwellers, 6; ideophones, 177, 178, 292; social versus empirical criteria, 151–52, 289; verbal dueling, 8
—artistic: 6; as part of goat pasturing for boys, 7; in arranging marriage, 8; with sexual innuendo, 7; women's use of double entendre, 96
—without inhibitions: compared to thrush, 224
—woman's: fearlessly, as old woman, 9; haltingly, as bride, 9
Speech: artistic, puns, 156
Storytelling: concept of interpretive intelligence, 31–32; concluding forms and formulas, 11–12, 29–30, 106; first and third person narration, 28; Haya criteria for adequate performance, 29; impersonation in, 28, 30; opening formulas, 27–28; performance context, 47–48, 292; spatial ordering in, 29; symbols for representing pauses in, 36–37
—modalities of: 35–36, 299n; symbols for representing, 37–38

—narrative style of: Benjamin Kahamba, 44; Kelezensia Kahamba, 44; Winifred Kisiraga, 45–46; Laulelia Mukajuna, 46–47
—narrator: audience cooperation with, 28, 29
Suicide: man's versus woman's, 152
Swamps: described, 4
Symmetry: in tales, 194–97; in "Kibwana," 198–99

Tales: metaphorical nature of, 30; presentation of, importance of juxtaposition, 25; songs in as controllers of boundaries, 69; spatial organization in Teaser, 125; symmetry in, 95, 194–97, 198–99; titles, choice of, 38–39
—Blocking the Wind: affect of child on woman's prestige, 73; burlesque of domestic, female power, 5; compared with Who Was the One Who Ate It? 289; example of narrative style, 46; interpreted, 194–97; text, 161; mentioned, 3, 4, 9, 13, 17, 18, 22, 23, 96, 99, 153, 201
—The Bride's Relish: interpreted, 149; text, 133; use of barkcloth in, 150; mentioned, 3, 99, 153
—Child of the Valley: duty in, 72; interpreted, 96; text, 91; mentioned, 5, 69, 130
—Crested Crane and Dove: example of narrative style, 47; laughter explained, 200–201; original text, 296; text, 168; mentioned, 3, 9, 15, 21
—Give-Him-Sweetness-If-He-Cries: interpreted, 68–74; original text, 293; text, 50; mentioned, 4, 11, 15, 21, 39, 201
—The Glistening One: as example of narrative style, 45–46; as full representation of landscape, 5; compared with Give-Him-Sweetness-If-He-Cries, 68; interpreted, 287; text, 232; mentioned, 10, 11, 22, 23, 99, 153
—Greens of the Cow Pasture: exclamations in discussed, 43; interpreted, 292; text, 257; mentioned, 3, 6, 12, 21, 22, 69
—Have You Not Seen Luhundu?: interpreted, 31, 154–55; text, 158; mentioned, 4, 9, 21, 22
—I Ate Minnows, Little Minnows: as example of narrative style, 45; interpreted, 151; text, 137; values expressed, 149; mentioned, 3, 6, 153
—I Shall Be Drinking from Them: direct expression of domestic, female power, 5; interpreted, 68–74; original text, 295; text, 65; mentioned, 3, 11, 15, 22, 50, 201, 301